Pathways

Sherrhonda Denice

Lily Bird Press
Redford, Michigan

This book is a work of fiction. Names, characters, places, and incidents are the product of the author's imagination or are used fictiously. Any resemblance to actual events, locales, or persons, living or dead is coincidental.

Unless otherwise noted, Scripture quotations are from the King James Version of the Bible

Copyright © 2002, 2007 by Sherrhonda Denice
All rights reserved.

No part of this book may be reproduced in any form or by any electronic mean, including information storage and retrieval systems, without written permission from the publisher, except by a reviewer who may quote brief passages to review.

Published by Lily Bird Press, P.O. Box 39055 Redford, MI 48239

First Edition: December, 2007

ISBN-13: 978-0-9801028-0-2
ISBN-10: 0-9801028-0-4

Library of Congress Catalog Number 2007902357

To order additional copies of this book or schedule a speaking engagement contact:
 www.sherrhondadenice.com or email: bookings@sherrhondadenice.com

Book cover photo by Tony Baker for Brand X pictures
Book cover design and interior by Donna Kitchen of deetoo design
Author photograph by David M. Simpson

Printed in the United States of America

This book is dedicated to Mommy (Beverly Faye), my mother, my sister, and my best friend. You taught me how to fly and always remind me that I can. And you are the wind beneath my wings. I love you more than I will ever be able to express in words.

Acknowledgments

To my Father, my Lord and Savior, Jesus the Christ, who was crucified that I may live, I love You Lord. Thank You for the gift of creativity. May I bring glory to Your name as long as I have Your breath of life.

To Mommy, I love you. Kisses. Willie, thank you for your love and caring. Pinkie and Mario, much love.

To my Man-of-God in training, L. J., I love you infinity times infinity times forever. You give your mommy so much inspiration. You are my "best" best friend.

To Daddy (John Martin), thank you for believing in my dreams and supporting me along the way. I love you. Pam, thank you for helping me to purchase my first computer, your generosity will never be forgotten. Love ya. Valerie, Ronnie, and Vickie, much love.

To Nikki (Nedra Nicole Womble-Slater), my best friend, I love you. You have truly been the best support system, listener, and advice giver for the last twenty-something years. And you keep it real! *"Nothin' but death could keep me from it."* Seek after God with your whole heart.

To Michele Smith, "Sis," I love you. Thank you for loving, honoring, and believing in me. You have been a walking inspiration and testimony. I thank God for you. *"You and me, girl, go a long way back!"* Thank you, Kevin, for being all that I prayed for.

To my big brother, Adren Harris, I love you. Thank you for loving me in a very BIG way. Jacque, thanks for being the best sister-in-law on the planet, and for your loving support. Kisses to Adelyn. Ma Marianne, thank you for helping to make the connection. Love ya.

To Auntie Barbara, my godmother, I love you. Thank you for all your wisdom and encouragement. Fonda and Tony, much love to ya.

To my cousins, who keep me grounded, Mark and Philomina Williams, Mike and Junitta Sumner, Herbert "Poochie" and Ree Williams, and Angela Martin, I love you.

To my spiritual godparents, Rev. Dr. G. Sebastian Vaughn and Ms. Daisy, I love you. Thanks for lifting me and holding me accountable.

To Pastor Nathan Johnson and First Lady Michelle Johnson, and my Tabernacle Missionary Baptist Church family—especially the Genesis Sunday School Class: Johnnie Brown, Patricia Doty, Carolyn Davis, Leanelle Simmons, Marion Jenkins, Cynthia Doty, Beverly Baul, Reverend Manuel and Annette Peace, Ed and Terri Sanders, Sharyn Green, Mona Chambers, Peggy McIntosh, Gwendolyn Lawrence, and Mary Wallace — thank you for your prayers, love and support.

To Nolan P. Smithers Jr., a strong tower of spiritual wisdom and realness, I love you. God bless you!

To Donna Kitchen, I can't say enough words to begin to describe what you have done to move this project forward. You are truly a birthing assistant!!! I love you. Thanks for helping me push, sister!!!

To Sis. Audrey McGresham, thanks for your commitment to this project, and good mid-wifin'!

To Sis. Danielle Hawk, thanks for being a "for real" sister. I love you.

To my BIG brothers in Christ, Reverend Willie James Hawk, Reverend Robert Walker, and Reverend Dennis Kitchen, I love you sooo much! Thank you for your "tiring" devotion as you *try* to keep me in line (ha ha).

To my Delta Sands, Aminah Steger, Cassandra Ingram, Monique Green, Candace (Cage) Cooper, Shannon (Major) Cannon, Dr. Danielle LaMarr, Stacie D. Wilson, Irene (Haynes) Martin, Carina Johnson, Cynthia Jenifer, and Elizabeth Walker, you all are the best sisters a girl could have. Thank you for encouraging me to write, and to see the beauty on the inside and out.

To the sorors of Detroit Alumnae Chapter and all other chapters across the nation. Thank you for your love and support.

To the D.P.S. School Social Work "Thursday Crew": James Appleton, Kathy May-Abler, Juanita Williams, Laura Black, Olinda Griffin, Linda Taki, Rochelle Rusan, Neenah Sabir, and Mary Brown, you guys have always supported and believed. I love y'all.

To some of the people that I have not had the opportunity to meet, but whose ministries and gifts have taken me to a higher level in Christ: Pastor Christopher Brooks and Pastor George Bogle of Evangel Ministries in Detroit, Pastor Juanita Bynum, Dr. Myles Munroe, P. Bunny Wilson, Francine Rivers, and Shirley Caesar—I thank you.

To some of the people who have been rocks or shelter, imparted wisdom, shown much love in their own special way, or helped me to grow: Big Sister Rose (R. A. W.) Davis, Big Sister Steffany "Many Moods" Muirhead, Diane Scott, Elizabeth Griffith, Ruby Nettles-Jackson, Irma James, Deborah Cahee, Emma Huggins, Kina Cosper, Wanonna "Noni" Gray, Florence Palmore, Kathy Hemingway, Alice McKenzie, Kim Ewing, Cheryl Davenport, Carolyn Phillips, Dr. Celestine May-Jackson, Mauritta Gardner, Ethel Burgess, Gwen Jones, Ruby Washington, Arezell Brown, Wilma Anderson, Terri Jones, Stella Byrd, Joe Johnson, Frederick P. Hodge, Jamie P. Tobin, Kimberly Kelley, Erica Buchanan, Felicia McDaniel, Linda Miner, Monete Hudson, Ashara Shepard, Raymond Brown, Jacqueline Ensley, Gwendolyn Moore, Tamara Jackson, Carla Henry, Charlotte Garner, James Culbreath, Angie Wilkinson, Yvette Carter, Sonja Johnson, Orlando Reeves, Triette Reeves, Patrick Bennett, Vickie Manley, Greg and Michelle Zonka, Mike and Tiffany Carter, Ted and Tish Mason, Charles and Ackoco Grace, Kellee Andrews, Kevin Forbes, Pastor Kevin and Lorie Jarrett, Aryan and Tracey Campbell, Cedric G. Fails, Michelle "Coop" Cooper, Renee Armstead, Deacon Antoine and Nicole Clay, Tracy Walker, Darryl and Julea Ward, Elaine Hudson, Steven and Marzina Clarke, Denise Davis, Edward Carter, Reverend Debra Carter, Dr. Nettie Wood, Reverend Beverly McCutcheon, Sister Irma Wise, Reverend Dr. Joy Davis, Stephen and Reverend Harriette Smiley, Reverend Dr. Emily Pardue, Reverend Barbara Brown, Reverend Jeraldine Jackson, Reverend Grace Moorman, Dr. Brenda Hague, Reverend Terry Robinson, Reverend Zachariah Johnson, and Reverend Johnnie Green II—thanks much.

To you, thank you for opening your heart to read a piece of my heart. I hope you are well pleased with this journey.

"Come unto me all ye that labor and are heavy laden, and I will give you rest. Take my yoke upon you and learn of me; for I am gentle and lowly in heart: and ye shall find rest unto your souls. For my yoke is easy, and my burden is light."
Matthew 11: 28-30, KJV

Chapter One

She was just sixteen when her mother put her out on the streets. It was the very same night her mother discovered that the young girl was pregnant. Her mother retaliated by beating her with a broomstick. With deliberate power, her mother cracked that wooden stick across the girl's body until it split in two, leaving horrid black scars dispersed over her cinnamon skin. The remainder of her mother's anger was released in a stew of curses and accusations—the impregnated revelation of hatred she'd felt toward the girl since she'd been born. The pregnancy had just been a convenient opportunity for her mother to rid herself of the girl for good.

Tonight, that night seemed as distant and as insignificant as a snapshot of someone else's past. And the pain of it had long since dissipated, as Dr. Genevieve Moss-Carpenter stood confidently at a Plexiglas podium in Petree Hall of the Los Angeles Convention Center. She looked out over the thousand-plus women that were in attendance for the final night of the Sixteenth Annual Women Rising Conference. She was still digesting the honor of having been chosen as the year's keynote speaker.

Poised, Genevieve addressed the audience of women who were watching and listening expectantly. Standing five feet seven inches tall, with smooth cappuccino skin and dark doe eyes, she was undeniably beautiful. Her naturally highlighted sandy brown hair was pulled delicately away from her face into a soft coil bun at the nape of her neck, which gave her a softened, girl-like look. The style complemented her radiant skin, which would still have been flawless without the expensive makeup she'd been coaxed into donning for public appearances. Not even remotely did Genevieve resemble her true age of forty-seven. Her well-toned physique erased the latter seven of those years. She was still as attractive as she had been in her younger days, having come a long way from the ungraciousness of her past.

Genevieve strolled across the platform authoritatively, encouraging the women to reclaim their lives from the strongholds of abuse, depression, and addiction. She rallied for them to take their lives back and discover their God-directed purpose. She recounted stories of how they had been beaten, raped, and mistreated—the hurts that had eroded their self-esteem. Convincingly, she talked about their lives like she knew each one of them personally. And she did, because more than sixteen years ago, she was one of them. Shameful, haunted faces stared fixedly back at her as she spoke. The sound of soft, repenting sobs wafted through the room as many of the women released their tears. Some cried out of embarrassment, others from the relief of not having to hide their secrets anymore. Genevieve had thrust them out into the open, exposing them, just as her mentor and long time friend, Dr. Denice Banks, had done to her at the First Annual Women Rising Conference.

Genevieve paused briefly as one of the volunteer hostesses discreetly approached the podium carrying an ice-cold glass of spring water. She winked graciously at the hostess for remembering to bring her a lemon wedge as well. "Thank you so much," she whispered as the hostess darted away quietly. Genevieve brought the glass to her lips, noticing a young woman who appeared to be in her late twenties sitting at a table in the third row left of the platform, watching her intently. The woman was deep brown with prominent features that sang of her African ancestry. She had strong, high cheekbones, succulent lips, and a widened nose. She was beautiful, but her eyes expressed an indelible absence that Genevieve understood. The two of them sank into one another's stare.

Genevieve could feel the young woman's writhe as doubt choked her hope. The young woman studied Genevieve, marveling at how good-looking and seemingly intelligent she was. How articulate she was. How much education she had. How expensive her clothes were. The young woman resolved that all the rhetoric about empowerment and self-esteem she'd heard over the weekend was unattainable for her, despite what Genevieve professed up on the platform.

Genevieve took a sip from her glass and placed it inside the podium shelf. "It takes time," she said directly to the young woman. "We are all beautiful. But it starts on the inside—remember that." Genevieve directed her attention to the audience. "Transformation is a *process*. It doesn't happen overnight. I know what I'm talking about because I've been there. I was *addicted* to crack cocaine. I prostituted to keep my habit up. I was *homeless*. Yes. That's what I *was*," she nodded boldly. "But I'm here to tell you that God is *not* a liar. And you can do all things through Christ who strengthens you," she said patting her chest for emphasis. "What you're looking at right now is part of a *process*. Before I accepted Christ into my life, I was a perpetual victim. I was used. Beat up. Kicked out. I didn't even like *myself*. I was so miserable that I tried to take myself out of here. I slit my wrist," Genevieve continued, pulling her suit sleeve back to expose a scar that served as a reminder of God's grace. "But guess what? God *loves* me. And guess what else? He loves you too. And you can change—if you want to. With His power you can!" she enthused the crowd before concluding with a prayer.

The audience of women rose to their feet in applause, including the panel of high profile lecturers and celebrity evangelists, several of whom were accomplished authors in their own right. But despite the media heavyweights in the room, a crowd formed around Genevieve, bombarding her with questions and requests to autograph her new book, *Moving Forward*, all eager to shake her hand and thank her for her inspirational message.

Genevieve was sorely exhausted, but she remained graceful, embracing each woman like an old friend as each took her turn to speak to her. Almost an hour passed before the crowd finally dispersed.

"You are absolutely powerful," Dr. Banks said, squeezing Genevieve.

Genevieve smiled proudly. "Thank You. I learned from the best."

"I'm serious. Every time I look at you, I am more convinced that God is real."

"And when I think about what you've done for me, so am I."

"Stop it. I think we've all cried enough this weekend," Dr. Banks said, blinking away tears.

The two of them mirrored sisters, though Dr. Banks had eight years on Genevieve. She was no less attractive, though. Fifty-five years hadn't tarnished her loveliness in any way. She still got those stares from men, sometimes younger ones, who were intrigued by her sophistication. A couple of inches shorter than Genevieve, Dr. Banks looked sharp in her navy business suit. Conservative, she stuck to blues, grays, and blacks, looking more like a Wall Street broker than a university dean. She had a natural look. She wore her jet black, perm-free hair in double strand African twists that she pampered with lavender and rosemary oil. She kept her hair short because she didn't believe that a woman her age should be strutting around with long hair. She thought it added years. She had no petty insecurities about aging, she just planned to give it a run for its money.

Her dark, sun-baked skin was one of her most prominent attributes. She had long rejected the color issues that people tried to impose upon her while growing up. Maturity had given her an appreciation for the rich dark color she wore. It was her birthright, as were her full lips and stone carved curves. Her shapely calves, hips and rear had come back in style. Now, women of other races were spending thousands of dollars every year to get the behind and lips she had rejected as a teenager because of foolish teasing. For that reason, as Genevieve's mentor, one of the first issues she tackled was self-acceptance. She'd found over the years that self-acceptance, or a lack thereof, was one of the main reasons that women turned to self-destructive vices and emotionally unhealthy relationships, eventually causing them to need a program like the one she had founded.

Dr. Banks had been Genevieve's greatest fan and motivator since the day they met. She still found the time to attend almost all of Genevieve's major speaking engagements *and* manage her responsibilities as Dean of Psychology at Greydale Christian College, the small university where Genevieve had earned a position as an adjunct professor. Genevieve's development as a woman and as a professional was still a priority to Dr. Banks. She'd become more than a mentor—their relationship had blossomed into a beautiful friendship that was valued equally. Genevieve was humbled by Dr. Banks' sincerity and considered their meeting to be one of the major turning points in her life.

It happened more than sixteen years ago, shortly after Genevieve attempted suicide. As a part of her treatment program, Genevieve was asked to attend the first Women Rising Conference. Her ticket had been donated by her therapist, Dr. George Kornblum, a longtime friend of Dr. Banks, who was the keynote speaker that year. Dr. Banks had written her third and most memorable book, entitled *Reclaiming Your Life*, for women in recovery. She'd founded Pathways Rehabilitation Center for Women in Lorton, Virginia, and had a seven-year track record of success. She'd used a great portion of her retirement savings, loans, and grant money to establish it. The center had been so successful that it had received national attention due to a *20/20* special. Dr. Banks took one look at Genevieve that evening at the conference and knew that Pathways was the place for her. And she knew that she was going to be instrumental in God's plan for Genevieve. She had so much faith that she personally covered the cost to relocate Genevieve from Detroit to Virginia so that she could take part in the program. And Dr. Banks' faith had not gone un-rewarded.

As the DC-10 fled the LAX runway en route to D.C., Genevieve and Dr. Banks collapsed in their first-class business seats. Genevieve wrapped the thin gray airline blanket around her shoulders, folded the small pillow just enough for it to be comfortable, and nestled her head against the window. She floated in Los Angeles' spectacularly lit skyline. The city looked like one huge Christmas tree adorned with millions of dazzling lights that gradually faded as the plane reached its proper altitude. Staring out into the darkness, Genevieve reminded herself that she hadn't been home in over three weeks. It was the longest time that she and her husband, Reverend Dr. Benjamin Carpenter, had been apart since they'd married seven years before. Genevieve had been in the middle of a fifteen-city book tour. She'd spoken at several different conferences in between, and had appeared on three nationally syndicated talk shows. She was wearing thin, but was grateful for the blessing nevertheless. The president of Greydale had called her the week before to tell her how great she'd looked on television and how glad he was to have her as a faculty member. Her book had been holding the number one spot on the New York Times Best Seller List for most of the year, propelling Greydale out of relative anonymity.

But teaching was Genevieve's second love. Her heart belonged to Pathways. It was her earthly inspiration. The gratification of being the director, handling the day-to-day responsibilities of the center and interacting with the women there, surpassed the satisfaction she would have received from just teaching alone. But teaching was a necessary part of what Genevieve felt she needed to do to ensure that the clinicians that Greydale graduated were well equipped to counsel the kind of women that she encountered at Pathways. She was fulfilled by the idea of impacting so many lives. And wearing the titles of both *Professor* and *Director* was almost an irony, considering where she'd come from. The thought of it caused her to smile on the inside. There was peace in knowing that she would never have to go back again, although her past still haunted her every now and then.

Her mother, Grace, had been waiting for her in the doorway when she came home from her part-time job at the drug store that evening. Grace's husky, overpowering frame was positioned in a war-like stance, clenching Genevieve's old denim-covered journal tightly in her left hand and a broomstick in her right. That was her weapon of choice that night. Genevieve didn't make eye contact with Grace immediately. She'd learned as a small child to keep her eyes on Grace's hands—that way she'd know just when a blow was coming. She was hardly ever caught off-guard that way. Genevieve focused on those huge, manly-looking hands that were rough and calloused from the years Grace had spent as an industrial housekeeper. As far back as Genevieve could remember, those hands had been symbolic of her fears. She braced herself and waited for Grace to strike.

Grace spewed venom each time she hit Genevieve, alternating between curses and Bible verses. She declared that Genevieve had sinned against God—that her soul was damned to hell. She called Genevieve's unborn child a "child of sin." She wanted to *cleanse* Genevieve of her sins that night by beating the "demons" out of her—or killing her. If there had been any way possible for Grace to kill Genevieve and get away with it, she would have. But it was Grace who had run Genevieve into the arms of a young man, searching for the love that she'd never received from her mother.

Genevieve dared to defend herself with words. "Mother, please . . . we're gonna get married . . . I'm sor—"

"WHOREMONGER!" Grace shouted back wildly, snatching a handful of Genevieve's hair, dragging her into the bathroom, where she forced her head into the toilet bowl. Her nails dug deep into the back of Genevieve's neck, pinning her face in the bowl. Genevieve held her breath as water splashed up from the toilet. She could feel the totality of Grace's burly, two hundred twenty-five pound frame, preventing her from escaping. Grace shouted Ephesians 5:5 as she attempted to rid herself of the one thing she hated most. "For this ye know, that no WHOREMONGER, nor unclean person, nor covetous man, who is an idolater, hath any inheritance in the kingdom of Christ and of God!" she preached. The harshness with which she quoted the scripture gave it no specific meaning at all, except to persecute Genevieve. That was the way Grace quoted the Word of God—without redemption. It always carried a sentence. And Genevieve suffered under it.

Ms. Lucille, Grace's next-door neighbor, saved Genevieve that night. Grace hadn't given Genevieve the opportunity to shut the door completely when she'd come in. Ms. Lucille had heard the commotion from the sidewalk when she'd let her dog out. "Grace, you gon' kill her!" Ms. Lucille shouted, pulling laboriously on Grace, throwing herself off balance, and sending herself careening into the wall behind her. She thumped hard against it before regaining her stance. Then she went to work on Grace again.

Ms. Lucille was a small-framed, fifty-year-old woman. She was five feet two inches tall, and no match for Grace in strength or size. At five foot nine, Grace towered over Ms. Lucille's frail existence. But Ms. Lucille continued to pull on Grace's arms until Genevieve was freed from her torment. Genevieve shot past Grace and took refuge behind Ms. Lucille while she regained her breath. Her chest heaved as her lungs took in air. Across from her, Grace breathed monstrously, cursing Ms. Lucille—her protector. Grace's eyes burned through both of them. Genevieve looked for some semblance of love in those eyes but there was none. "GET OUT!" Grace's rage reverberated. "Go back on the street where you belong!" she huffed. And Genevieve ran—right into a world that was just as merciless as her mother.

Mowing her way through Ronald Reagan National to the baggage claim area, Genevieve was glad to be almost home. She was excited about the ride back to Alexandria with Benjamin. Being with him would make the distance seem shorter. The vibration of her cell phone startled her. She smiled wide when she saw her husband's cell phone number on the tiny screen.

She sang her greeting. "Hi honeyyyyy . . ."

"Hey, Sweets," Benjamin returned, not sounding half as excited.

Genevieve picked up on his lackluster right away. "What's the matter? I thought you'd be happy that I'm finally home. I've been gone three whole weeks."

"I am. It's just that I've got a bit of bad news."

Genevieve let out a sigh. They'd been through this routine before. Schedules colliding like comets, choking their quality time. Disappointed, she asked for the news that she didn't want to hear. "What is it?" she asked, stopping in front of the luggage carousel.

"Last minute meeting here at the church. I'm sorry," he apologized.

Genevieve put in her earpiece, and slid her cell phone back in her waist clip.

"Honey, what are you saying?" she whined.

"I can't pick you up from the airport. And I'll probably be home later than I anticipated."

Disgusted, Genevieve made a smacking sound with her lips. "Ben ..." she pleaded, snatching up one of her bags.

"I'm sorry, Sweets. Really. Mother Peace and the twins are on their way."

Genevieve lifted her second bag from the carousel and sighed again.

"I'll get home as soon as I can. I promise. Love you."

"Love you too," she said half-heartedly, because her heart had just plummeted seven stories. She had anticipated seeing her husband. The life of a pastor and a center director/professor/author was starting to lose its appeal. Before the book, Benjamin had been the only missing-in-action family member, overseeing his church, providing counseling, and doing speaking engagements. Now, both of them were carting around PDA's, with their lives broken down to daily appointment schedules and other people's needs. Genevieve hugged Dr. Banks good-bye and stood at the curb saddened as she waited for Mother Peace and the children.

She forgot her disappointment when she saw the twins' faces. It seemed that they had grown some since she left them just three weeks ago. Joshua raced over to help her with her bags, while Faith questioned her as to what gifts she'd brought back for her and "her daddy." Genevieve had bought both of them new hiking backpacks just so she could fit in all their gifts. They hugged her quickly and then went searching through their backpacks to find the "cool new things" Genevieve had brought back from all the different places she'd gone.

While the twins busied themselves with their scavenger hunt, Mother Peace, the twins' longtime caregiver, informed Genevieve that she planned to take the children to the movies, and that they'd be spending the night with her tonight. Genevieve started feeling guilty. For the last three weeks she'd only spoken with them over the phone. She whispered to Mother Peace that it wouldn't be necessary now that she was home. Faith overheard her and insisted that she and Joshua would rather go to the movies and bake cookies with "Na Na" Peace tonight instead. Genevieve pursed her lips together while the twins waited for her verdict. She eased a smile after deliberating all of two seconds, swayed by their pitiful, anxious little faces. They jumped up and down like they'd won something.

Faith was a few inches taller than Joshua. Her large hazel eyes were filled with excitement. She showered Genevieve with kisses on her face. Genevieve looked at her reddish-looking hair and freckles and marveled at how much she looked like her father. Her slender little frame was starting to bud. Genevieve decided that it was time to toss the training bras and take Faith to a women's store to find a bra that would fit her more appropriately, now that she was filling out. She wondered what kinds of hormones were being injected into the food supply to make girls develop so fast these days. Faith noticed Genevieve's staring, and fidgeted uncomfortably with her beaded, crystal ponytail holder. She was self-conscious about her developing "new body."

"You're beautiful, sweetheart," Genevieve assured her, before Faith resumed pulling things out of the backpack.

"Hey, she's got half of my genes," Joshua joked.

"She sure does. And you are absolutely handsome," Genevieve said earnestly.

Despite the fact that Joshua had entered into the adolescent state where his arms and legs looked like extra-long extensions of his body, he was a handsome boy. But no matter what he seemed to eat, he remained scrawny. It didn't seem to bother him much, though. Benjamin had shown him pictures from his own childhood when he looked exactly like Joshua did now. Joshua could see how his father had grown from a geeky looking kid to a star football player. He was banking on that transformation for himself one day. He was a strange eleven-year-old. Benjamin had nicknamed him "Prophet" because his wisdom was well beyond his age. Benjamin said it was God-given. Joshua had even decided at the precocious age of eleven that it was his "calling" to be a minister. His oval-shaped, tortoise-rimmed glasses gave him a brainy, intelligent disposition. They seemed to fit ideally with his personality. Genevieve pictured him giving his first sermon. She smiled at him and ran her fingers through his coarse jet black curls before planting a kiss on his forehead. She'd missed the two of them more than she'd realized. But Mother Peace had won tonight.

Mother Peace had been helping to take care of the twins for Benjamin and his late wife Chloe since the day they came home from the hospital as newborns. Chloe was killed in a tragic car accident when the twins were just eight weeks old, and Mother Peace moved in with Benjamin temporarily. She was a sixty-year-old retired elementary school teacher, and she'd had plenty of experience with children, having taught for over thirty-eight years. Mother Peace had no children of her own, but she'd raised most of the children who had grown up in the church where Benjamin was now the senior pastor. She was a godsend to Benjamin. At the age of sixty, she had enough spunk to keep up with two newborns, and now, at the young age of seventy-one, she was still active enough to keep up with two adolescent "brainiacs." She still tooled around town in her four-door Honda Accord, doing her own shopping and taking pilates and aerobics twice a week. She'd moved back into her townhome when Genevieve and Benjamin married. It gave Mother Peace purpose to help out. Now that Genevieve and Benjamin were often out of town during the week, she spent a great deal of time at the house with the children. And Genevieve was grateful.

As the twins compared gifts in the back seat, ecstatic about the new iPod Nanos that Genevieve had picked up in New York, Mother Peace questioned her about her trip, and told her how many wonderful things she and the children had done while she was away. She also tossed in the gossip about what had been going on in church, like who died and whose daughter was *finally* getting married. Genevieve laughed a distant laugh that let Mother Peace know that she was miles away from their conversation.

Mother Peace's distinctive sandpaper voice brought Genevieve back to earth. "You are a million miles away, young lady."

"Oh, I'm sorry," Genevieve said, slightly embarrassed that she'd been only half-listening to Mother Peace.

"It's okay. One thing I understand is young love."

Genevieve chuckled. "I don't think forty-seven is considered young, Mother Peace."

"It is when you're seventy-one."

"Got a point."

The four of them listened to Mother Peace's big band CD, and Genevieve floated back to a space where she could concentrate on missing Benjamin. She thought about his famous red beans and rice. She'd been looking forward to a nice family dinner. That was all ruined now. She felt lovesick. She'd been hoping to put some "*stability*" back into their marriage tonight. But it seemed that God had rearranged all her plans. She knew that she could count on Benjamin being dead tired when he returned home from church. Stability would have to wait until morning. So she laid her head against the headrest and stole a few moments to reminisce. She glowed with a smile that only Benjamin could bring.

"You must be thinking about something awfully special, big as that smile is," Mother Peace teased over Duke Ellington's "I've Got It Bad and That Ain't Good."

"You better know it," Genevieve said before slipping back into her private thoughts.

Genevieve had barely retrieved her luggage from the trunk before Mother Peace and the children pulled off. The house was unusually dark except for flickers of light shining through the first floor windows. She mumbled to herself as she dragged her suitcases up the walkway. On the porch, she fumbled with her keys, reasoning as to why Mother Peace and the twins hadn't left any lights on. She stuck the wrong key in the lock, and then accidentally dropped the whole set between one of her suitcases and carry-on bag. When she stooped down to pick her keys up, the porch light sprang on and the front door opened. The suddenness of it scared her.

"You look like you need the assistance of a man," a familiar voice said.

"Well, only one will do." Genevieve exhaled, rising to meet the creature she'd been anticipating for three excruciatingly long weeks. Benjamin stepped out onto the porch and pulled her to him. Genevieve caressed him and buried her head in his chest, relieved. They re-familiarized themselves with one another, kissing long enough to make up for time that their lips had been separated.

"Maybe we should go in before the neighbors call the fire department," Benjamin joked in his husky, relaxed tone.

"I think so," Genevieve said, following him into the house. "I thought you had a meeting."

"I do. It's right here with you."

Genevieve's eyes widened with amazement as she stepped into the foyer. The entire house was illuminated with candlelight: Roman candles, pillars, tealights, votives, and floating candles. She walked around, inhaling the different scents, trying to imagine where Benjamin had gotten all the beautiful candles from, and when he had found the time to arrange them so perfectly. He had transformed the house into a romantic movie set. And the dining room table was set for two, with Genevieve's favorite red beans and rice on their very best china.

"Oh, honey, you are so sweet. I love you," she squealed.

Benjamin kissed her softly on her forehead. "Missed you."

"Missed you more," Genevieve said, wrapping her arms around him. And God answered her stability prayer in the most beautiful way.

Chapter Two

Cassandra "Sandy" Moss waited patiently outside of her therapist's office, perusing the same magazine that she'd read every Wednesday evening for the last few weeks, while she waited for Jody, her therapist, to open her office door, let her last client out, and invite her in. It was a predictable flow. People came and went like Jody was selling some valuable good. Every hour on the hour someone arrived to receive another dose of whatever it was that Jody provided that made them feel halfway whole—at least until the next week. Sandy laughed to herself about the fact that she always seemed to find an article that she hadn't read in that same magazine.

She'd been coming to therapy for three years in an attempt to deal with debilitating panic attacks. She was embarrassed initially, because as a Christian woman, she thought she should have been able to pray them away. But that never seemed to be the case. Over the last three years, therapy had helped to quell the frequency of the attacks and helped Sandy to begin to deal with what Jody referred to as "underlying issues"—like hating her mother—something she couldn't dare admit to Pastor Kelley. It was his suggestion that she see Jody Suggs, a psychiatrist who provided

Christian counseling. Before she began therapy, Sandy had fooled herself into thinking that she'd forgiven her mother. But talking to Jody every week seemed to prove otherwise. She wrestled with the fear of being a lifelong therapy patient like other people she'd heard about, but she was willing to do whatever was necessary to move forward and leave the panic attacks behind.

Six months ago, she coaxed her younger sister, Josette, into attending "family" sessions with her. Although Josette had made it clear that she was not interested in, nor felt that she needed, any kind of "therapy," she caved in under Sandy's guilt tactics, which included accusing her of being selfish and non-supportive. Today was a family session. Sandy knew that Josette was going to be late as usual. But she'd vowed six months ago that she wasn't going to let Josette's lack of commitment deter her.

Josette reiterated her feelings about therapy by not arriving on time. Therapy was not a priority for her. The only reason that she kept attending was because she'd let guilt get the best of her. Sandy was experienced at making Josette feel like a self-centered monster. Josette's participation in Sandy's weekly *liberation hour* was a dutiful chore, especially since she had her own problems to deal with now that she and her husband were separated. She'd moved in with Sandy three months ago, and the arrangement was beginning to strain their relationship. Between Sandy's obsessive-compulsive cleanliness and Josette being accustomed to having a housekeeper, a snapping of the rope was inevitable.

Sandy looked at the wall clock and placed the magazine back on the table. It was two minutes to show time. She stood up and walked over to the window facing the front of the building to stretch her legs. She was astonished to see Josette's black Range Rover pulling up in front. Sandy looked curiously out of the floor-to-ceiling window, pressing her forehead to the glass to confirm that it actually was her little sister hurrying into the building wearing black Prada pumps and a St. John's knit suit, with a Hermes bag slung over her shoulder. Josette's naturally curly brown locks pulled and sprang, obeying the direction of the September wind, as she high-stepped her petite self into the building with her eyes hidden behind Christian Dior sunshades. Sandy shook her head disdainfully at how much money Josette was wearing, and how many starving people she could have fed instead. Then her thoughts shifted. This was the first time in six months that Josette had ever been on time. She had used excuse after excuse to justify being at least thirty minutes late, cutting Sandy's liberation hour in half. It was always some big case she was working on, rush hour traffic, or a new client. The list went on.

But today, *Ms. Thang*, attorney Josette Moss-Kelley, was on time. Maybe it was because of the fight they had the night before, when Sandy screamed at the highest volume her voice could reach that Josette could find another place to stay if she didn't stop acting like she was the lone rare star hanging in the center of the universe. Sandy was prepared to gloat. Josette hurried into the suite at the same time Jody's door swung open. Even Jody looked confounded as she said good-bye to the Browns, a couple who had begun just four weeks ago.

Sandy could always tell how the Browns' sessions went by the look on Mr. Brown's face. If it was a good session, he usually spoke a few pleasantries when he came out. If not, there was just a nod of resignation. The couple looked so perfectly matched that Sandy wondered what kinds of marital problems they could possibly be having. But today, her usual habit of studying Mr. Brown was halted by the expression on her sister's face. Puffy red eyes that were previously hidden by three hundred dollar sunshades were evidence that Josette had been crying. Sandy guessed that

Josette had finally talked to her husband, Patrick. The two of them hadn't spoken in the three months Josette had been living with Sandy—not since the night Patrick put her out of their house. Sandy feared that Patrick would divorce Josette this time. And if he did, he had every right to. Josette's tears seemed to be a confirmation. Losing Patrick was the only thing that could make a normally brash Josette come close to dropping tears.

Josette hurried past Sandy and Jody and plopped down in the chair closest to the window in Jody's apartment-style office. It gave one the feeling of being in a friend's living room, causing Jody's clients to relax and let their guard down while she pried into the parts of their lives that they worked hard to keep secret. The color scheme was shades of blue. The walls were a deep subduing blue, while the plush carpet was powder blue with navy designs throughout in rectangles, squares, and circles. The furniture was an ocean blue-colored leather that almost looked like it belonged in a child's play room. Every piece was oversized. The room itself was unusually large for an office. It had been designed with a dual purpose in mind. Jody presented team-building workshops and other seminars for business executives. On one side of the room was a large gray conference table that seated twelve people. On the more welcoming side, nearer to Jody's desk, were the oversized sofa and loveseat. A lone chair sat in a corner by itself. It was always Josette's preference to sit in that chair, putting distance between her and *them*.

An assortment of plants lined the walls and shelves: spiders, yuccas, dieffenbachias, and tree plants, none of them artificial. Jody's love for art was evident as well. The walls showcased several paintings by well-known artists in originals and reproductions. She held an abstract gem by actor Billy Dee Williams that she'd purchased at a charity auction. Her favorite was Annie Lee's *Blue Monday* lithograph on canvas that hung behind her desk. It fit right in with the melodic blue tones in the room. A calming vertical fish tank stood next to the chair near the window, where Jody's "babies" swam carefree in confinement. They were Josette's only friends during the liberation hour.

Jody began the session by praying. Sandy closed her eyes and meditated on Jody's words. Josette watched the fish swim. As soon as Jody and Sandy had said their "*Amens*," Josette reached down into a shopping bag, pulled out a book, and tossed it into Sandy's lap.

With a balloon of sarcasm, she said, "Thought I'd bring you some *focus* today."

Sandy grinned, prepared to be sucked up to. "What are you talking about? Oh . . ." she said before reading the title. "*Moving Forward . . .* What? Is this your way of making up for last night?" she smiled.

"No, this is my way to help you get some closure so I can go back to kickboxing class on Wednesdays, instead of coming here. No offense, Jody."

"None taken," Jody said, fully aware of Josette's resistance.

Sandy looked at the back cover and gasped. "Oh my God—*where* did you get this?"

Josette's response was tight and curt. "Bookstore."

Sandy's emotions danced between relief and devastation. The feelings she thought she'd gained control over in the last three years were choking her. She felt a panic attack creeping up. Her fingers tingled. Her heart pounded fast and hard against her chest. She breathed in deeply and out quickly.

"I need air," she said before running out of Jody's office.

"*What* is going on? She's been off the Zoloft for two months!" Jody demanded.

"That's *her mother*," Josette said, sidestepping past Jody.

She hadn't meant to cause Sandy a setback. Sandy just needed to move on. She'd been in therapy long enough. Genevieve had moved on. Josette walked down the hall, thinking about what she'd just done. Not proud, but not necessarily regretful. She pushed the restroom door open.

"I'm sorry. I didn't know how else to tell you," she apologized, trying to scoop compassion from her empty vault.

Sandy paced back and forth with her arms wrapped tightly around her—comforting herself. Tears flowed down her honey-colored cheeks. Josette watched as Sandy repeated her ritual. *Step. Step. Step. Turn. Step. Step. Step. Turn.* Even in tears, Josette's big sister was regal at five feet eight inches tall with curves and fullness in all the right areas. She made those stretch denim jeans, simple white spandex and cotton t-shirt, and two-and-a-half-inch black leather ankle boots look like a Vera Wang gown and a pair of Jimmy Choo shoes. She could easily have been a model commanding a runway, instead of a thirty-one-year-old blubbering nurse who needed to let go of her past. Sandy smoothed her straight, shoulder-length hair behind her ears, and blew hard into the Kleenex she had balled in her hands.

"Sandy, I said I was sorry."

Sandy put her hand up in a stop motion. "I'm okay," she mumbled, sucking in a breath. "How long have you known?"

"Just today. I met a friend for espresso at Borders. I just happened to pick that book up. It was a fluke. I wanted to wait until we were here."

Josette remembered how the man at the counter had rambled on about a book that his customers were raving about, *claiming* it had changed their lives. He was selling the book like he was going to receive a percentage of the royalties. Josette blocked him out at first. She did that whenever strangers tried to make small talk with her. Her mind was on getting back to the office and going over a case. But the New Books display was right next to the counter. She figured it wouldn't hurt to get the book for Sandy, who frequently read self-help books. Seeing Genevieve on the back cover looking polished and professional delivered an unexpected blow. Josette had to hold on to the counter to keep from passing out right there on the floor. Trembling, she paid the cashier while her thoughts fought each other for forefront space in her mind. As she walked away, she heard the sales clerk talking about a book signing the upcoming week.

Josette had sat in her car for more than a half an hour trying to get *her* focus back. She'd forgotten where she was going and what she was supposed to be doing. The author bio kept ringing in her head. *Dr. Carpenter is an adjunct professor at Greydale Christian College and the director of a women's rehabilitation center in Virginia. She resides in Virginia with her husband and two children.* Josette had cursed under her breath about the fact that Genevieve had the nerve to have more children. She'd done enough damage to her and Sandy.

The restroom door pushed open again. "Let's finish the session. Obviously, we have a lot to talk about today," Jody said.

Sandy nodded. "I need a few more minutes please."

Jody acquiesced and Josette followed. Left alone, Sandy prayed aloud. "Father, why do you persecute me so? If you feel our pain, why do you allow me to hurt so much? Sixteen years, Lord. I don't want to hurt anymore." Then she remembered David. *Like as a father pitieth his children, so the Lord pitieth them that fear him. For He knoweth our frame; He remembereth that we are dust.*

Sandy spent the rest of the evening alone in her room, collapsed across her bed, drained from the session. She was wounded by the knowledge that Genevieve had more children after deserting them. She thought of reasons why Genevieve had never come back for her—hadn't tried to contact her. Maybe Josette was right. She was thirty-one years old now. What did or didn't happen years ago couldn't be changed. It was time for her to stop having a pity party about her lost mother. She'd spent thousands of dollars on therapy in the last three years, and what had it really changed? Genevieve had gone on with her life. If she had been any kind of mother, she would have contacted them as soon as she was in recovery. She could have come back. She could have checked to see if they were still *alive*.

Sandy needed peace. Josette had suffocated her with that book. *How could Genevieve just start all over? How could she do it?* Sandy held the book tightly to her breast, letting go of her tears. She needed answers—the ones only Genevieve could provide.

The Genevieve Sandy remembered was far from the polished looking woman on the back cover of the book she held. *That* Genevieve had been a slave to crack cocaine, ultimately allowing it to separate their family, causing her and Josette to become foster children. Sandy was twelve and Josette ten, the day a protective service worker and two police officers came to take them away. Genevieve had been gone over a week. She'd been in several treatment programs, but none had proven to be successful. Drugs had a stronghold on her then.

Josette was the one who made that final call to their family worker, who'd been working diligently to keep them together and help Genevieve overcome her addiction. Sandy had hoped that Genevieve would get better. Josette had given up. At the age of ten, Josette hardened her heart to any ideas of Genevieve getting better. She wrote Genevieve off. It was the only way she could cope with the scars Genevieve's addiction had caused her.

Sandy's childhood friend and confidante, Brian Joseph McKenzie, who was affectionately referred to by the nickname B. J., stood on the porch of their two-family flat in front of his mother, Sarah, looking on helplessly as the protective service worker escorted Sandy and Josette down the walkway and put them into the car. B. J. and Sarah lived in the upstairs flat, along with B. J.'s teenage brother, Craig, who ran the streets hustling. B. J. was the most feared seventh grader in the neighborhood. He fought at the drop of a dime, never losing a fight—earning his respect. The peril of their east side neighborhood demanded it. His brother Craig was already a certified thug at the age of sixteen. He had warned B. J. that once he allowed anyone to "punk" him, others would follow. So B. J. fought to prevent himself from becoming a perpetual victim like some of the other kids in the neighborhood who frequently had their money, clothing, and gym shoes taken by the *"fittest."* B. J.'s reputation simplified Sandy and Josette's life. None of the bullies dared to challenge them because they knew they'd have to deal with B. J.—or worse—Craig.

B. J. had been protecting Sandy since kindergarten. His first fight was with Tommy Green, a boy twice his size. B. J. whipped him good for kicking Sandy in her backside during reading. But the day he watched her and Josette being taken away, he couldn't do anything but try to hang on to his steel reputation that was being melted by his tears. Sarah comforted him by rubbing his shoulders and speaking mother words in his ear. She told Sandy and Josette to call her at least once a week, and promised that she'd still take them to the matinee on Sundays. Sandy hoped Sarah was telling the truth. She looked back at B. J. once before she got into the car.

She knew that if she never saw B. J. again, their bond was sealed tightly. He was like a brother to her and Josette. And he and Sandy loved each other in their own way. Even Sarah understood that.

Sandy hadn't seen B. J. cry in all the years she'd known him, not even when he had climbed on top of the roof in the fifth grade and fell and broke his leg. Not any of the times Sarah had put a Grade A butt whipping on him for not coming home on time. Not even when Craig caught him hanging around with the neighborhood drug dealers and boxed him all the way home like he was a man. Not a sound came from B. J. Just tears. Sandy beheld them like an eighth wonder. One of the most feared seventh graders on Detroit's east side shed tears for her. That was their good-bye.

Sandy and Josette were placed in an emergency placement with a woman the foster care social worker referred to as Ms. Betty. She received children who were newly placed in foster care until a permanent placement was secured. Usually, children didn't stay with her past twenty-four hours. Ms. Betty was a cheerful, sixty-three-year-old black woman. She was heavy-set with long gray hair that she wore in a single braid, which coursed down her back and reached her behind. She had a tiny two-bedroom house that was cluttered with a bunch of knick-knacks that she called "*antiques.*"

Sandy and Josette slept in her guest bedroom. The room was painted in a fading yellow color. It was safe and unisex in case Ms. Betty cared for a boy or girl. The furniture was oak, just a simple children's-sized dresser and twin beds. There were no paintings or any of her antiques on the walls or shelves, except a pair of prayer hands on the dresser that was a night light. Sandy and Josette lay awake in fear that night. They'd heard all the horror stories about foster care from other children at school. They knew that the likelihood of being split up or bounced around was high. They were afraid of being separated, so they made a pact in the illumination of those prayer hands that if they were separated, they would run away, neither one of them knowing where they'd run to. But the fact that they said it aloud gave them a sort of power when they had none. And powerlessness was still the feeling that prevailed when Sandy summed up all thirty-one of her years.

Linda and Roger Stevens became their first and only foster parents after their temporary placement with Ms. Betty. Both in their late forties, they were mature and believed in structure and discipline along with love. They were good parents. Roger worked midnights at an automotive factory on the assembly line, and Linda worked part-time at a flower shop that her family owned called Stop and Smell the Roses. Their home was located in a well-kept suburb of Detroit, in a newly built subdivision. It was a four-bedroom brick colonial on a cul-de-sac. The lovely house looked like it belonged in a Better Homes and Gardens magazine. The outside was exceptionally maintained, with a well-manicured lawn that was sprinkled with splashes of color from Linda's impatiens. Two stone statues of a little black boy and girl carrying flower baskets that overflowed with real pink and white impatiens stood on either side of the couple's French doors, inviting company in. The couple had done all the landscaping themselves.

Linda was meticulous about housecleaning and creating an environment that was homey. She prided herself on being a good homemaker and training the girls accordingly. Every few days, Linda cut fresh flowers from her flower garden in the back yard and placed them in various places throughout the house, which created an original, spring-smelling aroma that Sandy and Josette still remembered as adults. The house was alive with its own personality and a feeling of tranquility that the girls had lacked living with Genevieve.

Linda prepared home-cooked meals daily, enlisting the assistance of Sandy and Josette to help develop their housekeeping skills. It was a part of their household chores. Every Saturday was laundry day. Linda taught the girls how to properly sort, wash, and iron clothes. And she was particular about how she liked the towels and sheets folded. The linen closets were full of colorful, fluffy new washcloths and bath towels that were rolled neatly on the shelves. The sheets smelled of lilac and lemon and were folded in perfect squares. Sandy often opened the linen closet just to smell the fresh scents that reminded her of new beginnings. She couldn't remember a time with Genevieve when life had been so orderly. But the orderliness came with a price tag she and Josette were reluctant to pay.

Boot camp. That is what living with Linda and Roger was like initially. It was a tough transition—especially for Josette, the self-proclaimed rebel. The couple placed them on a tight schedule with homework, chores, *and* Bible study. And there were *rules*. Sandy and Josette were culture-shocked. Genevieve's addiction had enabled them to function as miniature adults. They governed themselves, watched what they wanted to on television, and went to bed when they wanted. That was their norm. But Linda and Roger were quick to enforce *their* household rules. Broken rules led to swift punishment. Eventually, Sandy and Josette adjusted, and discovered that life with Linda and Roger was beneficial. New clothes, weekly hair salon appointments, and allowances were just some of the niceties that helped to convince the two of them that life was better with Linda and Roger.

Fostering was Linda and Roger's calling. It wasn't about the money. They went above and beyond the girls' basic needs. There were family vacations every year, ski trips, and summer camps. And when it was time for parent-teacher conferences, school plays, and tournaments, they were there. Linda and Roger submerged themselves in every aspect of the girls' lives—even the mandatory therapy sessions that were required by the foster care agency. They were God-fearing Christians who simply loved children. They had successfully raised a son who was away at college when Sandy and Josette came to live with them. It was under their teaching that Sandy accepted Jesus Christ as a teenager. It was like moving from Genevieve's world to normalcy. But Sandy secretly wished that she could have the life she had with Linda and Roger with Genevieve. She would have traded the two of them for her mother back then.

Sandy's depression and panic attacks started then, but she was too young to understand what was happening to her. Family visitation at the agency was scheduled every Friday. Most often, Genevieve didn't show up. The girls' foster care worker, Mrs. Irma James, compassionately explained to them how difficult it was for a person who was addicted to recover. She told them that as long as Genevieve was using drugs, the chances of them seeing her for family visitation were slim. It was defeating to twelve-year-old Sandy to hear those words, but even now, she appreciated Mrs. James' honesty. It had always stayed with her.

Mrs. James was empathetic, but truthful. She didn't want to risk the girls getting their hopes up for a mother who was going to let them down every week—mainly so that Sandy wouldn't get her hopes up. Josette had stopped caring. On the rare occasions when Genevieve did manage to show up, Josette sat distant, refusing to speak until the hour-long visits were over. After the first year, Josette asked to stop coming altogether. But Sandy agonized over Genevieve.

By the time Sandy started ninth grade, Genevieve had gotten a job and began coming to the visits more regularly. Sandy's optimism peaked. Finally, she thought that the three of them could be a family again. But those dreams were shattered when Genevieve had another relapse. That's when Sandy gave up. Loving Genevieve was like being on an emotional roller coaster. Her grades suffered, and she withdrew emotionally. Her zest for life withered away under constant disappointments.

Linda and Roger supported them as much as they could, becoming involved in their therapy sessions to help them deal with the emotional baggage that stemmed from having their lives disjointed by Genevieve's addiction. Although they had given them love and a stable home environment, they both knew that neither of those things could replace the mother that Sandy desperately needed to help her to feel normal.

Josette's rebellion crept out during the therapy sessions. She ignored the therapist's questions, building an impenetrable wall around herself. She closed herself off from the world she had lived in with Genevieve, and wouldn't allow the therapist or anyone else to draw her back in. Josette's disposition after the hour-long sessions made living with her torturous. Days after she had endured unwanted prodding by the therapist, Josette wreaked havoc in the home. Linda's prized Sunday china would be "accidentally" broken during dishwashing, important messages would be disregarded, or one of the family members' "dry clean only" garments would mysteriously end up in the wash and ruined.

The therapist explained to Linda that Josette's hellish attitude was a result of her repressing the pain she had experienced. She called it "separation anxiety with displaced anger." She suggested that the family allow Josette the emotional space to deal with the trauma of Genevieve's abandonment. But Linda kept a short rope on Josette's short fuse. She made it clear that sassing and back-talking would not be accepted, regardless of therapy "issues."

And Josette knew how far to go before Linda's invisible rope snatched her back into submission. She didn't disrespect Linda like she had done Genevieve. *"Do not withhold correction from a child . . ."* Linda would say, warning Josette when her limits were being reached. They'd been told that their foster care parents were prohibited from using physical discipline. But Linda had responded very bluntly, "I don't care what that social worker told you two. The bottom line is that Roger and I run this house and we're not taking any mess. The Word of God is the guide here. And it plainly states that when correction is necessary, the rod is to be used. And it will be," Linda said, paraphrasing. That was her way of reminding them who was really in charge. Although, due to their circumstances, she hadn't intended to hit either one of them, but her speaking those words kept things in check.

Sandy looked at Genevieve's face on the back cover of the book again, and made her decision to phone the psychology department at Greydale. It took her two days to finally make the call. The fear of rejection threatened her. Just when she got her nerve up, it ended up being fruitless anyway. A secretary answered and explained that Genevieve was on an extended leave to promote her new book. When Sandy ended the call, she held the phone in her hand and looked at Genevieve's face on the back cover of the book. She wondered who she was and what series of events had turned her life around and made her the kind of woman she hadn't been with her and Josette. Sandy was fifteen years old the last time she saw Genevieve. It was the day that the court took Genevieve's parental rights away permanently.

Sandy read the book, trailing her fingers gently over the environment-friendly paper, searching for clues as to who Genevieve was *now*. The very words she read were precious because they were a part of the mother whose love she'd longed for since she was twelve. Genevieve's absence had left her hollow. She wanted to fill that hole up with something permanent if possible. She obsessed over the "what-ifs," pulling and twisting strands of hair from the nerve spot in the middle of her scalp where a patch of her reddish brown hair was much shorter than the rest because of her constant nervous picking. She even tried calling information before realizing that she didn't know what part of Virginia Genevieve lived in.

Mid-way through the first chapter of the book, she had an epiphany. She turned to the Acknowledgement page. There in black and white was what she needed. *Thanks to my publicist, Seth Campbell.* Her best guess was that Seth Campbell was either in New York or California. God smiled on her persistence. Seth Campbell was the owner of the Seth Campbell Agency in New York, New York. It was already past eight p.m., so she waited until the next morning. She lied and said she was interested in obtaining Genevieve's services for a speaking engagement. After being on hold for almost half an hour, she convinced Seth that she was an old friend of Genevieve's who didn't know how else to contact her, and she apologized for lying to his secretary. She left her name and number with him and prayed that somehow he'd get the message to her. He probably represented a hundred people, but Sandy hoped that he'd have some sympathy for her. It was a calculated stab in the dark.

At least a week had passed since she'd made that call. Sandy accepted the fact that Josette was right. Punishing herself for being home alone on a Christian Singles-Mingle Friday, feeling dejected, she sulked. But she thanked God that Josette was in D.C. for a law conference and would be gone for a whole week. Then she showered, donned a pair of Joe Boxer pajamas, and walked down the spiral staircase of her two-story detached condominium. She'd had it built just three years ago, out in the suburbs, where ducks parlayed in her backyard. It was a twenty-six hundred square foot, three bedroom, two-and-a-half bath home with hardwood flooring in the foyer, living room, dining room, and kitchen. The two-story family room was Sandy's main entertainment area, with its vaulted ceilings and red brick fireplace that crept up the wall. A plush beige carpet made it even cozier. Being practical, Sandy had chosen rust colored leather furniture for this one room. She hated leather, but she cringed at the thought of one of her church members spilling something on her sofa during a dinner party or "pamper" night.

Her artwork, as well as pictures of herself, Josette and Patrick, her foster parents, and foster brother, were scattered throughout the room on the fireplace mantle, end tables, and walls. There was a multi-picture photo screen that held at least a hundred photos of her and Josette's extended family, near her Bose stereo system. The kitchen was a chef's dream, with maple cabinets and black granite counters with specs of beige and silver. Her maple covered refrigerator blended in with her traditional looking cabinets, while the rich looking stainless steel Wolf stove gave the kitchen a modern edge. An island in the center of the room was where she and Josette *used to* have girl talk over ice cream atop Sandy's wrought iron bar stools—back in the days before Josette had invaded her home.

Sandy mulled around the kitchen with her furry yellow Big Bird slippers on. His round, feathered head bobbed on each foot as she walked over to the cabinet, pulled out an antique whistler, filled it with water, and placed it on the stove. Having an old-fashioned whistler made her think of the good old days that never were. It made her feel like life was simple when it wasn't. She took the last bag of chamomile tea out of the "goodie" cabinet and dropped it in her favorite mug, which read: *My cup runneth over.* She sat on one of the bar stools with her feet dangling and waited for Betsy to whistle. She imagined that she was married and that her husband and children would come running through the door any minute, interrupting her "mommy time." Her husband would tuck the kids in, read them a story, and then return to their master bedroom suite and create a love story with her. That was how it was supposed to have been. But no, God had this master plan that she still hadn't been privy to after all these years of serving Him.

Sandy was tired. She thought about Genevieve and decided that she was going to crash one of her book signings and let her fans know the truth about her. No more playing *Ms. Nice Christian.* She was going to let Genevieve's fans know just what her triumphant little story cost her and Josette. Her anger rose and switched gears. She thought about the man who had made a mockery of her love for four years, and wondered just what kind of plan God had for real. She hated even thinking about those years. Then a scripture came to mind. *For I know the thoughts that I think toward you, saith the Lord, thoughts of peace, and not of evil, to give you an expected end.* Sandy looked upward and said, "Yeah, right!"

The whistler screeched in agony. She poured the hot water in her mug and added a teaspoon of sugar. Fake sugar equaled cancer. Her motto was: "Everything in moderation"—except for sex, of course. That was another little incidental her Father had denied her. It had been so long, she'd forgotten what it was like to be emotionally and physically synced with someone. She had given sex up along with her marriage and nasty divorce, so she could please Him. She thought about that same scripture again. Then her thoughts switched back to her drug-addicted mother, growing up in foster care, and her unfaithful ex-husband. "Sure," she said, stirring her sugar in. She repented immediately and said, "Daddy, please forgive me, I'm just tired."

Her phone bawled, interrupting her gripe session. She had every mind not to answer it. "Is that You calling to scold me about what I just said?" she chuckled. She walked over to the wall nearest the family room and picked the cordless up from the base, trying not to make the caller feel like she could care less about what he or she wanted in the middle of her gripe session. She turned her "nice nurse" voice on before saying a very polite "Hello." She pretended that she was glad to have someone calling at ten-thirty p.m. on a Friday night—even if it was in the middle of her complaining to God.

"Cassandra Marie Moss . . . is that you?" a shaking voice queried. It was the one Sandy hadn't heard since she was fifteen. The one that had haunted her dreams. Dazed, Sandy slid down the wall until she was sitting on her behind with her knees tucked into her chest. She pushed her head forward between her knees so that she could breathe more easily, and held the phone close to her ear like it was a lifeline.

"How could you just forget about us?" she said, unable to hold back the flow of anguish creeping down her face. Her soul ached. Grief overtook her. The next few moments were filled with the sounds of Sandy and Genevieve's crying and sniffles.

"I'm so sorry," was all Genevieve could repeat through her tears.

Sandy wanted to forget herself and her Lord, spray Genevieve with curses and make her feel guilty about what she had done. She wanted to hurt her like she had been hurt. She wanted to be cold and vicious like Josette would have been, but that inner calm wouldn't allow her.

Hours passed while the two of them waded back through the years, through Genevieve's story, Sandy's story, and Josette's story. By two a.m. Sandy was exhausted, more so emotionally than physically. She wanted to get off the phone, but Genevieve kept asking questions about her life as if she was trying to fill in all her empty spaces where there should have been memories. Sandy told Genevieve about her marriage and divorce. She told her about therapy. She told her about Josette and Patrick. She told her about the hate that she'd been carrying around until she had started therapy. They talked for another half hour, both of them tired and overwhelmed, before finally deciding that it would be best if they met in person. It was only fitting that what had to be said was said face to face—woman to woman. Genevieve owed Sandy that much.

Genevieve had a book signing in Chicago in two weeks. They planned to meet then. Sandy phoned Josette in D.C., asking if she would come.

"Jo, I think it would be better if we did this *together*. I need you to go with me," Sandy said.

"NO!" Josette scowled amid colorful expletives. "I ain't got NOTHING to say to that woman. You hear me!" Josette yelled into the phone.

Sandy didn't challenge Josette's feelings. She'd learned that in therapy. *"Each person is entitled to express his or her feelings as long as it does not hurt or interfere with the expression of another,"* Jody's voice reminded her. It was fair. Josette was entitled. But she had to see it through.

Chapter Three

Josette left the courthouse and drove down East Jefferson to Belle Isle Park. She sat in her truck, not sure what to do with her time. She reclined her seat back, kicked her shoes off, and watched six middle school girls play soccer. Bony James' "Into the Blue" serenaded from the radio amidst the laughter and screams of the zealous adolescents. She took a quick gulp of the Vernors she'd purchased at the Mobil Mart up the road and let out a loud throaty "Aaah . . ." as the ginger burned her throat. In an effort to maintain her 115-pound, size-four frame, she hadn't had one in weeks. It was her own special treat to herself for finally letting therapy with Sandy go. To think that Sandy had the audacity to ask if she would join her in meeting with Genevieve was ridiculous. That was the last straw.

She could have gone to kickboxing—the class she claimed she'd been missing the last six months because of Sandy—but she couldn't drum up enough energy. Life was setting in. Her husband was good as gone. And Sandy had stung her two weeks ago when she told her, "You've got to be the dumbest woman on the planet to lose a man like Patrick Caleb Kelley. Good women like me sit around praying for a brother like Pat—man of

God, fine, and financially stable, while chicken heads like you get him and are so stupid, you can't keep him. It's a shame before God."

They came close to throwing blows that night. A real live cat fight. They were up in each other's faces, screaming like two adolescents, daring one another to pass the first lick. Josette resented Sandy and her unsolicited opinion. She wanted to scratch her holy eyes out of her head. She was sick of her talking about God, praying, and sticking her nose in her business. None of that mattered now. Not even the secrets she'd kept that were destroying her marriage—causing the best thing that had ever happened to her to walk right out of her life.

Josette gently bumped her head against the headrest, trying to think of a logical reason as to why more than fifteen years were washing down the drain. She'd had a good man. Period. Their arguments were few and minor. Their main disagreement had been about when to have children—and sometimes about God. Ambitious, Josette wanted to press full speed ahead into her career. Patrick wanted a family, and he wished his wife would at least come to church with him *sometimes*. But that was no reason for her to do what she'd done. At least none she was ready to admit. A stupid affair. It was tearing her life apart like a demolition team. She couldn't go back, and couldn't face what was just up the road. Life was a blur.

She remembered the first day she met Patrick "Preacher Boy" Kelley. She and Sandy had been living with Linda and Roger for four years. It was summer. Josette was starting ninth grade that fall. She stood out in front of the house practicing cheerleading routines with the neighborhood girls, Jasmine Davis, Ramona Carter, and Penelope Smalls, while Sandy watched from the porch. Josette had aspirations of becoming a cheerleader when she got to high school. She had been on her middle school cheerleading team since sixth grade. For her, it was a natural progression.

It was eighty-seven degrees that day, but the humidity made it feel ten degrees hotter. Heat stretched across the sky like a canopy, but youthful energy was not deterred. The young tree in the front yard provided no relief from the sun, but it didn't matter to them. They were caught up in their own carefree world. In the middle of Josette scolding Ramona about her timing being off on a jump, she saw the most beautiful creature she'd seen in her entire fourteen years, walking down the middle of the street in a cutoff Lions jersey, gripping a football. He had a gym bag slung over his shoulder. Josette was frozen by miles and miles of muscles underneath a worn out Billy Simms Lions Jersey with #20 sprawled across it in faded white lettering. Patrick's stomach was cut perfectly. It looked as if a tailor had sewn his skin on top of all his muscles. His athletically sculpted physique was so tight and toned that Josette garnered a new appreciation for the male anatomy that day. She was catatonic staring at his delightful looking showcase with a honey brown face that was just as handsome. It seemed that God had personally formed him out of the dust.

"WHO is *that*?" Josette inquired of Penelope Smalls, the neighborhood junior investigative reporter, with her hands mounted on her size-four hips.

"That ain't nobody but Preacher Boy," Penelope smacked her lips. "And you might as well close your mouth, because he don't get down like that. All he do is play football and keep his nose stuck up in a Bible. His daddy a preacher. He can't have no girlfriends. I don't even think he want a girlfriend. He is *lame*," she reported.

"He look too good to be without a girlfriend. He need to be with me!"

"I told you, Preacher Boy ain't talkin' to *nobody*."

Josette had stopped listening to Penelope. She watched in awe as Patrick walked across the street to Keith Cooper's colonial and rang the doorbell. Keith poked his head out and said something. Patrick walked back down the walkway and sat on the curb. He placed his football down by his feet, pulled a small Bible from his gym bag, and began reading. Josette had never seen a man besides her foster father, Roger, read the Bible that intently. She made up her mind right then that she was going to get to know him.

"Where you goin'?" Sandy had called out as Josette strolled across the street.

"I'm 'bout to introduce myself to the new neighbor."

Sandy laughed. Even at fourteen, Josette was brash and invincible. When she saw something she wanted, she went for the take.

Josette stood right over Patrick. She could hear laughter emerging across the street, but she was brave. She didn't care. There was no plan of failure. She stood so close to Patrick that he would have knocked her tiny frame over if he had tried to stand up. She looked down at him and said, *"Blessed is the man who walketh not in the counsel of the ungodly, nor standedth in the way of sinners, nor sitteth in the seat of the scornful. But his delight is in the law of the LORD; and in His law doth he meditate day and night. And he shall be like a tree planted by the rivers of water, that bringeth forth his fruit in his season; his leaf also shall not wither; and whatsoever he doeth shall prosper. The ungodly are not so: but are like the chaff which the wind driveth away. Therefore the ungodly shall not stand in the judgment, nor sinners in the congregation of the righteous: For the LORD knoweth the way of the righteous: but the way of the ungodly shall perish."* Then she backed out of his space coolly, giving him just enough room to stand.

He rose, smiling, towering over her at six feet. "Psalm 1," he nodded, impressed with her. And she was just as pretty as she could be, all five feet two inches, with her thick curly hair pulled back into a bushy pony tail

She dissected him with her hazel, feline eyes. "Absolutely correct."

Patrick was grinning ear to ear. He could feel her energy.

"My name is Josette Moss. But my friends call me Jo." She extended her hand, expecting him to plant a kiss on it, like gentlemen did in the movies.

Patrick's forehead glistened with sweat, not from the heat, but from the nervousness that the pint-size beauty was causing in him. His voice cracked when he spoke. "I'm Pat—I'm Patrick Kelley," he said, turning her hand sideways, giving it a shake. "And I've never heard that scripture quoted so beautifully."

Josette stared him straight in his eyes, increasing his nervousness. He shifted his weight and looked toward the ground. "Thank you," she said, giving him another thorough look over. When she saw Keith coming out of the house, she stepped an inch closer to Patrick and said, "We'll talk later." With that, she swayed her hips back across the street. She could feel his eyes watching her. Her entourage wondered what she had said, but Josette wouldn't tell. And she just knew that Patrick Kelley was going to be *hers*.

Roger had taught her and Sandy that scripture. He said that it was their measuring rod for choosing a husband or boyfriend—*when* they were permitted to date. Josette kept it in the back of her mind, not sold on God or His Word. But seeing Patrick reading the Bible that way stirred her.

She watched for the next two hours as Patrick and some of the other boys in the neighborhood played football in the street. Patrick stood out from the others. He dominated them. The nervousness Josette had witnessed earlier disappeared under his command of the game. His aggressive nature rose quickly as he charged down the middle of the street with that football gripped tightly. The cockiness that seeped out when he scored excited her. And that self-assured smile convinced her that he was the kind of *man* she wanted.

Patrick lagged behind the others when the game was over. He walked over to Josette and whispered, "I'd like to talk some more, Jo."

"What's wrong with right now?"

He looked around at Sandy, Penelope, Jasmine and Ramona. "Well ..." he said, outnumbered, "I was kinda hopin' that we could talk alone." He seemed embarrassed, looking past her as if he were looking for someone down the street. Josette saw God's meticulousness in the brown eyes that were trying to avoid her.

"They can go home," she countered before turning toward them. "Bye y'all. See y'all tomorrow," she said, waving them off.

They dispersed, snickering, with their pom-poms in tow. Sandy took her novel and lemonade into the house, closing the screen softly behind her. Josette was left on the porch, talking to the man-boy that was sweaty all over from playing football, and from fear of her. He stumbled over his words when she asked him questions like what kind of *woman* he was looking for. His shyness kept him from making eye contact when he spoke. He tried to hide his vulnerability by looking up at the sky.

Patrick and his father, Reverend Joseph Kelley, had recently moved into the neighborhood so that they could be closer to their newly built Morning Star Baptist Church, where his father was the pastor. The football coach at Lathrup High School had recruited Patrick from the small Christian academy he had attended since grade school. The coach all but guaranteed Reverend Kelley that with Patrick's skills, he would earn a full football scholarship, have the opportunity to play for a top-notch college team, and fulfill his dream of playing in the NFL.

Lathrup had been the number one team in the state for the last three years. Patrick's excitement rose as he talked about football to Josette. He budded for her, giving her access to even his previously guarded spaces. He shared that his mother had divorced his father when he was just three years old, and had left him behind as well. Patrick hadn't seen or heard from her since then. Josette listened and compared their lives. They were parallel in some ways, but she didn't open her own door of pain. Instead, she made Patrick laugh a hearty cartoon laugh with her realness. Josette stamped that beautiful smile on a memory card, along with that laugh and the part of him that wasn't nervous or cautious. There was something incredible about him that was beyond his handsomeness. He was like no other fourteen-year-old she'd ever talked to. He was mature beyond his years. His conversation was substantive. He quoted scriptures with the confidence and faith of a minister, and recited Langston Hughes and Khalil Gibran like he had written the words himself. Penelope had said that he was "lame," but everything about him moved Josette.

It was nine-thirty p.m. when Linda came out on the porch to see who Patrick was and do a thorough investigation. Respectfully, Patrick rose to his feet when he saw Linda.

"And who are you, young man?"

"Ma'am," he nodded, "I'm Patrick Kelley. I live around the corner." He shook her hand firmly.

"Who are your parents?"

"I live with my father—Reverend Joseph Kelley."

"Ump. Pastor of Morning Star Baptist?"

"Yes ma'am."

"Are you active in church?" Linda continued with her investigation.

"Yes ma'am. I serve on the usher board and the youth evangelism team."

"I guess your father *makes* you participate in all those activities," Linda poked.

"No ma'am. *I* decide which activities I participate in. A *man* has to know and serve the Lord for himself."

Patrick's humility, laced with straightforwardness, took Linda. And Josette was positive that she was in love at that very moment. Patrick's silent authority convinced her that he was *the one*. And Linda was satisfied as well.

"Sounds like you've got a good head on your shoulders, Patrick Kelley," Linda conceded. "Jo, I want you in the house at ten. You don't need to be on the porch talking to anyone save Jesus after that."

"I was going to leave at a respectable time," Patrick defended.

Linda checked him with mother bear fierceness. "I'm making sure."

Patrick received it with graciousness. "Yes, ma'am. It was nice talking to you. Hope to talk to you again soon."

Linda smiled on the inside, but kept her mother bear eyes glaring at him. "Same here. Good night."

Patrick didn't have to say another word that evening. Josette was sold. She'd already learned the two things that transformed this fourteen-year-old boy into a man: God and football. Unaware that night, she would become the third.

Linda, Roger, and Sandy joined Morning Star Baptist a few months later. Josette joined Morning Star's Wednesday night Youth Bible Study, just so she could be close to Patrick. She admired his passion and fire for

God. He didn't go anywhere without his slim, burgundy, leather Bible. Whenever people congratulated the star running back about his performance in a football game, he just shrugged and told them that the Lord was his strength.

He and Josette were remarkably different. Patrick was a quiet soul; Josette was emphatically outspoken. He liked the simple things, like sitting in the park, people-watching, and reading. Josette thrived off of being in the middle of something—anything. But Josette had a way of pulling Patrick away from his quiet space. She had a way of pulling all the people around her away from their quiet space—especially Linda when she boldly defied her authority. And Sandy found herself being sucked into Josette's agenda even though the backlash was costly.

Linda ruled with a strong but loving hand, but Josette stretched Linda to the outer realm of her sanctity. Josette was still fourteen and Sandy sixteen when Linda came close to exercising her biblical authority to use "the rod." And it didn't matter to Linda that they were both teenagers, considerably past the ages that most people felt physical discipline was still effective. Josette was barely in the ninth grade, but she'd had the nerve to sneak Patrick into the house. Roger had been away at the nursing home visiting his father. Linda had gone to the flower shop to help her sister because both of the afternoon workers had called in sick. Normally, Linda trusted the girls to be alone for a few hours. But they were under strict rules. There was to be absolutely no company in the house unless she or Roger was home—especially not any one of the opposite sex. Linda said it was a set up for the devil to start *trouble*.

The no-company rule applied to Patrick as well. And Linda could have cared less that Patrick's father was the pastor of her church. She was well aware that Josette and Patrick called themselves a *couple*. But the house rule was that there was no formal dating until age sixteen. Josette, however, had a history of doing exactly what she wanted to do. She coaxed Patrick into coming over against his righteous judgment. She figured that Linda wouldn't return home until at least seven that evening. Stop and Smell the Roses closed at six o'clock. Josette calculated that it would take Linda a good forty-five minutes to get home. But the surprise came when Linda showed up earlier than Josette had figured. Not only had Josette broken one of Linda's cardinal rules by having Pat over, the two of them were *tongue* kissing. Josette had mowed Patrick's guard down. His petite angel caused him to compromise and do what he knew was wrong.

Sandy had been upstairs in her room studying for a chemistry test. She'd nodded off to sleep at her desk on top of the elements chart when Linda came in, yelling at Josette and Patrick. She was careful to stay planted at her desk so that Linda wouldn't think that she had been an accomplice to the crime. She didn't want any part of that. She had just turned sixteen, and Linda had promised her that she could start dating. Sandy had her hopes up for Vincent Townsend, a senior track star. He had already asked her out twice, and she didn't want to mess up a good thing now that Linda had given her the dating green light. She had prepared to wait it out until it was quiet, but time kept ticking by. After Linda finished her tirade with Josette and Patrick, she called Reverend Kelley.

When Reverend Kelley arrived, the four of them sat down at the kitchen table for hours, talking about sin, fornication, and obedience. Sandy peeked out of her room a few times just to see what was going on. She heard Reverend Kelley's deep baritone voice say to Patrick, "Son, I'm greatly disappointed by your actions. You have embarrassed me to the utmost." He'd said it with such a defeated voice that Sandy felt sorry for *him*. She knew that Patrick had to have been feeling like a snake, because Reverend Kelley had a reputation for being level-headed and soft-spoken. He was the one person they hated to get chastised by. In the calmest, softest voice, he made them realize how they had completely violated God. While he spoke in that soft, non-threatening voice, they would be thinking about all the other terrible things they'd done in the past.

"Pop, and Mrs. Stevens, I'm sorry for my actions. I'm a *man* of God . . . I should have thought things out . . . please forgive me. It won't happen again," Patrick said humbly. "I would never violate the Lord by compromising Jo's virginity or mine. We just shared a kiss. That's it. That is all that happened here," he continued, taking Josette's hand, looking so sincere that Sandy was jealous that he loved Josette so much.

But Linda's response to Patrick's God-fearing confession was, "Space and opportunity create temptation. And temptation leads to sin." She talked about the infamous "*Point of No Return*" as if it were a real place on the map. She went on about how lust could shut down their young brains and make them forget about what God wanted. *"But every man is tempted when he is drawn away of his own lust and enticed. Then, when lust hath conceived, it bringeth forth sin: and sin, when it is finished, bringeth forth death,"* Linda said, as Sandy stood with her door cracked just enough to hear what was going on downstairs, repeating the verse silently to herself. Linda had made them memorize James 1:14-15 when she gave them the "sex talk." When the whole ordeal was over, Josette was on punishment for three weeks.

Linda opened Sandy's door and asked, "Sandy, did you know that Patrick Kelley was in this house?"

Sandy couldn't lie to Linda after all that talk about sin. "Yes, ma'am," she said.

"Well, you'll be sharing a punishment with your sister. If Jo robbed a bank and you were with her, you'd go to jail just like she would. Understand?" Linda said.

"Yes ma'am."

"You get a lesser sentence. Two weeks for you."

Sandy was crushed. There was a Junior Class trip to Montreal, Canada, coming up. Vincent Townsend was going. Her whole world had been hanging on that trip. But the verdict had been handed down. She could have killed Josette. She cursed herself for not doing what she had started to do—tell her little sister, "No—no company." She resigned that she got what she deserved. But it wouldn't happen again.

Josette was what some people considered to be "free spirited." To Sandy, she was just plain old selfish, spoiled, inconsiderate, and self-centered. She had always been that way. Nothing much had changed about Josette except her age. She was still her number one priority. That was the main reason that her marriage was in such a horrendous mess.

Linda had seen it coming when Josette was young. She'd done her best to prevent Josette from making a mess of her life. She'd shared the realities of life, sex, and getting an education with both of the girls as if she were their own mother. Sandy took Linda's advice. Josette was another story.

Linda made them work at the flower shop after school. She taught them how to save money and she opened up bank accounts for them. By the time Sandy was about to begin her freshman year at Michigan State, she had saved up three thousand dollars. And she was able to secure an academic scholarship. Linda sent her a monthly allowance for the first year. Then, she and Roger told Sandy it was time to get a job. Linda figured it would take Sandy at least a year to adjust to college. She was adamant about Sandy completing her degree, but she wanted her to be responsible. Linda wasn't a supporter of economic outpatient care. She gave them extra money and bought clothes from time to time, but she was more concerned about preparing them for the real world.

Josette wrote letters to Sandy, angry that Linda wouldn't buy her Coach purses, Gucci bags, or some other designer wear that her friends were sporting. Linda made Josette save the money that she earned working. But that process was too slow for Josette. Sandy would feel sorry for her and send her money that she'd saved. Sandy treated Josette like a daughter instead of a younger sister. For that reason, Josette had never been good at *saving* money. And Sandy was partly to blame. Josette had grown accustomed to depending on her older sister. Looking back, Sandy could see how she had helped Josette turn out to be the monster that she was. But it was time for her little sister to grow up. They weren't kids anymore. It was time for Josette to stop playing "As Jo's World Turns," and take life more seriously.

Josette finished the last of her Vernors, thinking about the other side of her man-of-God husband—the side she'd seen the night he'd told her to get out of his house, and she'd been so afraid of him that she left without taking anything with her. She had sent Sandy back a day later to pick up her clothes. She'd first seen that dark side of Patrick when they were just sixteen. It was their junior year. Patrick "Preacher Boy" Kelley almost got himself suspended from school and kicked off the football team because of her. He'd gotten into a fight with Felix Redd, star player on Lathrup's basketball team. Felix was a senior being wooed by no fewer than ten colleges. Cocky and arrogant, he'd had his dark chocolate, six-foot-six sight set on Josette since her sophomore year. Felix's sister, Regina, was co-captain of the cheerleading team with Josette. And Josette made the mistake of sharing with Regina that she and Patrick had never had sex. It seemed that all the other popular students were, but Patrick maintained that it was a sin before God. Regina shared her and Josette's conversation with Felix, hoping that it would work to his advantage, but the information earned him a beating instead.

Josette had sweet-talked Patrick into hanging out at The Quest, a movie theater and arcade where most of the juniors and seniors congregated on Friday nights. Patrick preferred the quiet theater across town, where he and Josette would be the only students from their school. That way he'd feel like they really had shared some "alone" time. But he gave in to Josette. They were leaving when Patrick handed Josette his letterman to put over the thin sweater she'd worn. The brief rainstorm that had come and gone while they were in the theater had left the night air chilly. Patrick and Josette were a few feet away from Patrick's Nova when Felix pushed a button that started a war that he was unprepared for.

"Preacher Boy, you better start handlin' that before yo' girl be wearing my letterman."

Pat shrugged it off. "Whatever."

But Felix took that plunge. "Yo, Pat…you handlin' yo' business?"

"You better mind yours," Patrick said back with finality—the warning that Felix was too busy taunting to heed. A loose crowd gathered to see what exchange was going on between two star athletes. Tension swarmed.

"This *boy* is over here walking next to all that behind, and ain't hittin' it." There was laughter from the crowd. "I'd be takin' care of that *daily!*"

Those were the last words Patrick heard Felix speak. They had to peel him off of Felix. A black eye and a badly split lip is what Felix walked away with. His face was monstrously swollen from the punishment Patrick inflicted upon him. It happened so quickly that no one had been able to step in between the two of them. Josette's pleas were smothered under Patrick's rage. It had taken one of Felix's teammates and two of Patrick's to keep him from doing more serious damage to Felix. Their teammates tussled with the two of them until they were separated. Afterward, they calmed the crowd and sent the teens scattering to their vehicles in order to avoid a run-in with the police. It would have been a matter of minutes before Patrick and Felix were carted off to jail.

Patrick had been a wild, uncontrollable animal that night. Not a visible scratch had been left on him, but there had been one left on the inside. He had muddied his witness for the Lord with his anger. *"For the wrath of man, worketh not the righteousness of God,"* he said. That thought was more devastating than the idea of being kicked off the football team for conduct unbecoming an athlete.

Josette blamed herself. She hadn't told Regina that she and Patrick weren't having sex to embarrass him. She'd said it as a matter of fact. So she settled the problem by setting up a private meeting with Principal Williams, whom she already had eating out of the palm of her hands. She had served as an aide for him since her freshman year, running errands, filing, and helping him manage his personal affairs, like sending his wife roses. She was his favorite student. He'd watched her develop into a bright, articulate young woman. His wife, Edna, had come to regard Josette in the same manner. Edna was an attorney who participated in the school's career mentoring program. She was Josette's mentor and Josette was her "baby." Josette earned work credit by accompanying Edna to her office and to court when permissible. But Lathrup had a strict policy regarding athlete conduct in and out of school. Fighting and disorderly conduct could lead to being benched or kicked off the team. Josette put her negotiating skills to work. She told Principal Williams that Felix had been *sexually harassing* her. That was the truth.

"He's made several inappropriate comments that I have overlooked, but I know what my rights are," Josette said, showing Principal Williams the school code of conduct, which clearly stated that any form of sexual harassment was grounds for a school transfer and criminal charges.

"I see," he said nodding.

"Patrick had every right to *protect* me. But Lathrup doesn't need any negative publicity. If you bench two star players, questions will be asked. *We* need Felix for the championship games that are coming up, *and we* need our star running back. I figure that if we could all agree that the two of them will stay away from each other, and that Felix will write an official letter of apology to me, as well as a ten-page term paper on sexual harassment—all confidential of course—everybody can go back to normal. No parental involvement necessary. That's how I see it, seeing that the incident was not on school property or during school hours," Josette said, sitting across from Principal Williams with her legs crossed.

He smiled. "Sounds like a plan. But what am I going to do with you, Josette Moss?"

"Sir, I have no idea," Josette said, batting her eyes playfully and taking a handful of Skittles from his "relaxation" jar.

"I'll meet with the guys and their coaches in a few minutes. You hurry up and get to forensics class before you're late. And if I ever need an attorney and Edna isn't available, I'll give you a call," he said, watching Josette bounce out of his office. He shook his head. "That girl is too smart for her own good." He looked up at the academic scholars list on his wall. She was still carrying a 4.0 average.

Life was good back then. Now, it was complicated with Josette's secrets. Pulling up next to Sandy's BMW in the garage reminded her that her life was out of order. She should have been pulling next to Patrick's Corvette or one of his other toys. But her penchant for playing with fire had turned everything upside down. Living on the edge had backfired. Sadly, she was the only one who wasn't aware that she was dangling.

She was a senior in high school, a few weeks shy of graduation, when Linda called Sandy at college, crying, feeling like a failure because she'd found out that Josette had been skipping school. At first, Linda assumed that Josette and Patrick had been skipping *together,* but further investigation revealed that Patrick was not her co-conspirator this time. The two of them had broken up. Josette had still been pressuring Patrick about having sex, but he wouldn't budge. She thought that he didn't love her enough to compromise that one thing for her. It would have been the ultimate proof of his love. But he wouldn't put her before God. Josette needed to know that he would do *anything* for her.

To Linda's dismay, Josette had secretly been seeing an older man she'd met at the flower shop. He was ten years her senior. But that was only part of the reason that Linda was so torn up. Josette had been lying to Linda, telling her that she couldn't work some days because of cheerleading practice, when she really had been going out with the man she'd been dating. Linda found birth control pills in Josette's room. Sandy had to pretend that she was shocked and unaware of the whole situation as she listened to Linda bawl on the other end of the phone.

Linda had asked them repeatedly to come and talk to her *before* they considered giving up their virginity. She said that a woman should only lose her virginity to her *husband.* She had taught them 1 Corinthians 6:18. *Flee sexual fornication. Every sin that a man doeth is without the body: but he who committeth fornication sinneth against his own body.* How many times had she explained that taking a man into their bodies would be defiling the temple of God? She had tried to drill it into them. It was important to her. To think that Josette had been having sex, after all she'd done to prevent it, was disheartening.

The fact that the man was from one of the most prominent families in the city didn't make matters any better. He was Paco Kimbrough, son of millionaire businessman, Lance Kimbrough. The Kimbrough family was well known in business and socialite circles, being one of the few African American families in Detroit who headed privately owned multi-million dollar companies. Lance was the founder and owner of Kimbrough Construction, a commercial construction company. The family had expanded their business to include ventures in land development, real estate and the entertainment industry, which operated under the umbrella of Kimbrough Enterprises and was run by Lance's six sons and four daughters. They were best known and applauded for igniting the revitalization of downtown Detroit with the building of new master-planned communities and businesses.

Paco was the third youngest of the Kimbrough clan. He had stepped out of his father's shadow and had become co-owner of Elephant City, an upscale restaurant in downtown Detroit that catered to a young, professional, and elite crowd. He was on every single woman's hit-list. Sandy had never figured out why he was so fascinated with Josette. He could have had any *woman* he wanted. But he loved Josette. Initially, Sandy thought that Josette and Paco's relationship was based on the ploy of an experienced man's attempt to manipulate and control a beautiful young girl. But she learned otherwise.

Josette had lied to Paco from the beginning. She'd told him that she was twenty. He didn't find out the truth until it was too late for both of them. Sandy had met him and talked with him in depth about his relationship with Josette once, when he'd driven Josette up to campus to visit. She came right out and asked him why he wanted to be with an eighteen-year-old that wasn't quite out of high school yet. He sat down on the edge of Sandy's dormitory bed, with Josette securely on his lap. "What does age have to do with love? My mother is several years *older* than my father. She's Puerto Rican and he's African American. You think their families wanted them to be together? Jo is eighteen, not fifteen. Legally, she's grown. If she weren't, I wouldn't be sticking my neck out like this, risking my reputation. Ten years from now, what will it matter?" he challenged Sandy. She couldn't think of a rebuttal, so she left it alone. He had more to lose than Josette did.

Josette had always been physically mature for her age. Though petite, she was shapely. She'd started developing when she was just nine. By the time she was ten, physically, she looked thirteen. At eighteen, Josette easily passed for twenty or twenty-one. The slightest hint of make-up placed her at least two to three years beyond her actual age. And she was an intellectually mature young woman. She had interned at Edna's law office throughout high school. She was used to having conversations of substance with people that were years older than she was. She was a well-read honor student with an inviting personality.

Josette knew all the right things to do and say to get a man's attention—even an older man like Paco Kimbrough. But that was no consolation to Linda. She was furious with Paco. She blamed him for *stealing* Josette's virginity. But Josette had known full well what she was doing. She'd had sense enough to go to the clinic and get birth control pills *before* she met Paco. And Linda had no idea that the reason that Josette and

Patrick had broken up in the first place was because Josette claimed that Patrick didn't love her enough—that he was moving "too slow." Josette said that she was ready for them to take their relationship to the *next level*. She was eighteen years old, complaining that she needed to be with a *"real man."* But Sandy didn't dare tell Linda that. It would have broken what was left of her heart.

Despite Linda's tears, Josette continued to see Paco. She'd been accepted to Spelman on a four-year academic scholarship. Patrick had received a full football scholarship to the University of Michigan. Josette claimed that she and Patrick were not a couple, but were going to remain *friends*. While in their first year of college, the two of them seemed to go back and forth with a long-distance relationship, lying to themselves about what they truly meant to one another. And Paco was always there on the sidelines. Instead of him toying with Josette's head, it seemed that, as young as she was, she had the upper hand. Paco flew her to exotic locales like Hawaii and the Fiji Islands on semester breaks, took her shopping in New York, and spoiled her with designer clothes and jewelry. When Linda refused to purchase something for Josette, Paco bought it. Linda finally gave up on trying to "guide" her. Josette kept a high grade point average and made it clear that who she slept with was none of Linda's business.

Linda tried to retaliate by cutting off all economic support to Josette. But Josette didn't call home for money. Paco took care of her. Sandy was convinced that was the only reason Josette kept him around. She never believed that Josette was actually *in love* with Paco. Josette's heart had altogether belonged to Patrick Caleb Kelley. Sandy reasoned that Paco had to have known that. But his love for Josette kept him from caring—or maybe it was his hope. He loved to love her. He thought the distance between her and Patrick would give him the upper hand, but it only made Josette long for Patrick more.

Josette felt a deep emptiness without Patrick. She was incomplete. No man she dated could replace the feeling of being with him. So the summer after her freshman year at Spelman, she transferred to the University of Michigan. Edna ensured that she obtained a pre-law scholarship, covering the remaining cost of her undergraduate studies. Josette made all the arrangements herself and kept it a secret—even from Sandy. She'd made up her mind and wasn't interested in anyone else's opinion. She drove all the way from Atlanta to Ann Arbor by herself. She went straight to Patrick's dorm. She hoped that he was alone, because she had decided that this day would be their turning point. She'd been a Spelman hopeful since middle school. She left her dream for Patrick because she couldn't stand to be without him.

She knocked softly on his door, listening to see if there was anyone in the room. Two bookworm-looking young men on their way to the library passed her, admiring her slyly. She heard one of them joke that he was going to change his major to football. They laughed. Josette smiled back, accepting the compliment gracefully. She pressed her ear to Patrick's door and heard the sound of a television. She could hear Moe of the Three Stooges scowling at one of the others. Then she heard Patrick's laughter. It made her smile. She smoothed her white cotton T-strap sundress with her palms and smoothed her hair back. Then she pressed her ear to the door again. There were no other voices. She knocked, harder this time. Patrick yelled twice, "Who is it?" But Josette waited in silence. She wanted to see the look on his face when he saw her standing there.

Aggravated, Patrick snatched the door open, thinking that one of his dorm buddies was playing a prank. "Stop play—" he started. His aggravation faded instantaneously. He smiled hard as Josette took him in. He was wearing a white tank with a pair of Michigan shorts. His honey brown skin was darkened from the football practices in the summer heat. Easy on Josette's eyes.

She acted as if they hadn't spent the last year of their lives apart, trying to make sense of the love that they had for one another. "Hey," she said casually, like she'd just seen him the day before.

Patrick blinked slowly, taking *her* in. Head to toe. Toe to head.

"It's me. You ain't dreaming."

"Prove it," he said friskily.

One year of college had matured him in a different way. His confidence was full blown. Josette stretched on her tiptoes, crisscrossed her arms around his neck and kissed him. "I love you, Patrick Caleb Kelley. I need you . . . and I *want* you," she spoke in that low voice that weakened him like Kryptonite. "I left Spelman for you—if you still want me . . . here I am."

And Josette officially became Patrick's girl again—in the way that *she'd* wanted. Patrick prayed hard afterward, crying over his failure, battered by the way his convictions had been torn down brick by brick, kiss by kiss. He stayed away from Josette for two whole weeks, repenting and fasting. Then he found himself lusting after that forbidden fruit. He couldn't hide from it. Couldn't run from it. He gave in eventually, and split himself in two.

Josette wanted to empathize with Patrick, but she couldn't. She wanted to feel that fire he had for God, but she didn't. She had said those words at church when she was fourteen, *"I accept Jesus Christ as my Lord and Savior."* That's what every tired and worn-out soul said. They all had confessed their sins. That is what had to be done. She was baptized, still full of uneasy questions and doubt. Josette was missing something that she saw on everyone else's face. She had looked over at her sister dressed in that white ceremonial robe as she walked past her, on her way to that "watery grave." There were tears of joy in her eyes, a reflection of redemption and happiness. Josette was confused. She just wanted to be with Patrick. She knew that he wouldn't be with anyone with whom he was "unequally yoked." He had told her that the first night she met him. He hadn't said it to pressure her. It was a part of who he was.

Linda and Roger said that Jesus would give Josette's life meaning. They said that there was so much that He wanted to give her. They promised that He could take the pain away—all the things Josette wouldn't talk about in therapy when she was placed in foster care. She wanted to please them, too. They'd been good to her and Sandy. They were her family. So she did it. When the minister lifted her up out of the water, he shouted, "Rise and walk in the newness of life!" But there was no newness in Josette's spirit—just the things that had been there before. The horrible things that God hadn't protected her from. They didn't go away when she came out of that water. She hadn't believed they would. She didn't trust God. Still didn't. Now, He was punishing her for that by taking Patrick away.

Patrick was drafted into the NFL right after his senior year at U of M. He asked Josette to marry him right after he signed with Detroit. But Josette was ambitious. She'd told him that she wanted to go to law school. She wasn't ready to have a family. She had already been accepted to U of M's Law School, and she wanted more than anything to obtain her law degree. She didn't want to toss her dreams aside for the sake of having a family. She wanted it all. But she was in love with Patrick Caleb Kelley, star running back. She didn't want to lose him. She knew she had something special. Patrick promised that he wouldn't interfere with her study time or pressure her about children until she had completed law school, so she said "yes."

They were both just twenty-two. And for Josette, being married to Patrick was too good to be true. They were best friends. When Patrick wasn't on the field and Josette wasn't at the law library, the precious few moments they had were genuine. It was just the two of them, instant millionaires, still eating sweet-and-sour chicken out of Chinese food cartons while watching *The Three Stooges* on cable. Sometimes, Patrick would even let her win at chess after he got tired of whipping her. He still sparked that same fire in her that he had when they were teenagers. Their love was strong. Josette had no regrets about becoming *Mrs. Patrick Kelley*.

She still couldn't explain why she'd jeopardized that. Starting a family had been their only strain. Patrick wanted to start a family after seven years, and Josette was nowhere close to having children. She'd never admitted it to Patrick, but she wasn't sure *if* she even wanted children. Secretly, she'd been taking birth control pills. When Patrick found out, he was so angry that he barely spoke to her for two whole days. But then she apologized, convincing him that she'd been worried about maintaining her status at the firm. He knew it was hard for a woman to muscle her way to the top in a man's world. And Josette reminded him that he was living out his childhood dream while she was still working to achieve hers. It was true. He reluctantly agreed to give her more time.

But Josette's time ran out the night of Patrick's NFL retirement party. The affair that she'd had and ended, resurfaced when her disgruntled lover called Patrick and told him about the affair. Josette had no defense. Patrick knew dates, times, places. Johnnie Cochran couldn't have defended her behind all of that evidence. It had ended months prior, but it was brand new for Patrick. Curses and threats overrode his soft-spoken nature.

Josette didn't know that Patrick. He roared at her, asking why she'd done it. *Hadn't he taken care of her? Hadn't he been faithful, despite the fans and the groupies?* She had no answers for him. That was the first time Patrick had ever put his hands on Josette that way. Her silence had enraged him so much that he pushed her out of their bedroom and into the hallway. He closed the door and told her to *leave*. For moments she stood on the other side of the door listening to him trash their bedroom. The breaking of glass and the knocking over of furniture jolted her. His curses rang out over the sound of him destroying the material things that had represented their love for one another. Josette screamed out an "I love you" through the door. It was a heart reflex. Those were the only words that shot out when she opened her mouth to speak. They had come from nowhere. But they were enough to send Patrick spiraling.

In one swift movement, he snatched the right side of their French bedroom doors open, collared Josette by her oversized Betty Boop T-shirt, and cursed her, killing her with words he never would have said to her before. "Get out of my house!" he shouted. "I swear if you stay here another minute, I'm gonna hurt you. I don't want to hurt you, Jo…I don't want to hurt you." His words ripped her down the middle. Her Patrick was gone. A stranger stood over her, breathing heavily, with tightened muscles and clenched fists.

There was murderous look on his face. Josette imagined him killing her with his bare hands, sans remorse. As a criminal attorney, she'd seen that look on the faces of clients that she had interviewed in jail who'd been charged with murder or some other hideous act. She could look into their eyes and know that they were guilty. That was the look she saw in her husband's eyes. So she left.

Chapter Four

Genevieve checked into the Park Hyatt Hotel on North Michigan Avenue. The lobby was faintly scattered with uniformed employees sporting tin name badges and polite smiles. Carefree guests breezed in and out of the front entrance on perky salutations from the hotel staff. Genevieve stood in front of a young desk clerk distracted, fidgeting with the silver charm bracelet on her left wrist, making jangling noises. Each charm was an expressive reminder of the loves she held most dearly, comforting her as she touched the silver symbols. The cross was an ever-present confirmation of Christ's sacrifice. The silver, diamond-cut bumble bee evoked delicious memories of her "honey," Benjamin. The violin was for Faith, whose gifted musicianship soothed and lifted Genevieve's spirit. And the crown was for Joshua, whose wisdom reminded Genevieve of King Solomon. Then there were the two stars welded together, reminding her of the distance that separated her from the two little girls she left behind years ago. One of them would be walking through the lobby door in a few hours.

Genevieve watched people come and go, guessing her fate. She stared at those glass doors, wondering what the outcome of her meeting would be. The attractive young desk clerk waited for Genevieve to make eye contact again before patiently saying, "Dr. Carpenter, here is your key. John will take your bags up for you." The softness of her voice refocused Genevieve.

Genevieve smiled politely. "Excuse me. I'm sorry," she said, taking the key from the young Puerto Rican girl. Before Genevieve turned away from the counter, the girl leaned forward and spoke in a low, raspy voice coated with a thick accent. "My name is Eva," she said. "I ran away from home when I was sixteen . . . because of the things my father used to do to me. I lived on the streets for awhile, but I'm starting to get myself together now." Her eyes shifted downward. She looked a bit uneasy about divulging her private life to a stranger, but she felt a kindred spirit with Genevieve from reading *Moving Forward*. "I work here full time and go to community college at night. I'm studying business," she said hurriedly, trying not to take up too much of Genevieve's time. "I saw your book at the library and read it. I'm only nineteen, but it really helped me a lot. It helped me to see that I've got a lot of years ahead. And that I can start over. That's what I'm trying to do. I've been reading the Bible and everything." Eva looked relieved that she had said it all.

Genevieve's eyes softened. "Praise God! That is just wonderful." Eva's testimony intensified her euphoria. She reached in her leather tote for a book. She placed it on the counter and autographed it. *To Eva, whose testimony filled my heart with the greatest joy. Keep your eyes on Jesus.*

Eva thanked Genevieve with a hug, realizing that it wasn't exactly the *professional* thing to do. The two of them laughed at the way they were stretched across the counter. Then Genevieve gave her a second autographed copy of *Moving Forward*. "Give this to someone else who would benefit from reading it. Blessings are meant to be shared," Genevieve said. She was proud of what God was doing in the life of this beautiful young girl. Eva was yet another confirmation of God's purpose for her life. She strolled to the elevator re-energized, thanking the Lord for using her as an instrument to uplift other women. She felt joyful about what the Lord was doing.

But as soon as she settled in her suite, Satan tried to steal that joy. Genevieve's optimism about seeing Sandy after sixteen years was being chased away by ghosts. Second thoughts pushed through. She wondered why she'd asked Sandy to meet her *before* her book signing. Several times she contemplated calling Sandy on her cell phone and asking if they could reschedule, but she didn't want to risk giving her the impression that she was trying to back out. The last thing she wanted to do was to make Sandy feel that their meeting was not important. But the odds of their reunion going sour became more real to her than the fantasy ending she'd imagined.

She had been completely comfortable talking to Sandy over the phone. The flow of the conversation was a sign that maybe Sandy had forgiven her—or at least wanted to forgive her. There had been brief moments of tension, but the two of them had established a level of respect and understanding. Those two strengths alone could give them a firm foundation to stand on. But hypothetical what-ifs invaded. What if Sandy seeing her led to a verbal war? What if her daughter still hated her? Genevieve would have to go to her evening book signing rattled and discombobulated. It'd be unfair to her fans and herself. She wanted to greet them with the surety and freedom God had given her years ago. She wanted them to see the woman she'd become—the woman God had lifted out of the pit. A teary-eyed, frazzled author was not the impression she wanted to make tonight.

The guilt chains tightened. Genevieve paced the room, asking herself questions aloud, reasoning with herself. It was a nervous habit she'd developed as a teen. She plopped down on the edge of the bed, then immediately hopped up and began pacing again. A wave of nausea passed over her. In a moment, her hands were wet with perspiration. Her heart pounded. She was weakened by dizziness. Genevieve leaned her head against the wall near the bathroom. She felt her insides rebelling against her, forcing her breakfast up. "Lord, God . . . please," she supplicated, stammering over the toilet. Then she dropped to her knees in front of it, hanging her head over. Her body jerked as she gave up her breakfast. This hadn't happened to her in years. She had gotten control of these dreadful things. Now, her control was being undermined. She sat on her heels for a moment with her head still hung over the toilet, hoping to get it all out at the same time—the pain and the food she was regurgitating.

Genevieve was paralyzed for ten minutes before she felt a resurgence of strength. She turned the sink faucet on full blast. She refreshed herself, dampening a cloth with cold water and pressing it firmly against her face. She walked back into the suite and rummaged through her toiletry bag until she found her toothbrush and paste. She returned to the bathroom, placed a double heap of toothpaste on her brush, and worked vigorously to eliminate the foul taste that had been left behind. She avoided looking in the mirror, not wanting to see herself this way. She had crumbled so easily, and the emotional debris was a reminder.

When she was done she lay sprawled across the bed, crying. Her past lashed her one frame at a time. It came back in bits and pieces. All the things she had buried. She saw herself standing in front of the judge the day that the court took permanent custody of her girls. She remembered the pull of the addiction, and the numerous sexual indiscretions that had been necessary to sustain that beast. Genevieve cringed. She'd made a mistake, thinking that she could do this. Thinking that all was forgotten. Thinking that she could face her oldest daughter. Josette was right to hate her. And Sandy shouldn't be coming either. It was all a mistake.

"My grace is sufficient for you," Genevieve heard a familiar voice say, and peace chased away the doubt and confusion. *"Pray,"* He said in a whisper. *"Pray."* Genevieve slid off the bed, onto her knees. The floral print bedspread slid compliantly with her. She took a corner of it and wiped her eyes. She prayed to the Lord, thanking Him for His tender mercy, which had been renewed that very day for her. She praised Him for loving her and keeping her. She petitioned Him for His peace, asking Him to bless her and Sandy's meeting this afternoon. She gave God back the burdens that she had unsuccessfully attempted to bear alone.

Genevieve stepped out into the lobby renewed, knowing who she was, and to whom she belonged. She was expecting Sandy at one o'clock sharp. She was fifteen minutes early. The two of them would have plenty of time to talk before her six o'clock book signing. She found an inconspicuous spot to sit, where she could watch the door without being noticed. But before she had the opportunity to get comfortable, a tall honey brown woman with shoulder-length hair glided across the marbled lobby, wearing a brown pantsuit. In the woman's stride was the assurance of a thousand Egyptian queens. She encompassed all the boldness that beauty and age permitted. Determined as a runway model, the young woman eyed the room casually, oblivious to the stares of the men who passed her by, wanting. She was so attractive that Genevieve was delighted that they were a part of one another.

With tiptoe anticipation, Genevieve followed Sandy's steps with her eyes. She watched her pass a handsome man impeccably dressed in a fine

Italian business suit, yacking away on his Blackberry, with his briefcase in tow in the opposite hand. She knew it was Italian-made the way it hung superbly on him. It had to have been tailor-made. He was six feet two inches tall with a lean, muscular build. His dark Hershey-bar skin was complimented with jet black hair. He was crisp and sharp. Genevieve thought of an old saying. "Ain't a spec of dirt on him," she mumbled to herself.

The gentleman noticed Sandy and stopped abruptly, ending his call. He said something to her that caused her to swivel around curiously. She waited for him to catch up to her.

"You've got to be the most beautiful woman I've ever seen in my life," he flirted. "You look *exactly* like my wife—and I've never been married." He gave her his hand. "I'm Lamont Drake." His commanding demeanor caused Sandy to smile. The two of them shook hands and Lamont lingered with Sandy's hand in his. His gaze was sure. He held Sandy in it until her eyes averted.

Nervous, Sandy giggled girlishly. "I'm Cassandra Moss," she blushed. She slowed her breathing with deep drags.

Lamont inched forward, closing their spatial gap. "I'd like to get to know you, Sandy." His stare was penetrating.

"Well, actually . . . I'm not from Chicago. I live in Detroit. I'm here for a business meeting."

He was quick to extinguish her excuse. "That's not the other side of the world," he said, smiling wide. He surveyed her again, taking in her honey brown skin that looked soft to the touch, and curves he imagined underneath her suit. Satisfied with his preliminary findings, he said devilishly, "Besides, I'm always game for an adventure." His gaze was almost lustful. His directness unclothed her. But she gave in to his pursuit without asking all the standard questions she should have asked, like if he had a relationship with the Lord, and a regular place of worship. But the two exchanged business cards anyway, and Lamont promised to call her and arrange a date.

The concierge had been looking on enviously. He gave Lamont a congratulatory nod as he walked toward the glass doors to exit the lobby. The conqueror nodded back victoriously. Sandy watched him until he was out of sight; then she searched the room for Genevieve again.

Genevieve stood up. Instinctively, Sandy zeroed in on her and hurried in her direction. Genevieve wondered what Sandy was going to do when she reached her.

"Hi," Genevieve said, extending a trembling hand.

Sandy embraced her instead. And the opportunity to hold Sandy was more than Genevieve felt she deserved. No words were spoken. Genevieve let go of her fears in her daughter's arms. She hadn't seen her since she was fifteen, but the love hadn't left. She felt a resurgence just holding her. The delicate exchange was confirmation that Sandy was still her little girl—her firstborn. She had agonized over Sandy and Josette for so many years. It was unreal holding her. She squeezed Sandy deeply, assuring herself that the moment was not some dream she'd conjured up in her sleep—that this beautiful woman was her *baby*. Tearful, they pulled apart to examine one another.

"Nice suit," Sandy said, reaching in her purse for Kleenex. She divided the small travel-size pack and handed half to Genevieve. Both of them pat-dried their faces, careful to avoid smudging their make-up. They smiled at each other uncomfortably.

"Thank you. It was a gift from Benjamin. *You* look beautiful."

Sandy gave Genevieve a thorough look over. "Thanks. You do too.

What a coincidence that we both wore brown today."

"It's my favorite color."

"Mine too."

"I remember," Genevieve said, blotting the corner of her eye where she was sure her supposed "twenty-four hour" mascara had run. "It looks good against your skin. You look so beautiful."

"Thank you," Sandy said, studying Genevieve with her dark brown eyes, the way she used to do when she was a child, trying to figure something out. She looked for the Genevieve that she knew years ago, but there were no traces of her. Just the woman that looked like her—better than her. Sandy couldn't believe that this woman was her mother. "I can't believe how good you look."

"A lot has changed," Genevieve said humbly.

Sandy nodded in agreement. "I see," she said, continuing to study Genevieve.

"Why don't we go up to my room where we can talk more privately," Genevieve suggested. She could tell by looking at Sandy's face that there were a hundred questions behind those pensive brown eyes. She reminded herself not to allow Sandy's questions to turn into a character-bashing session. She had to remain in control of that. That wasn't the purpose of this meeting. She had to make sure that was clear, in the most delicate way possible.

They entered the suite and Genevieve took off her shoes. She waited for Sandy to get settled and said, "Sandy, I want to be able to answer any questions you may have, but I don't want to be on the defense. If we can't talk everything out in a productive manner today, we can always get together again. I want to be at my best for the signing this evening,"

"Look, I didn't come here to fight with you. I came here to put some closure to some of the things that have been holding me back as a person. I've been in therapy for three years, and I want to get on with my life."

Genevieve digressed. "Okay, thank you," she said.

She and Sandy sat down at the small table right across from one another, like they were going to conduct a business meeting. Sandy had written most of her questions out on index cards. She placed them in a neat stack in front of her. Genevieve squirmed in her chair and took in a deep breath.

"I tend to forget my thoughts when I get emotional," Sandy explained. "This is not an interrogation."

"Okay," Genevieve said back. But the seating arrangement and the note cards made her uncomfortable. She felt like she was on trial. She did abandon her children. She couldn't deny that. Still, she didn't have to allow herself to be abused, no matter what the circumstances. She fidgeted with her charm bracelet again, mentally preparing herself to answer the first question she knew Sandy was going to ask. The one that was surely going to be the main point of prosecution. *Why didn't she come back for them?* But Sandy surprised her.

"How did you finally get clean?" Sandy said without looking at the index cards.

Genevieve calmed, relieved that Sandy had chosen something less laborious to start off with. She adjusted herself in her seat and relaxed her shoulders. She went back to a time that was so distant from the present that she was almost completely disconnected from it.

It was winter, one year after the state had taken permanent custody of Cassandra and Josette. Genevieve was deep into her addiction, working "work today/get paid today" jobs. Most of the temporary agencies had banned her. They knew about her habit. It didn't take long for word to spread from one supervisor to the next in those small temporary employment companies. Genevieve lived from place to place, caught up in the lifestyle she had created for herself. It was a self-constructed prison.

The snow had come down in chunks earlier that day, covering every outdoor object, both man-made and God-hewn, like a soft white blanket, providing a false sense of peace. But a fierce cold front had ushered in since then. Genevieve's demons tormented her as she walked up Linwood Street, looking for someone to sell her soul to, just so that she could escape the cold. It had stopped snowing, and it seemed that she could feel the temperature dropping. A wind chill advisory was in effect until morning.

Genevieve made exaggerated steps in the snowy sidewalk blanket that had accumulated to six inches. She wiped at her nose by brushing it across the arm of her thin spring jacket so that she didn't have to remove her nearly frozen hands out of the pockets. She had only walked a few blocks away from an apartment where she'd outstayed her welcome and had been subsequently discarded, but it felt like miles the way the wind chill razor-sliced her face. Her skin tightened. She felt a burning sensation on the tip of her nose and her ears. She had no idea where she was going to go. The beginning of frostbite yanked tears from her eyes. She searched the block for "regulars" but the streets were nearly empty. Even the locked-down corners of drug dealers were barren. The scarf she had tied around her head did not shield her from the inclement weather. She felt like her scalp was freezing. She shook her head a few times to knock the chill off. She adjusted the green nylon duffle bag that she carried on her right shoulder. Everything she owned was in it: a change of clothes, and addict essentials—drug paraphernalia. The longer she walked, the more the cold ate away at the two pairs of socks she had on. The consummate union of snow and cold stung Genevieve's toes through her gym shoes. She needed to go someplace warm and figure out her next move.

Genevieve headed for the neighborhood Coney Island, which was still a half a block up at the intersection of Linwood and Davison. She could sit down and think of a plan, maybe get a ride to a shelter. Even though they'd be overcrowded with people like her—and worse—on a night like this, it would be better than the cold. They wouldn't turn anyone down in these conditions. She had two dollars in change in her pocket—just enough for a cup of coffee and a donut so that she wouldn't get booted for loitering. Genevieve hastened her walk, but slowed her pace when the slippery bottoms of her gym shoes caused her to lose footing. She viewed the Coney as an oasis as she cut through the Speedway gas station on the corner closest to the small establishment. Its purple neon Coney sign was a welcome fixture. She concentrated on it until a car swerved so quickly in front of her that she screamed, thinking that it was going to hit her. It had come so close that if she had extended her feet an inch farther, the front tires would have rolled right over them.

The window eased down on the passenger side. The passenger was Ray, one of the largest west side drug dealers in the city. He was the supplier of "temporaries"—things that made people forget their problems short-term until his "goodies" had worn off. Even dressed in an expensive fur coat, he still looked like a natural-born thug. He had a street reputation for having a short fuse. He was feared by the other hustlers and everyone else who had been unfortunate enough to be caught up in his business web. It was Ray's darker secrets that terrorized Genevieve, however. The sadistic ones were revealed when she was alone with him. On an infinite number of occasions, he had been brutal.

"Genny . . . whatchu got yo'self out here for? Don't you know it's a wind chill warning in effect?" Ray laughed gregariously out of the passenger window.

The young man behind the wheel of Ray's 500 Series Mercedes laughed too. He didn't look old enough to drive. Genevieve placed him at about fourteen years old.

"I ain't got nowhere to go," Genevieve said back, staring at the young man who was driving. He looked exactly like the kid she had bought drugs from the day before.

"That ain't nothin' new. You been looking for me?" Ray asked.

"Yeah, but the streets are empty."

"Freakin' hook. Temporary interruption of business the last couple days, Genny. Ol' Ray gotta lay low. And I know it's plenty crime they could be fighting instead," he said, holding a cigarette out for the young boy to light. The young boy held the car's cigarette lighter steady as Ray put a Kool Mild in his mouth, pushed it into the lighter, and dragged on it. He blew smoke in Genevieve's face.

"Ray, it's cold," Genevieve said, shaking her head again.

"No sh—oops. I'm trying to stop cursing," he said. "My moms say that sh—oops—it ain't polite." The young boy nodded in expected agreement. Ray looked at Genevieve with the only kind of empathy he knew. "You wanna party tonight, Genny?" he asked.

Good common sense should have made her say no. She knew what Ray was capable of doing to her. It could be dangerous being alone with him. But the fierce cold and the lure of getting high swayed her. And Genevieve settled into the back seat of his 500 Series Mercedes anyway, not having enough energy to think about what she was going to do when he was done with her—if she wasn't half dead.

It was in the bathroom of Ray's two-thousand-dollar-a-month loft that the question, *"what next?"* clawed at Genevieve. Her frame had whittled down to a measly 102 pounds. She should have been at least 130. The streets had taken a toll on her. She was only thirty-two, but her youthfulness had been zapped by the men and the drugs. Genevieve was a shell of a woman. She could hear Ray outside in the master suite clapping and singing to the music that was playing loudly in the background. He called for her twice. She stuck her head out and bought more time.

The smell of marijuana was strong. That was the only drug Ray used, but he kept others for "company." She wiped the fog off the mirror to get a good look at the woman who had stolen everything from her. "*What do you have to live for?*" the woman asked Genevieve. "Nothing," Genevieve said back, ashamed. "*So why are you still living?*" the woman scolded. "I don't know," Genevieve answered. The woman laughed at Genevieve, mocking her. She convinced Genevieve that God had made a mistake by allowing her to be born in the first place. So Genevieve searched Ray's medicine cabinet for something to right the error. She found Ray's fourteen-carat-gold, monogrammed razor. She opened the head, took the blade out, and examined it. It was thin and unthreatening-looking, but deadly enough to bring an end to her suffering. She held it tightly between her thumb and forefinger, positioning it properly before slicing into her left wrist twice. Her body plummeted to Ray's marbled floor with a thud.

When Ray discovered Genevieve, he tied neckties around her wrist to slow the bleeding and drove her to the nearest hospital. He dumped her out at the emergency area and sped off to avoid being linked to her in any way in case she died. That would have been bad for business—or worse, landed him in jail for something he didn't do. He didn't need the police snooping around in his life, interfering with his cash flow. She wasn't worth that.

When Genevieve awakened in the hospital a day later, she lied to the staff on the hospital's psychiatric unit when she told them that she didn't remember who she'd been with the night she'd tried to kill herself. She was later released into an in-patient drug treatment center facilitated by the hospital. It was there she met psychiatrist Dr. George Kornblum.

The first time Dr. Kornblum attempted to assess Genevieve, she stared at him in silence for the entire hour. She was insulted that he thought he knew anything about her life, let alone could help her. She looked at the plaques and certificates that covered his office walls. He was a privileged man whose only interaction with the world she had lived in was case studies. She reasoned that he had probably come from a good family, had gone to the best schools, and was now living the American Dream—the dream of some. She ignored him and his "treatment approach." But her silence did not rattle him. "I get paid to do a job. Now, if you sit here in silence for an hour, that's quite all right with me. But I'm going to talk. When our time is up, I'm going home with a clean conscience," he had told her. He continued his assessment, jotting his notes down on a yellow notepad and speaking them out loud. "Genevieve Moss is a thirty-two-year-old black female, addicted to crack cocaine. She was hospitalized for attempting suicide by cutting her wrist with a razor. She is electively mute during this session, and presents as withdrawn and detached . . ."

Genevieve intrigued Dr. Kornblum. And breaking through to her was a challenge that he welcomed. He refused to end any session because of her resistance. But their fifth session was interrupted by an emergency phone call. Dr. Kornblum's two-year-old daughter, Rose, had fallen down a flight of stairs at home and had injured her head and broken her arm. Genevieve listened as he talked to his wife on the phone. That was the only time he had ended one of their sessions early, even when Genevieve shut down. His eyes had welled with tears. Genevieve saw him vulnerable, like her. "I need to see about my princess," he said before rushing out of the office. When she saw him a week later, she surprised him when she asked about Rose. Her broken silence shocked him. "Oh, she speaks," he said, smiling, knowing that her stubborn resolve was disintegrating.

Dr. Kornblum took a personal interest in Genevieve. And before Genevieve was released from the inpatient facility, he worked with her discharge planner to help secure housing for her. Genevieve's aftercare social worker found a place downtown that was near a college, where the rent was three hundred dollars a month. Six months rent had been paid for under a special grant from a local community agency. Dr. Kornblum made arrangements for Genevieve to continue to see him at his private office free of charge until she got on her feet and found a job with health care benefits. Every Monday afternoon, she took the bus to the city's outer limits, and transferred to the SMART bus, which covered the suburban areas.

Genevieve attended weekly NA meetings, sometimes four a week to keep herself balanced. Her place was just a studio apartment, with a worn-out futon. It was a shoebox, but it afforded her the opportunity to live alone and think about what she could do with the rest of her life. It took two months for the aftercare worker to help Genevieve find a job. It was at a light assembly plant that serviced the automotive plants in the city. It paid seven dollars an hour with no benefits. But for six months it seemed that her life was on the upswing. She had saved five hundred dollars and purchased a clunker from one of the college students to get back and forth to work, and to see Dr. Kornblum. She looked forward to Monday evenings with him, but a terrible emptiness remained. She knew that she couldn't work as a light assembly worker forever. She felt like she was just kidding herself, allowing Dr. Kornblum to convince her that she was someone she wasn't. She was playing a role in his American Dream. But when the curtains came down at night, she was still an addict.

After six months of lying to herself, Genevieve gave in to that feeling of unworthiness and slipped back into using drugs again, ending up in the same circle of people that had helped to keep her addicted in the first place. They didn't want anything else out of life and didn't want her to want anything else either. But she felt she belonged with them. No matter what Dr. Kornblum said, they understood her. They were her.

Genevieve missed three Monday night sessions in a row. She'd spent her rent money and was thinking about selling the junk car she had purchased. She knew that Dr. Kornblum was going to be disappointed. She lay on her futon in her cramped studio apartment looking at the scar on her left wrist, wondering why God hadn't just allowed her to die. She thought about trying again. There would be no one to save her here at her own place. The desire to use drugs had more control over her than she did. That demonic pull made her not want to live. She couldn't force herself to live up to Dr. Kornblum's expectations.

The fourth time she missed a session, she cried because a part of her knew she needed to go back to therapy and deal with her relapse, but another part wanted to go someplace, get high again, and just forget about everything. She fought on the inside with demons. She knew that if she used drugs again that night, she would live the rest of her life that way. But that night was supposed to have been a big night. She was supposed to have accompanied Dr. Kornblum to a motivational conference for women. He'd told her that an old college buddy of his was the guest speaker. He said it would be positive for her. Genevieve had marked it on her calendar. But there she lay in bed, fighting the urge to give her life and soul back to her demons.

Banging on her door frightened her. She knew it was Carol down the hall, probably needing a ride to buy some temporary relief. That was her sign as to who she was. She got up to open the door, accepting the life that God had allowed her to have. And there was Dr. Kornblum, wearing an expensive, tan, cashmere coat and scarf. His long coat made him appear even shorter. His stomach protruded, stretching his button stitching. He scolded her like she was a child. "It's not nice to waste someone's time, Genevieve," he said, disgusted by her pathetic-looking state. His blue eyes tore into her. "Get yourself together right now. We are going to this conference. And after that you can do whatever you want to with your life. I don't care!" His normally pale face was colored with anger. Genevieve hadn't seen him like this before. He had always maintained a certain level of calmness. She gathered her clothes assiduously before scurrying into the bathroom to get dressed. She tried to figure out why her life concerned him so much. He had driven all the way to downtown Detroit just to pick her up for some stupid conference. She didn't see what the big deal was. But she obeyed anyway. And she was positive that he knew the reason why she had missed her sessions.

At the conference, Dr. Kornblum's old college "buddy" turned out to be Dr. Denice Banks, Dean of Psychology at Greydale. Her book, *Reclaiming Your Life*, was the topic for the evening. She spoke about women reclaiming their lives from whatever it was that had them bound. She said that they could take their lives back and start over. Genevieve listened to her talk about *her* life. She felt as if she were in church listening to a sermon that had been written especially for her. She was unclothed by Dr. Banks' words—the mini-sermon that had turned the conference into a church service, eliciting "Amens" and shouts from the audience.

Two women who had been involved in Dr. Banks' seven-year-old program shared their experiences with the audience. Both of them had *transformed* their lives. Genevieve swam in confusion. She was torn between believing them and accepting her life as it was. Michelle, the first woman, had been an addict. She was now an elementary school teacher working toward a master's degree. Carolyn, the second woman, confessed that she had been a victim of incest and subsequently suffered from manic depression for most of her life. She had endured abusive relationships. But she had married and was living a full, healthy life.

Genevieve imagined having a life that had meaning and purpose, but then she conned herself into thinking that the two women possessed some exceptional quality that she lacked. She didn't think she could ever be like them. But their stories gave her hope. The women made her want to *try* to do something different with her life. She was flooded by her own fears. She wanted to cross-examine each one of the women. She hoped that their stories weren't media hype to sell Dr. Banks' book, because a part of her wanted to believe.

When the conference was over, Dr. Kornblum introduced Genevieve to Dr. Banks over coffee at a restaurant across from the conference center. His stiffened disposition was supplanted with laughter in Dr. Banks' presence. Genevieve noted how beautiful Dr. Banks was with her dark-chocolate skin. She eyed her clothing and her perfectly manicured nails as Dr. Banks sipped from her coffee cup. It was just a simple French manicure, but it was feminine. She was well put together. She looked like a *woman*. Unconsciously, Genevieve looked down at her own clothes and nails in comparison. When Dr. Banks noticed Genevieve, she spoke the words that Genevieve still repeated at every one of her speaking engagements. "It takes time, Genevieve. We're all beautiful. But it starts on the inside. Remember that." It seemed that Dr. Banks had read Genevieve's mind. And before the night was over, she'd made the commitment to Dr. Kornblum to relocate Genevieve to Virginia so that she could take part in the Pathways program.

Dr. Banks' book was based on seven years of success with Pathways. She'd written the initial grant for the program and was acting as the Executive Consultant. Before she accepted the position of Dean of Psychology at Greydale, she had served as the Executive Director for Pathways. She hired Alicia Payne to replace her. The facility continued to receive much of its money from private sources, and had partnerships with three local churches: True Faith Ministries, Christ's Kingdom, and Bread of Life Baptist Church.

Pathways was located on one hundred acres of farmland in a secluded area of Lorton, Virginia. Dr. Banks had come upon the estate by happenstance one evening as she was driving through the neighborhoods, admiring the pre-Civil War architecture of the historic home sites. The main building was an old farmhouse. Although it had been renovated with modern office amenities and newly decorated, it still retained its farmhouse charm, with its whitewashed cedar clapboards and vaulted ceilings. It was charismatic sitting in the middle of a vast open land of lush green grass, surrounded by wildlife and over three thousand feet of river frontage.

The farmhouse contained three administrative offices that had previously been bedrooms, and four other bedrooms that were occupied by senior residents. The senior residents held leadership positions in the home, and had completed the two-year program. A twenty-million-dollar annex had been built to accommodate at least seventy women and their children in dorm-sized rooms. Its outside architecture mirrored that of the original farmhouse. Inside there were fifteen classrooms, an exercise facility, and a state-of-the-art computer and technology lab.

Upon entering Pathways, each woman had to agree to live on the property for at least one year. Pathways offered intensive treatment intervention programs for drug dependent, battered, and homeless women. The program components were designed to equip women with the skills they needed to be successful once they left. It gave them an opportunity to create new lives for themselves and their children.

The maximum time a woman could stay on the farm was two years, unless she was promoted to senior resident. It was expected that within two years time, a woman would find her own living accommodations, with assistance from the staff and a transitional support team. Women received support services and were monitored for two years after their completion of the program.

Pathways used some of the same principles as most twelve-step programs, but the major focus was on gaining emotional stability through faith in Jesus Christ and intensive therapy. Part of the women's contract included serving on a service committee through one of the churches involved, or being involved in one of the community outreach programs Pathways offered. The process of selecting residents was stringent because of this.

Each woman and child had a daily list of chores. Self-Improvement classes were required. They were taught by senior residents and volunteers from some of the local service agencies and universities. Classes on topics ranging from self-esteem to cooking were available. For the first six months, the women were not allowed to work outside of Pathways. This time was referred to as the stabilization period. Afterwards, they were connected with agencies that had been chosen by Pathways to further help them meet their goals. Genevieve completed her General Equivalency Diploma her first year at Pathways.

She began community college the year after. That was the year that she came to know Jesus Christ as her Lord and Savior. She was sitting in a Bible study class at True Faith Ministries, as she had for many weeks. It had become routine. But she liked the camaraderie that the group offered. That night, as she kneeled and listened to Reverend Rose Davis pray, she experienced a peaceful, urgent fire. It tugged at her. Invisible arms encircled her, squeezing, validating. Genevieve wanted to rest in those arms. She was afraid that when the prayer was over, that incredible lifesaving feeling would go away. Tears poured out from the comfort those arms provided. Genevieve wanted to retain that feeling of security.

When she rose from her knees, her whole body weakened. She fell to her knees again, stretched her arms upward, and called on Him. "Lord Jesus, please save me!" she heard herself shout.

Reverend Davis rushed over to Genevieve, placed her hands on her head and said, "*If thou shalt confess with thy mouth the LORD Jesus and believe in thine heart that God hath raised him from the dead, thou shalt be saved.* Genevieve, do you accept that you are a sinner and repent of your sins?"

"Yes . . . yes," Genevieve cried.

"Do you believe that Jesus Christ is the Son of God, who lived and was crucified, and was raised from the dead for your salvation?" Reverend Davis asked.

The tears continued to pour from Genevieve's eyes. "Yes, I do," she whimpered.

Reverend Davis pulled Genevieve to her feet and shouted, "Welcome to the body of Christ!" She blessed her in a victorious prayer.

Genevieve was baptized the following Sunday. Grace had forced Genevieve to be baptized as a child without her fully understanding what it symbolized. Genevieve was baptized this time on her own accord, to bear witness that she had accepted Christ in her heart and understood the gloriousness of the gift of salvation. Still, it took her two years to relinquish her psychological dependency on drugs. She struggled, but the Lord blessed her not to have a relapse.

She graduated from Junior College in two years and began attending Greydale, where she continued to study liberal arts until she decided upon a major. Life was wide open. She was overwhelmed by all the choices. She knew that she had the power to be successful in any arena she chose. She found that going to school and studying was relatively easy for her, although it required a great deal of discipline on her behalf to balance a full-time job and maintain high academic averages in her classes. She had not known that kind of responsibility before then.

She was hired by Pathways as an administrative assistant to Alicia Payne, the center's Director. Alicia had chosen her because of the typing and organizational skills she had acquired in the program. The center offered Genevieve the opportunity to live on the property as a senior resident and pay a reduced rate for rent, as a part of her contract. She declined because she had already found a nice, affordable apartment close to Greydale in nearby Alexandria, Virginia. Besides that, she relished the independence of living alone. She had gotten over her fear of failure and was ready to take on her new life. She wanted to feel in control of her life, no matter where she lived. Staying on the property would have provided a security blanket that she needed to come out from under in order to flourish. But she volunteered at Pathways in the evenings as a self-esteem coach.

Dr. Banks encouraged Genevieve to study psychology. Genevieve had expressed an interest in discovering what motivated people, including her, to do certain things, or make the choices they made. Listening to other people's life stories fascinated her, so she pursued her undergraduate studies in psychology. She was thirty-seven years old when she received her bachelor's degree.

The day Genevieve walked across the stage, it seemed that every woman that had been involved in the Pathways program was at her graduation, cheering for her. Two members of the executive board were there as well. But her biggest coup came when she looked out into the audience and saw Dr. Kornblum, his wife Sarah, and his daughter Rose in the audience. Genevieve beamed with pride. She had come so far. Just five years earlier, attaining a degree had been far from her thinking. As she was handed her mock diploma and posed for the photographer, she thought to herself, *Five years ago, I was ready to take my own life.* She had no idea of the blessings that the Lord had prepared for her.

The staff and residents threw a big celebration party on Pathways' campus for all of the women who had completed the two-year program or had graduated from community college or a university that year. Balloons and streamers floated in the spring air. The grounds were covered with tents, where specialty dishes had been prepared by caterers. A Christian jazz band filled the air with good music that made Genevieve feel like she was on top of the world. She scanned the grounds, unable to hold back her tears. She stole away from the guests and residents and found a quiet spot near the river, where she filled the air with music of her own—praises and thanksgiving to God who had brought her this far, and had walked with her along the way.

Later that evening, when the celebration was over, the center held its residents-only Success Book Ceremony. The Success Book contained photographs and biographies of some of the women who had completed the Pathways program and had volunteered to have their information available to residents as a source of inspiration. It was updated as the women accomplished more of their goals. And today was Genevieve's turn. She gleamed as they added her degree to her biography, along with an article about her life that had appeared in the Life Stories section of the newspaper. A classmate had been so touched by Genevieve's story that she had shared it with a relative who worked for the local newspaper. Not only had Genevieve recovered from a drug addiction, she had also graduated with her bachelor's degree, and had received a full academic scholarship to pursue a master's and doctorate degree at Greydale. She'd planned to become a psychologist like Dr. Banks.

Alicia Payne, the executive director and Genevieve's direct boss, resigned from Pathways two years after being diagnosed with breast cancer. Prior to that, Dr. Banks and the executive board had allowed Alicia time off to undergo treatment. They had planned to keep her position open until she was well enough to return to work. But being diagnosed with cancer caused Alicia to realize just how precious life was. She chose to stay home and raise her two sons with her husband after she recovered from the treatments. Up until that time, Genevieve had continued her job as assistant to the director while she pursued her graduate studies. She handled the majority of Alicia's responsibilities. She knew most of what Alicia's job consisted of because she had accompanied Alicia to meetings and taken notes. She'd handled her schedule, and assisted with the budget, payroll, and grant writing projects.

Alicia's position was posted at the university and in the newspaper.

Pathways

Genevieve had already completed her master's degree, so she applied for it. No one had asked her to apply. No one had even suggested that she should apply. She expected shock to follow the submission of her resume packet. But she knew about the day-to-day responsibilities of running Pathways. She'd functioned as an assistant for four years, and besides that, educationally, she was qualified for the position. And she was a product of Pathways. If nothing else, she had the women's trust. She had proven herself trustworthy in handling some of the organization's finances, including making huge donation deposits that came in from philanthropists.

Genevieve interviewed along with the other applicants. She made it to the final selection of three candidates. The other two candidates were women who had been directors of social service agencies and drug rehabilitation programs. They were educated women. One had a PhD already. The other had a master's degree and was currently working to complete her PhD, just as Genevieve was. But the one thing that the other two candidates lacked was the experience of being on the other side of the couch. Genevieve had been where the women that Pathways served were. She had been an addict and a battered woman. She knew what it felt like to be homeless. She related to them. She was a role model—someone they could see and touch. Dr. Banks and the exec board knew that Genevieve understood the women in a different way. But Dr. Banks distanced herself from Genevieve during the application process. Genevieve wasn't sure how Dr. Banks felt about her applying for the position to become the director of a program that she founded. She didn't expect Dr. Banks to do her any more favors. She had done more than enough for her over the years.

During her group interview, Genevieve floored the committee when she asked them to forget that she was a former client of Pathways, but instead to remember her professional job experience with the organization, as well as the fact that she had been an addict. She wanted her life and the transformation of her life to speak for itself. What she had done with her life was proof of her determination and commitment to the program.

She waited a week for the decision. She told herself that if they didn't decide to give her the position, she wouldn't be bitter. She resolved that she would continue her job as an assistant, and evening therapist until she completed her PhD. Genevieve promised herself that she wouldn't give in to self-pity, but trust that the board had made a decision that was best for the agency.

She was at the center working the day that the news came. She had just returned from a funding meeting with the executive board members of the churches that were involved with the center, along with Fred Carter, a member of one of D.C.'s community development programs. It was eight-thirty p.m., well after work hours, but Genevieve wanted to write her report on the meeting while everything was still fresh in her head. She had temporarily moved into Alicia's office since she was handling most of her responsibilities.

She looked around at the tastefully decorated office, with its mauve walls and expensive mahogany office furniture, and sank into Alicia's huge suede office chair. She smoothed her palms over its soft fabric, imagining. Then she pushed the thought out of her mind. But the thought felt comfortable—natural, even. So she pleasured herself by kicking off her shoes, putting her feet atop the smoked glass-top desk, and smiled as she finished the remainder of the Häagen-Dazs that had been in the office freezer. Strangely, there was a knock at the door. It caught her off guard because the main building was locked. She had watched the security guard lock it herself. She hadn't heard the entry alert on the alarm system either. But before Genevieve could take her feet off the desk and investigate, Dr. Banks walked in with Alicia Payne, whom Genevieve hadn't seen since she had gone on medical leave. Both of the women wore disappointed looks. That told Genevieve what the news was. She took her feet down and put the lid back on her ice cream carton. She braced herself with a deep breath and sat up straight in the chair.

She spoke before either one of them had a chance to. "You know, I've already decided that I'm going to continue working here as the assistant until I finish my doctorate. I have a small caseload in the evenings, and this works well with my school schedule. No other job is going to allow me the flexibility that I have here. I need the time to study anyway."

"That's what we came to talk to you about," Alicia said.

Genevieve's heart sank.

Alicia turned her back to Genevieve as if she were overcome with emotion. She reached over and pulled some of the pastel-colored Puffs from the box on the corner of the desk and started to sniffle.

Dr. Banks intervened. "Genevieve, you know that we value you a great deal here at the center, but we're making a lot of changes. Finding someone to fill Alicia's position permanently is only a small part of what we need to do to continue to move this project forward . . ."

Genevieve didn't want to hear another word. She wanted so badly to ask Dr. Banks to "please be quiet." She'd already accepted the fact that they probably needed someone with more experience. And maybe her being a recovering addict affected their decision negatively, instead of the way she'd hoped. She wished the two of them could read her mind. She had come so far. She didn't want to hear about her failures. She just wanted to move on past this day. She didn't need to be petted like a child. She felt like screaming out to Dr. Banks to just get it over with.

But Dr. Banks continued on anyway, despite the look on Genevieve's face. ". . . You see Genevieve, we need a woman with a lot of experience," she said, avoiding Genevieve's eyes. Tensed, Dr. Banks clasped her fingers together, inverted them, and stretched them out. "We think we found the right person . . ." she continued in a defeated tone. "The only problem is that she has the authority to choose her own assistant . . . I'm sorry . . ." her voice trailed off.

Genevieve felt flustered. She could feel heat dispersing throughout her limbs. She ran her fingers through her hair. What were they saying? Not only had they come to tell her that she didn't get the position of director, but she was losing the assistant position as well. *How could this happen?* She loved her job. She hadn't even considered the fact that she would be replaced when the new director was hired. She was stunned. *God, what are You doing? Why are You doing this? You brought me all this way to push me back farther?* She'd trusted Him. How could He let this happen?

Genevieve tried to maintain her professionalism, but some of her anger seeped out, "So what are you two saying?" she demanded.

"We're saying . . . you aren't the director's assistant any longer," Dr. Banks said, regretfully. Alicia never turned to face Genevieve.

Genevieve started to protest. "Why didn't you warn me that this could happen? I love my job. Now what am I going to—"

"You are the NEW DIRECTOR!" Dr. Banks yelled.

And finally Alicia spun around with an incredible smile on her face. "CONGRATULATIONS!" she screamed.

It took sixty whole seconds for their words to register. For sixty whole seconds Genevieve was frozen, until her brain printed out the words, IT WAS A HOAX; YOU GOT THE JOB! Then Genevieve screamed out in complete hysteria and every other emotion that came along with winning—finally. The three of them jumped up and down in the center of Genevieve's new office, screaming and crying like fanatic teenagers at a rock concert.

Both Genevieve and Sandy were teary eyed. Sandy wiped her tears and took off her suit jacket. "You think I could get some water, or a pop—soda?" she said, moved by her mother's incredible story.

Genevieve stood. "Soda? Oh, I'm sorry. I should have offered you something earlier," she said, walking over to the mini-bar. She pulled out a Diet Sprite and a water bottle. She handed them to Sandy.

"Thank you. I'm parched," Sandy chuckled.

"Would you like room service?"

"Come to think of it, a BLT sounds good right about now. And maybe some fries," Sandy said as she looked through her index cards.

Genevieve's nervousness had dwindled. She was ready for any question Sandy might throw at her. Even the one that she wasn't sure she could answer. *Why didn't she come back for them?* She dialed room service and ordered as she watched Sandy get up and stretch her legs. She followed her with her eyes as she walked over to the window to take a look at the view. She was beautiful. Genevieve smiled. "Okay, lunch will be here shortly," she said, resuming her seat at the table.

Sandy sat down across from Genevieve again. She spoke seriously, looking Genevieve directly in the eyes. "Tell me about Benjamin . . . and your other children," she said. Her smile was gone.

Genevieve hesitated. She could hear the dejection in Sandy's tone. She knew what she was thinking—that she'd had more children and forgot about her and Josette. But that wasn't what happened. She first met

Benjamin while working as Alicia Payne's assistant. Alicia had worked with Benjamin on a host of faith-based community projects through his church, Bread of Life Baptist. Genevieve spent four years as Alicia's assistant, taking notes during her and Benjamin's meetings and making follow up calls to Benjamin about projects the two were involved in. She and Benjamin became better acquainted when she became the director of Pathways.

Genevieve had considered Benjamin to be an attractive man since the first day she met him. But when her job caused her to spend extensive amounts of time in meetings with him, she found that she had a greater attraction to his spirit. She surprised him the first day she met with him as the executive director of Pathways. She walked into his office and took the seat that was usually reserved for Alicia. Benjamin looked at her curiously and said, "Are you going to take notes from there?"

"No, actually I'm going to *meet* with you from right here. I've been promoted to director. My assistant is running a little late."

Benjamin laughed, covering his mouth, slightly embarrassed. "Well, excuse me, Ms. Moss. I need to stay abreast of what is going on in the world," he said playfully.

And Genevieve noticed his perfect white teeth and genuine smile. His quiet spirit was enchanting. Her nervousness disappeared in his light-heartedness. The easy camaraderie they shared laid the foundation for their transition from casual business associates to friends. After several meetings and brainstorming sessions, Benjamin asked Genevieve out on a date. She'd quickly told him that she needed to pray about it and would give him an answer later. She wanted to make sure that she was doing what the Lord wanted her to do. Was she emotionally ready to date? What about her past? When she prayed, the Lord had given her a sense of peace, so she called Benjamin back one afternoon and accepted his invitation—three weeks after he'd asked.

Genevieve felt absurdly awkward when Benjamin arrived to pick her up from her apartment. It was the first date she'd been on as a woman of God. She had cleaned the apartment twice, and re-cleaned it, arranging plants and end tables in different areas of the room, wanting it to look perfect in case Benjamin stayed awhile. At her suggestion, they went to the zoo. She hadn't been since Sandy and Josette were toddlers. She and Benjamin had a picnic lunch. Benjamin had cooked corned beef and made two hearty sandwiches, along with potato salad. Thoughtful, he had also brought along cheese and crackers, fresh fruit, and sparkling grape juice to toast their first date. He confessed that he'd had his eyes on her for over a year.

The two were inseparable from that first date. It was confusing and exciting all the same. Could she be falling in love? And after three months of dating, Benjamin caused even more of a stir in Genevieve when he expressed a desire to define their relationship. He said that he wanted to be *more* than friends. The word *exclusive* circled Genevieve. If Benjamin wanted to become serious, she'd have to tell him about her past. He stood waiting for an answer as Genevieve looked at him confusedly. It wasn't the reaction he'd hoped for.

"Pray about it and let me know," Ben had said quietly before walking away from her apartment door, disappointed.

Genevieve stayed up that night reeling, not certain if she was emotionally ready to be in a serious relationship with a man. Her life before Jesus had been dysfunctional. All of her relationships had been plagued with abuse and self-gratification. She didn't know *how* to be in a relationship. She hadn't learned that at Pathways or in graduate school. For the last seven years since being involved with Pathways, she hadn't desired male companionship—not until Benjamin asked her out.

Benjamin was a wonderful man of God that she respected and cared for. He had treated her respectfully. But she feared that telling him about her past would change things between them. Doubts were heavy. She sought counsel from Dr. Banks. *"For God hath not given us a spirit of fear; but of power, and of love, and of a sound mind,"* Dr. Banks quoted 2 Timothy 1:7. She reminded Genevieve that she was a new creature in Christ and that her old life had passed away. "There is no reason to fear your past, Vee. It's over," Dr. Banks encouraged.

Genevieve received those words and prayed that when the opportunity came for her to tell Benjamin about her life, he would receive it with the love of God and not judge her for it. She stalled for a week before agreeing to go cruising with him on his boat. It was Benjamin's only luxury. He'd sold most of the land that he'd inherited from his father to purchase it. His sixty-foot joy swayed buoyantly as gentle waves caressed the bottom and sides. Sitting next to Benjamin on the aft deck, looking out at the blackened, magnificent sky, Genevieve made the speech that she had practiced in her head for a whole week. It was the speech that might send him—the man that she was surely falling in love with, walking out of her life. She kept her eyes on the stars as she spoke until she felt that she had unchained every weight. Benjamin listened quietly as Genevieve released. He paused before responding to be sure that she had said everything she'd wanted to say. When he was sure that she was finished, he scooted closer to her, took her hands in his, and kissed them. He cupped her face in his hands and said, "Genevieve, you still haven't given me an answer yet."

Genevieve collapsed in his arms, crying, holding on to him for dear life. He was the first man in her life who had accepted her for who she was—even the part on the inside that she'd hidden from everyone but God. And Benjamin kissed Genevieve with an urgency that stayed on her mind long after their evening together had ended.

Less than eight months later, Benjamin proposed, right in the spot where they'd had their first picnic. They married the following month in a small evening ceremony at Benjamin's church. Faith and Joshua were four years old. Genevieve had gotten to know them over her and Ben's courtship and had fallen in love with the dynamic duo. Being a mother to them was effortless. It was like having a second chance.

Chapter Five

Sandy couldn't have imagined a better meeting between her and Genevieve. She even accompanied Genevieve to her book signing, careful to blend in with the rest of the autograph seekers. She was flabbergasted watching Genevieve sign autographs and mingle with her fans as though she'd always been a famous author, and not the woman that Sandy remembered in her dreams. Genevieve and her fans had a passionate love affair. She prayed, laughed, and cried with some of the women. She'd changed so much from the woman Sandy remembered. For the first time in a long while, peace found a space in Sandy's heart. It was the peace of having answers. Though the pain of her childhood hadn't completely dissolved, it no longer engulfed her. She and Genevieve had enjoyed a productive meeting and good conversation.

Sandy had to admit at least one truth about all the money she'd spent on therapy sessions in the last three years. If nothing else, it had helped her to identify the things in life that were important to her. She'd learned from Jody that facing her feelings and accepting them was a sign of growth. She wanted to be free of the emotional trap she'd been in, and therapy had been the start she needed. She'd worn the "victim" hat since

Genevieve's addiction. She'd been the victim child, the victim wife, and the victim girlfriend. The "yes girl"—the sacrificial lamb. She felt like she could take those hats off and start living life by her own rules now.

She planned to start with Lamont Drake. She needed an outlet, and it wouldn't hurt to have one that was chocolate-covered. Having Josette as an extended guest was a parenting job. The peaceful and quiet unwinding time Sandy used to relish after work had been bombarded with Josette unwinding with the Bose system blasting. Sometimes it was agonizing love songs, other times it was some rap artist that Sandy figured Josette should have outgrown a long time ago. She wondered what the other attorneys at the law firm Josette worked for would think if they saw the "flipped script" of Josette Moss-Kelley, their darling little protégé, bouncing around the house with that *Tupac Lives* t-shirt on, rapping.

It became a monotonous habit, Sandy screaming at Josette to turn the music down like she was some teenager. And Sandy wondered how she had acquired the title of "maid" since Josette had moved in. She found herself picking up behind Josette: dirty dishes left in the sink, Manolo Blahnik and Jimmy Choo shoes all over the house, hair brushes in the kitchen, and un-made beds. It was a sad ritual.

Josette was accustomed to having a housekeeper. Sandy didn't know that she had inadvertently signed up for the job. She wished Josette would have thought about these things *before* she got herself kicked out of the house where the housekeeper was. Sandy needed her space back. If she had to tolerate anyone working her last good nerve the way her little sister was, she wanted that person to be at least six feet tall with baritone, and not hard to look at—like Lamont.

She felt ready to date again. She welcomed the idea of going out to dinner with a man for a change. It had been four years since she'd been involved with anyone. She still had hopes of having children, praying that the Lord didn't hold against her what she'd done to the first child that He'd blessed her with. She still carried the shame from the abortion she had while she was *married*. The only person she had heart enough to tell was Josette. It was one of those sins that she'd confessed to God but still clung to. Sometimes she felt like her singleness and childlessness was God's divine way of punishing her for that horrible deed.

She was twenty-six years old then. She'd been married to Terell for four years. She'd cried through the whole union. A week before she found out that she was pregnant, she caught Terell cheating on her for the *third* time—that she knew of, anyway. She knew she couldn't stay in the marriage anymore. It had drained the life out of her—all the lying and sneaking around—not to mention the embarrassing trips she'd made to the doctor when Terell had brought his street life home to her. Her marriage was a disappointment and a shame. She couldn't see herself bringing a child into the mess she and Terell had. She couldn't see God's plan in it either. Now, she couldn't forget the day that she allowed a gift of life to be torn right out of her body. It was still her secret shame.

Sometimes she blamed God for the way her life had turned out. She was a good Christian woman. She'd been a virgin when she married. She'd saved herself just like Linda had taught her—just like it said in the Word. And most importantly, Sandy had wanted to please God—tried to please Him. She studied her Bible and concentrated on developing a deep, intimate relationship with the Lord. She served others, doing the things that were taught at church. But God had left her on the planet with a mother who was a drug addict and a husband who'd misused her like she was nothing. Even now, Sandy couldn't quite figure out exactly what she'd done to deserve it all.

Her divorce from Terell had been just as emotionally costly as Genevieve's abandonment. It stripped her of her dignity and self-worth. Terell's infidelities caused her to develop the "not good enough" syndrome, which pushed her further into depression. The worst blows came from other Christians. Sandy felt like a leper the way she was stared at and whispered about at *church*. A few of the women she'd had friendships with stopped calling her altogether, like divorce was contagious. It was as if they were afraid that Sandy was going to contaminate their marriages.

Sandy left Terell's church and the memories of the life she'd had with him, and returned to Morning Star Baptist, her childhood church. A part of her regretted the abortion, but the other half of her was satisfied with the fact that she and Terell didn't have a child binding the two of them together. She wouldn't have been able to heal with Terell running in and out of her life every other weekend for visitation. She would erase all the memories of her past if she could—just to have peace within.

Despite serving her Lord, Sandy's life had taken a wrong turn somewhere and she couldn't quite figure out where or why. Josette had been blessed with everything—the niceties of life and a good man—and hadn't appreciated any of it. Sandy had given herself to the people she'd loved and hadn't received anything in return. Their lives were a scale of unfair balances, and Sandy was the loser. Even her best friend had disappointed her, just like Genevieve. Just like Terell.

Sandy and B. J. kept in contact by phone when she and Josette were placed with Linda and Roger. B. J. and Sarah moved back to Florida to be closer to their family. The mean streets of the Motor City had proven to be too rough for a country girl. Determined to preserve their friendship,

Sandy and B. J. wrote each other every week and called once a month.

During Sandy's sophomore year at Michigan State, B. J. called with the sad news that Sarah had died of a brain aneurysm. He wanted Sandy to fly down for Sarah's funeral. The two of them split the cost of Sandy's plane ticket so that she could be there with him on the day he buried his mother. Sandy was right in the middle of final examinations when she got the call. She had to schedule a meeting with her psychology professor to ask if she could take her final exam early so that she could be with B. J. He needed her.

Sandy waited anxiously outside of Professor Hodge's office in the psychology building. She had already purchased her plane ticket. She didn't know what she was going to do if he told her "no." She couldn't afford to let her grades slip, and she couldn't let B. J. down either. Her palms were moist with perspiration. She stood up to shake off that feeling that came over her when she worried about something. She took deep breaths and wiped her moist palms on her jeans. She thought of lies she could tell that would make Professor Hodge more sympathetic to her situation. She wondered if telling him that Sarah was her aunt, as opposed to a family friend, would make it a more acceptable excuse. She felt guilty about having to lie. Linda had always admonished them to "be truthful in all things." It was the godly way to handle a problem. Sandy sighed, hoping Linda was right.

When Professor Hodge walked up and saw the flustered look on Sandy's face, he knew he wasn't dealing with the usual student excuse to head to Florida early for spring break. Sandy opened her mouth to explain her plight and all of her history came tumbling out. She found herself telling Professor Hodge her life story, like how Sarah fed her and Josette when Genevieve had been too high to care, or had pulled one of her infamous disappearing acts. She told him that she had to pay her last respect. She owed it to Sarah and B. J.

Professor Hodge listened to Sandy's story despite her rambling, nodding his head periodically, taking in all that she said. But before he gave her his final decision, he looked in his record book. He repeated her student number to himself as he searched the book. When he finally came across Sandy's number, the look on his face indicated that Sandy's grades were impressive. She was in the top ten percent of his class, and was the student who had set the curve on the last two examinations. Even if she failed the final, she still could have passed the class.

"I admire your strength, Cassandra," Professor Hodge said, nodding in agreement with himself. He handed her the final examination, "Strong black queen, handle your business," he said.

"Thank you, sir," Sandy said gratefully. But her face was contorted, looking at Professor Hodge like he was from another planet. A blue-eyed, middle-aged white man had called her a "strong black queen," and had said it with reverence.

Professor Hodge smiled at Sandy's surprise. "The whole world isn't going to hell," he said while shaking his finger playfully at Sandy. "I marched with Dr. King, young lady," he said proudly, reaching across his desk to hand her a brass, two-picture frame. One of the pictures was a snapshot of him in his younger days, marching behind King. The other was a family photograph of him, his wife, and their twin daughters. Sandy was outdone. She never would have guessed that Professor Hodge was "down for the cause," married to a sister, *and* raising two black queens of his own.

"Thank you again," Sandy said, smiling about her discovery.

She took her exam, and afterward, she waited in the hallway, chewing her nails, while Professor Hodge scored it. He opened his door twenty minutes later and told her that she'd scored a ninety-three percent. He said that he'd deducted seven points off the written portion because she could have given more detailed answers. Indebted, Sandy shook Professor Hodge's hand, relieved that she was on her way to see B. J. She was happier about that than she was about having a final grade of an A. And that feeling that always came when she worried had left.

The small church was packed with mourners. Every wooden bench was crowded with relatives and friends. They were all squeezed together hip to hip, raising the temperature as the sun beat its way through the beautiful stained-glass windows. Two large wooden-paddle ceiling fans spun the heat around like a web. Dow Funeral Home church fans fluttered busily across the sanctuary, creating individual pockets of cool air, as chords of "Sweet Hour of Prayer" awakened the pipe organ and prepared the hearts of the people for worship at Sarah's homegoing.

B. J. was broken. It was the second time in Sandy's life that she had seen him cry. Quietly, B. J. cried a man's cry. It anguished Sandy to see him paining that way. He tried to retain some of his strength by sniffing it back in deeply, broadening his shoulders, and holding his head erect. But his pain kept escaping in tears. He looked right through the mourners who had tried to console him with hugs and kind words after they had taken their last look at his mother. He just said, "Thank you," as graciously as he could with a distressed voice, never taking his eyes off Sarah's pearl-colored casket.

Sandy sat right next to B. J. Big Mama, his grandmother, sat on the opposite side. They created two strong, buffering walls around him. Every so often, Big Mama took the edge of her handkerchief and gently blotted B. J.'s tears. Sandy was still as she could be, allowing B. J. to rest against her when grief grabbed him. From time to time during the service, B. J. lifted his head and squeezed Sandy's hand tightly, then dropped his head again. He was not the same feared, freckle-faced boy she'd met in kindergarten. He was a man dealing with the upset of life's trials—trials that Sandy knew all too well at the age of twenty.

She knew the emptiness of losing a mother. She understood the loneliness B. J. was facing. She knew what it felt like to be afraid, without the person you loved most. Every time B. J. squeezed her hands, she felt his thoughts in her spirit: "*What am I going to do now?*"

A repast had been prepared at Big Mama's home by her church members. After leaving the cemetery, the family had planned to remember Sarah by looking through Big Mama's memory trunk, which contained precious mementos like Sarah's first doll, her prom dress, and other items Big Mama had saved from Sarah's childhood. It was their family tradition. They did it after every funeral. Big Mama was in high spirits. It seemed that she was looking forward to the family's last good-bye to Sarah. But B. J. had made it clear to Big Mama that he was *not* going to attend the repast and memory trunk celebration. He had decided that at the hospital when he'd watched life slip from his mother. He had to let go of Sarah in his own time, in his own way. It had all been depleting. It was too heavy a burden for him at twenty—the flowers, the cards, the neighbors coming by to console him. He couldn't take another hour of mourning relatives and neighbors talking about the things Sarah *used to* do. "I need to be alone" was all he said when Big Mama reminded him of the family's plans as they left the cemetery chapel. He planted a soft kiss on her forehead and gave her a hug.

"Ain't no reason to be sad, son. Sarah gone with the Lord now. Ain't no mo' crying. Ain't no mo' tears," Big Mama said as B. J. helped her down the chapel stairs.

"I know. I just need some time to myself," B. J. said back.

Big Mama yielded to B. J.'s need to grieve in solitude. "Okay. You a grown man now. Got to make yo' own choices. But if you change yo' mind, come on by," she said.

The family members organized themselves quickly and quietly, so that B. J. could ride back alone to the home he and his mother had shared together. Sandy packed in one of the other family cars with Big Mama and some aunts and uncles she'd met the night before. She had no intention of imposing on B. J.'s time to grieve alone, regardless of the fact that she'd come all the way from Michigan.

As they neared the main road, the family car that B. J. was in stopped abruptly. B. J. emerged and jogged over to the car carrying Sandy and Big Mama, and tapped on the window. Big Mama looked puzzled as she fumbled with the power window button.

"You change yo' mind about joining us?" she said, smiling.

"I need to talk to Sandy," B. J. said, looking past Big Mama.

Sandy felt guiltily embarrassed. She wondered what Big Mama was thinking. Her eyes darted back and forth between Big Mama and B. J. who had already opened the door and was waiting for her to step out of the car. But she was iced in her seat by her imaginings of Big Mama's thoughts. Aunt Donna and Aunt Cassie cut eyes at one another, then at Big Mama. Sandy remained seated next to Big Mama like she was attached at the hip.

"Come on," B. J. said, gesturing with his head.

Sandy didn't budge. She kept watching Big Mama, waiting for her to respond. Aunt Cassie and Aunt Donna whispered to one another as they too waited for some response from Big Mama. B. J. was the only one of them who wasn't waiting for Big Mama's response. Big Mama twisted her lips, mulling over the thought of two young adults alone at a time like this, when emotions were heightened.

B. J. disregarded the look on Big Mama's face and kept his focus on Sandy. "Sandy!" he shouted, attempting to beam her back down to earth. He looked at Big Mama to see *if* she had anything to say. He and Big Mama had had these discussions before. In some respect, he was considered to be a grown man. He had a full-time job and had been helping to support Sarah by working at an auto-mechanic shop. He had taken the trade in high school and had been successful, graduating right into a good paying job. He'd worked at the same shop since graduation and even had health benefits. Most of the down payment on the house that Sarah had purchased came from money B. J. had saved. He made more money than Sarah did working as an office assistant. So he found it strange that he was considered "grown" when it was convenient for Big Mama. She had a hard time letting him go when it came to matters like these.

"Go on," Big Mama conceded reluctantly, nudging Sandy.

B. J. helped Sandy out of the limousine. "I'll call you later," he said to Big Mama.

"You do that."

The ride back to Sarah's was cushioned with understood silence. B. J. rode quietly, staring blankly out of the window at the countryside that moved past him with the same swiftness as Sarah's death. God had taken his mother without warning. Without provocation. Without cause. Where was the love Big Mama preached about? Where was this God of mercy?

They were resting comfortably back at the house when B. J. broke the silence with teasing. Sandy lay across the sofa reading a copy of a campus magazine on women's health issues. B. J. had engaged himself in a game of solitaire at the small kitchen table until he was sidelined by the peaceful expression on Sandy's face. She reminded him of a little girl reading a fairy tale story. She'd stolen his attention away from his attempt to fill his mind with nothingness. Could she be the same little girl that he had walked to school with everyday from kindergarten to seventh grade? The cute one with the single ponytail twist that was tied with a white ribbon and clipped with a white butterfly barrette?

"Big Mama got you scared?" he asked. He stood up and walked over to the kitchen counter peeking under the Reynolds Wrap and plastic that covered the food that Sarah's neighbors had sent over.

"No . . . I just didn't want her to think—"

"Think what?" he asked, lifting an apple pie in the air. It was a gold mine discovery. Sandy got up and joined him at the counter. He handed her the apple pie.

"That I was loose or something," she said, taking it from him. He passed her a knife and she cut two huge chunks for both of them.

"Why would she think that?"

"Well, she didn't look too happy about the idea of us being alone together."

"If you ain't noticed, I'm a grown man. And I don't remember *asking* nobody what they thought," B. J. said, sticking a forkful of pie in his mouth.

Sandy meditated on his declaration for a moment. She hadn't *looked* at him since she arrived. Her plane had come in late the night before. They hadn't had the time to share more than menial conversation. Sarah's house had been filled with relatives, neighbors, and friends. And B. J. had kept his distance from all of them. He'd wanted the day of the funeral to come and go. Sandy had sensed his need to have space and had kept her distance as well. It wasn't until the moment that he'd said, "*I'm a grown man*," that she noticed that he *was* a grown man. The last time she'd seen him in person was the day before he and Sarah had moved back to Florida. They were thirteen years old.

Most of her memories of B. J. were of him being awkward and grungy. Now, his reddish-brown freckles were barely noticeable on his golden complexion, and the unkempt hair he sported from elementary to middle school was neatly trimmed. His hair was less fiery than she'd remembered. And his grey-green eyes no longer appeared weird-looking, but were kind of attractive instead. He had sent her a couple of pictures over the last two years, but they hadn't done him justice. He was much more handsome in person.

Sandy smiled at him. "So I noticed," she said.

"Noticed what?"

"That you are a grown man."

He inched his chest out playfully. "That's right! So, *Ms. College Woman*, have you decided on a major? Last time we talked you were undecided."

"Nursing," Sandy said.

"You'll make a great nurse."

"Thank you. What about you? What are you going to do with yourself?"

"To tell you the truth, I don't know yet. Craig died of AIDS in prison. Now mama's gone. Life keeps throwing me these curve balls."

Sandy nodded, realizing that Sarah's death was another defeat. She quickly changed the subject to something lighter, and suggested that the two of them change into some sweats and head to the video store. They rented a bunch of old movies that Sandy loved as a girl: *Sparkle*, *Flashdance*, and *Fame*. But they found themselves playing catch-up more than they paid attention to the movies. The two of them sat on the area rug, philosophizing and debating world issues. Occasionally, Sandy would catch B. J. staring at her. When she asked him what the problem was, he just shrugged it off and said, "Nothing."

But B. J. was thinking about how different Sandy looked from the last time he'd seen her. She was beautiful. Even in a pair of sweatpants and a university logo T-shirt that had been washed so much that the letters could barely be made out, she was beautiful. There was a certain chemistry between them—an adult chemistry.

It embarrassed Sandy to think of B. J. in any way other than the brother she'd grown up with, but she had to admit that he was attractive. The feeling was mutual. B. J. couldn't keep his eyes off of her. The fluctuation of emotions that he'd experienced over the last week had put him in a different mood. He wanted a safe haven to rest in. He wanted the kind of comforting that only a woman could bring. The commonality of pain that he shared with Sandy drew them to one another. While Jennifer Beale danced around in leg warmers, their lips found each other and their tongues played a chasing game. Sandy let out breaths of "Oh, please . . . more . . . more" without uttering a single word.

B. J. put his cool, soft lips on her neck. And without hesitation, Sandy turned and twisted her neck to give those lips room to touch more of her skin. A forbidden rush of pleasure pulsated through her. As quickly as their lips had met, they were knocking on the door of the place Linda used to warn her about. Sandy could hear Linda's voice saying, "*Sandy, deep kissing is dangerous. It leads to other things.*" 1 Corinthians 6:18 flashed on the screen in her head, then James 1:14-15. The verses disappeared slowly as Sandy kept falling into that feeling. The sound of her and B. J.'s soft panting dominated the quietness. She felt herself slipping deeper, entering that point of no return, as she and B. J. caressed each other.

When Sandy was positive that it was too late to pray, the phone rang. At first they ignored it, concentrating only on one other. Six pestering rings later, B. J. answered. He cracked a half-smile, looking at Sandy pleasingly. Ashamed of the thoughts that she knew B. J. could hear, she covered her face with her hands. Gently, B. J. pulled them away, admiring how pretty she was, as he talked to the person who had trespassed on his moment. "Talking," he said, trying to convince Big Mama. "Yeah, I know," he continued as Big Mama rambled on. "I know," he kept repeating before handing Sandy the phone.

Sandy cradled the phone between her neck and shoulder. She walked over to the refrigerator and filled a glass with water to put out the fire B. J. had started. As she greeted Big Mama, B. J. wrapped his arms around her waist and whispered in her ear. "Saved by the bell," he said. The sensation of his body so close to hers, and the warmth of his breath in her ear, caused a sort of aftershock vibration. If she hadn't sat down at the kitchen table, her knees would have buckled. She watched him disappear into Sarah's room. She had to compose herself.

"Cassandra, I just wanted to remind you that B. J. is mournin' his mother," Big Mama admonished her. "Men act out they grief different. You hear me?" Big Mama stressed. "This the time Satan try to get in—when peoples be feelin' low. Don't y'all give the devil no opportunities."

Sandy's thoughts drifted between the words Big Mama spoke and the imagination of her and B. J. making love. "Yes ma'am," she answered.

"Cassandra . . . I'm gonna ask you somethin' and you ain't got to answer me if you don't want to. But I'm gonna ask it anyway. Are you a virgin, young lady?"

"Yes ma'am."

"And I know you tellin' the truth 'cause the Lord done already told me that. And if you been savin' yo'self fo' yo' husband, you keep right on savin'. Whatever worth havin' is worth waitin' fo'. The Lord wants you to stay as pure as you are right now—hear me?"

"Yes ma'am," Sandy said, convicted.

"Well, good night. I just called 'cause the Lord put it on my heart. Good night now," Big Mama said, ending her lecture.

"Good night."

B. J. stood over Sandy, looking serious. "Did Big Mama tell you that the Lord told her to call?" he asked, pulling Sandy up from the table.

"Yep."

"You believe her?"

"Yep."

"Strange as it may sound . . ." B. J. started, shaking his head, "I do too." He smiled a defeated smile and kissed Sandy's hand. "You can sleep in Mama's room. I'm going to hit the sack in my own room tonight. I moved your suitcase in there already."

Sandy had slept in his room the night before, and he had slept on the couch in the living room, along with some of his other cousins who had made pallets on the floor.

"Oh, no. I wouldn't feel right," she protested.

"It's cool. Mama would want you to. I made the bed for you already."

Sandy gave in, knowing that Sarah wouldn't have had it any other way. Besides, this sleeping arrangement would keep her out of B. J.'s bed and out of trouble.

"Thank you," she said, following B. J. down the hall to Sarah's room.

B. J. surprised her when he turned and kissed her, not holding his lips to hers more than a second. "Good night," he said, before walking away. He'd made a difficult choice since Big Mama had called. And it had been made reluctantly. He was still full of sexual tension and anticipation.

Sandy stood in the hallway watching him walk toward his room. "B. J., I love you," she said quietly, but not quietly enough for those words to slip past him.

He hurried back down the hall toward her. "What did you just say?" he asked seriously.

Nervous, Sandy repeated the words she hadn't expected to say in the first place. "I said, 'I love you.'"

Softly, B. J. pressed her into the wall with his body, whispering to her as if someone else might hear his confession. "You wanna know something? I've *always* loved you," he said, breathing hard into her ear. "Did you know that?"

Sandy was intimidated by him. She wiggled her leg nervously.

B. J. held her hand tenderly, with his body still pressed against hers. "Ever since kindergarten, I've loved you. Can't express it in words. It's a sin for me to show you the way I want to. So . . . go in that room, lock that door, and get some rest." He turned the knob and pushed Sarah's door open. "Good night, Sandy," he said again, ordering her inside.

Sandy walked in and closed the door behind her, locking it before she walked over to Sarah's bed, minimizing the likelihood of getting into trouble. Because if B. J. had tried to persuade her with those delicious kisses again, she might have forgotten all about waiting for her husband. She lay in Sarah's bed with mixed emotions. She thought about Linda telling her how important it was to save herself. Then she thought about what it would feel like to be with B. J. in that way. She wanted to feel him next to her and fall asleep in his arms. There was no other person that she would have chosen to share that experience with. She drifted off to sleep thinking about it.

Sandy left Tallahassee still as pure as the night she arrived. Big Mama accompanied her and B. J. to the airport. When B. J. got out of the car to retrieve Sandy's suitcase from the trunk, Big Mama turned to her and asked in a stern voice, "Cassandra, are you still a virgin?"

"Yes ma'am."

"Thank you Jesus!" Big Mama said, looking up toward Heaven. Sandy watched her say a prayer.

Sandy and B. J. called each other every day after she returned to Michigan—until it became too expensive. They slacked for a while, and B. J. grew distant in the interim. The letters that used to come at least once a week weaned to once a month before stopping altogether. He struggled with Sarah's death. It changed him, destroying the small amount of faith he'd had in God. Sandy blamed herself for not being able to support him more. They were miles apart in every sense.

When the two of them did talk, Sandy frustrated B. J. with questions about what he was going to do with the rest of his life. Sarah had left him the home that was paid off through a death benefit policy, in addition to a fifty-thousand-dollar life insurance policy. Sandy encouraged him to be wise with the money and home he'd inherited. She'd taken a few economics classes and talked to him constantly about investing. She had even gone so far as to send him financial books and magazines. B. J. appeased her by promising that he would find a financial advisor.

It wasn't a lot of money, but properly invested, it could have helped him to get ahead in life. That's what Sandy wanted for *them*—a better future. But B. J. felt pressured by his new responsibility and God's cruelty to him, snatching Sarah away the way He had. He viewed Sandy's concerns as nagging. After she'd harassed him about registering for a few college courses or enrolling in a community college, B. J. told Sandy that he had no plans of going to college.

"You shouldn't shrink from going to college, just because you find school challenging. You can't expect to fix cars for the rest of your life," Sandy retorted.

"Look, I'm grown. I don't need you to tell me what to do with my life or my money. Just mind your own business!" he yelled. The words had spun out before he could harness them. And they left Sandy bruised. In all the years she'd known him, he hadn't spoken a harsh word to her. Not one time. He'd always been her protector.

The fifty-thousand-dollar inheritance had caused him to grow complacent. He didn't talk about his dreams or goals anymore. Sandy noticed the changes in him. Whenever they had a disagreement about anything, he'd bark at her, reminding her that he was a grown man. He missed work regularly. He'd stay out all night drinking, and would be too hung over to report to the job that he'd once taken pride in. He tried to drink and party away his pain, sometimes finding comfort in strange women.

Big Mama had called Sandy to see if she could talk to him. She said that the devil had gotten a hold of him, and he was running through his small inheritance like water. She told Sandy that she was still praying for B. J.'s salvation, but that he had stopped coming to church.

Sandy tried talking to B. J., but his arrogance and insensitivity to any suggestions from *Ms. College Woman* trying to run his life, created a barrier between them. She was greeted with the voices of various young women when she called. He finally bludgeoned her by telling her that he was going to be a *father*. That was all Sandy's heart could take. Secretly, she had hoped that the two of them could be together after she graduated from college. That was the reason she had hounded him so much about his future—it was their future. She wanted him to prepare for *them*.

Sandy realized that she was in love with him the day that he broke her spirit. She loved him like a woman loved her man. It wasn't the childhood friendship she'd had with him. It wasn't kid stuff anymore. Destroyed, she vowed never to call him again so that he could concentrate on taking care of his family. And the years sped by. Sandy forgave him in her heart and wanted him to share her wedding day. But B. J. didn't show. That was the second pain of her life.

Chapter Six

Josette sat at her desk, fuming. Rochelle, a business acquaintance and undercover enemy, had just phoned to *purposely/inadvertently* let her know that she'd seen Patrick out with another woman, at Elephant City the night before. Josette couldn't decipher if she was angrier about Patrick being out with another woman, or the fact that Rochelle had the audacity to call and rub her nose in it. She couldn't believe her supposed *man of God* was taking *this* route. It had been four months of silence. She wished that Patrick would file for a divorce and get it over with if that's what he wanted to do. She didn't need the embarrassment of people talking about her marriage woes behind her back, or to her face, like Rochelle had just done on the sly.

Josette worked over in her mind the possibilities: a groupie, someone who had been around all along, or someone new to help him to forget about her. It didn't matter which. She wasn't going to take this kind of humiliation lying down, whether she deserved it or not. Being separated was one thing; Patrick flaunting his woman around was another. No, Josette didn't want a stupid divorce. She wanted Patrick, but there had been no talks of reconciliation—nothing since the night her life changed.

Josette threw some files into her brief case, locked it, and snatched it off of her desk. She stopped by the receptionist's desk and told her that she'd be gone for the rest of the day. She jumped in her Range Rover, hitting speeds that should have gotten her a ticket, two-wheeling around corners and gunning through yellows. She knew just where she could find her husband—at the building that was slowly being transformed into Pat's Place, his new restaurant. She hadn't had any contact with him in the last four months, but today he was going to face her. Today he was going to do what needed to be done.

Although the inside of the building was still under construction, Josette was sure that he'd be there overseeing the project. It had been his baby since he'd decided to retire from the NFL. He'd poured all of his energy into it. Josette hadn't wanted it to come down to her confronting him at his place of business, like Bernadine in *Waiting to Exhale*, but that was how it was going to be today. Patrick had forced it.

A volt of electricity shot through her when she pulled up to the restaurant. The sign was already up outside. Pat's Place was spelled out with huge bronze letters in a fancy cursive script that looked edgy against the dark brown brick. It had urban character with a touch of class. They were supposed to have picked out the sign *together*. No doubt that he and his *woman* had picked it out together instead. Josette sped past what was going to be the valet booth and drove around to the back of the building to the future V.I.P. entrance. Patrick's XJ8 Jaguar was parked in a space that had a thirty-six by thirty-six-inch bronze sign that read: *Owner*, with his signature blazoned underneath. That had been her idea in the first place. And there should have been two signs up, not one. "He's really taking this thing far," Josette said aloud as she stepped down out of her truck. She was thrown off balance when the heels of her Borbonese snakeskin boots got stuck between the cobblestone crevices in the lot. She had advised him to go with a regular paved lot. This just supported the preponderance of evidence that he was determined to omit her from his life.

The floor in the back entrance was being laid, and dust covered every inch of the building on the first level. Her boots would have to go straight to the shoe shop. She looked around at the few construction workers leaving the building for a lunch break. The building was quiet aside from their chatter. They greeted Josette with pleasantries, but she nodded and waved only. She didn't want Patrick to hear her voice. He may have run out to avoid her like he'd been doing the last four months.

Josette bypassed the bronze door elevators, deciding that the sound might alarm Patrick, and walked gingerly down the long corridor and up to the second level where his office was supposed to be—according to the blueprints they'd gone over *together*. She knew he was there. She could smell him. It was his personal fragrance. Keturah, an African woman that owned Keturahscents Perfume Shoppe, created individual scents for her clients from natural herbs, oils, and plant extracts. She had created a cologne especially for Patrick with some of his favorite scents. The aroma reminded Josette that she hadn't made love to her husband in over four months. It was a mixture of chamomile, myrrh, and other fragrances that Keturah refused to share the names of, for fear of duplication. And Josette knew why. Keturah had an elite clientele who paid three hundred dollars an ounce for her creations. It was so sexually intoxicating that Josette almost forgot the reason she'd come.

The sound of Patrick's foggy voice floated toward her. The emptiness of the building caused it to echo. His tone was low and gentle, but professional. He was talking to a woman. Josette had familiarized herself with the several different tones her husband used. The one she was hearing now was his business voice—the one he used when he talked to women. It was the kind of tone that could easily cause even the shrewdest businesswoman to let her guard down. It was quiet and yielding. It could have been mistaken for flirting, but it was just Patrick's nature. He was still a true gentleman—despite the infamous night he'd thrown her out.

Reality was a slap in the face. Patrick looked at Josette like she'd just risen from the dead. She surprised him in an unsettling way. He stammered over his words, telling the other party that he needed to call her back later. Before he could make sense of what Josette was doing there, she sliced into him.

"We don't have to play games, Pat. Why don't you just be a man about the whole thing!"

Pat huffed. "A *man*? The kind of man you're talking about would have hurt you for what you did," he sliced back, staring at her like she was repulsive to look at. He leaned back in his chair.

"Look, if you want to go out with another woman, that's your business. All I want you to do is be a man and tell me what is going on. It's been four months and I'm sick and tired of this silent crap!"

Patrick rocketed out of his chair. His bottom lip quivered. He bit down on it to hold his composure. Josette had pushed his buttons. "You've got nerves on top of nerves to waltz up in here telling me I'm not a man! Who's the man, Jo? That punk you slept with? Huh? Some lame brother that slept with *my* wife and had the audacity to call me up and tell me about it!"

Josette's head spun. *This is going all wrong. He is about to get out of control. I didn't come here for this. I just want to know what is going on. That's all. That's not too much to ask. I don't want to fight anymore.* She calmed herself, and changed her tone to one that was more humble. "Pat, I need to know what we are going to do. Four months have gone by."

"Yeah? Well, I needed to know that my wife was so unhappy that she had to go out and sleep with another man!"

All Josette's energy fled her body. She couldn't take another fight. He used to reverence her, be gentle with her. "Pat, what are you going to do?" she asked, holding her tears back.

"I DON'T KNOW!" Patrick's voice reverberated. He quieted with a tightened jaw, and spoke through clenched teeth. "And I am NOT about to talk about this right NOW!" he said with finality. When his phone rang, he snatched it up quickly and slammed it back down.

Josette flinched. "I'm still . . . your wife . . . and I need to know what is going on," she protested quietly.

Patrick shook his head in disgust. "No. You're not my wife. My *wife* belongs to me, not to any man that can get her in bed." A tear cascaded down his warm skin. "I hope every second of it was worth our marriage, Jo," he said before knocking every single item off of his desk. "You're not my wife. You are NOTHING to me, JOSETTE *MOSS!*"

Patrick's use of her maiden name conveyed to Josette that she was no longer *Mrs.* Patrick Kelley. Veins protruded from the middle of his forehead. His eyes blazed. He warred on the inside. Josette had witnessed that same look in his eyes the night she left their home. Patrick restrained himself, but a part of him—that dark part—wanted to punish her for violating their covenant. Careful not to come within arms' reach of Josette, Patrick stayed behind his desk, constructing a safety barrier for both of them. He clinched his fists tightly. His chest rose and fell as he breathed heavily, releasing the fighter in him in a breath of air. The objects he knocked to the floor had taken Josette's place. She looked down out of the corner of her eye at the marble, globe-shaped paperweight that had just barely missed her foot. She imagined Patrick leaping across the desk and choking her to death. She deserved it.

She scanned the room for safe spots. There were only two, the bathroom behind Patrick, and the door she came in. She knew that she couldn't safely make it to either one if he came across their barrier. The security guard that Patrick hired after street thugs and vagrants had been found wandering around the building, was standing in the doorway of Patrick's office trying to assess the situation. He was a young, lanky white man with ice-blue eyes. His adrenaline was still kicking from his sprint up the stairs. He was in good shape. The flight of steps hadn't cost him his breath. Josette had never seen him before, but from the look on his face, she was sure that he knew who she was. He had done his homework. He hesitated, not quite sure how to handle the situation. He shook nervously, easing his weapon back into the holster on his hip. Patrick turned his blazing eyes away from Josette and bore into the security guard. "Out!" he shouted.

The young man nodded obediently and eased backward at a snail's pace, with his eyes on Josette. He wanted to ask if she was okay, but he couldn't stop shaking. He saw the look on Patrick's face and was just as scared as Josette was. He didn't want to challenge that two-hundred-something-pound statue of solid muscle that just happened to be his boss. Josette looked back at the guard, giving him the impression that she was safe, although she wasn't sure that she was.

"GET OUT!" Pat yelled again, with a voice so powerful that it seemed to push the young man backward. This time the young man found enough courage to move his jellied legs. He turned around slowly and jogged back down the stairs.

Josette couldn't hold her tears any longer. "What am I supposed to do,

Pat?" she cried, unable to keep her voice from cracking.

"Go back to the real man," Pat said smugly.

Josette bolted out of the door. She couldn't let him see her break down. She couldn't move fast enough to get out of that building and out of Patrick's life for good. She screeched out of the lot, almost hitting a woman driving a white Porsche who was pulling in. Josette wanted to ram her truck into something. Break something. Hurt somebody. Her husband didn't want her anymore. And it was her fault. She had erased more than fifteen years, just like that, because of some stupid tryst that she still couldn't explain to herself.

A part of her had been missing since she and Patrick separated. And she knew now that it was not going to return. She drove aimlessly through traffic, without any particular destination. The freshness of the day had abandoned her. A few weeks ago, she'd admired all the beauty of fall. Now, the spectacularly colored leaves looked only mediocre. Patrick had taken the remainder of beauty from her life. He'd snatched all of her dreams away in seconds. Her marriage was over.

Josette found herself at Belle Isle again—the same park she'd frequented every Wednesday evening since quitting therapy. She sat in her truck and cried to herself for as long as she could before its confinement became suffocating. She walked to a nearly deserted section of the park and sat atop a worn picnic table with her feet resting on the bench. Through blurry eyes she watched the multicolored trees blow in slow motion, not caring that her constant crying had caused her M.A.C. makeup to smudge all over her face, or that the chipping wood of the picnic table she'd chosen had snagged her fifteen-hundred-dollar Escada sweater dress. She doubled over, put her head in her lap and squeezed her knees together to brace herself for the constant stabbing of her stomach. She felt like her organs were shifting around on the inside.

Why didn't I just go home that night? Josette beat the top of her head with her fists to steady her thoughts, and to get that song out of her head—her and Patrick's song. "Forever Mine." She could still hear the O'Jays crooning, serenading her and Patrick as they danced their first dance at their wedding reception. That was their love song. She'd let the best thing that ever happened to her walk out of her life. "I love Pat!" she cried aloud to no one in particular.

Chapter Seven

Sandy was awakened by the sound of Josette wailing. She sat up against her cushioned leather headboard, grunted, and twisted her night stand lamp on. It was the fourth night in a row she'd been robbed of her sleep by Josette and all of her drama. She felt like she was babysitting. Josette hadn't been to work in three days, vomiting like she was suffering from stomach flu. But Sandy knew better. Consequences were the only things Josette was suffering from. Sandy had peeked in on her right before she'd gone to bed, and had found her balled underneath the bed covers asleep. At least she was quiet then.

In the past three days, Josette hadn't got out of the bed except to use the bathroom and to throw up. There'd been no music blasting, no television, and no phone calls—just constant crying. Sandy refused to console her the first two nights. The only thing she'd been kind enough to do was to call the firm and tell them that Josette had stomach flu and was going to take the rest of the week off to recuperate. She figured Josette was getting just what she deserved. Maybe now she'd know that someone's love was nothing to trifle with. It was a well needed lesson that had been a long time coming.

Sandy had her own problems to think about, now that Genevieve was back in the picture, pressuring her to meet again. She'd spent two weeks dodging Genevieve's calls, not sure if she wanted to pursue a relationship with her anymore. Now, Josette was falling apart. She hadn't bathed or combed her hair. Sandy had every intention to call Dr. Greene in the morning to inquire if Josette fit the symptoms of someone having a nervous breakdown. Last night had been the only time she'd shown her little sister any sympathy. She was awakened by Josette screaming out Patrick's name, declaring that she didn't want to live anymore. Sandy wished that it had been an act. But last night, Josette had seriously worried her. It had taken Josette four months to realize the gravity of what she'd done to her marriage.

Sandy had held her little sister tightly in her arms last night, rocking her, telling her that everything was going to be all right, while thinking to herself that divorce was imminent. If Patrick was going to reconcile, he would have already. Maybe he'd used the last four months to detach himself from Josette so he'd have time to grieve and get used to life without her. Sandy had warned her little sister about her ego months ago. But Josette had deluded herself into thinking that the whole thing between her and Patrick was going to blow over in a few days and that he'd take her back. But four months had passed. She'd misjudged him.

Sandy prayed. She had to get some sleep tonight. She couldn't take another night of being up to the wee hours of the morning with Josette. It was too draining. "Father, I need your rest and peace right now, in the name of Jesus," she prayed. She didn't have the energy to pray longer; she hoped that what she'd said was enough, or both she and Josette were going to have nervous breakdowns. Groggy, she pushed her covers back and swung her legs over the edge of the bed. She stretched her arms out and yawned. The clock read 3:27 a.m. She had to be at the hospital by seven—less than four hours away.

Sandy walked down the hall to the guest room and listened at the door. It was completely quiet, so she knocked on the door and pushed it open simultaneously. "Jo, you okay?" she asked. She walked over to the bed. "Jo . . ." she whispered. Josette didn't answer, but Sandy could hear a light snore from under the covers. "Thank you, Jesus," she said sincerely before turning around and going back to her room. She knew for sure that God had answered her prayer. And at least she could get a couple more hours of sleep.

She wondered what kind of plan God had in store for her life, because right now, her life was disjointed. The only thing she'd been looking forward to lately was spending time with Lamont, the handsome specimen she'd met in Chicago a few weeks earlier. She'd talked to him every day since then, and they'd managed to sneak in a few lunch dates when he'd come to Detroit to hammer out a business deal with one of the Big Three. He seemed like the kind of man who could add some spice to her life. But Josette's problems had been throwing a monkey wrench in her program.

Worried about Josette, Sandy had cancelled her weekend plans with Lamont. The two of them had planned to go to Windsor and take a train to Toronto to catch the last showing of *The Phantom of the Opera*. She'd seen it on Broadway on two occasions, but Lamont had never seen it. She couldn't believe that a man as well rounded as he was had never seen *Phantom*. It was such a treat. The music and costumes were superb. Sandy had gotten excited about their excursion. But it was all for naught. He was going to have to catch it another time because she needed to stay home and keep an eye on Josette.

She hoped that Lamont didn't think that she was brushing him off.

She'd tried to explain the situation to him delicately without telling him *all* of Josette's business. He'd sounded so disappointed when she'd broken the news to him—but not as disappointed as she was. She couldn't remember the last time she'd been on a real date, so much so that it didn't bother her that much that he didn't have a regular place of worship. He'd said that his business often took him out of town on weekends, which made it particularly difficult to establish roots in a church home. But he assured her that he had accepted Christ as his Savior in grade school. A few years ago that would have been a red flag to Sandy, but now she felt like her clock was ticking. She was thirty-one, not twenty-one. The prospect of being married again and having children seemed to be vanishing as she aged. And what was so wrong with having male company and companionship?

Sandy wanted to hear baritone on the other end of the phone sometimes. She had long tired of attending concerts and plays with women. She thought about holding a man's hand or being in a man's arms—some of the time. She'd already told Lamont that she was celibate and that she planned to stay that way until she was married. She figured she'd get that out of the way early just in case he wanted to bolt. Telling a brother—even a *Christian brother*—that she was celibate and not interested in changing her situation, sometimes gave him an all-expense-paid ticket in the opposite direction. And that was good. It saved her from heartbreak down the line—after all the time and emotions had been invested. There was no sense in holding that information back. After compromising in the past, she'd promised herself that she was going to do things God's way—even if He was holding back everything that she desired.

Lamont had assured her that her celibacy wasn't a hindrance, and that he admired her spiritual convictions. He seemed to be just what she needed right now—someone to freshen up her stale life, which mainly consisted of work and church. He was articulate, charming, and ambitious. He owned his own marketing firm. But Sandy had told him that he'd missed his calling as a comedian, because he kept her in stitches whenever they talked. It was the first time she'd laughed with a man in a long time. It was refreshing. She anticipated seeing him again. *Soon.*

Chapter Eight

It had been over a month since Genevieve had met with Sandy. But since she'd returned home, Sandy had been avoiding her. She hadn't returned any of her phone calls. Genevieve couldn't explain what had gone wrong. She was positive that their meeting had gone well. She'd felt it in her spirit. Benjamin had advised her more than once, "Let God work it out." But just what did that mean in *this* situation? Just sit back and do nothing? She didn't want to pass up this chance that she'd been given to restore her relationship with her daughters. She thought she had been allowing God to handle it. After all, it was Sandy who'd found her. She had put her faith in God by meeting with Sandy after all these years, even though she had risked the chance of it ending in failure.

Genevieve felt like God had deserted her. She'd prayed about the situation so much over the last month that she'd grown weary—irritable. It was almost as if the Lord had teased her with the possibility of reuniting with her daughters, then took it all back again. But Genevieve knew her Father better than that. He didn't want to see her hurting the way that she'd been. She couldn't help but feel that maybe things should have been left the way they were. If Josette had never found her book, her life would still be halfway normal. She wished it had never happened.

When she left Detroit years ago, she forced herself to accept that that part of her life was over. She'd lost her girls. And all of a sudden, there they were. She'd felt redeemed. But now they were gone again. She'd been tossed back behind the starting line. And lately, her relationship with Benjamin had been in a pressure cooker. It was bad enough that Benjamin was away from home so much. But when he had been home, she hadn't been much of a wife. Maybe a vacation without the kids would give them better standing ground. They'd both been working hard, with little time for one another—just hits and misses.

Genevieve sat in bed occupied with travel brochures she'd picked up that afternoon, hoping that she and Benjamin could coordinate their schedules, cancel appointments or whatever else was necessary, to sneak in a Seaborne Cruise. Then the guilt of leaving the children burdened the thought. While tossing ideas back and forth, she heard the front entry signal. Benjamin had made it home. The children were asleep. She should have been asleep herself, but the ordeal with Sandy and Josette had kept her up. When she wasn't thinking about them, she was thinking about how much she and Benjamin needed to get away together.

She heard Benjamin creep softly up the stairs, trying not to disturb the sleep that she should have been enjoying. He cracked the door open and peeked in, smiling because she was *alive*, looking dead at him.

"If I had known that you were up, I would have jogged up the stairs the way I usually do instead of tiptoeing," he joked.

"Hey, honey." Genevieve surveyed Benjamin's face. He was exhausted. There was no point in trying to have a discussion about quality time, because he would probably fall asleep during the conversation. Then she'd be angry that he didn't think that what she had to say was important enough for him to stay awake and listen.

Benjamin took off his clothes hurriedly and scooted under the covers. "How long are you going to be up, Sweets?" he asked. That was his way of cueing her to turn the lamp off. He couldn't sleep with it on.

Genevieve collected the travel brochures and put them away in her nightstand drawer. She reached over and turned the lamp off without a rebuttal. It was nearly one a.m. Benjamin had just flown in from a three-day convention. He had an early morning meeting with the city's housing project director to discuss plans for a new senior housing complex that the church was planning to build. Genevieve stared up at the ceiling in the darkness, listening to Benjamin snore for as long as she could bear it, before going down to the nook to make herself a cup of French Vanilla coffee.

She stood in the nook in front of the patio door, sipping her coffee, staring out into the blackness. If she wasn't so paranoid, she would have stepped outside onto the first level of their two-story cedar deck and savored some of the fresh morning air. Benjamin had designed and built the deck himself when they were first married. He loved family barbecues and get-togethers. The deck was perfect for entertaining. Their bedroom was just above the kitchen. When the weather was nice, they'd have breakfast together on their bedroom deck. Those were the irreplaceable moments in their marriage that Genevieve loved.

Every now and then she would wake up early and walk around her house, marveling at how much her life had changed. Materially, it was filled with all the things she'd ever wanted in life. But that wasn't what made her feel so elated. The things that she'd been looking for all her life were in her house—God, love, acceptance, and peace. It was a place of refuge. It was her quiet spot, the one place she knew that she could come to when everything else in the world was chaotic. She could come home, find security, and feel valued. She thanked God for all that He'd done for her through the years, even those painful ones. She thanked Him for her hideaway and her family. Benjamin and the children were just extensions of the love, grace, and mercy that God had shown her. The real security was in her heart, knowing that the Spirit of God dwelled within her.

Genevieve had experienced plenty of failures in her life since coming to know Christ. But the inside of her had stayed intact. It hadn't changed. She had a constant feeling of belonging. The physical materialism she now had represented only a minute amount of the gifts God had given her. And the most important gift was the knowledge that she didn't have to take on the burden of trying to run her life or figure out how to make the world work for her, like she'd done in her past.

Before she came to know Christ as her Savior, she'd spent so much time planning, figuring, and anticipating, not understanding that God wanted to be in charge of her life. Now, people could look at her and know that God could do anything. He had taken a worthless, shameful woman who had committed all these terrible acts in life, and said, "*Come home. It doesn't matter where you've been or what you've done. Come home.*" He was the parent who stood in the window waiting for a wayward child to come home, ready to forgive. Genevieve was glad that she'd made that choice to accept His forgiveness. She wished that Sandy and Josette could forgive her.

Chapter Nine

Sandy had been screening calls, purposely avoiding Genevieve still. She'd slipped once and picked up the phone without waiting for the answering machine to come on, and Genevieve had caught her. She decided that she was going to get that Caller ID thingy, the one that all of her friends laughed at her for not having. She hadn't needed it until now. But maybe it was worth the extra six dollars added to the phone bill. Genevieve had bombarded her with all these questions as to why she hadn't answered her calls. Sandy couldn't give her an answer. She was still unsure about what a relationship with Genevieve would accomplish at this point in her life. Linda and Roger were her parents—Mom and Dad. It had been that way since she was twelve. She didn't know where Genevieve fit in.

Before she reunited with Genevieve, she'd had an internal vacancy from unanswered questions. Now that those questions had been answered, the emptiness had disappeared. And maybe all she needed was closure. Genevieve had all these grand ideas about Sandy coming to Virginia and meeting her family. But Sandy didn't see that oasis in the near future. She'd told Genevieve honestly that she felt pressured by her. She asked her for space. Genevieve hadn't handled that announcement well. She'd pleaded with Sandy to give their relationship a chance. But that caused Sandy more duress. She'd ended the call abruptly amid Genevieve's teary pleading.

Everyone wanted something from her. She was a mere factotum—a sponge that everyone else squeezed dry. The rueful assignment was oppressive. Didn't she deserve more than that? She couldn't get away from it. She'd be avoiding Josette too, if they weren't under the same roof. But at least Josette's depression kept her quiet most of the time. Besides going to work, Josette didn't do much else. She'd stopped eating and was starting to look sick. She was already down to a size two from a four. She couldn't stand to lose anymore weight without looking like she was addicted to something. The "completely polished from head-to-toe" woman had vanished. Josette barely existed. The expensive clothes and make-up were camouflage.

Nowadays, Sandy didn't have to beg her little sister to go to therapy. Josette had started coming back to their family sessions *and* had started individual sessions, trying to deal with the mess she'd gotten herself into. She was malleable. Knowing that Patrick was gone made her that way. This time it was real. He didn't want her back. Patrick had told Sandy that face to face after she'd tried to play the big sister role and intervene on Josette's behalf. "*Jo is history.*" Those were his exact words to Sandy the day she paid him a surprise visit and had gotten a surprise of her own.

Sandy had dropped by early one morning—unannounced, hoping to catch Patrick right after he had prayed and meditated so that he'd be more open to discussion, and less put off by her intrusion into his personal business. Over the years, she'd stuck her nose in when she felt that he and Josette needed an objective view. Patrick had always received Sandy's input graciously. But this time, his mind was made. Sandy knew that when she saw his beautiful *houseguest.*

The woman had peeked out from the kitchen when Patrick opened the door to let Sandy in. Then she sauntered playfully up the stairs toward the bedrooms with her coffee mug in hand, sending a secret message to him. Patrick was blasé, keeping his eyes on her until she was out of his view. Sandy held the woman's gaze long enough to notice that she was wearing a pair of Patrick's sweat pants and one of his T-shirts. It was obvious that she'd spent the night. It was nine o'clock in the morning. Both she and Patrick looked like they'd just awakened. But Patrick was not the least bit embarrassed by the woman's presence—not like he should have been.

Sandy deduced that Patrick and his houseguest had just eaten breakfast. The remaining aroma of bacon still lingered. Sandy photographed the woman with her eyes, mentally comparing her to Josette. There were no visible similarities. Josette was short and petite, with a natural flair. Patrick's houseguest was about six feet tall—Patrick's height. She was an Amazon. Tall and thick. Her build reminded Sandy of Phyllis Hyman. And she had wild, jet black hair that swelled past her shoulders and down her back in ringlets. It was sexy and untamed. *Maybe from the night before.* Sandy had a feeling that she'd seen the woman a dozen times before, but she couldn't quite place the face. The wild hair threw her off. Maybe she'd colored it or something. She could have been an actress. Patrick sometimes socialized in those pretentious circles. Sandy hoped the woman wasn't someone that both Patrick and Josette knew. That would have been a low blow despite the precarious state of their marriage.

Patrick was unshakably calm. He led Sandy into the nook area of the kitchen, being casually polite. "Can I get you anything?" he asked, pouring himself another cup of coffee.

"No, thank you," Sandy replied, eager to get to the point. She cleared her throat, looked at Patrick, and said, "Pat, I know this thing with you and Jo is none of my business. But I just came to ask if you'd consider talking to Jo. She's not doing well."

Pat looked at Sandy like she was missing a few screws in her head and said, "Neither am I."

"You look like you're doing pretty well to me," Sandy fired.

"Sandy, don't go there. It's not about *me*. It's about that sorry sister of yours."

"I'm sorry."

"Look, I don't want Jo anymore. I loved Jo. Took care of Jo. Jo doesn't want to be loved. That's the bottom line."

"Pat, I know what it *looks* like. All I'm asking is for you to just talk to her. Even if you file for a divorce, you still need to talk about it."

"I don't need to. The truth is as plain as day. Jo does not want to be married—at least not to me. Sandy, you know full well that this isn't the first time that this has happened," Patrick said, daring Sandy to lie. "Yeah," he nodded confidently, "I know about New York—back when we first got married. I didn't want to believe it at the time, but I've always known."

Sandy had lost her train of thought in between Patrick's words. She was careful not to comment on the New York *scandal* one way or another. She had no idea that he'd known about it or *how*. And she wasn't about to say anything alluding to the fact that she had been in cahoots with Josette, because she hadn't been. She had stopped speaking to her sister for a whole month because of it.

Sandy had dragged Josette to a spiritual conference for women in New

York. She'd decided to go out to dinner with some of the other women she'd met at the conference. But Josette had connected with one of her Morehouse admirers who lived in Manhattan. Sandy knew when Josette came back to their hotel room that she'd done something stupid. Her shifty-eyed, nervous answers to the questions Sandy hurled at her were a dead giveaway. Sandy scolded Josette like a mother instead of a sister, and vowed that she would never go out of town with her again, so that she couldn't be used as some scapegoat for Josette's mess. She warned Josette about ruining her marriage.

Sandy took the high road with Patrick, skipping over the New York scandal altogether. "Pat, Jo and I had a bad childhood. Some of the things that she does, believe it or not, are a result of the things that happened to us back then. That's why we've been going to therapy," Sandy explained. "Please just talk it out one last time," she begged. Patrick stood at the island without an expression on his face. Unmoved. Not listening. Every word Sandy spoke floated over the top of his head on its way to a graveyard of abandoned memories.

It was dismally uncharacteristic of Patrick to entertain another woman in the home that he had shared with his wife, or pleasure himself with some extraneous soul in his marital bed. His walk with the Lord had been evident to those who knew him, and those that knew about him. He'd made every humanly possible effort to be that light for others. Be the man that the Lord had called him to be. But his relationship with the Lord had been catastrophically weakened by his wife's infidelity. His holiness had obviously been stained by an errant lifestyle. And under the veneer of indifference and collectedness was his weakening faith. It had been shaken like the palms of trees thrashed about during a hurricane.

This evening, Sandy planned to relax and not think about anyone else's life. It was time for her to start working on hers. She missed Lamont. He'd hinted that he needed to see more of her. She hoped he hadn't put her on his cancelled list, considering the number of times she'd cancelled dates with him because she'd been babysitting Josette. But tonight, Josette was quiet. Music played *softly* in the guest room. No crying. No drama. Good. Sandy couldn't believe she'd literally been babysitting a grown woman.

This was another Friday night that she would be forced to curl up with a good book instead of having dinner with a fine man. She'd called Lamont several times, but he hadn't returned any of her phone calls. It made her think about how Genevieve must be feeling. Disgusted, she turned in early. It was just five o'clock. *Darn shame.* She smacked her lips and pouted like some child who had been ordered to bed early as punishment for some offense. She propped herself up against the headboard, took the latest Sandra Brown novel out of the nightstand drawer, and dove in to escape her miserable life.

She had nearly read herself to sleep when someone lay on the doorbell. She dragged herself out of the bed to see who the culprit was that had lost his or her mind. Through the peephole she spotted a sister with a head full of dark brown zillion braids with auburn streaks, sporting a sweatshirt that read: *Don't Let Life Boss You Around.* It was Dr. Faye Duncan, one of Josette's sorority sisters. Sandy could stand only two of the ten that had pledged with Josette. Faye Duncan was one of them. The other ally was anchorwoman Candace Cage-Cooper. As far as Sandy was concerned, the rest of them were a bunch of bourgeois, spoiled misfits—like Josette.

Faye was a doctor of internal medicine. She owned Duncan Medical Center with her husband, Damon, a gerontologist. She was an everyday, average-looking woman who happened to be extremely intelligent—

packed full of brains. She was curvy with dark brown skin and dreamy eyes. More inwardly attractive than she was physically, Faye's most outstanding characteristic was her caring spirit. She was a people person—a steward who genuinely enjoyed caring for others at the medical center and in the ministries that she and her husband were involved in at Morning Star Baptist.

The demands of work and family prevented her and Josette from getting together as much as they had when they were younger, but Faye still came by whenever she could. She'd been proactive in her approach to save Josette from the heartache she was experiencing now. Faye had shared with Josette personal experiences that had helped her to build and maintain a strong marriage. She warned her about the pitfalls that could sometimes destroy a marriage little by little. But Josette couldn't handle that. She had a hard time dealing with people who told her the things she *didn't* want to hear. And Sandy was glad that Faye was there. It gave her an opportunity to get out of prison. She opened the door cheesing. Faye knew the motivation behind that smile.

"Hey, how's Jo doing?" Faye asked.

"About the same. And I'm glad you're here. This inmate needs to get out of her cell for a while. Maybe I'll take myself to the movies or something."

"No problem. I'm off for two days. I was hoping to spend the weekend with Jo. Damon and Damon Jr. are gone camping with Damon's father," Faye said.

"Hey, sounds good to me."

Faye closed the door behind her and took off her driving gloves. The rock that danced on her left hand was blinding. It was almost as huge and brilliant as Josette's. Sandy had seen it before, but it was so exquisite that every time she saw it, she was in awe. She shook her head. *At least three carats.* It was a simple emerald-cut center stone on a platinum band. Sandy wondered if it would ever happen to her. She didn't have to have a ring that glorious. She just wanted to be loved.

Faye's husband, Damon, was a good man. Saved. Fine. Family oriented. The kind of man Sandy wished she could get her hands on. She marveled at the way some women could strike gold when it came to men. She shook her head again. *Where am I when brothers like that are walking down the street?* She watched Faye bounce up the stairs with a bag of oatmeal raisin cookies from Mrs. Field's. She knew that wasn't going to cheer Josette up. She'd already tried that. Sandy trailed behind Faye to tell Josette that she was going to step out for a while. Josette nodded her head without looking at Sandy or Faye.

Sandy hurried into the shower. She adjusted the water so that it was as hot as she could possibly bear it, hoping that the forceful stream of heat would rejuvenate her. She felt like crying over nothing in particular, but life itself. It sounded stupid, but the tears came anyway.

"Sandy... *Lamont* is on the phone... he says it's really important!" Faye yelled into the bathroom, startling Sandy.

When Sandy's heart started beating again, it lifted. "Okay, tell him to hold on... I'll be right out!" She rinsed the remainder of her shower gel off, towel dried, and raced to the phone. She stumbled over her Big Bird Slippers almost falling onto the bed.

"Hello," she said, trying not to sound too excited or exerted.

"Hey, beautiful, I've been missing you. What are you up to?"

"Nothing—just got out of the shower, actually."

"Oh, do you already have plans?"

"Sort of," she said. She didn't want to sound too available. "I called you all day long."

"Oh . . . I've been in meetings. I accidentally left my cell back here at the hotel. Sorry about that."

"Hotel? Where are you?"

"New York. And I was hoping to see you tonight."

Sandy laughed. "Unless you can do magic, we won't be seeing each other tonight, Lamont."

"I can do more than magic."

"What are you saying? Are you planning to fly here or something?"

"Nope. *You* are going to fly here."

Sandy laughed again, wondering what kind of game this man was playing with her. "First of all, regular working people don't just plane hop. It costs to fly."

"I'm not a *regular* man, Sandy."

She endured him. "I see . . ."

"Why don't you get dressed and pack for the weekend? There'll be a car waiting to pick you up at six."

"What?"

"Just get dressed. Oh, and bring a few pairs of jeans. We'll be doing some *regular* stuff this weekend," he laughed.

Ordinarily, she would never have accepted a date at the last minute. She hated when men did that, as if she were just sitting around like the Maytag man waiting for them to call. But Lamont was different. For him, she relaxed the rules. They'd discussed the possibility of the two of them spending the weekend together—in separate rooms, just because of the distance. A long-distance relationship was better than no relationship. And they'd talked every day—three to four times a day, since they'd met. Sandy felt like she'd known him for years. Lamont even offered to put her up at a hotel if she was uncomfortable staying at his place. It was a bit premature, but she was long overdue for a date. And tonight was the perfect time to start being *grown*—not the babysitter. She pulled her Coach overnight bag out of the closet and packed hurriedly, feeling giddy.

Private jet. It had been three years since the last time Sandy had been on a private jet. A fashion designer had flown Josette and some other NFL wives to Paris for the couture shows, and she had tagged along. It wasn't something she experienced on a regular basis. She wasn't Josette. She didn't frequent costly celebrity theme parties and music award shows or keep company with multi-millionaires. That was Josette's life, not hers. And that is what unglued her. Lamont hadn't mentioned anything about a *jet* before. She needed to conduct better dating interviews. What had she gotten herself into?

She'd thought that Lamont was the finest man walking the planet until she saw his older brother, Brian. He was just as tall and good-looking as Lamont. Same complexion. Same straight white teeth. Same model smile. She averted her eyes to avoid staring. *Looks run deep in the family.*

"I see that Lamont is trying to tempt me tonight," Brian said, helping Sandy up the steps onto Eve, a Gulfstream IV. "My brother didn't tell me I'd be picking up such a beautiful woman. I'd better call my wife before I forget I'm married," he joked.

A slender, leggy flight attendant stood at Brian's side dressed in an above-the-knee uniform, with her sleek short hair sculpted to the back. She greeted Sandy with a widened, practiced smile and handed her a purple gift bag with metallic wrapping paper poofing out of the top. "Ms. Moss, this is for you," she smiled.

"Thank you," Sandy said, returning the smile and trying not to seem so brand new. But she was a fish out of water.

Brian played the part of a proud host escorting Sandy through the luxurious fourteen-passenger, stand-up cabin. He first introduced her to the pilot and co-pilot, who turned from toying with the instruments on the control panel long enough to welcome her aboard. Sandy made an extra effort to maintain her composure and avoid looking like a goofy, inexperienced underling. But her nervousness increased as she inched behind Brian. She eyed the details of the custom-designed black and cream interior with careful observation. From the glossy ebony-stained wood design that trailed the length of the cabin walls to the cream-colored linen wallpaper, Eve was extravagantly arrayed. The ultra-modern gourmet galley was suitable for a home with quartzite counters and black cabinetry with rope-like sterling silver handles. The flooring matched the ebony-stained wood design on the walls in the seating area of the cabin, trimmed with light oak. And the marble-topped vanity and gold faucet in the lavatory reminded Sandy of a powder room in a swanky hotel. The cabin had a stereo system and two built-in television screens that were bordered by three-dimensional leather matting that made them look like framed art. The leather seats and sofa were cream with black leather piping. Eve took the saying "First-class flight" to new heights.

Sandy's short but impressive tour ended with Brian seating her in one of the extra-wide seats that could almost accommodate two people. She reclined the seat back and tried to concentrate on *enjoying*. She watched as Brian took a seat at the small conference table, where he busied himself on his laptop. Then she looked through her "goodie bag" that was filled with a bunch of her favorite candy treats and magazines: *In Style*, *Black Issues Book Review*, and *Today's Christian Woman*, along with an autographed copy of her favorite author's latest novel that wasn't for sale yet. She gushed like a teenager and added ten mental points to Lamont's scorecard.

    Brian offered her refreshments, but still aflutter, she declined. She took out the novel and began reading. That always seemed to relax her when she was wound up. Brian folded his laptop, moved to the cushy sofa, and stretched out. Sandy pretended to be engrossed in her book, but when Brian called his wife, she hung onto every word he spoke. His conversation didn't last more than three minutes. "Miss you too," Brian said. "Yeah, hug the boys for me. Yes, you know I love you. See you soon. Good bye," he continued, while patting the flight attendant on the behind when she walked past. He got up and followed her to the galley. Their laughter floated towards Sandy moments later. The two of them interacted with a deep familiarity that was played out in touches and brushes up against one another. Sandy grunted under her breath. Brian returned with a drink, perched himself back on the sofa, and called another woman whom he told he would see shortly. He kissed into his cell phone, winking at Sandy when their eyes met. She hoped that Lamont was nothing like his brother because Brian had the word *Player* written across his forehead, among a few other words that weren't befitting for a Christian woman to be thinking.

    "Comfortable?" the flight attendant asked after they were airborne.

    "Yes, I'm fine. Thanks," Sandy said, relaxed. She'd managed that by pretending to be Josette. She crossed her legs and enjoyed her reading like she was a seasoned veteran of this kind of luxury. Brian didn't pick up on the fact that she was a novice either. He flirted with her relentlessly before finally falling asleep. She wouldn't have paid much attention to him if he hadn't said, "Yeah, Lamont better keep you close, or else Big Brother may have to teach the young man a lesson." He was disgusting. His slime overshadowed his handsomeness. *Creep.*

When they landed in New York, Lamont was waiting for Sandy outside a black, chauffer-driven Escalade. He hugged her close and whispered into her ear. "I hope Brian behaved himself," he said.

"Yes," she whispered back. But that wasn't the complete truth.

Lamont kissed her on the cheek and caused a current to flow. She remembered that she'd forgotten to put her slim pocket Bible in her purse. She was going to need it. She started thinking about *real kisses*, then quickly erased the thought and replaced it with scripture. "…*Ye shall therefore be holy; for I am holy.*"

Brian hopped in the front of the SUV while Sandy and Lamont climbed in back. When the chauffeur pulled in front of The Carlyle hotel on Madison Avenue, Brian conveniently disappeared with an African woman who had been waiting for him in the lobby. Sandy recognized her immediately. She was Fatima, a model. And somewhere along the way, someone had slapped the word *"Super"* in front of it, to go along with her super-nasty attitude. Sandy had heard all about her tirades and drug use on the cable entertainment channel. Fatima and her best friend, Simone Montgomery—the other supposed *"Super"* model—stayed in the tabloids for one reason or another: Fatima, for her tantrums on photo shoots, and Simone for her loose habits with wealthy men. Sandy rolled her eyes. *What a pair.* Fatima made a lackluster attempt to conceal her identity with shades and a fedora. Sandy couldn't believe it. *Like that makes her unnoticeable. She should be ashamed of herself, sleeping with a married man.* It didn't surprise Sandy one bit that Fatima was with a creep like Brian.

She refocused her attention on Lamont as they rode the elevator. *Was he this fine?* She had to calm herself in order to engage in their desultory elevator conversation. And if she wasn't mistaken, he seemed just as infatuated with her.

"So how was your week?" Lamont asked, taking her hand. He held it momentarily then let it go gently.

Sandy could feel the fine hairs on the back of her neck stand at attention. She tried not to look at him so directly, but then again, how could she not? *Gosh, he's sexy.* She felt like Silly Putty—soft and pliable. *Oh my goodness.* "A little stressful. Glad to be away from home," she said swallowing a nervous lump. The elevator doors dinged and she was grateful.

Lamont escorted her to a suite—down the hall from his. She added ten more points to his scorecard. She played calm until she closed her door. It was a Louis XV period room with antique reproductions in the living area and bedroom. Sandy twirled whimsically around the suite before free-falling backward onto the bed. The sophisticated French provincial furnishings and décor were dainty trimmings in the fairy tale abode. The hand-carved silk upholstered sleigh bed was queenly, painted in antique white and gold leaf. The marble-topped bedside tables were also antique white with scroll toes. A double door armoire stood opposite two side chairs that were covered with a soft rose and mint floral print. The elegant room was an appropriate haven for this modern-day Cinderella. Sandy hopped up suddenly and ran to the window. She parted the rose-colored silk drapes and peered out. She would have an awesome view of Central Park in the morning. But for now, she took in the city lights of New York and welcomed a new adventure and a new man. She couldn't wait to don the thick, plush, terrycloth robe and those terrycloth slippers after she'd had her bath tonight.

She slipped into a modest little black dress, but her ample curves turned it into a ferocious little black dress. It had taken her all of fifteen minutes to freshen up and touch up her make-up and hair. Lamont took a step backward from her suite door as she stepped out into the hallway wearing that black dress that was singing his name. He shook his head in admiration, turning her around slowly. "Whoa . . ." he nodded approvingly.

"I guess this is where I say thank you," Sandy said modestly, smiling.

"No, this is where I say thank *you*. You look gorgeous," Lamont said, swallowing Sandy with his eyes. He'd dated many beautiful women—models and actresses alike. But her beauty was natural. She didn't need an extra helping of make-up to be gorgeous. She was that without trying. He had an arm piece tonight.

They dined at Restaurant Daniel on 65th Street. And from the moment Sandy entered the majestic bronze studded mahogany doors, she knew she was at a four or five star restaurant. It had elaborate pilasters and columns with deep crimson-colored velvet drapes—the flair of Italian Renaissance style. She could tell by the way Lamont walked through the lobby without gawking at the art work or the architecture that he'd been here before. He didn't look at all like he was taking it in for the first time. They were seated in an area that gave Sandy the vantage point of being able to see all around the room.

"This is a *really* nice place," she said looking at the soft, creamy-yellow color on the walls, and the gold brocade drapes. If he had set out to make tonight memorable, he had accomplished the task.

He looked at her unreservedly. His plans had been successfully executed. He had her smiling. "I wanted to do something special for you since we finally have this chance to spend some time together."

"This is really special," she said. She couldn't think of anything more intelligent to say. "Oh, and thanks for the 'goodie bag'—I'm sorry. I forgot to tell you earlier. That was really thoughtful."

He studied her while she spoke—swallowed her with his deep-set eyes. "I'm glad you are enjoying everything. I'm just glad to have you here."

Glad to be here. "Thank you."

For their appetizers he ordered smoked quail and wild mushroom ravioli. They both decided on the Guinea hen with glazed chestnuts for dinner. Sandy hardly wanted to touch her food at first. Everything had been presented so artistically that it seemed destructive to put a fork in it. Each dish was a miniature art painting. Lamont appreciated her humility. Her sexiness. Her conversation. He couldn't stop looking at her the way he was—greedily. He digested the way she sipped her drink, spoke, then sipped her drink again. The meal was delicious, but not as delicious as she was. His staring unraveled the threads of her composure.

She paused curiously. "What's the matter?"

"You are so beautiful. Sorry if I'm making you nervous," he said.

"Thank you. And yes, you are making me a bit nervous," she chuckled.

"Well, it is a definite pleasure to be in your company tonight, Cassandra. It's been hard pinning you down."

"I'm sorry. Life has been hectic since Jo has moved in."

"I understand," Lamont nodded. "I hadn't given up—I don't do that easily. Now, I have you to myself the entire weekend. What a coup!"

Sandy smiled, this time swallowing *him*. Deep brown. Chiseled face. Strong jawbone. Bushy eyebrows. Dark brown eyes. Thick lips. *Perfect.* She kept her mind from traveling into dangerous territory by asking him about his business. And he was a little boy talking about his favorite toy. He lit up excitedly, giving her the history of Vision Marketing. He and

Brian had started small but had turned it into a powerful marketing machine over the years. He never said he was a *millionaire*. But Sandy knew full well that rinky-dink companies didn't have their own jets. She wondered why he hadn't mentioned it before. Then again, she thought that maybe it wasn't exactly wise for a single, wealthy man to broadcast to his dates that he was loaded.

Lamont and Brian had started Vision ten years ago. Since then, they'd done major advertising campaigns for top-notch companies, developing commercials and marketing campaigns for almost everything: gym shoes, banks, and sporting events. Lamont reminded Sandy of a commercial that had been popular a few years back that starred a famous basketball player running all over town in sneakers, doing errands for his grandmother.

"I came up with that idea myself," he said proudly.

"Very creative," Sandy said, swallowing his chocolate flavor again.

Lamont bragged playfully. "I'd like to think so."

"That sounds cocky."

"Just confident," he laughed.

"Watch it. Too much confidence might get you into trouble."

"As long as it's with you," Lamont flirted, reaching his hand across the table, touching hers, heating up Sandy's cool.

Nervously, she tucked her hair behind her ears and looked away. Lamont read her nervousness and pulled his hand back, continuing to fill her in on Vision. He didn't want to ruin this one. He was going to take his time with her.

Lamont attributed much of Vision's success to what he'd labeled the "Be Down Era." He explained to Sandy how hip-hop had changed the face of marketing, now that it had reached suburban white teens. Hip-hop mania had white companies scrambling to search out black marketing firms and advertisers to develop campaigns that would target the hip-hop population, capturing both the black and the white dollar. Because of that trend, Vision had made millions. Sandy was engrossed in conversation with him. She admired the passion he had for his job—something she lacked.

"You haven't told me about your girlfriend," Sandy said.

Lamont looked baffled. "Huh?"

"Eve."

"Oh, *Eve*," he chuckled. "Actually, she doesn't belong to me alone. She's a shared woman," he smiled.

"Explain."

"Well, she's sort of like a timeshare property," Lamont explained. "Vision pays a yearly fee for her use and we have her at our disposal when we need to." He pulled out his wallet and showed Sandy his charter membership card. "It's called fractional ownership. It's almost like she's all mine. But she's got many others," he said, returning it to his wallet.

"So you like sharing?"

"No, I don't. I'm working on getting a woman of my own."

"A jet all to yourself?"

"That too."

Lamont was suave. Sure of himself. Self-made. Sandy liked that about him. She had to keep reminding herself to stay focused during dinner. He caused some sort of natural phenomenon in her, stirring up feelings she hadn't felt in awhile. Made her feel like she was in the middle of a school-girl crush. Made her hope again. Made her think about marriage and babies.

The chauffeur cruised around New York after dinner, while Lamont gave Sandy a backseat version of a genuinely unprofessional nighttime tour of a city he considered his second home. She couldn't keep herself from laughing when she periodically asked him questions about a particular building or historical fact, and his answers were all the same. "I don't know. I forgot," was his mantra.

"I need to brush up on some New York history." Lamont said, laughing at his lack of knowledge as they navigated through Chelsea.

"You know what they say . . . don't quit your day job."

"Definitely not." He took Sandy's hand in his and rubbed her palm with his thumb.

A thousand electric-eel currents flowed though Sandy. It had been over four years since a man had touched her that way. She felt parts of her awakening. Felt scary. Felt good. She put a reign on the emotions that were eager to be let out of the starting gate. She didn't want to screw up something that had the potential to be *something*.

She was Cinderella leaning against Lamont like he belonged to her. He pulled her closer to him and put his arm around her. She hoped he couldn't feel her heart beating. Being close to him was comforting. It felt real. Travel-hypnosis swooped down on her quickly. She couldn't fight the sleep that was pressing her. She snuggled herself under Lamont's wings and pretended that he was hers.

Sandy was awakened by room service at nine a.m. Lamont had ordered it for her before he and Brian had gone to a business meeting with the producers of a mini-series that would be airing in a few months. He'd left a note under Sandy's door letting her know that he'd be back by noon. On the note he'd asked that she dress comfortably. When he returned a few hours later, Sandy was wearing a pair of Gap jeans, a black knit sweater, and a waist-length leather jacket. She waited in her suite while Lamont changed from his business suit into a pair of faded jeans, a fleece pullover, and walking shoes. Outside, in the front of the hotel, Lamont talked privately with Brian just before he and Super Witch eased into a silver Porsche Carrera GT, with tinted windows. Trying not to stare, Sandy turned her attention toward the lobby. She blinked twice. She thought she'd seen Simone Montgomery or someone that looked like her. But as quickly as she'd seen her, the woman had disappeared.

As the driver ushered Sandy into the backseat of the SUV, the temptation arose to question Lamont about Brian's blatant disrespect for his marriage and his lack of discretion. His flaunting had dug a hole underneath Sandy's skin. But she told herself to mind her own business. Lamont noticed the irritation on her face.

"First of all, Brian and I are two different men, Cassandra," he volunteered as the driver closed the door behind him. "What Brian does is his business. I'm not condoning it and I'm not supporting it. He takes care of his family. But I've got enough to do keeping myself in line. He isn't on my priority list for counseling."

"I'm not holding anything against you."

"Well, the look on your face conveyed something else."

"Okay. To be honest, I was wondering if you thought his behavior was acceptable, because it's not to me."

"It's not *acceptable* to me either. Listen, let me be honest…I'm looking for a woman that I can settle down with. I'm doing everything in my power to make sure that I choose the right one, so that when I do marry, I don't have to get my needs met anywhere but home. I'm not Brian."

"Thank you," Sandy said. She needed to hear those words, to be assured that this was something that *was* going to turn into something. Some of her irritation subsided.

"You're welcome. And in all fairness to Brian, it's not totally his fault."

Sandy's irritation returned. "Well, just whose fault is it—his wife's?"

"That's not what I'm saying, Cassandra," Lamont said firmly.

Sandy snapped. "What are you saying?"

"Some of that he learned from our father."

"Okay. He's a grown man now. He needs to make better choices."

"That may be true, but parents have an impact on their kids. My father had his fair share of women outside of the marriage. When we got older we knew what was happening. But he always took care of home. And Momma probably stayed because being with him was better than nothing."

"I think I would have just settled for nothing."

"Whoa . . ." Lamont said. "You said that like it was a warning."

"Nope. I've just dealt with the crap before. Not going to do it anymore."

"I sense some hostility."

"None intended." Sandy was aggravated. She scooted away from Lamont and pretended to be looking out of the window.

"Hey..." Lamont said, taking Sandy's hand, pulling her back next to him. "I'm looking for my *wife*. I'm not out here dating just to be dating—it's not about sex, either. It's about finding the mother of my children. The woman I'm going to grow old with. There is a method to my madness."

"A wife?"

"Yes, a wife. But I realize that a friendship needs to be developed first.

I thought that's what you and I were doing," he said, stroking Sandy's cheek, melting her guard.

"Okay," she nodded. She liked what he'd said. And Lamont erased the remainder of her concerns with the gentle way he held her hand and kissed her cheek.

They spent the remainder of the day shopping. Against Sandy's better judgment, she allowed Lamont to buy her a red silk wrap dress from the Roberto Cavalli boutique that was way too expensive for the status of their *friendship*. Knowing that men often used that kind of bait as a bargaining tool for sex in the future, Sandy accepted it anyway, after Lamont didn't give in to her protests. She prayed that she hadn't just set herself up for something she wasn't particularly ready for down the road.

Lamont made a fuss over Sandy, having the salespeople attend to her like she was some sort of rock star. And Sandy wanted to enjoy the attention while it lasted. She wanted to feel loved again. She'd been missing that. She needed it. If the wanting was wrong, she was guilty. But she was still a woman. Still human. And Lamont was breathing on the needs that had been neglected for too long.

They flew into Chicago that evening, and Brian's wife, Stacie, picked them up in a black Rolls Royce Phantom. The personalized plate ironically read: *HELUVME*. Sandy smacked her lips quietly as she watched Stacie squeal with excitement over the small gift box Brian handed to her before kissing her and lifting her off of her feet. Sandy rolled her eyes. *If she knew the whole truth and nothing but the truth, maybe she wouldn't be so happy to see the creep.* Brian fell into the husband façade effortlessly, telling Stacie how much he had missed her and loved her, trying to convince himself. Sandy twisted her lips. *Hmph. Just last night he had his hands all over some other woman's behind, and had his tongue down her throat this morning. How's that for love?*

Stacie was a gorgeous yield of Asian and African-American parents. She was deliciously attractive, with black eyes that bore a slight slant. Her cocoa hue was unblemished. She had silky black hair, that had been cut into a bob that moved freely as she deep-kissed her husband. Sandy evaluated her as Brian wrapped his arms around her tiny waist. She had a figure that rivaled that of any star Sandy could think of, and she wasn't at all what Sandy had pictured in her mind's eye. Brian's reckless behavior had caused her to expect some chunky, dowdy-looking housewife with bifocals. But Stacie was a showstopper. Sandy halted from wondering what could possibly be wrong with Stacie, and focused on what was wrong with the creep the poor girl had married.

Stacie looked surprised to see Sandy standing in between Brian and Lamont. She raised her eyebrows at Lamont as he introduced the two of them. Lamont hugged Stacie and told her how beautiful she looked. Then the two of them exchanged kisses on the cheeks. Sandy smiled a polite smile and noticed that Stacie and Lamont were communicating to one another without talking. Stacie let loose a series of silly giggles that stirred up Sandy's irritation. She wondered what the hidden sidebars were about.

"Forgive me for being so silly, Cassandra. It's just that I've been trying to hook this brother up for the last few years. I'm just surprised to see him with someone," Stacie said, wiping her lipstick print from the side of Lamont's cheek with her thumb.

"It's nice to meet you," Sandy offered. "Lamont has told me a lot about your famous sweet potato pie." *But you need to ditch the loser.*

"Well, as usual, I set it out for my baby," Stacie said with her arm around Brian's waist. "I made an awesome dinner. You guys are welcome to come over."

"Actually, I'm going to cook dinner for Cassandra myself, and I have ice cream to go along with that pie you packed for me in your car," Lamont said, putting his arms around Sandy.

"Lamont Drake, how did you know that I brought you some pie?" Stacie asked with her hands on her hips.

"Oh, I just had a feeling," Lamont laughed.

"Hey, you better watch it, man. I might get jealous," Brian said, playfully putting his fist in Lamont's face.

Stacie kissed Brian. "But you've got me, baby."

Sandy could have gagged. *You and America's "Top Witch."*

"Lamont, are you sure that you don't want to come over for dinner tonight?" Stacie pushed.

"Yeah, I'm gonna take a rain check. My housekeeper is on vacation, and I'm not sure how my guest rooms are looking. I may have to clean up a little, you know . . . make sure Sandy won't be sleeping in a jungle tonight. The boys were over last, remember?"

"*Guest room?*" Brian said under his breath.

Stacie elbowed him. "Well, in that case, we better get you home so that you can take care of your business. Because your nephews don't even clean up at their own house," Stacie said.

Sandy was relieved that Lamont mentioned the guest room, in case there had been any doubts floating in the air. She was spending the night, but she wasn't *spending the night*. She planned to keep her promise to God. She hoped Lamont understood that more than anyone else.

She started having second thoughts as soon as they arrived at his greystone located a half a block off of Lake Shore Drive. She wondered if her staying would be a mistake. She wanted to ask Lamont if it would be all right if she stayed at a hotel tonight instead, but the words wouldn't come out. *What am I doing? Am I crazy? This could get me in BIG trouble.*

Lamont didn't notice Sandy's internal struggle. Maybe she was smiling too much for him to see that she was afraid—not of him, but of herself. It had been so long since she'd been held, kissed, or touched. *I won't kiss him. I want to kiss him. I can't kiss him. No kissing.* Sandy kept a plastic smile, careful not to show any emotion. She didn't want to insult him. She didn't want him to be angry about allowing them to drive all the way to his home, and then not trust him enough to stay overnight like they'd planned. It seemed like a good plan over the phone. And Lamont hadn't tried to compromise her in any way in the last twenty-four hours.

Too late. She was in. Stark white walls and white marble flooring greeted her. White suede furniture. A clear glass and steel elevator. It was a museum. Not what she expected from a bachelor. Invisible *Do Not Touch* signs were posted on every wall. There was no sign of any item being out of its proper place. Not a magazine on a table or a bill left on a counter—nothing. Aside from it being furnished so tastefully, there was no indication that someone actually lived there. It was too perfect.

The greystone had the faint essence of a woman—interior decorator or girlfriend. It had a woman's touch. Sandy had to keep her mouth from dangling open as she followed Lamont. All four floors of the museum were exotic. Each room had its own motif that ranged from African to Southwestern. It seemed that every wall had been wallpapered with art work that Lamont had collected from his various globe-trotting escapades. Lamont held Sandy's hand as he explained where the different masks and other art pieces were from. He beamed with pride, telling the history and origin of each piece like he was the head curator.

"I have a passion for collecting."

"I see. Gosh, you've been to so many places: Africa, Italy, Australia, Brazil, and Paris? I'm jealous. And you've researched all the pieces. That is impressive." Sandy said, nodding.

"You can thank my mother for that. I developed the interest from her. We travel together at least once a year."

"Cool."

Lamont flirted, kissing Sandy on the cheek. "Like you."

Lord, help. Sandy picked up a statue from the built-in shelf along the second to third floor staircase to take her mind off Lamont's flirting.

"You better be careful with that," he teased. "You're holding a fertility statue. It's from Senegal."

Sandy's mind wandered off somewhere in the middle of a jungle with Lamont holding her so close that she could barely breathe. *He touched his lips to hers. The sound of African drums beat out a mating song.*

"I'm sorry. Am I boring you?"

"Oh, no. I was just thinking about Africa."

"It's beautiful. I think that every black person should make it a priority to take a trip to the Mother Land. There is so much history there it's incredible."

"I'd love to do that one day."

"What's stopping you?"

Sandy paused for a moment. She didn't have an answer to that question. Most of her life she had been her own worst enemy—unsure of herself, self-conscious, afraid. "Nothing really."

"So just do it. I like a woman who's sure of what she wants," Lamont continued to flirt.

Sandy didn't respond. She just flashed a smile. It was best to keep her lips closed. She followed him down the hall. He stopped, opened a door to a room, and closed it right back. He did the same thing to the room next to it.

"Well, Cassandra, I think you are going to have to take my room tonight, because my guest rooms are worse off than I thought. I'm going to kill my nephews."

"Wherever you put me is fine. But please call me Sandy. I've been meaning to tell you that. Cassandra is so formal. And I'm starving," she laughed.

"My apologies, Sandy. I could have given you a tour on a full stomach. Spaghetti is your favorite, right?"

"Good memory. Yes."

"Coming right up," Lamont said before showing Sandy to his room.

Painted in a smoky grey, it was dark and enclosing. The black furniture was ultra-modern with odd shapes and art-deco accents in brushed silver. Lamont's king size, low platform bed was only a few inches off of the floor. Sandy had imagined him sleeping in a room like this when they'd stayed up late at night talking on the phone. It was a true bachelor's nest, more masculine than the rest of the house. Two side by side plasma screen televisions floated over the black marble fire place—classic man stuff. She didn't even bother to ask why he needed two televisions right next to one another. She'd dated enough men to know that the ability to watch any two sports games at the same time—pub style, was like a kid being in a candy store.

Lamont went down to the kitchen to work on dinner. After showering and changing into sweats, Sandy made her way down to see if he needed her help, but he didn't. The noodles were draining in a steel strainer, and Lamont was putting the finishing touches on the meat sauce. She could smell the garlic bread warming. Lamont put another pinch of oregano in the pot, stirred the sauce with a large wooden spoon, and scooped some out for her.

"Taste," he said, beckoning her over to the stove. He fed the meat sauce to her, eyeing her lustfully.

She teased him by smacking her tongue against the roof of her mouth like a taste tester.

Lamont laughed at her playfulness. "You really look cute doing that, you know."

"Really?"

"Yes. So how's the sauce?"

"Good. Very good."

"How's *this* . . ." Lamont leaned in and devoured Sandy with a kiss that made her senses go wild. And she kissed him back like their lips were a natural pair. She couldn't believe what she was doing. *I said no kissing.* Sandy tried to pull back but Lamont pulled her in closer, and squeezed her tightly against him. She could feel his heart pounding. His breathing hastened. *I should have stayed at a hotel . . .* Surely this was going to get her into *trouble. Lord, help.* She was completely lost in Lamont's kiss, completely molded to his will, when he finally pulled away slowly by his own volition.

He smiled mischievously. "I've wanted to do that over a month. You said you wanted to stay celibate. You didn't say we couldn't kiss."

Sandy caught her breath. "Kisses like that could make staying celibate a problem. Warn me next time."

Lamont chuckled. "Sandy, I'm *never* going to do *anything* to you that you don't *allow* me to. I just needed to get that out of the way before we ate—so I can concentrate on our conversation and not on what your kisses feel like."

"Now you know."

"Oh, yes," he nodded, entertaining a thought that he needed to keep to himself because of Sandy's convictions. She was beautifully different. A good Christian woman. That made her all the more enticing. "Let's eat," he said, focusing.

Sandy waited in the dining room while Lamont prepared their plates in the kitchen. He'd lit the white taper dinner candles and had removed all the place settings at his six-seat dinner table set except for two. He'd turned on some soft jazz and set out a bottle of Black Rooster label, Chianti Classico Riserva that he'd brought back from Castle Il Palagio in Tuscany over the summer. They'd just said grace when his phone rang. Lamont was agitated by the interruption.

"This better be important," he said to Sandy before going into the kitchen to answer it. He spoke politely. "Hello . . . she sure is."

Sandy could overhear him. She sat back nervously, wondering what had occurred back at home that would warrant Josette or Faye calling her here. She'd left Lamont's home number and cell on the refrigerator in case of an emergency, with the assumption that there wouldn't be one. Her stomach started to feel queasy. She hoped Josette hadn't done something ridiculous. She couldn't think of any other reason they would call her here.

"Hello," Sandy said, half holding her breath.

"Sandy, I'm sorry for calling you like this, but it's just that I really think we should talk. I know that you've been purposely avoiding me. If I said or did something wrong, I deserve to at least know what it was. I just want us to be adult about it," Genevieve said.

I'm acting like a child? She's the one hunting me down. Sandy decided that she would kill Faye, knowing full well that Josette was not responsible for this. "Look, this really isn't a good time to have this conversation."

"Sandy, please don't do this . . . come on. Don't do this," Genevieve pleaded.

Sandy blew out her frustration and the curses that were going through her mind. *Why is she doing this right now? I don't want to deal with this. I can't get away from Jo or Genevieve for a moment. Why won't they just let me have some space?* "This could have waited, Genevieve."

"No. It couldn't have. If you don't want this to go anywhere, then say that. And I'll walk away. But I need to know why you even bothered to look me up in the first place if that was the case."

"I'm trying to have a relaxing weekend. I don't have time for this right now," Sandy said sternly.

"Is everything all right?" Lamont whispered.

Sandy nodded and continued to listen to Genevieve tell her how important their relationship was, and how they needed to meet again so that they could talk things out.

"Look, I don't know when I'm going to be free to do that. I have a lot on my plate."

"*Cassandra*, are you saying that you just want to stop right here—this is it?"

Sandy couldn't feel the tingles from Lamont's kisses and touches anymore. Genevieve had blown her high. "Right now, that's what I'm feeling. I'm sorry." *I don't owe you anything.*

Genevieve took that statement hard. For a few moments she didn't speak. She swallowed and said, "Take care of yourself. I really wish you well. And . . . I love you."

"Bye," was Sandy's response.

Lamont waited casually for some explanation. But Sandy felt the tears starting. *I don't want to do this in front of him. He's going to think I'm unstable or something.* She took a deep breath. "I need a minute alone, please," she said without looking at him, and ran up the staircase.

Too many demands. Too much pressure. She couldn't take care of everyone and make their lives right. She couldn't spend any more time taking care of other people. It was what she'd always done. It was what she did at work and at home. Had anyone ever stopped to think that maybe when the day was over she needed someone? Didn't she deserve to be on the receiving end sometimes? Josette and Genevieve were sucking the life out of her. And where was Genevieve when she'd needed her all those years? And now, she was supposed to stop the world for her?

Fifteen minutes passed before Lamont knocked on his bedroom door. Sandy's face was flush with embarrassment. *I've brought all my problems with me. He must think I'm crazy. I've brought nothing but drama to what was supposed to be a getaway. Get away from what?* Life kept following her. She wiped the remainder of her tears and tried hard not to look like the basket case that she was at the moment. "Come in."

Lamont took one look at her face and said, "What was that about?"

"You weren't supposed to see those."

"Too late. Can I help?"

"No. I think I can handle it. I'm just tired of dealing with everyone else's problems."

Lamont sat next to her. He took her hand and planted a kiss on it. "You want to talk about it? I hear therapy is good for you," he smiled, pulling his fingers gently through her hair.

I should know; I've been at it for three years. "Oh yeah? What are your qualifications?"

"Now, that's a good question," he laughed. "Besides being a good listener, I don't know what other *credible* credentials I have." He wiped the tears from her eyes.

She wanted to trust him with her soul right then. But she was afraid. She didn't want him to see *that* Sandy. She wanted him to see the Sandy that was strong. Inside the crying ball of confusion was strength—somewhere. She needed to find that reserve button. But she gave in to the desire to let go of some weight, while Lamont served as the substitute therapist.

They talked about her failures, her childhood, her marriage, and the other relationships that didn't last. Sandy sat with her legs stretched across Lamont's lap, while he rubbed her feet, listening to her pain. She hoped the divulgence would help him to understand her better, and not backfire on her at a later date. She'd just shared information that she usually only discussed in the confines of Jody's office. She hoped that he was sensitive enough to protect it. It was still early in their relationship, but she felt like she could trust him. She hoped she wasn't wrong.

They finished their conversation over the spaghetti Lamont had prepared. Sandy drank the last of her wine. "This is the best wine I've ever tasted."

Lamont picked up the bottle. "It is good, isn't it? It's the grapes and the aging process. See, there's only a handful of wine producers in the world who are able to bear the Black Rooster label or have their wine labeled as Chianti *Classico*," he said, thumping the rooster logo. "It's made with ninety percent Sangiovese grapes. And they have to come from a particular terrain in Tuscany. I've had more expensive wines, but I've got to admit this is my favorite. I've got bottles of this stuff."

"You tryin' to keep me around?"

"Whatever it takes."

"I guess that's what Genevieve is saying too. *Whatever it takes.* Whew. I can't believe she called me here. Don't you think that was overstepping boundaries?"

"Honestly, I think you're running. Maybe you don't want to deal with what really happened and accept Genevieve for who she is now," Lamont said, filling Sandy's glass with more Chianti.

"I don't know . . . you could be right. Maybe I'm not over it. I thought I was over it." She put her hand up to cue him to stop pouring.

"Sometimes things are not what they seem."

"All the money I've spent on therapy, you'd think that all my problems would be solved by now. I don't want to be a lifetime therapy patient."

"I think you should try to get to know Genevieve all over again. Life is too short to hold on to pain of any kind. You two could have a decent relationship if you both put forth the effort—like with any relationship."

Lamont was only partially right. But right now Sandy didn't want to think about it one way or the other. All she wanted to do was rest in his arms. Lamont put their plates in the dishwasher and the two of them lay on the double chaise lounge in his den watching HBO reruns on a plasma screen until both of them were snoring. Late into the night Lamont adjusted himself, pulling Sandy out of the comfort of her sleeping position. He picked the remote up off of the floor and aimed it at the screen. Dustin Hoffman faded to black.

The satisfaction of lying next to a warm body anesthetized Sandy. Lamont had intertwined himself with her and brought back that incredible sense of safety that she'd been missing.

Lamont whisper-kissed Sandy's ear. "I think it's time for us to hit the sack."

"Umm… I'm comfortable right where I am."

"Yeah, but you feel way too good for me to allow you to stay right here. I couldn't be responsible for my actions. You wanna stay celibate, right?"

"Yes."

He stood up and pulled Sandy to her feet. "Time to go."

Sandy stood up and leaned in to give him a good night kiss.

Lamont stepped back. "Don't tease me," he said. His eyes were serious. "I'm going to try to walk this 'celibacy walk' with you—for now. But I can't and won't make you any promises. I'm not where you are."

Sandy wasn't sure how to respond to his boldness. "Okay," she said, turning toward the staircase. *What am I going to do with him? Pray.*

Chapter Ten

Two months had passed since the day Josette stormed in and out of her husband's restaurant office. She was healing. Six months after the storm that tore her life apart, she had to move on. She had started going to the gym again, and her appetite had picked up. She'd gained five pounds back. Her body was beginning to look good again. Faye attributed it to her prayers for Josette. But Josette didn't believe that. There was nothing magical or spiritual about her getting back to a place of stableness except for the fact that she'd been real with herself. Patrick wanted a divorce, and that's just the way it was.

Josette plunged herself into her work to help keep her mind off of her marriage. Criminal law was time-consuming. It was beneficial at a time like this. And the diversity of her clientele still thrilled her. She'd represented all kinds of people who intrigued her. From white-collar criminals to murderers, it was never dull. Her career never lacked that rush she got every time she entered a courtroom. She lived for it.

Josette high-stepped down the street, away from the courthouse and into the Starbucks around the corner. She'd just left the pretrial conference for the John Paul Dozier murder case. She had a smile on her face. She felt good—invincible. John Paul Dozier, who went by his street name, J. P., faced a murder charge for the death of his wife of seventeen years, Gina Dozier.

John Paul had been one of Detroit's most notorious drug dealers in the eighties. He'd done ten years in prison for trumped up drug charges because the prosecution couldn't stick anything to him that would have sent him away for life—like they'd wanted to. The rumor mill on the streets claimed that J. P. had at least two loyal fall guys that were serving twenty-year sentences for drug trafficking and other illegal activity related to their involvement with J. P.

He'd been out of prison for six years. And he'd kept a low profile. He had re-established himself as an entrepreneur with several reputable businesses. He owned two barber shops, two car washes, and a laundromat on the west side. His primary business was real estate. John Paul owned three eight-unit apartment complexes, several flats, and a dozen single-family homes that he rented out. That, coupled with his knack for "flipping" properties, secured him a standard of living that was significantly above that of most working people and small business owners. He made his living that way—and it was all legal.

J. P.'s estimated worth was $4.7 million, a long way from the estimated $100 million empire he reigned over at the height of his drug career in 1982. He owned a half-million-dollar home in Indian Village, a historic neighborhood on the east side. His neighbors portrayed him as a quiet man who kept to himself. Most of them were unaware that they had an urban street legend living right on their block.

J. P.'s business records were impeccable. His lifestyle was a squeaky-clean transformation from what it had been in his drug heyday. He claimed that he had found God and had turned his life around. Said that he had been born again. That he prayed every day. He had faded from the minds of most, except when an occasional discussion of the "Amazing Eighties" came up. He had been the *man* back in the day. Josette remembered J. P. from her childhood. She was ten years old when he used to ride through the poor neighborhoods in stretch limos, passing out money to kids. He had no fewer than four bodyguards with him at all times. J. P. and his entourage could be seen on any given day sporting heavy gold artillery around their necks, and full-length mink coats when it was cold. He was an urban superstar. Now, he was Josette's client.

J. P.'s wife, Gina, had been found strangled to death in her Mercedes in a mall parking lot. Mark Major, the prosecuting attorney, was planning to convince the jury that J. P. murdered his wife. Josette was all too familiar with Mark's style. She knew that he was going to argue that J. P.'s motive was an affair. It was common street knowledge that Gina had a loose reputation. But J. P.'s alibi was a football game, and it was locked tightly as far as Josette was concerned. Josette knew that Mark was going to attempt to make the jury concentrate on J. P.'s past, remind them that he was known for getting back at his enemies, having them hanged, killed execution-style, or tortured—things that were never proven.

Josette was sitting at a table by herself sipping espresso when Mark Major strolled in. He saw her and beamed. He ordered and sat with her.

"I knew you'd be here. What's happening, kid?"

"Nothing much. How 'bout yourself?"

"Can't complain," he said, placing his cell phone on top of the table. It prevented him from missing calls.

"You know I'm walking on this one," Josette laughed.

"We'll see."

"I got this J. P. case locked down tight, baby," Josette teased.

"You braggin'?"

Josette took another sip from her cup. "Yeah. Remember the Williams' case? You were struttin' around the courtroom like some rare black peacock with your Brooks Brothers' suit and Johnston Murphy shoes on."

"Yeah. I did you in," Mark said with a proud smile. "But today, Judge Velasquez couldn't even concentrate. I think he was looking at your legs. I hope he's paying attention when this trial starts."

Josette laughed. "You know, you're silly. He's seen them before—I've presented plenty of cases in front of him."

"I couldn't tell," Mark laughed. "Looked like it was the first time he'd seen those legs, girl. Maybe it was the heels."

"Hush."

Josette and Mark had a friendly rivalry. Not even J. P. could rattle that. Secretly, Mark admired her. However, he had kept it to himself, never being less than professional with her. They had developed a sort of friendship in the last three years. He couldn't lie to himself though; Josette was a fox. A fool could see that. He'd told her that on more than one occasion, but he'd never stepped out of line. He loved her fire, as most men did. She was a heavy hitter in the world of criminal law—brassy and arrogant, but just as delicate as a flower. Her femininity—the sway of her hips and the curves of her body caused a man to take notice when she walked into a room. That made her more appealing. Mark had taught himself how to admire women like Josette without crossing boundaries. He believed in love. He respected the sanctity of marriage. But the thought of loving a woman like her crept into his thoughts from time to time.

"We need you on our side, Jo," Mark said earnestly, staring into her soft hazel eyes.

"I like this side."

"I used to too. Then I asked myself what my law career was all about. Justice? Or money and power? Because on the other side, all I saw was money and power being the vehicle that allowed people to get away with things that they shouldn't. People got away with murder just because they were able to pay for a beautiful, intelligent attorney like you who just happened to work for Marty Pipes, one of the richest and smartest criminal attorneys in the country."

Mark's defect plea was not enough to sway Josette. "Maybe one day, Mark. Not any time soon."

Mark's cell phone vibrated its way across the table and over to Josette. He shook his head disappointedly that he wouldn't be able to finish his conversation with her. He was enjoying her company. He stared at her with a puppy-dog face as he reached for his phone and answered it quickly. *Business.* Josette saw it in his eyes. Mark stood, picked up his coffee cup, and retrieved his coat from the back of his chair, nearly tipping it over. He steadied it and backed hurriedly away from the table, winking at Josette. She winked back as he headed back to the courthouse.

As far as Josette was concerned, J. P. was going to walk. A man had a right to change. He had proven that for over six years. He had led a crime-free life since getting out of prison. And he'd told Josette that he didn't do it. Not that it mattered. She would still have a job to do if he was guilty. But Josette believed him. She was looking forward to the trial. That's where she was going to put her energy. John Paul Dozier was going to be her man for the next few months.

Chapter Eleven

Genevieve stared at her reflection in the mirror as she pinned her hair up and prepared for bed. She went through her four-step skin cleansing ritual thinking about the last few months of her life. It seemed to be falling apart now that Sandy had rejected her. And in everything that had transpired, she still couldn't find a lesson in it all. She was beginning to think that there was no lesson. She didn't know what God's will was in her situation. The only thing she knew for certain was that she'd been neglecting her family because of her depression. Her mind had been elsewhere. Her optimism and zeal had fizzled out. Benjamin had attempted to encourage her by leaving scriptures on note cards for her to meditate on throughout the day. It was a thoughtful thing for him to do, but lately she hadn't felt like meditating on anything.

She had cried so much in the last few months that she couldn't even force herself to become excited about the family trip to Florida that Benjamin had surprised her with. She had tried to look thrilled when Benjamin showed her their itinerary, but she'd been far from enthused. She felt like going on a vacation by herself to sort out the thoughts that kept her from feeling whole again.

She completed the last of her ritual by applying her overnight moisturizer with her finger-tips. She did it hurriedly, bypassing the care that she usually took, foregoing the two-finger, upward, circular motion technique the beauty consultant had taught her. It wasn't important tonight. Did her skin look healthier and younger like the consultant promised? That didn't matter either. She was stuck in a spiritual rut.

Genevieve slid into bed, and before she could slip into a dream, Benjamin snuggled up behind her. He had showered and was wearing Cool Water, her favorite cologne. Even though it was a relatively old fragrance, Benjamin still wore it because Genevieve still loved it. His wearing cologne just to come to bed was a not-so-subtle way of letting her know what his *agenda* was. Tonight, however, Genevieve wasn't in the mood. She hadn't been in *that* mood since her life had been infiltrated and then left barren. She hated to deny him, but she wasn't feeling herself.

"Sweets, you up?" Benjamin whispered.

Genevieve tried to relax and hoped that nature would take its course. "Barely," she said.

Benjamin kissed the back of her neck. "I need some Q.T. . . . are you up enough for that?"

Usually, that one simple show of affection would start her motor. *Quality time?* Tonight she was cold. She felt like she was grieving. *Due benevolence*. Ben continued to kiss her. Genevieve squirmed a little, hoping that Benjamin would think that she was half-asleep. Maybe they could pick up some other time.

"Sweets, I want to plaaay . . ." he said, sounding so cute that Genevieve almost wanted to laugh. Then he would know that she was awake and trying to avoid giving him the body that belonged to him in the first place.

Genevieve turned to face him. "Hon, I don't know if I can be much fun tonight," she said seriously.

The fluorescent light from the deck outside their bedroom cast a neon glow on both of them.

"You sure? *Kiss.* It's been a while. *Kiss.* Maybe I could change your mind," Ben said, more determined.

Genevieve felt pressured. *How long had it been since the last time? Maybe three weeks?*

"Sweets, it's been a month. Don't let what's going on with Sandy and Josette separate us like this . . . please."

She certainly was convicted. *The wife hath not power of her own body, but the husband: and likewise also the husband hath not power of his own body but the wife.* Genevieve couldn't remember a time when Benjamin had not given in to her, even when he'd been dead tired. Whenever she said the words, *"I need you,"* he obliged her. So she forced her mind to float to a worriless universe where she could focus on the wonderful gift of a husband God had given her and be lulled by his affection. But knocking at their bedroom door interrupted her focus. Benjamin was oblivious to the intrusion, but Genevieve's maternal ears were fine-tuned.

"Ben . . ." she whispered, breaking away from his kiss.

The knocking continued more loudly. Ben eyed the clock. It was after midnight. "What in the world . . .?"

It occurred to Genevieve that it had to be Faith because Joshua would have said something by now. But before she could communicate that thought to Benjamin, he responded to the unwanted interruption.

"Yes!" he said frustrated.

"My stomach hurts," Faith whined through the door.

Ben pulled away from Genevieve. "I don't believe this."

"You want me to handle it?" Genevieve asked.

Benjamin got out of bed and retrieved his robe from the bench at the edge of the bed. "No, I'll take care of it."

Benjamin nudged Genevieve. She'd fallen asleep in the twenty-five minutes it had taken him to give Faith some medicine and talk her back to sleep. Sleepily, Genevieve propped herself up on her elbow. "What took you so long?" she yawned.

"Long story. I guess you're not in the mood anymore, huh?"

"I'm just sleepy, Hon. I'm sorry."

Benjamin sighed. "Just forget it, Sweets. Just forget it."

He was angry. And Genevieve would have been more concerned if it hadn't been for the fact that she was halfway in dream zone. She rationalized. *Maybe in the morning.*

Benjamin was gone when Genevieve awakened around seven a.m. There was no index card on their dresser with a scripture on it, like there had been the last few weeks. It was a sign that her husband was surely angry. No love note stick-um on the bathroom mirror, nor next to the coffee maker in the kitchen.

Faith and Joshua were both asleep in their rooms. There was an empty bottle of Maalox on Faith's nightstand that Benjamin had given her. Genevieve wondered how she could have slept so late. She was usually up by five a.m. every morning for prayer and meditation. Today she was sluggish. She remembered that today was supposed to be Guys and Girls Day. She'd planned to take Faith to the spa for a manicure and pedicure, then maybe to lunch and to a movie. Genevieve smiled when she thought of how silly Faith laughed when the manicurist touched her feet.

She wondered what Benjamin and Joshua were going to do as she looked in the refrigerator and found it almost empty of breakfast food. She knew they weren't going fishing because both of them would have been gone already. She closed the refrigerator door and scolded herself for not going to the market the day before. She put fresh grounds in the coffee maker and added bottled water. She browsed through circulars as she waited for her coffee.

This was the first weekend of the month, their designated family weekend. Normally, she would spend the day with Faith while Ben and Joshua spent the day together, and then the four of them would come together in the evening for family time. She hoped she and Benjamin could work out their *problem*.

Genevieve poured Irish Crème in her coffee and leaned against the counter, drinking. Benjamin entered the kitchen through the garage.

"Good morning," she said cheerfully.

Benjamin was dry. "Morning," he said, placing two grocery bags on the kitchen counter.

"Are we not in a good mood this morning?"

"No, we're not," Benjamin said, placing a carton of eggs, pancake mix, and a half-gallon of Genevieve's favorite orange juice on the counter.

Genevieve walked over to Benjamin and reached out to help him prepare breakfast. "Can we talk about it?"

Benjamin moved her hands gently out of the way. "I've got it," he said. "There's not much to talk about, Genevieve."

Genevieve? What happened to Sweets? "Well, obviously there is, because you're angry."

"I'm not angry. I just think that a whole month is too long to *not* be able to make love to my wife. I feel like I'm on some kind of punishment.

What do you want me to say?"

"Ben, I fell asleep. Gosh. You're making such a big deal out of nothing."

"It is a big deal. I'm supposed to be able to be with *my* wife."

Joshua strolled into the kitchen. "You guys having a fight or something?" he said, rubbing his eyes. "I mean . . . disagreement?" he corrected himself.

Benjamin took the griddle out of the bottom cabinet. "No. Your mother and I are just talking."

"Have you washed your face and brushed your teeth?" Genevieve said.

"Huh?" Joshua said as though Genevieve had just spoken Japanese.

"Go," she said pointing toward the stairs.

Benjamin mixed the batter and poured it onto the griddle in neat circular shapes. "You are not off the hook, Genevieve," he reminded her.

"I'm sorry. I just haven't been feeling like myself."

"Well, I want to feel like myself."

Genevieve took another sip of coffee. "Hon, I don't want to fight about it."

"I don't want to fight either. But you have been giving me excuse after excuse. I've tried to respect where you are. I wish you would do the same for me."

Benjamin's tone was firm. It was a serious issue for him. Genevieve wished it wasn't because she couldn't give him any answers. She walked over to him and watched while he flipped the pancakes over. When he finished, she circled her arms around his waist and slid her hands into his jean pockets. "I'll make sure we put in some Q.T. tonight, I promise," she said.

"I don't want charity, Sweets. I want it to be like it was before. Last night, I had to practically coerce you. I felt like you had to concentrate in order to make love to me. What on earth is that about?"

"Ben, I wasn't concentrating."

Benjamin pulled away and took four plates out of the cabinet. "That's how I felt."

"I said tonight, Ben."

"I need your attention at *home*, Sweets. That's all I'm saying."

Genevieve's ire rose. *I said tonight already. What does he want from me?* "You never hear me complaining when you're at church all day and half the night and forget that we've planned to do something." She regretted the words immediately, but they had been released into the universe already.

"That's different and you know it. I belong to God *first*. It's not like I have a regular job." Benjamin said with restrained anger.

Genevieve's apology was sincere. "I'm sorry."

Benjamin was sarcastic. "Yeah, me too."

"I'm not hungry anymore," Genevieve said, storming out of the kitchen.

Genevieve and Benjamin having separate activities with the children, was the saving grace of the day. At least that had gone well. They had taken them to a movie afterward, being cordial to one another at best. At home, they all turned in early so that they could get enough rest for the eight a.m. service.

Benjamin didn't come to bed. He sat in the sitting room off the master suite watching television. And after a long soak in the garden tub,

Genevieve prayed for peace between them. She took her journal out and then put it away. She didn't feel like writing about anything that had happened today. Maybe she and Benjamin could talk after church tomorrow when the kids went over to Mother Peace's for their Sunday visit. Maybe then they could stop this foolishness and talk things out like two adults, without trying to win an argument. But right now, things were a mess.

Chapter Twelve

Sandy eased into Lamont's rhythm effortlessly. Weekends in Chicago. Off days in Chicago. By midweek, she'd already be packed. Their relationship consumed almost all of the time that she used to have too much of. A gap was closing and she was happy about it. She loved every second of it. And she'd kept her commitment to the Lord. She knew that Lamont's feelings for her were genuine because she hadn't given in to what her flesh had wanted on many occasions. And he was still there.

Sandy woke up with excitement. It was the first day of her weeklong vacation. And Lamont was in Los Angeles securing a large cosmetic account that would amount to a seven-figure deal for Vision. It was a business move that would make Vision a formidable contender for contracts just as hefty in the future.

Sandy twisted the mini-blinds open and sunlight splashed her face. She thought to go over to the bed, but the sun beckoned her, so she kneeled down at the window and prayed. She said a special prayer for Lamont and thanked God for keeping her pure. She asked God to soften Lamont's heart so that he would be moved to build a stronger relationship with Him. Asked God to lead him to a church home.

At Sandy's suggestion, they had visited several churches in the Chicago area. It pleased her that Lamont seemed to have a particular affinity toward Trinity United Church of Christ, whose pastor was the charismatic Jeremiah Wright. She hoped that Lamont would root himself someplace that taught good, sound doctrine. It could only make their relationship better.

Since they'd been together that first weekend, Lamont had arranged his schedule so that he hardly worked on weekends for any reason. He promised Sandy that he would belong only to her from Friday to Sunday. He'd kept that promise. And she was feeling that he could be *the one*. Lamont was working hard for her heart. He made the world stop when they were together. And when they were apart, the love notes, cards, and calls in the middle of the day let her know that she had secured a special place in his heart.

Sandy started her morning off properly by cooking herself a two-egg omelet, with tomatoes, green peppers, and onions. She set the bar counter with her Waterford Crystal plate, grabbed a gold-rimmed goblet from the cabinet, and filled it with non-alcoholic champagne. Josette was gone to work and the house was peaceful. She walked over to the Bose system and turned on some jazz. She grabbed her latest *Newsweek* to see what was going on in the world. After tiring of reading about cloning, she made an appointment for herself at Butterfly Day Spa. She told Rita, the receptionist, that she wanted The Works package: a facial, manicure, pedicure, and an hour-long, full body massage. Afterward, she'd treat herself to some serious shopping at Neiman Marcus.

The day was alive with promise. Sandy felt it in the air. She was glad that she'd taken this week off from work even though she wasn't actually going on a real vacation. She needed the rest. She read her daily meditation until her doorbell buzzed. She tightened her silk kimono, walked over to the door, and peeked out. She saw a private courier dressed in a baby blue and navy uniform standing on the other side smiling. *What has Jo ordered now? She needs to stop spending all that money like she's still married to a millionaire.* Sandy cracked the door open.

"I have a package for Cassandra Moss. I need someone to sign for it," the man said, holding a large box with a cutout top. Yellow and gold paper jutted out, temporarily hiding what couldn't be mistaken for anything else but a flower arrangement.

Sandy smiled hard and opened the door wider. "Oooh . . . Good morning, that's me," she said. The slim young man's grey eyes roamed over her kimono while she took the electronic pad and pen from him and signed her name. He reverenced her with stolen glances that he couldn't control.

"Ms. Moss, be careful. The package is marked fragile," he said, shaking off Sandy's spell. He handed her the box carefully.

Sandy took the box from him. "I will. Thank you. Have a nice day."

"You too."

She rushed to the kitchen bar and moved her plate and goblet over to make room for her surprise. She reached down into the box and pulled out the heavy arrangement that was held tightly by a block of packing foam. She tore the paper excitedly. Two dozen purple roses bloomed out. "Oh . . . these are gorgeous," she said lifting the vase carefully out of the foam block. She gasped when she beheld it fully. It was a purple and fuchsia, hand-blown, Murano glass vase that she'd spied in a Chicago gallery just Saturday while shopping with Lamont. The store owner had assured her it was an authentic piece from the factory in Venice, as he encouraged her purchase. It was two thousand dollars too expensive for her taste, so she'd passed on it without a second thought. Lamont had been off in another section of the gallery looking at pieces for himself. *How could he have known?* "Oh my goodness," Sandy said, snaking her fingers over its deep crevices and raised surfaces that looked like three-dimensional ocean waves. "I don't believe this." She lifted a second package from the original box. She pried it opened to find a music box covered with faux rubies and stones. Gently she lifted the lid, and the little black ballerina, dressed in a white and silver tutu, spun around, dancing for her. "Oh, I am like . . . falling so hard!" she shouted.

Sandy took the card from the roses, while the ballerina danced to an enchanted melody. The card read:

Can't stop thinking about you.

Lamont

And she'd been thinking about him. "Where in the world did he find *purple* roses?" she said aloud. She couldn't wait to hear his voice, but she knew that he was probably still in his meeting. She was full of anticipation as she dressed and left the house, beaming as she drove to the day spa. She was soaring so high on a Lamont Drake cloud that later, she planned to return Genevieve's calls, taking the advice that Lamont had given her months ago.

Freddie's massive but soft-to-the-touch hands kneaded Sandy's back like bread dough. Freddie's large build came with strokes of power. Sandy let out sighs of tension that had built up from work stress over the last week. Every place that Freddie rolled and nudged expelled toxins from her body. Frustration. Anger. Fear. She drifted off to sleep under Freddie's hypnotic ritual until he began to work on her feet. He flexed each one of her toes. Sandy squirmed a bit because her feet were ticklish.

Freddie paused for a moment and said, "Don't stay away so long next time."

"Right," she giggled. She'd been long overdue for Freddie's magic. When she adjusted her head to the right, she noticed Jennifer, Freddie's assistant, sitting quietly by the door. If she hadn't seen her, Sandy would never have known that she was there. Jennifer had been sitting so still that Sandy hadn't even felt her presence. She started to tell Freddie that but thoughts of Lamont took first place. Jennifer signaled to Freddie that she was stepping out of the room momentarily. Freddie nodded and Jennifer eased out as quietly as she had been sitting.

"Freddie, your hands are magic."

"I know. That's what Jo and Dr. Duncan said when they were here on Saturday."

"Jo was here? Good for her," Sandy said, glad that Josette was back to being herself. Sandy had to admit she missed the old Josette—a smidgen.

"Yeah, I was getting worried about Jo—with everything that's going on between her and Patrick."

"She told you about that?"

"Baby, everybody tells Freddie *everything*. I'm a therapist," he laughed.

"The way you got me feeling right now, all a sista can do is agree with a brotha."

"Well, one thing is for sure, it doesn't go any further than right here. That is code."

"Not even for the right price?"

"Not even for my wife. Don't tell her I said that."

Sandy's whole pampering process took over three hours. But when she left, she felt glamorous. A little sexy. Sensuous. Her cell phone catapulted her out of a Lamont Drake daydream.

She answered blissfully. "H-e-l-l-o."

"Hey, beautiful, how's the first day of your week off going?" His baritone rang through her whole body.

"Fine. And thank you for the gifts. They're beautiful. The flower arrangement is gorgeous, the vase unbelievably elegant, and the ballerina . . . well, she's the most precious gift I've ever received. You didn't have to do that. I mean the vase alone was so expens—"

Lamont cut her off. "Unh-unh. Don't . . . I did that because I wanted to. Because I can. And because you deserve that and more, baby. This is real, Sandy. Just let me love you the way I want to, okay?"

Sandy was subdued by his earnestness. *Did he just say the L word?* "Okay," she said, easing into the valet lane at Neiman's. If there was a motive behind Lamont's spoiling she was in trouble, because she was hooked like a worm on a fishing line.

"Guess what?"

"What?"

"I'm missing you. Can you believe it?"

"You just saw me yesterday. But I guess I'm a miss-able girl."

"No doubt. And guess what else?"

"Yes . . ."

"A celebration is definitely in order."

"You got the account?" Sandy asked, stepping out of her BMW 745i. She handed the valet her keys.

"Yes *we* did!"

"Oh, I am so proud of you!"

"They loved our ideas. We nailed it from the moment we walked into the room. And I want you to celebrate with me."

"Okay . . ." Sandy said, not knowing exactly what she was agreeing to. With Lamont, she never could tell.

"You need to get packed—enough for a week in the sun," Lamont said, grinning a smile that Sandy could only imagine.

"Packed?"

"Yes, packed. We're going to meet Brian and Stacie in Jamaica tomorrow."

"Jamaica?"

"Yep. We'll be staying in a little villa at the Half Moon. It'll be fun."

Sandy hesitated. She worried about being alone with him in such a beautiful place for a whole week. Her righteous resolve would be stretched like a rubber band. "I'd love to but I—"

"There is enough space for you to have your own room if you don't trust yourself," he joked. But I *need* you to be with me." His tenderness sweetened the pot.

Needs me? Think girl, think. "Okay . . ."

"Your flight to L.A. leaves in four hours. Northwest, flight 702."

"Oh, I'm flyin' commercial?" Sandy joked.

"First class. Brian has some last minute business in New York this evening, and Team One, our main go-getters, will be flying out too. We promised them an all-expense-paid trip to anywhere they wanted to go. The schedules weren't gelling. It's like I said, Eve gets shared a lot."

"So where is Team One going?"

"Aruba."

"Aruba? Been there. Done that. If I were on Team One, I would have chosen someplace exotic like Paris or Fiji—especially since you're paying and all."

"Baby, if you were on Team One you would have already been to both of the places you just named."

"Well dang, maybe I need to work with Team One, Mr. Drake, sir," Sandy teased.

"Nah. All you got to do is be with me. I'll take care of the rest—I'm gonna take care of you. I promise you that. So I'll see you soon, okay? I love you."

"Love you too." *Did he just say, love? Did I just say it back?*

Love was hitting her like a hammer, but it felt so good. Sandy closed her flip phone and floated into Neiman's. Floated into the dressing room. Floated up to the counter. Floated all the way home.

She could hear the phone ringing as she entered the kitchen. She had so many packages that she dumped half of them in the center of the kitchen floor in order to make it to the phone. She managed to reach it just before the answering machine picked up. She told Genevieve that she'd call her back. She could hear the disappointment in her voice.

"Listen, I'm not trying to put you off. I'm on my way out of town and I need to get to the airport so that I don't miss my flight," Sandy explained.

Genevieve pinned her down to a specific day and time when they could get together again. Sandy agreed to meet with her after she returned home from Jamaica. And it satisfied Genevieve for the time being.

Chapter Thirteen

Josette dressed in a black Dolce and Gabbana halter dress that chain-hooked around the neck and dipped low in the front. She searched through her shoes, trying to decide which ones would go best. She settled for a pair of black, tie-around-the-ankle Manolo's. Josette primped in front of the mirror. She looked good. She ran her hands along the curves of her hips. She was getting back the body that she used to work hard to keep. She was ready. No more crying herself to sleep at night. She was going to get out and move beyond her life with Patrick.

She donned her black diamond mink and headed for anchor woman Candace Cage-Cooper's surprise birthday party at Elephant City. It didn't even matter to her that Patrick would be there in support of Candace's husband, Keith, forward for Detroit's basketball team. He and Keith had been best friends since high school. But Patrick wasn't going to keep her from living any more. She'd avoided visiting Candace for months, afraid that she might bump into him. But she could no longer allow Patrick's relationship with Keith and Candace to keep her locked in some cocoon.

Candace had been like a sister to Josette since they'd met at the University of Michigan during their sophomore year and pledged the same sorority together. Candace was a local celebrity, being the youngest black female anchor to hold down the six o'clock spot on channel four. She and Josette had a lot of catching up to do. Josette couldn't hide out tonight.

Security was tight. Elephant City was packed with wall-to-wall celebrities: professional ball players, record company executives, models, actresses, and a host of bodyguards for the few elite friends Keith had invited. Lana Porter, special events planner, had decked the posh restaurant out in an Egyptian Queen theme. The tables and chairs were covered with gold lame and the wait staff was dressed in Egyptian garb, with headpieces and sandals. Elephant City's ninety-eight thousand dollar, two-story limestone waterfall added glamour to the beautifully renovated former warehouse. Josette saw several people she hadn't seen in awhile, including her old friend Priscilla. As soon as Josette asked her when her next album was going to be released, the lights blinked twice to signal that Keith was walking Candace in. The room went black. It was standing room only. Josette was pressed so close to Johnathan Carter, center for Chicago, it had to be illegal.

"Josette Kelley, you better get away from me. I don't want that husband of yours trying to kill me," Johnathan joked.

"Shut up," Josette said, elbowing him playfully. "Where's Sheila?" she continued, just above a whisper.

"At home with the baby; she's got a fever."

"So what are you doing all the way in Detroit?"

Johnathan was interrupted before he could answer. "Get ready . . . on three," an anonymous voice shouted out of the darkness. The room quieted. On the count of three the guests yelled "Surprise!" and the lights flipped on. Candace covered her mouth in shock. Her inquisitive nature could spoil a good surprise party. But tonight, she'd been totally unaware.

Keith made sure that the party planner had kept information regarding the party mum. The exact location wasn't even divulged until two hours before the party.

Candace cried. She buried her head in Keith's chest, happily embarrassed by all the people who had come out to celebrate her thirtieth birthday. Then she raised her head and flashed a big smile. "Thank you!" she yelled into the crowd, blowing kisses. She stood on her tiptoes to give her six-foot-nine husband a kiss for his thoughtfulness, and he bent down like a giraffe to accommodate her lips. They deep kissed and the crowd went crazy cheering them on, shouting and clapping.

Josette pushed her way through the crowd toward Candace.

"Hey girl, what's up?" Candace said, squeezing Josette, when Keith had released her. "Look at you. Think you cute, don't you?"

"Uh-huh. Tryin' to be like you," Josette said, inspecting Candace's red GiGi Hunter dress that clung to her body like skin. Her shoulder-length hair was pinned in the back and spiral curls framed her face. Keith kept his arm locked around Candace's waist. She was his and they were still in love. Josette missed those days with Patrick. She forced a smile again to chase away the thought and the heartache that came with it.

As soon as she saw Patrick approaching from across the room she backed away slowly. She was relieved that Priscilla had managed to hone in on her. She could avoid Patrick without being too obvious. Priscilla walked Josette over to a table where she introduced her to ten other people, including Greg Stone, her new man and manager.

"How is Pat doing, Jo?" Priscilla asked.

"He's fine," Josette said, sounding genuine. She had to be careful about what she said to Priscilla because Priscilla had no discretion when it came to other people's business. Josette didn't need a news bulletin put out tonight.

"So, when are you two going to have some babies?" Priscilla questioned.

"That's kind of on hold right now," Josette said, noticing that Patrick was walking in their direction. She thought of ways to escape.

"I'm going to tell Pat he better get on his j-o-b and put in some overtime. I'm ready for godbabies. And I've been waiting for *too* long," Priscilla said.

Josette laughed a phony, cocktail-party laugh. To her dismay, Patrick had gotten close enough in proximity for Priscilla to spot him. Priscilla screamed across the room, waving her hands at him.

"Pat, get over here!" Priscilla screeched. Her voice was so irritatingly loud and high-pitched that Josette wondered how she transformed into a songbird when she sang. She had lungs. Patrick looked as if he could hear Priscilla over the music and noise of the crowd. Disenchantment crossed his face. He looked at Priscilla, then at Josette.

Priscilla put her fists on her five-foot-ten hips. "Yeah, you. Get over here!"

He put on a mask of a face to disguise his disgust and walked over like life was *normal*. "Hey, lady," Patrick said, kissing Priscilla on the cheek.

Priscilla squeezed him. "Hi, sweetie," she said. "I was just over here asking your wife how come we don't have a bun in the oven yet. I'm ready for godbabies," Priscilla repeated for the second time.

Patrick smirked. He rubbed his goatee and waited for Josette to respond to Priscilla's statement.

Josette's smile inverted, but she was determined not to let him win. *I'm not going to take it there tonight, Pat. Sorry. Joke's on you.* "Baby," Josette said with all the sweetness she could muster, "I told P that we've kind of put that on hold for the time being." *Now. I'm not going to play your little game.*

"Hmph. I don't see why. The man is retired now. Y'all got plenty of time to make babies," Priscilla insisted.

"Well, Jo's career is really important to her. And her attention is a little *divided* these days."

A tension cloud rose. Josette looked away for a moment to see if there was someone nearby that she could talk to. Patrick was taunting her. He wanted to make it known that she was the *bad wife*. She couldn't look at him another second. *Honey brown. Armani slacks. Hand-knitted turtleneck. Rolex watch. Diamond-encrusted cross pendant by Jacob the Jeweler. Silver link bracelet. Gucci shoes. His own special smell.* She fought to keep herself together. When she looked back at Priscilla, she locked eyes with Candace, who rushed in for the save.

Candace reached out for Josette's hand and pulled her away from Priscilla and Patrick. "Hey, I need to borrow my girl for a moment," she said.

"No problem," Patrick said.

Candace walked Josette to an area of the room that was less crowded. "You okay?"

Josette inhaled and exhaled. "Yeah."

"You looked like you were about to pass out for a minute."

"Felt like it."

Candace fluffed a few of Josette's curls. "Well, just lay low. Nobody knows anything. And it's not like you and Pat are normally up under one another when you guys go out. People will think that you two are just mingling."

Candace was right. Josette re-committed herself to the decision she'd made earlier. Pat would have the power if she ran.

"What was he doing over there, anyway?"

"Priscilla called him."

"For what?"

Josette rolled her eyes. "Talking about *babies,* girl."

Candace unwrapped a mint. "That girl and her mouth. What did Pat say?"

"He just told her that I was concentrating on my career or something in his own little snide way. I don't think P picked up on it though."

"Good. How are you feeling?"

"Okay."

"You guys still haven't talked yet?"

"Nope. Nothing productive."

"Well, relax and try to have a good time. We'll do breakfast in the morning—make that lunch because I'll probably still be celebrating with my boo."

"I bet."

Candace left Josette standing near the live band. Josette pushed herself into a corner so that she didn't look like an idiot standing alone or bump into any of the couples who were dancing. She tapped her feet to the groove of the band. The music quieted before fading out completely. The lead guitar player announced that the band was going to take a break to give the DJ an opportunity to honor a song request from the birthday girl. And when the record started to spin, Josette wanted to faint. It was bad timing. *This can't be happening.* If she were on *Name That Tune,* she'd be a winner. But not now. This wasn't the time. *Why didn't Candace choose another song?* Josette felt hot tears coming. *Maybe if I don't listen to the words . . . Maybe I should have stayed home . . . Maybe I'm not ready for this yet.* The O'Jays' "Forever Mine" played on. *"Don't you ever think about leavin' . . ."* Josette stood still where she was, despite the fact that couples had swarmed all around, dancing close to one another. Some were reaffirming a commitment, others hoping to solidify one. *Shoulda stayed home. If I don't move, I won't cry. Just be still.*

"Hey, can we dance?" a rusty, all-too-familiar voice said in Josette's ear from behind.

What is this about? What is he doing? I'm not going to let him see me falling apart like this. "Sure," she said, turning around. She stared at him nervously, wondering where love went when it left people.

Careful not to dance too close to her, he said, "You look good."

"You do too," Josette said. He was still strikingly handsome.

"How's life been treating you lately?"

"Not so good."

"It gets better."

"Yeah, well, I'm not convinced."

"Well, are you convinced that I still love you? I mean, as a friend."

"I'm not sure."

"Well then, life really has been treating you bad."

"I thought you knew."

"What's going on with you?"

Josette swayed to the beat, feeling more comfortable with him. "Too much. Long story."

"I've got time."

Josette's eyes gave in to emotion. "Pat and I are separated."

"Oh, no. What happened?" he said, concerned.

"I messed up."

"Aw, Jo . . . Can you work it out?"

"I don't think so. I think this is the end of the road for us."

"I'm sorry to hear that, Jo," he said, moved by her tears. "I've always wanted you to be happy."

The tears flowed more steadily. "Well, happiness and *me* are not synonymous," Josette said.

"Hey, don't do that. Let's talk about something else. I didn't mean to get you all upset."

Josette wiped her tears and tried to pretend that life was going to be all right. But she knew she was lying to herself. "I really love Pat, Paco. I don't want to lose him like this."

Before Paco could respond to Josette's confession, the two of them were abruptly and forcefully separated by Patrick, who had grabbed Josette under her arm like a teenager caught at a party. "Excuse me. I'd like to talk to my *wife* for a minute!" Pat said, pulling Josette away, drawing an invisible line between him and Paco.

Josette's heart beat fast. *Two hotheads in the same space. Not good.* Paco respected Patrick. He'd always respected his and Josette's marriage. But he wasn't the type of man who liked to be fronted or ever backed down when he was challenged. Josette's eyes pleaded with Paco. *Don't.* She doubted if he could handle Patrick. *No. Paco, don't get embarrassed in your own establishment. Let it go.*

Paco looked at Josette and humbled himself. He threw his hands up in the air, staying on his side of the line. "No problem," he said.

Another tension cloud rolled in from the east. A storm was brewing. Patrick pulled Josette through the crowd and into the hallway where the restrooms were. "WHAT do you think you're doing?" he said with veins popping on his wrinkled forehead.

"What!"

"You heard me! How dare you disrespect me in public!" He turned his attention to a couple that was attempting to get to the restrooms. "Restrooms are closed!" Pat said, holding his huge arm straight out, blocking their path. The couple changed directions without a hassle.

"I was just dancing, Pat. Pac and I are friends. You don't have the right to—"

"WHATEVER!" Pat interrupted. "Let me tell you one thing, Josette MOSS," he continued with his finger pointed so deeply in Josette's face that he was only a half a millimeter from touching it, "I don't need my business in the street. Now if you want to go around acting like a—" He caught himself before the words came out and rephrased what he was feeling. "I'd appreciate it if you do what you do behind closed doors!" He walked away, leaving Josette standing in a frosty spot.

Josette didn't respond. It wasn't worth it. She stood still until she had enough energy to lean against the wall and cry. She pressed her cheek against the wall and dug her fingers into the crevices of the textured wallpaper, like she was holding on to someone who could keep her from falling.

"Jo, you okay?" Paco said, prying her off the wall. "What happened?"

Josette didn't answer. "I need to go home. I can't go back out there," Josette said, looking at the emergency exit at the end of the hallway.

Paco walked her in that direction. "Jo, what happened?" he asked again.

Josette shook her head. She couldn't bring herself to think about the word that her husband had almost called her.

"Hey, I'll talk to Pat. He knows I wouldn't disrespect him. We just played ball together at the club the other day."

"Pac, just leave it alone. It's not about you. It's about me."

"Jo, I feel bad. I'm sorry. Pat and I have been cool for the longest. He's never approached me like that," Paco said, taking a small set of keys out of his pocket and unlocking the emergency door so that the siren didn't go off.

"Forget it, Pac," Josette said, stepping out into the biting cold without her mink. She'd get it tomorrow. *Pac will return it in the morning.* She swallowed another dose of reality. *He might as well have said it. Is that what my husband thinks of me?*

Chapter Fourteen

Genevieve helped Sandy put her luggage into the trunk of the rental car. She'd flown all the way to Detroit just to meet with Sandy again. She couldn't help but notice how much Sandy was glowing. She looked mellow. She'd gotten a tan. Her skin was a deep golden brown, but she was dressed for the reunion with the Michigan winter. She was wearing a pair of stonewashed blue jeans, a crisp white shirt, red ankle boots, and a red leather jacket with a mink collar and lining. Her hair was pulled back into a ponytail. Sandy was so busy fumbling with her bags, she hadn't noticed a man standing with his wife, sneaking a peek at her.

"Thanks for letting me pick you up," Genevieve said.

Sandy slid her carry-on bag off of her shoulder and into the trunk. "You're welcome."

Genevieve closed the trunk. "Have you eaten?"

"Not since earlier. I could go for some waffles. I know the perfect place."

Sandy directed Genevieve to a place called The Flap Jack Shack. She called it a "hole-in-the-wall" joint. She admitted that it was located in a not-so-nice neighborhood, but assured Genevieve that the food was delicious. They seated themselves in a booth where the red cracked vinyl seat and back cushions had been covered with duct tape. Sandy watched for an adverse reaction from Genevieve, but there was none.

"So, how was your vacation? Did you have fun?" Genevieve questioned, as a waitress slid two menus on the table without speaking, and then walked briskly to the next booth.

"Oh, yes. Lamont is special. It was great just relaxing on the beach with him, you know. We went horseback riding, snorkeling, biking—it was fun. It's been a long time since I've had someone in my life."

"Sounds like he's an adventurous kind of guy."

Sandy closed her eyes momentarily and summoned a memory. "Very attentive," she said, returning her attention to Genevieve. Another waitress returned and took their orders.

"I'll have the Papa Pancakes," Genevieve said closing her menu. Buckwheat pancakes sounded scrumptious this mid-afternoon. The waitress looked at Sandy with a certain remembrance.

"Let me guess . . ." the waitress started. "You want The King's Omelet?"

Sandy smiled. "Yes, I do."

"How's your sister doing?" the waitress questioned politely.

"Fine. Just fine."

"Good. Tell her I said hello. I'll be right back with your fresh-squeezed orange juice," she said before prancing off.

While Genevieve gathered more details about Sandy's weeklong stay in the sun, Sandy received a call from Lamont.

"Good afternoon, Mr. Drake," Sandy said softly.

Genevieve watched the laidback princess transform into a giggly schoolgirl. She tried to imagine what Lamont was saying that made Sandy blush so. Continually, Sandy answered "yes" to whatever Lamont said on the other end. And she said it in such a submissive way that Genevieve's curiosity was aroused.

"I'm sorry. I won't be much longer," she whispered to Genevieve.

Genevieve smiled. "Go ahead." She was getting to know her better this way—just observing. Sandy was so vibrant and beautiful. Genevieve tried to take her in all at once. She took note of all of Sandy's idiosyncrasies, like the way she twisted her lips playfully, and the way the blinks of her eyes lasted a split second longer than normal. Genevieve wondered about Lamont. *He should be honored to have her attention this way. I wonder if he knows what a jewel he has.* It was obvious that Sandy was into him. Genevieve hoped the thrill was mutual.

"I love you too," Sandy said softly. She closed her cell phone. "That was Lamont," she said to Genevieve.

Genevieve could count every last one of Sandy's teeth. She listened while Sandy talked about her trip and how her relationship with Lamont had blossomed since they'd met in Chicago. "I'm glad he makes you happy," Genevieve said.

"He does," Sandy said resting her elbows on the table. The rickety contraption wavered. "Oops," she laughed. "May not be the Whitney, but the food is the best."

Minutes later, the waitress placed their meals on the table. Genevieve buttered her pancakes and poured on a good helping of syrup. She took a bite and swallowed.

"Mmm . . . delicious. Quiet as it's kept, this kind of place is the best place to get a good meal—contrary to popular belief."

"Gotta appreciate the 'hood,'" Sandy said, eyeing the meager-looking establishment. It could have used a new paint job and a new ceiling. The once-white ceiling tiles were stained with grease, dirt, and brown water spots where the roof leaked when it rained. And the floor had missing tiles that could have been replaced. That, however, didn't seem to bother any of the patrons. The small eatery was filled with a variety of customers, some run-of-the-mill folk, and some suited businessmen who had found a cheap treasure.

"What's it been, about three months with you and Lamont?"

"Yep," Sandy nodded. It seemed longer than that. They were using the "L" word already. There'd been no *major* relationship discussions other than Lamont promising Sandy that exclusivity was something that would be brought to the table when the time was right, so that there would be no guessing—if they got to that point. For now, they'd both agreed to enjoy each other's company as friends—special friends.

"You really like him?"

"Yes, I do. He's sweet. Very attentive. He's *fine*," Sandy smiled. "He's really articulate and intelligent. He's a go-getter. And he treats me like an absolute queen. So yes, I have strong feelings for him."

Genevieve laughed at the puppy-love look on Sandy's face. "Can I just be myself and say something without you being offended?"

Sandy's smiled disappeared. "Sure," she said after hesitating.

"I can just feel the energy you have for him. And I think it's wonderful. But you know as a Christian woman you have to be careful about spending that kind of time alone with someone that you're so drawn to. Emotions can get out of control, and I know from our first meeting that you don't want to displease God."

Sandy was noticeably aggravated by the unwanted advice from the mother who had abandoned her and left her rearing to someone else. The air had grown cold in a matter of seconds. "I haven't been to bed with him—if that's what you're implying, Genevieve. I was saved *before* you came back in my life, remember?"

Genevieve recoiled. "I'm sorry. I know that you're a grown woman. I just sense something in the way that you say his name even," she smiled. "Please don't be angry."

"Look, Lamont and I have already talked about the celibacy 'issue.' He's okay with it. So there's no problem. We spend good quality time with each other. We're both satisfied with that."

"Okay," Genevieve retreated. She didn't want this to sour because of her intuition. "Sandy, you are a beautiful gift from God. I just hope Lamont knows that. That's all."

"Thank you. He does," Sandy said, remembering how much of a gentleman Lamont had been in Jamaica. She'd been hesitant about staying with him at first, but he'd proven himself to be worthy of her trust. And she'd shared an experience with him that caused her to open her heart more.

She'd been up one night too cranked up to sleep. It was past midnight, but the exhilaration of being surrounded by luxury in the six bedroom waterfront villa, along with the emotional intimacy she'd shared with Lamont over the past few days, had her wide awake and tightly wound. Lamont and Brian had invited a few business associates and their wives to spend a couple of days celebrating with them, but Lamont's attention had not been diverted away from Sandy. He'd gone out of his way to make her feel comfortable and make sure that she enjoyed her time with *him*. The other couples left and Lamont had spent the entire day with her, lounging around, talking, and building emotional bridges. Not even the sensual sound of Marvin Gaye pleading to his "Distant Lover" piping through her iPod, had been able to lullaby her that night. She was on an adrenaline high. Love was invading her heart, filling a four-year vacancy. It was the feeling couples always remembered after their love had aged. It gave them a reference point to get back to when love needed to be reignited.

Sandy had gone down to the kitchen to covet another slice of rum cake. She was still listening to the iPod that she'd clipped onto her pajama pants, while she stood looking out at the picturesque waterfront, eating cake with her hands, when she felt a ghoulishly frightening fire shoot up her spine. Her yelp would have been amplified if her mouth hadn't been full of cake. Lamont had walked up behind her unexpectedly and put his hands on her shoulder to get her attention. But he nearly caused her a heart-attack instead.

"Shh…" he said turning her to face him, with a finger over his lips.

Sandy's eyes were plate saucers. She pulled her earphones off. "Whoa… you trying to scare me to death?" she whispered, catching her breath.

"No. I didn't mean to scare you, baby. I'm sorry," he admitted with that boyish, devilish grin on his face that Sandy hated to love.

"What's funny?" Sandy said poking him in the chest with her finger.

"You were scared out of your mind, baby. But you didn't drop that cake."

She cracked a reluctant smile. "You make me sick. You know that?"

"That cake must be awfully good, baby."

"It is," Sandy said still holding on to a quarter of a slice.

"Give me some," Lamont said taking Sandy's hand, leading it to his mouth. She fed the slice to him and he sucked the remainder off of her fingers before kissing her. He hugged her. "You can't sleep or just having a midnight snack-attack?"

"Both."

"Same here," he said. "Wow! You smell good. What is that?"

"It's called Heavenly—by Victoria Secret."

He buried his nose in the crook of her neck and inhaled again. "That stuff is *wicked*, baby."

Sandy's heart thumped. She melted like wax when he was close to her.

Lamont pulled back and cupped Sandy's face in his hands. "You got me on another planet, woman. You know that? You are simply amazing. Man, I'm lucky—blessed. But if I don't get any sleep tonight, I ain't gon' be no good at golf in the morning, and Brian will brag all day long."

"I guess its time for you to go back to bed then."

"I can't sleep without you…come to bed with me." His request was spoken calmly, directly.

Sandy had fixed her mouth to protest. Had he tricked her into coming to Jamaica on the pretense of spending a *friendly* vacation with him, while he'd plotted some diabolical plan to get her in bed? She was disappointed. "Lamont, I thought you understood—"

"Wait, baby—hear me out first. Just listen," he said, cupping her face in his hands again. "I'm not asking you to have *sex* with me. I just want to hold you—that's all—I swear. I will *not* get out of line. I'm not playing games, Sandy. I just want to hold you—just sleep next to you. That's all… please. If I do *anything* that makes you feel uncomfortable at any time, I'll put you on a plane back home—I swear. I'm not trying to violate you or anything that you believe in. You can go put on some extra clothes if you want to," he smiled. "But please, just trust me, baby."

It wasn't a wise move to make—it was careless even. Not spiritually astute at all. Temptation to the tenth power. It could have gotten her into a mess she would have regretted later. But she believed him—trusted him. And it was beautiful. Lamont had slept spooned behind her with his arm around her waist and his hands locked in hers—a position he did not deviate from the entire time. The scent of her was all that he needed to let his guard down. He shrugged off his "player rules" and allowed his heart to do the talking. She'd pulled his heart string. He spoke into her soft hair that she'd freed from her ponytail at his request. "I want to be the best man I can for you, Sandy. I want to love you like you deserve to be loved," he said. Those simple words had given her so much hope. She'd fallen asleep on that profession. Lamont awakened her in the morning before anyone else got up, so that she could return to her own room without having to feel ashamed if Brian or Stacie saw her leaving his room. She'd found a note on her pillow:

That was one of the most beautiful times I've had in my life.

Love, Lamont

The thought of that night was still precious. Sandy didn't need Genevieve's advice, because Genevieve didn't know anything about Lamont. She derailed from that conversation altogether. "I want to know about our father," she said to Genevieve.

Genevieve grimaced. Hardly any of her memories of Lou were good. It had begun innocently, with delicate sprinkles of infatuation. Genevieve was sixteen when she met Lou Stiles while working at Checker drugstore after school. He was tall and slender with jet black skin. He wore his blackness like a banner, proud of his dark hue and the kinky afro he sported. He had a self-assured gait that mirrored his street bravado and his slickness. He had a way with women.

Lou began his quest for Genevieve the first time he saw her behind the counter with her doe eyes and cappuccino skin, paying close attention as Edna Mae trained her on the cash register. She was beautifully innocent, with almost every inch of her body hidden by a long black skirt and button-up sweater that had left him with only imaginings.

"The weather's getting a little nippy, huh?" Lou said, making small talk with Genevieve as she rang up his order under Edna Mae's watchful eye.

"Always be nice and polite to your customers," Edna Mae whispered to Genevieve. "You gotta make eye contact and smile—and keep your eyes on the register at the same time."

"Yes ma'am," Genevieve affirmed quietly before making eye contact with Lou again. "Yes, sir, the weather has gotten a bit colder in the last few days," she smiled.

"That's right . . . good," Edna nodded, watching Genevieve successfully press the right keys on the register and give Lou the correct change while keeping an easygoing smile on her face.

The way Lou stared at Genevieve made her blush on the inside. Edna Mae hadn't noticed, but Lou gave Genevieve a penetrating look that she felt like tremors of an earthquake. Genevieve's palms moistened. She rubbed them gently on her skirt, and toyed with the buttons on her wool sweater.

Lou took the change from Genevieve, holding the stare that made her feel naked. "Have a nice evening, *beautiful*," he said before walking away from the counter.

Genevieve watched his cool stride, intrigued by his charisma. He was dressed in a pair of black polyester pants, a multi-print black and white polyester shirt, a pair of black and white Stacey Adams, and a three-quarter-length black leather jacket. He had a weekly routine of coming into the drugstore to pick up the local newspapers and purchase cigarettes. And after seeing Genevieve for the first time, he made it his business to find out her work schedule. He accomplished this simply by slipping

Edna Mae a ten-dollar bill. He made a point to stop by the drugstore on the days Genevieve worked.

Lou was the first person Genevieve could recall who had ever taken a genuine interest in her. He was twenty-two years old—six years Genevieve's senior—but he spoke to her as if she were a woman. Her maturity impressed him, but her innocence and shyness excited him in a carnal way. He charmed her by asking her opinion about the happenings that were going on in the city or about articles he'd read in the newspaper. And he listened to her responses as if she were the authority on the subject matters they discussed. He stood in front of Genevieve's register so attentively, looking her right in the eyes as she spoke, complimenting her on how articulate she was for a girl just sixteen years old.

Genevieve was drawn to Lou's handsomeness—but drawn even more to the way he made her heart lift when he spoke her name, and the gentleness with which he talked to her. It seemed to Genevieve that Lou noticed everything about her. If she wore her hair in a different style, he commented on it, telling her how becoming it was on her. He told her that she was a beautiful *woman*. Before she met him, she hadn't allowed herself to *feel* beautiful. Living with Grace, she'd felt everything but beautiful. But Lou apprehended Genevieve with his low, flattering voice. His very presence ignited her.

He earned her trust over lunch dates and stolen moments. She opened herself to him slowly, sharing her private thoughts and her dreams. She looked forward to the moments when she was the center of Lou's attention—when he would hold her hand and smile that smile of his that mesmerized her and made her feel like she was loved. Genevieve played a dangerous game, sneaking off with Lou when she had half-days at school, lying to Grace, telling her that she was at the library studying. And yet, to be with him, seemed every bit worth the risk.

Lou earned a living working on the assembly line. He had his own apartment on the northwest side. But Genevieve was more impressed that he had his own car. It was a white, '74 Chevy Impala. It was two years old, but it still looked and smelled brand new. When he drove it, he exuded confidence and control. He leaned ever so coolly with one hand resting on the wheel, and the other clasped inside Genevieve's. She fell in love watching him drive—watching his power. Sometimes she snuck off with him after school and he took her for long rides. She would stretch her neck out of the window and allow the wind to blow against her face. She felt free of Grace. Free of the abuse she'd suffered since she was a small child. She thought about all the possibilities that life could bring her with Lou. She loved being with him. She loved him.

Grace had stripped Genevieve of feeling over the years. She'd made her withdrawn and numb. The unwarranted beatings and verbal lashings had broken Genevieve's spirit and forced her into a self-protective shell that was encompassed by the memories of being locked in closets, made to go days at a time without food, and convinced that she was destined for hell. But Lou chipped away at that shell until it relinquished its precious pearl.

Initially, Genevieve was afraid of what Grace would do if she found out. But that fear began to subside when she and Lou became intimate. She felt empowered being with him that way. Grace didn't matter to her then. All the fear and punishment that Grace had controlled her with evaporated in the space between her and the man who had become her lifeline. Genevieve longed for that feeling of being connected to someone—of being needed by someone. She *needed* to be with Lou more than she understood the danger of it.

When Grace threw Genevieve out, Lou took her in that same night. Grace had been rigid and punishing, isolating Genevieve, not allowing her to have friends. Genevieve saw Lou as a savior. He'd taken her in when she needed someone. But the beatings and brutality followed Genevieve. Lou's gentleness and tenderness vanished just as quickly as their relationship had started. He was just as controlling and abusive as Grace had been.

Lou made sixteen-year-old Genevieve wish that she had never been so trusting of a stranger. In a short period of time, the precious creature she once anticipated seeing every day had turned into a monster. But her naïveté and fear kept her in bondage. Between him and Grace, Lou was the lesser of the two evils.

His transformation had started with harsh words, escalating to pushes and shoves—slaps and punches. He imprisoned Genevieve in his apartment, not allowing her to go anywhere without him. The physical violence, like the black eyes and the bruised ribs, caused her to fear him even more than she had feared Grace. Genevieve spent many nights with sprains and bruises that she had earned from "offending" Lou.

Lou's rancor was not limited to the confines of the apartment he jailed Genevieve in. Once, he had taken her to a movie, and a young male attendant's eyes lingered on Genevieve as she handed him her ticket stub. In a jealous rage, Lou backhanded her right in the theater lobby, accusing her of flirting. Genevieve stood in the middle of the floor with her head swirling, shocked and embarrassed—humiliated by what had just happened to her. When Lou turned to see her tears, he shoved her toward the restroom, complaining that she was embarrassing *him*.

Genevieve thought that the whole nightmare was over, until they returned to Lou's apartment. He started in on her again about being disrespectful—this time after having had way too many beers. He took off his thick leather belt and whipped Genevieve with the buckle end until he had tired of hitting her. She lay on the floor in the bedroom crying until she couldn't feel the emotional or physical pain. And Lou put those beatings on Genevieve at will—even while she carried his child. Two years and two children later, Lou casually disposed of an eighteen-year-old Genevieve without a second thought—like she was trash.

"I haven't seen him since," Genevieve said, pushing the memory back. "Your father was abusive. And your grandmother was too. But that was all I knew. I was just a young girl."

Sandy reflected on Genevieve's words before she spoke. "Is that what caused you to use drugs?"

"Partially. I had experienced so much hurt, I just needed to find a way to numb the pain—before I knew that God could erase it all."

Sandy looked at Genevieve with empathy. "I'm so sorry that you had to go through all of that. When Jo and I were kids you were like a mystery to us. You never answered any of our questions when we asked about your childhood. In my heart, I knew that you loved us . . . but you changed. It seemed like I woke up one day and you were someone else . . ." Sandy's voice trailed off. She closed her eyes to keep the tears from coming. The memory of Genevieve back then was still crushing.

"I was someone else, Sandy. I was trying to find my way and didn't have a clue as to where to start. So I looked outside of myself—outside of God. I wish I could go back and undo every single thing, but I can't."

"I felt so empty. It was like you didn't love us enough to stay clean."

"Addiction is powerful, Cassandra. It isn't just a matter of being clean for those you love. It is about loving yourself enough to have the will to stop. I didn't have that then. That is where I was at that point in my life."

"But you never came back for us when you got off drugs. Why?"

That question sank into Genevieve's heart and immobilized it. She'd been caught off guard this time. She'd been prepared for it at their first meeting. But today she wasn't ready. She sighed heavily. "Sandy, I'm not sure you are going to understand my answer. I'm not even sure if I understand my answer." Genevieve rescued a tear in the corner of her eye with her forefinger.

Sandy met Genevieve's eyes with compassion. "I need to know."

"You need to know that I pained over the decision not to *interfere* with your lives. My rights as a mother were gone . . . I thought it was the best thing to do—just let everyone start over."

Sandy couldn't quiet her anger. "How do you think a child starts over without her mother, knowing that she's out there somewhere? Did it ever dawn on you that maybe you should have gotten in touch with your children—the ones *you* birthed!"

"Cassandra, I understand your hurt, but—"

Sandy's voice continued to elevate. "Do you?"

"Cassandra, let's not do this right here," Genevieve said in a gentle but undaunted tone. She glanced at the booth next to them where four businessmen were watching her and Cassandra's exchange. Genevieve reached into her purse, pulled out a fifty dollar bill, and laid it on the table. She grabbed her coat and purse off of the seat. "Let's go," she ordered Sandy. The sound of Genevieve's heeled boots against the tiled floor was a legion of soldiers marching. She pushed the fingerprinted glass door open, stepped out into the cold, and inhaled. She spun around as soon as she could feel Sandy behind her. She let loose the words she'd suppressed back in the diner. "You listen to me, young lady. I admit who I was—what I was. I admit that I did not come back for my children. I did what I thought was best at the time. You asked me why. I told you why. Now you grow up and accept what you asked for! Then let it go!"

"Are you serious? What? You think it's that easy!"

"Do you think it was easy to be beaten and raped? To be homeless? To be so far gone that all you live for is getting high? To hate yourself so much that you try to kill yourself? Let it go! I did!"

"I wish it were that easy!"

"You're the only one holding yourself back. All we have is right now. We can build something or tear it down before we start. It's up to you. But I'm not going to be beaten and badgered about my past because I can't go back!"

God softened Sandy's heart. "I'm sorry."

Genevieve's tears revealed her frustration. "Let's just get to know who we are right now. Can we just try to do that today? I don't think God has brought us this far for nothing."

Sandy wondered what it all meant—if her life would ever be normal. The only constant she had was God.

Chapter Fifteen

Sandy sipped eggnog while she watched Lamont wrestle with his nephews. The boys yelled and laughed simultaneously as Lamont lay across both of them, pinning them to the floor. Sandy imagined him frolicking with *their children*. She imagined holidays, and birthday parties, and family barbecues.

The live, seven-foot Blue Spruce was an exceptional department store display with neat gold bows and beaded gold garland. White lights blinked intermittently, giving it a celestial glow. Lavishly wrapped gifts topped with satin, velour, and silk ribbons overflowed from the base of the tree. Others were stacked in corners on either side of the great room. Sandy was still astonished that Lamont had invited her to spend Christmas Eve and Christmas at his parents' one hundred acre Indiana estate. Earlier that day the two of them had walked one of the equestrian trails and played in the snow like children, making angels and throwing snowballs at each other. She felt at home there.

She'd first met his parents at their fortieth wedding anniversary party that Lamont and Brian had thrown for them a week before Thanksgiving. Lamont's mother, Theresa, had acted as if Lamont had walked in with Halle Berry the way she fussed over Sandy. Theresa spent half the night interviewing the woman that her son was so enchanted with that he'd brought her with him to a *family* affair. She couldn't remember the last time she'd met one of Lamont's women. She knew, of course, that he'd had many of them over the years—he had his father's genes. But she surmised that he hadn't come across one who was *worthy* of being brought home—until Sandy. Lamont solidified his mother's intuition that Sandy was *the one* for him, simply because of the metamorphosis that took place in him while he was in her company.

Theresa had always considered him to be dedicatedly serious. But with Sandy, Lamont was humorous, easygoing, and gentle—not the rigid businessman his father had trained him and his brother to be. Theresa had watched Sandy and Lamont dance and remembered what it was like to fall in love. There was no question that this was *different.* Lamont rarely left Sandy's side all night during the party. And when he had, it had been to dote on her—like when he'd ordered one of the waiters to *find* some Cool Whip just because Sandy preferred that on her strawberry cheesecake, as opposed to the brand the hotel had used. Even Lamont's father, Winston, had a hard time getting him away from Sandy that night. Lamont playfully hassled Winston when he'd asked Sandy for a dance. From that first meeting, Winston wagered a bet with Theresa that Sandy would be their new daughter-in-law. There was something about her that tamed the man Winston raised. Every man needed a woman like that.

Sandy was overjoyed to be spending yet another holiday with Lamont. He had warned her during their first few phone calls not to take it personally if she didn't meet his parents for a while. He'd said that dating was a *private* issue for him. He didn't take every woman he dated home to meet his family. He'd said that if and when she had the opportunity to do so, she'd know that their relationship was progressing to *another level*. Sandy had been honored to attend the Drakes' anniversary party and Thanksgiving dinner. But she was even more honored to be spending Christmas Eve with them. It was a lovers' holiday—a family holiday.

"Cassandra, come on in here and help me with these cookies," Theresa called from the kitchen. Theresa wiped sweat from her brow with her apron corner. Her fair skin was smooth. The heat in the kitchen had moistened her black hair, deepening her natural waves, which looked sexy in a classic bob. Her hips had widened over the years, but Theresa had a lovely shape. It was plain to see why Winston had fallen in love with her.

Sandy rose from the sofa and walked into the kitchen. She watched Theresa pull three cookie sheets from the convection oven. Theresa handed her an apron from one of the drawers. "You can help me decorate these holiday cookies when they cool. Do whatever you want to them. There's glitter and sprinkles on the counter. The decorating icing is in the cabinet. And I'll put these chocolate chip cookies on top of the stove for Lamont—they're his favorite."

"May I sample one? I love chocolate chip cookies when they're hot, fresh out of the oven."

Theresa scooped three cookies off of a cookie sheet and placed them on a plate. "So does somebody else," she said, motioning toward Lamont, who had walked in. He stood behind Sandy. "The boys giving you a break, Monty?" she said, smiling at Lamont.

"Yeah, they went out to the horse stables with dad."

"Your father and those horses."

"You know he's got to go out there and check on his babies."

"Sandy, did you know that my husband has a state-of-the-art, heated stable for his *babies?* Complete with plasma screen televisions and music? I swear he pays more attention to those horses than he does me," Theresa complained.

"Never that, Mommy," Lamont said, taking a cookie off of the plate that Sandy was holding like a prized possession. He put it in his mouth and savored it, sucking in cool air at the same time. "Mmm . . . you taking notes, baby? Mommy has spoiled me with these things. Homemade. None of that modern-woman, boxed stuff. My wife has got to know how to bake these."

Theresa raised an eyebrow at that word. *Wife.* Lamont wrapped his arms around Sandy's waist, pulled her closer to him, and kissed her softly on the neck.

Sandy felt waves. It moved her that he was so affectionate—even the way he and Brian still called their mother "Mommy." It wasn't just a commonplace title. It had become her nickname. It showed Lamont's soft side. The strong businessman wasn't embarrassed by the nickname that even his father addressed Theresa by. Sandy thought it was cute. "I think I could be good with a little practice," she said, looking up at Lamont lovingly. "I wouldn't want to deny you these—they are delicious."

Lamont brushed his lips gently across Sandy's ear and whispered, "So are you."

Sandy wondered if Theresa could see the heat rising from her body.

Theresa studied them and raised another eyebrow at Lamont. Would she have another daughter-in-law soon? And maybe a granddaughter this time? She hadn't seen Lamont act this way with anyone, let alone be so brazen with his public display of affection.

Brian buzzed in on the intercom. "Mont, what are the boys doing?"

Lamont walked over to the wall and pushed the talk button on the black box. "They went out to the stables with dad."

"What are Stacie and Sandy doing?"

"Stacie ran out to get more eggnog. Sandy's right here in the kitchen with me and Mommy."

"Great. Sandy, come on up here. I need a woman's opinion on something while Stacie's out."

"Okay," Sandy said toward the intercom.

Theresa rolled her eyes. "He does the same thing every year—with his last-minute self. He should have been done choosing *and* wrapping gifts."

Brian's reputation made Sandy hesitant about being alone with him. Lamont read her. "I'll be right up, baby," he said.

When Sandy was out of earshot, Theresa walked up close to Lamont. "I've never seen you carry on like this before."

"What are you talking about, *Theresa?*" Lamont teased.

"Don't get slapped, boy."

Lamont laughed. "I'm just kidding, Mommy."

"I know. But seriously, what's going on? Should I be looking for a new dress?"

Lamont leaned against the wall, smiling at his mother. "A dress for what?"

"For a wedding."

Lamont laughed again. "It's only been a few months. Look at you. What are you trying to do, get rid of me? What? You don't want to vacation with me anymore?"

"No and yes. I want to know what's going on. You seem so . . ."

"Happy?"

Theresa nodded. "Yes."

"Well, Sandy is definitely special. And she is *definitely* wife material. I mean, a brother would have to be an unadulterated fool to let a woman like her get by him."

"Well, don't you be the *unadulterated fool* and mess it up."

"Mess it up?"

"Yes," Theresa said emphatically. "I know men. I married one and raised two. And sometimes you all just don't think straight. You feel yourself falling in love, get scared of that commitment, and mess things up. Sandy seems like such a sweet girl."

"I hear you. But I ain't tryin' to mess it up. Believe that."

"Don't. When you find something special, you don't need to go looking for anything else—just put your energy into the good thing you've found so that you can make it even better."

"I'm not looking for anyone else, Mommy."

"I do read those silly celebrity magazines sometimes, you know."

Lamont looked surprised. "What are you talking about?"

"I've seen you a few times in the 'Who's Dating Who?' section of a certain magazine."

"Mommy, *whoever* you saw me with is old, old news."

"Yeah, well, keep it that way, because I wasn't impressed. Those kinds of women may be pleasurable in bed, but they don't have what it takes to be a good wife and raise a family. Don't be like your father in that respect."

"Mommy . . ."

Theresa placed her fingertips over Lamont's lips. "Lamont, I'm not stupid. I am well aware of *all* the things that have happened outside of my marriage. I was the good wife. I stayed. I stayed for you and your brother. And I stayed because I chose to. But if I had to do it all over again

. . . I don't know. I love your father dearly, but . . ." Theresa paused. "All I'm saying is that the thrill of having a 'trophy woman' will fade. A real woman is going to stand by you until one of you takes your last breath. I believe that Sandy is that kind of woman. I just have a gut feeling."

Lamont read the unspoken words between the lines. He looked at his mother with sincerity. "Mommy, I hear you, and I'm *listening*. Okay?" He kissed Theresa on her cheek. "Let me go check on Sandy."

"I love you," Theresa said.

Lamont held his mother's hand. "I love you." He looked up and saw Sandy strolling back into the kitchen. "Wow, that was quick," he said.

Sandy looked relaxed, which let Lamont know that all had gone well with Brian. "I hope you didn't eat all the cookies up, Lamont," she said.

"Yep, I ate them all. You have to wait on the next batch."

Sandy scrunched her face. "You didn't!"

"I'm joking, baby. I left you some."

"I was going to kill you."

"Ooh, hurt me, baby!"

Sandy shook her head. "You are so bad."

"I know."

Theresa took in their love play, fully persuaded that she was going to have another addition to the family soon. Lamont and Sandy slipped away to the family's walnut paneled library where they lounged on Theresa's prized swing sofa that hung in the center of the room from exposed ceiling beams, which matched the dramatic paneling on the walls. An oversized cobblestone fireplace that made Sandy think of a castle, took up half the width of the west wall. The room was enclosed on the north and south by window walls that framed the expansive area outside. Lamont had brought in a bottle of Sandy's favorite sparkling apple cider and two champagne flutes. He lit the fireplace, filled their glasses, and snuggled up close to Sandy on the sofa. They rocked slowly back and forth, with the deep cushions of the sofa enveloping them like body gloves, pushing them closer together as they sank into the fabric.

Lamont gently traced Sandy's face with his fingertips. "You know, I've really enjoyed having you here."

"Me too. This is one of the best holidays I've had in a long while."

Lamont considered his next sentence carefully, pausing to gather his thoughts. "You know, I'm usually not at a loss for words . . ."

"What is it?" Sandy asked.

"You—this is wild. I feel like a young buck again. I think about you all the time. I love being around you. Love the way you smile. Love the way you talk. Love the way you smell. Love the way you feel when I hold you. I love everything about you, Sandy."

Blood rushed from the tips of her toes, through her veins, to her cheeks that blushed red. "I feel the same way about you," she said full of butterflies.

Lamont took her hand in his. "I know we agreed to put commitment on hold until we knew where we were going with this. And I told you that I wasn't even going to play that game without being *sure* that's what I wanted to do. But with you…I just feel like it's time to take this to the next level. I'm not seeing anyone else. And I don't want you seeing anyone else either. I think you and I have got what it takes to build a future together. I want to cultivate that. I want you to be my lady." His old-fashioned courtship request was as sweet as honey.

Sandy laced her arms around his neck, just as giddy and excited as she would have been if he had popped *the question*. "I would love to, baby."

Lamont smiled. "Good. 'Cause I don't take 'no' well." He kissed Sandy deeply, savoring the taste of cider.

New Year's Eve was grand, with sparkling lights and exquisite holiday decorations in the Cobo Hall Riverfront Ballroom. The view of the river was breathtaking. The Black Businessmen's Association held their annual black-tie affair honoring the muscles of business and industry. Tonight, Lamont and Brian were being honored for their contributions to urban communities and their college mentoring project that gave black students an opportunity to "earn and learn" at Vision Marketing. Lamont was impeccably dressed for the occasion in a black Gucci tuxedo, and Sandy was the perfect accompaniment, dressed in a black, velvet, Richard Tyler gown that clung to her curves. It was just one of the gifts that Lamont had spoiled her with on Christmas. He loved her in black. And she was beautifully stunning in it. Her hair was pinned up loosely, with a few tresses dangling, exposing the lovely two-carat diamond studs from Tiffany that Lamont had also given her on Christmas. The two of them were the perfect pair for a perfect evening.

Sandy watched Lamont mingle with the go-getters—all the men and women who were keeping the country running with high-powered deals and investments. They were people who were not only successful, but who were making a difference by giving back to their communities. She watched him ease in and out of conversations, making connections that would lead to new business deals. Sandy assimilated into that high-powered world easily, being the enviable arm piece that every successful man desired.

The sultry sound of Anita Baker's "You're the Best Thing Yet" filled the room as Lamont held Sandy lovingly in his arms, dancing close.

Sandy found herself floating once again on a Lamont Drake cloud. She'd found that safe spot that she'd been longing for. Being in Lamont's arms felt like being wrapped in a security blanket. She could be this way with him forever.

They danced until well after two-thirty a.m. before finally leaving the BBMA gala and heading to Sandy's condo. Josette was away babysitting Damon Jr., freeing Faye and Damon to enjoy hosting the Duncan Medical Center's New Year's Eve Party. Still elated from the energy of the festivities, Lamont and Sandy turned on the satellite radio and tuned it to a slow-jams station. They continued to slow dance in the middle of the family room with the lights dimly lit. Sandy laid her head on Lamont's chest. He loosened her hair and worked his fingers through it, massaging her scalp soothingly.

Sandy cooed. "Mmm . . . that feels nice."

Lamont's voice was low and easy. "Really?"

"Yes," she said, floating.

"I have a confession to make."

Sandy looked up at him and searched his eyes. "Yes?"

"I'm in love," he said, swaying her to Luther's "Don't You Know." "I'm ready for a wife like you."

"So soon?"

"It feels like forever."

"It does to me too. I haven't felt this way in a long time," Sandy said.

Lamont's low and easy baritone had dropped an octave. "Show me," he said into Sandy's ear before scorching her with a kiss that was like kerosene on an open flame. Eagerly his hands roamed her body with wanting, caressing her soft flesh. Deep kissing alone would not suffice tonight. No. Tonight he was going to have what he'd been waiting for. His anticipation had mounted, and it was going to be satisfied.

Sandy was dizzy with passion. She tried to will herself not to get lost in it. She repeated the Shulamite girl's warning in her mind. *I charge you, O daughters of Jerusalem, that ye stir not up nor awake my love until he please.* She had prayed hard about *this* all day long. She'd known since morning that tonight would be her greatest challenge. She'd felt it in her spirit. Things were so perfect. And Lamont was such a loving man—so giving. They'd bonded so much since they met. They were right for one another. She wanted to express to him what he'd done for her since he'd come into her life. How he'd given her more motivation to be beautiful. The motivation and security to open her heart again. She wanted to give back to him that feeling she got every time she heard his voice. Every time he said something sweet. Every time he'd treated her like she was the only thing that mattered to him. But she heard that inner voice say, *"No."* Sandy pulled back gently. "Lamont . . . I can't."

Lamont covered Sandy's ear with his lips and moaned. "Baby, I *need* you tonight. . ." His baritone was persuasive, rattling Sandy in a sensual way. He eased his lips from her ear to her neck to her mouth again, kissing her softly—deliberately, preventing her from backing away from the emotions that had her re-thinking the commitment she'd made to the Lord. The more Lamont felt her easing back, the stronger he held her, tightening his hold on her like a boa constrictor, confining her to space where there were no boundaries between them.

Sandy fought to keep her prayer from dissolving, to keep from falling into that bottomless pit. And Lamont fought harder against her reasoning. He used that kiss as a weapon to obliterate her righteousness—her defense. His kiss was a fiery dart that ignited her, persuading her to forget about her commitment—forget about celibacy. Forget about God. It had been so long. She fought with her own thoughts. She painted intimate images of the two of them in her mind. She wanted to yield to them. *"No."* She heard that voice again and pulled free.

Breathlessly she said, "I'm sorry . . . I can't." Shaking, she crossed her arms over her chest and shook her head to free the thoughts that kept tempting her. She dropped her head and pressed her chin to her chest.

Lamont lifted her chin with his fingertips. "Sandy, baby, I love you. I'm not going anywhere. It's just me and you, remember?"

"It's not about that, Mont. It's about God."

"Sandy, it's not like you're seeing a bunch of different men. It's just me, baby—right?"

Sandy nodded reluctantly. "Yes."

"We've got something special. You're *my lady*. I want to make love to my lady. It's natural, baby."

"It's not to God."

"Come sit down," Lamont said pulling her over to the sofa. "What are you saying? I'm never going to be able to touch you—make love to you?"

Sandy switched on the lamp. "No . . . I'm saying that I can't share that part of myself with you unless we're married. That's all."

Lamont rubbed his temples. "Sandy, have I once pressed you for sex since we've been dating?"

"No."

"And haven't I treated you like a woman is supposed to be treated?"

"Yes."

"Because I've been busting my behind trying to let you know that I'm into *you*. I work my business schedule around you, baby—devote every weekend to you, and some weekdays if I'm able to fly into the city. The trips, the shopping sprees, the jewelry—all of that has been to show you how I feel and let you know that our relationship is not about sex."

"I know that. I haven't taken any of that for granted. But I told you, I made a commitment to the Lord."

Lamont reasoned with her. "Baby, making love is beautiful and *natural* for two people who feel the way we do about one another."

Sandy shook her head. "No, Mont. The Word says in marriage only. I can't compromise on that."

"I told you that we're headed in that direction, baby. Do you think I would have invited you out to my parents' for Thanksgiving—Christmas, if I didn't think this was real?"

"No. Mont . . . please . . . don't. Let's not fight about this. We're not going to agree."

"I'm not fighting, Sandy. I'm just trying to understand why you don't want to make love to me."

"I would love to make love to you, Mont, trust me. I'm just making a *choice* not to so that I can please God. Please try and understand that." Sandy stood. "My den has a let-out bed. I prepared it for you this *morning.*" She turned around and walked up the stairs without another word. Lamont sat simmering. He was frustrated in the worst way.

Upstairs, Sandy closed her bedroom door and prayed. "Thank You Lord for keeping me. Thank You for Your strength. Help me to stand strong, that I might please You with my actions." When she climbed in bed, she cried herself to sleep. The warring of the Spirit and flesh had been exhausting.

Chapter Sixteen

Josette sat on the edge of the bed with the phone in her palm. Her head hurt from the anxiety her decision had caused. She inhaled deeply and released her breath slowly before dialing the numbers. She listened to the rings and waited for that voice to answer, hoping it wasn't the recorded one this time.

"Pat, I love you. I don't want to lose you. I want our marriage," she said as soon as he picked up the phone.

His voice came back cold and indifferent. "What happened, Jo? Did he get tired of you, and now you want to come running back to me?"

"Pat, there is no *he*. I've told you everything. That was done with a long time ago." Her words were choked in her throat. "I have been alone for the last seven months. And I've had a lot of time to think about my life," she sniffled. "I want you back, baby. I want my life back. I'll do whatever it takes to make us work . . . please."

"It's a little too late for that."

The dial tone brought a fresh new pain. No reconciliation. Josette lay back on the bed and cried silently. *How can a man who loves God so much be so cold? So unforgiving?* It finally occurred to her what had been happening between her and her husband for the last seven months. She understood the true motivation for his silence. It was uncomplicated now. Patrick was forcing her hand. He wanted her to end it. She was the one who had broken their bond. He wanted *her* to finish it so that he could be left blameless, keeping his impeccable reputation as a man of God—a man who'd been done in by the woman he loved. That way, he'd be released from taking any responsibility for their marriage or their divorce.

Josette ached over the debris of her life. She'd have to rethink the wholeness that she thought she'd gained, and the ridiculous notion that a few therapy sessions could help her heal and move on without Patrick. What was it that God had against her? He'd stopped loving her when she was just ten years old. Josette wondered why as the tears rolled from the corners of her eyes.

Sandy tapped on the door lightly.

Josette didn't attempt to hide her tears. "Come in."

Sandy slid onto the bed and patted Josette's hand. "Not having a good day?"

"I don't know if there will ever be a good day without Pat, Sandy."

"It might feel like that now, but there will be."

Josette sat up, wiped her tears, and cracked a half-smile. "Well, until then, this is the Heartbreak Hotel."

Sandy stroked her face. "Jo, I love you. Just want you to know that I'm here for you. We haven't really talked in a while."

Josette changed the subject to something her heart could handle. "I heard that you've been enjoying yourself lately," she grinned knowingly.

"Is that right?"

"Yep. And I'm hurt because I don't have any *details.*"

"This sounds like an ice cream conversation."

"Bring it on!"

Josette sat opposite Sandy on a bar stool in the kitchen, with a heap of butter pecan ice cream in a crystal bowl, while Sandy spooned French vanilla from an extra large coffee mug. It had been eons since the tension between the two of them had loosened enough to enjoy one of their favorite pastimes—girl talk over ice cream.

"So, I hear you're in *celeb* status now."

"What?"

"Faye told me that you've been seeing *Lamont Drake*."

"You know him?"

"I know of him. Who doesn't? He has a brother named Brian—who is mangy as a dog." Josette rolled her eyes. "He's dated a few women I know, while he's been married."

"Yep. That sounds like Brian. Anything I should know about Lamont?"

"Na. From what I hear, Lamont lays pretty low. He dated Simone Montgomery off and on for a couple of years. And you know what they say about her—there aren't too many wealthy men that she hasn't dated. Sleazy. No class. I don't know what they see in her."

Sandy mashed and stirred her ice cream to soften it. "Well, for one thing, she is very beautiful," she said, licking her spoon.

Josette's mouth was full of ice cream; her words sounded coded. "So are you, Sandy! You are a hundred steps above Simone." She swallowed. "Has he ever mentioned her?"

"No. He just said that he'd dated some actresses and models before—but the relationships were no big deal."

"Well, I heard from my friend Jackie who works at *Entertainment Magazine* and whose sister knows Fatima, Simone's best friend, that Lamont and Simone were engaged once and Simone broke it off."

"That didn't make the celebrity news?"

"Jackie said that it only lasted a day. The two of them were supposed to have eloped. But then Simone flounced off with some shipping magnate."

"Hmm. That's interesting. He acts as if this is the first time that he's ever been in love."

"*In love?* Did he say that?"

Sandy nodded. "Yep."

"Well, go on with your bad self."

Sandy looked at Jo seriously. "He's been very good to me, Jo. First time any man has been this good to me."

"You deserve it."

"Yeah, well, I just hope that I can *maintain* until we get married."

Josette bucked her eyes. "*Married?*"

Sandy laughed. "Lamont said that I am the kind of woman that he would like to spend his life with—that we are working towards that."

"Wow. He must be serious to be talking like that."

Sandy put another scoop of ice cream in her mug. "Celibacy is a big issue right now. I think he's getting restless."

"Well, big sister, like you always tell me—do what is right. For you, that means doing what the Bible says. You've been a good girl for four years straight—no slip-ups, right?"

"Right."

"A few more months won't hurt. Maybe he'll step up to the plate with a ring sooner than you think."

"Wow. That's amazing advice, coming from you."

"What did you expect me to say, Sandy? 'Forget about what you believe in. Just do it! Do it! Do it!'" Josette laughed.

"Yes."

"Nope. I've learned a lot in the last few months. And if I had done the right thing, I would still have my husband."

Sandy embraced her. "Jo, it's going to be all right," Sandy said as Josette cried weakly on her. She prayed, "Father, God, consider the prayers of the weak. Forgive us of our sins and bring comfort from our pain, oh Lord. Only You can heal the broken hearted. In You I put my trust. Correct with loving mercy, Dear Lord, so that we might be what we should. In Jesus' precious name. Amen."

Chapter Seventeen

Genevieve tried her best to talk to Benjamin in code on her cell phone while the twins watched *I Robot* on the DVD player in the backseat. "Well, honey, *the person* said that they wanted one of *those meetings* with me. And this time, *the other one* has agreed too."

Benjamin decoded from the other end. "So Sandy wants you to participate in a family therapy session, and Josette is willing to participate too?"

Genevieve pulled her Lexus 330 SUV into Mother Peace's complex. "Yes. That's right, honey."

"Well, Sweets, how do you feel about it? It's really up to you, you know?"

"I'm not sure yet. I know *the other one* is still angry. I don't want to be attacked. I've had enough of that all my life."

"Did you let them know that?"

"Well, *the other one* has always been a little headstrong. I don't think much can be done about that."

"I see. So Josette could be a problem? Have you prayed about it?"

"Yes, but probably not as much as I need to. I feel like I need to be protected from something."

Benjamin wanted their lives to be normal again. "Well, I'll do whatever it takes to support you, Sweets, but in the end it's your call."

The twins became restless in the back. "Mama, come on!" they said in unison, excited about their report cards, anxious to show Mother Peace.

"Okay, honey, we're here. We'll talk later. Love you."

"Love you."

Genevieve rang the doorbell. The twins stood side by side, knocking. When Mother Peace didn't answer, Genevieve used her emergency key. Joshua and Faith rushed in and crowded around Mother Peace with their report cards stuck out, while she slept peacefully in her Lazy Boy chair. Genevieve nudged her gently. Mother Peace's soft face held a gentle smile.

Genevieve felt something unnerving grip her. "Mother Peace . . . wake up . . ." She placed her ear against Mother Peace's chest and closed her eyes. She listened for the lively beating of Mother Peace's heart. But it was still. Genevieve checked Mother Peace's pulse. Again, there was nothing. She stood up straight with her eyes fixed on the sweet sleeping beauty and shook her head in disbelief. Tears came as quickly as a rushing wave.

Joshua shook Mother Peace harder. "Na Na Peace! Wake up!"

Faith stared at Genevieve, waiting for her to speak, but Genevieve couldn't think of what to say. Joshua reached over and took Genevieve's cell phone from her waist clip and phoned his dad. Genevieve drifted off. She began to think about every letdown that she'd experienced in her life, wondering why God seemed to be pitiless toward her at times.

Joshua looked at his mother and became the parent. "Mama, call an ambulance!" His words brought Genevieve back to the space she needed to be in. Animated, she went into the kitchen. She pulled the phone from the base and dialed 911. She rested her head against the refrigerator to collect her thoughts. What was she going to say to the children? How was she going to approach telling them that they'd never have any more weekends at Mother Peace's? *No more chocolate chip cookies from scratch. No more Sunday dinners with fresh homemade rolls. No more of Mother Peace's famous Friday night adventures.* After giving the dispatcher Mother Peace's address, she took weighted steps toward the children, wanting to shrink from the task at hand. Faith was still cemented in her same spot with her report card stretched out in the air, waiting for Mother Peace to open her eyes, laugh, and perhaps say, "Gotcha!" But that was just the last hope of shock.

"Come on, baby," Genevieve said, pulling Faith into her arms. "She's gone..."

And when Genevieve said those words, Faith let out a siren—one that pierced Genevieve to the bone marrow. She grabbed hold of Genevieve's arms and screamed repeatedly. And with each one of her shrills, Genevieve felt like she was being assaulted. Faith dug her nails so deeply into Genevieve's arms that she broke the skin.

Genevieve grabbed Faith's hands and pulled them to her sides. "Faith!" she shouted, securing her tightly in a bear hug, burying Faith's face in her chest, muffling the sirens slightly.

Joshua dropped Genevieve's cell phone onto the end table next to Mother Peace, and stood right in front of her lifeless body—staring at the woman who he had come to regard as his grandmother. She'd been his caregiver, almost since his birth. He reached his hand out slowly and stroked Mother Peace's hair. Then he kissed her forehead like he'd seen his father do a thousand times, and began to pray with a loud voice. *"I will bless the Lord at all times. His praise shall continually be in my mouth.*

Lord, we give You honor and glory right now, because You are a good God. You are the giver and taker of life. We thank You Lord, for giving us Na Na Peace. We thank You. We thank You for all Your blessings. Lord, right now, I ask that You touch my mother and my sister and remind them that the death of a saint is merely sleep. God of mercy, be with my family at this time. In the name of Jesus . . . IN THE NAME OF JESUS! IN THE NAME OF JESUS!"

The fervor of Joshua's prayer caused Faith to quiet. His loud voice had boomed through Mother Peace's living room, sounding just like his father. He was an anointed authority, calming both Faith and Genevieve. Genevieve was amazed by her man-of-God-in-training. She marveled at the gift the Lord had given him.

Benjamin bolted through the door on the heels of the paramedics. Genevieve and the twins were quieted in a prayer circle, giving the Lord praise. Benjamin prayed over Mother Peace's body. Then he joined his family in their prayer circle as the paramedics carried out their duties.

Two days had passed since Mother Peace's death. Genevieve called into the office for the fifth time that day to make sure that everything was running smoothly. Amanda, her assistant, assured her that she didn't need to be hovered over. Then she said a prayer for the family. Amanda communicated in a tactful way that Genevieve had set Pathways up so efficiently that it could function for a few days without her presence, but it would be missed nevertheless.

Genevieve hung up the phone with a smile. She had done an astounding job with the center. It was something to be proud about. She sat quietly in the nook, relaxing with a cup of coffee. Faith had finally fallen asleep after crying all morning and afternoon. Benjamin had taken Joshua to the funeral home with him to finalize the arrangements for Mother Peace. Genevieve protested against it initially, thinking it would be too much for Joshua to handle. But Benjamin assured her that Joshua had asked to go. She had sent them with one of Mother Peace's cream-colored suit, and jewelry. She sipped her coffee and reflected back on her day with Faith. The poor thing had been so grief-stricken that she hadn't even eaten. She'd asked Genevieve repeatedly, "Why did God do this?" And Genevieve's attempt to explain God's omniscience was of no consolation to Faith. Unlike her brother, it was too much for her to take in. And she needed to be angry at someone for taking Mother Peace away.

Genevieve was watching a television program when Benjamin and Joshua came in, toting dinner from a fast food restaurant. They'd taken care of all of Mother Peace's arrangements, since she didn't have any living relatives. The funeral was going to be held the coming Saturday.

"Ben, are you sure that enough people will know about the funeral, considering that it will be held before the next church service?"

Ben chuckled. "We thought about that, and we came up with a plan."

"What?"

"We stopped by Ms. Lula's house on the way home and gave her all the information."

Joshua nodded in agreement with his dad. "Uh-huh."

"Shoot, the way Ms. Lula can spread a word, the people in Africa will know the funeral arrangements," Genevieve said.

Benjamin smiled, but there was something hidden underneath. Genevieve tried to discern it but couldn't. "Joshua, go check on your sister and wash your hands," Benjamin said.

Genevieve sensed that something was wrong. She waited until Joshua was gone. "Ben, what's the matter?"

"Mother Peace's insurance."

"She doesn't have any insurance?"

There was a strained expression on Benjamin's face. "No. She's got plenty of insurance. There's no problem with that."

Genevieve moved in closer, taking Benjamin's hands. "Well, what's the matter?" She feared something was seriously wrong.

Benjamin leaned against the counter. "Mother Peace left us something and I don't know how I feel about it." He walked over to the table and sat down. "I don't feel right."

"What, Ben?"

"It's almost a million dollars."

"What? Ben, what are you talking about?"

"Mother Peace has left this family nine hundred and seventy-eight thousand dollars."

Genevieve laughed incredulously. "What? What was Mother Peace doing with that kind of money?"

"Retirement benefits, investments, insurance policies. I added it up again just to be sure. We are the beneficiaries."

"Oh, my goodness…" Genevieve said stunned. She sat at the table next to Benjamin.

Mother Peace had never discussed figures with them. She'd told them that she had their names on her policies, but they hadn't paid her much attention. Genevieve figured that it was probably just enough to take care of her burial arrangements. Benjamin had admonished Mother Peace every Christmas for spending too much on the children. He feared that she was spending too much of her retirement savings.

Benjamin scratched his head. "I've got to think about this. This whole thing has made me uncomfortable. I hope Mother Peace knew that everything this family ever did for her was from our hearts, not because we expected to receive something when she passed. If anything, she was more of a help to us. I wasn't expecting one red cent. We are doing okay, especially with you writing and all. I hope she knew that—I wasn't expecting any kind of repayment—none."

"Ben, honey . . . Mother Peace knew that. As headstrong as Mother Peace was, you think she didn't know that? She was a part of this family. Families help one another without expecting anything in return. What Mother Peace has done is beautiful, Ben—certainly nothing to feel guilty about."

Ben dropped his head in his hands. Genevieve stood up. She comforted him by rubbing her hands over his back, realizing that he'd lost two mothers in his lifetime—his own mother, and now Mother Peace. That was the root of his guilt. "Honey, I love you and I'm here for you," she said.

Benjamin rose and embraced his wife. She was so beautiful to him. Her strength and tenderness reminded him why he had fallen in love with her in the first place. It erased some of the distance and isolation he'd felt. "I thank God for you," he said softly in her ear, forgetting that he'd been feeling estranged from her for the last few months.

Genevieve could feel the wetness of Benjamin's tear against her skin. She squeezed him. "I'm here for you through whatever," she said. She felt renewed in her love for him, sorry that she'd allowed circumstances to separate them. She regretted the months that had gone by without them reaffirming their love for one another in the union that God had ordained. She planned to recommit to her husband tonight. She would give herself freely.

Chapter Eighteen

Everyone was on time for the session—even Josette, who was modestly dressed in a pair of jeans and a sweater. Her face was without make-up. Her trademark curly hair was blow-dried straight and pulled back into a ponytail. She looked void of the diva attributes that had once been synonymous with the mention of her name. No flashy diamond jewelry. No expensive designer clothing, aside from the waist-length mink jacket she wore. And her wearing it was more a matter of staying warm than making a fashion statement. She was disquieted. Her confident stride was gone; all that was left was dread.

Genevieve and Benjamin were already seated next to Sandy in the waiting area outside of Jody's office. They stood to greet Josette. She kept her distance, both emotionally and in proximity. She stood in front of Genevieve and Benjamin peaceably, saying short "hellos" to them before walking over to the window and staring out, rethinking this decision. Her mind was more focused on Patrick than on rehashing her childhood with Genevieve.

This is what Sandy wanted. She said that she needed to have this session to move forward once and for all. She was ready to discontinue her sessions with Jody altogether. This was her closure. She had even asked Patrick to join them today, hoping it'd be beneficial for him to take part in this session where she and Josette would discuss their childhood openly. Maybe he would understand his wife better. Maybe it would move his heart enough to consider saving his marriage. She'd promised him that all he had to do was *listen*. But he hadn't shown up.

Josette stood alone stoically, checking the part of her that wanted to grieve, grateful to hear Jody's voice in the background talking with Sandy, Genevieve, and Benjamin. Jody was in her normal therapist mode, with that serious voice that sometimes pricked Josette's nerves. "Why don't we come in and get started. This is going to be a long session," she said.

Josette took off her jacket and laid it over her arm before turning around to join the others. She paused uncomfortably when she saw her husband entering the suite. She lowered her eyes to avoid looking at him. Just a minute ago she had mourned the fact that he hadn't shown up, and now, she didn't know how to feel about his presence. She stepped past him without a word and took her usual seat in Jody's office—the corner chair—away from everyone else. She could hear Jody telling Patrick how pleased she was that he had decided to come, but she drowned their voices out. She thought to herself. *What am I doing here anyway? This is stupid.*

Patrick humbly introduced himself to Jody, Genevieve, and Benjamin before taking a seat on the larger sofa next to his sister-in-law. Sandy hugged him, thankful that her conversation with him had weighed heavily enough on his heart for him to grant her this last request. Sandy kept her eyes on Benjamin, who looked as if he was afraid of something—maybe afraid for his wife. She watched him squeeze Genevieve's hand and whisper something reassuring in her ear. Genevieve was visibly nervous.

Sandy could see her shaking, even though Benjamin was attempting to calm her with comforting words.

Josette was a quiet storm. She looked as though she would release the wind and rain on the first person she chose. She kept her eyes on the vertical fish tank, wishing this intrusion of mind to be over quickly.

Jody sat back in her bright blue chair observing each one of them, scrutinizing the way they interacted or didn't. She adjusted her rimless glasses and spun her chair around to grab a pen off of her desk. It seemed that she could see right through each of them. They were all nervous. Afraid. Eager to get the session over with. Each worried about being vulnerable. Jody cleared her throat and prayed. Afterward, she laid down the ground rules. "Today and tomorrow we will be doing something groundbreaking in family therapy. I want to give everyone an opportunity to talk. But please, be respectful of one another."

They nodded in unison, except for Josette, who was still fixated on the fish swimming in the tank.

"Okay, let's get right into the session," Jody said. "Sandy, is it okay if we start with you?"

"Yes." *No. Why did I say yes?*

"Sandy, why are you here today?"

Sandy looked at Genevieve. "I want some peace."

"To get to the peace we have to go through the pain," Jody said. "What is your most painful memory of your childhood with Genevieve or without her?"

Sandy paused and took in a breath. She looked at Genevieve. And Genevieve looked back with so much sorrow and repentance that Sandy had to take quick short breaths to keep from crying like she always did. She recalled the feelings of hurt and anger that Genevieve's abandonment had caused—some things she'd already shared with Genevieve and some she hadn't. Genevieve took it all in, acknowledging her daughter's pain, accepting that she'd caused it. For over thirty minutes, Sandy beat Genevieve with her memories.

"I've hated you for so long," Sandy swallowed finally, stinging her mother. "I've hated you because you left me."

"Okay . . . good," Jody nodded. "Josette, I want you to share before we talk to Genevieve." She asked Josette the same questions she'd asked Sandy. "Why are you here? And what is your most painful memory related to Genevieve?"

Josette wiped the tears that had crept out while Sandy was revealing their mother's sin against them. She looked directly at Jody when she spoke. Jody handed her a box of Kleenex covered with cartoon characters. Josette wiped her face. "I'm here because I want some closure—from this whole thing with Genevieve—and my marriage too. I just want to wake up tomorrow and let life be however it's going to be."

Jody nodded. "Go on."

Josette closed her eyes. Stress lines etched across her brow. She opened her eyes and blew out air. "My worst memory . . ." she started quietly, taking in deep breaths and letting them out slowly. She closed her eyes again to hide herself. She spoke through quivering lips. "I . . . um . . . was . . . ten. I was ten years old. Genevieve had taken me with her to the house where she used to buy her *stuff* from."

Sandy scooted to the edge of her seat, clinging to Josette's words. Patrick sat straight up against the back of the sofa, watching his wife.

"I didn't want to be there with her. I knew what was going on. The dealer's name was Doug . . . yeah . . ." Josette nodded to herself. She took her eyes off Jody and stared into her own lap. "He and Genevieve got into an argument about something. I wanted to leave, but it had gotten dark . . . so I stayed with Genevieve. Doug kept giving me these strange looks that made me feel so dirty. I felt like someone had dumped me in the sewer the way he looked at me. Genevieve kept telling him 'NO' over and over. Then we left. Genevieve was walking so fast, pulling me so hard," Josette cried. She broke down, sobbing loudly, covering her face with her hands, rocking back and forth in her chair. Sandy stood up to walk over to her, but Jody intervened.

"No, Sandy. Let her finish," Jody said. "Josette, go on please."

They waited in silence for Josette to gather herself. She swallowed hard. Sandy cried with her sister from across the room. Patrick made circles on Sandy's back with his huge hands.

Josette's voice cracked, "...I was walking to school a couple of days later," she said breathing in and out again, not bothering to wipe her face this time. "I had walked by myself that day because Sandy left me. I had taken too long getting dressed," Josette sniffed. "Sandy's first hour teacher, Ms. Crown, had threatened to suspend her if she was late one more time . . . so I went alone. And Doug . . . he . . . he grabbed me . . . and he... raped me. He raped me . . ."

Tears streamed down Patrick's face. He stood. "Jo . . ."

Jody stood blocking Patrick's path. "Please sit down, Patrick. We need to do things this way."

Patrick complied reluctantly, looking pitifully at his wife. The one who had given herself to another man. The one he had loved with every fiber of his being. The one he'd asked God for. He watched helplessly as she sobbed in her chair. She squeezed her legs closed tightly and covered her face with balled-up fists. Her legs shook violently, creating a soul-aching rhythm. She ripped more tissue from the box and blew hard.

Genevieve had buried her head in Benjamin's chest to quiet her own sobbing. He wrapped his arms securely around his wife and rubbed her shoulders, still whispering the words that were unable to bring comfort. His eyes were full of tears for all of them.

Jody tried to refocus the session. "Josette . . ."

"No more . . . please . . . no more . . ." Josette cried, looking into the fish tank.

"Okay," Jody nodded.

The entire room was paralyzed, filled with an ominous silence. Each soul was restrained by distress. Sandy would have told her little sister how sorry she was for her, but Josette wouldn't acknowledge any of them anymore. She'd finished playing her part in this painful game—this unfolding drama. And her husband was pulverized under all the secrets and revelations. He rubbed his hands over his head and covered his face. He couldn't touch his wife, so he squeezed Sandy's hand instead. Dumbfounded, he looked at Genevieve, unsure what to think about her. It was his first time meeting her. And so far, nothing good had come from this meeting that was supposed to have set them all free emotionally. Instead, Patrick feared that more damage would follow.

Sandy cried guilty, remorseful tears, blaming herself for what she'd just heard. She'd been betrayed by both Josette and Genevieve, not having known about her little sister's secret. Memories came rolling in like waves. Whenever they had come in contact with Doug back then, Josette would stiffen apprehensively as if she were afraid to cross his path. Her lively countenance was marred by something Sandy couldn't put her finger on. Sandy assumed that it was because Josette blamed Doug for supplying Genevieve with crack. She was wrong. Then there was that strange morning that had puzzled Sandy until now. Josette was fifteen. Sandy had awakened and found her at the kitchen table reading the Sunday paper before church as she did every Sunday morning. She usually started with the comics. That morning, however, Josette hadn't made it to the comic section. She was thunderstruck by the front page, crying like someone had died.

Sandy had picked up the paper and read the headline and article.

SATURDAY NIGHT SHOOT-OUT.

Alleged drug lord, Douglas Williams, was killed by police at his home after he opened fire on two officers while they were responding to a domestic violence call from his girlfriend…

Josette's tears had soaked through the page, blurring the image of the monster she had feared and hated. She still harbored the shame of having her purity vitiated by a slime of a man who had seemingly gotten away with raping a ten-year-old child. Now he was gone. Sandy thought her reaction to the news of Doug's death was strange—inexplicable. But for Josette, the bittersweet taste of vengeance was recompense for the sin against her, and a reminder of what had been stolen from her.

Sandy's sympathy for Genevieve was destroyed by the secret Josette had hidden from her and Patrick. All that remained was anger—a brutal anger. Their lives were Genevieve's monster. She was the reason Sandy had spent three years in therapy and the reason Josette had been raped at the precious age of ten—possibly the reason why Josette's marriage had fallen apart.

They spent another thirty minutes half-listening to Genevieve talk about her abusive childhood, abusive relationships, and her addiction. The horrors of Genevieve's life, including the reason that Grace had hated her, seemed trivial in comparison to what Josette divulged. But they had agreed to listen to *everyone's* pain. The emotions that had been brewing inside of Josette since she was just ten years old prevented her from feeling any sympathy for Genevieve.

Patrick was distraught, trying to process all that he'd heard, trying to figure out how it was relevant to his marriage. He looked upon the woman he loved with compassion. He was still in love with her. He fought hard against that truth, but it remained.

After two hours, the session was over. Josette sprinted out of the door. Patrick's eyes followed her. Sandy watched him, seeing all the love he felt for her little sister in his eyes. Patrick moved to get up from the sofa and his knees buckled. He balanced himself, and Sandy helped him get his arm in the sleeve of his jacket. Still in shock, he walked out of Jody's door in successive still shots. He didn't hear Jody remind them of tomorrow's session.

Chapter Nineteen

Josette walked over to the water cooler, took one of the Styrofoam cups off of the table, and held the lever up on the water cooler until the cup was filled. She gulped it down and practiced a breathing technique she'd learned. She heard Sandy walk up behind her quietly.

"Jo, you okay?"

Josette swallowed her emotions. "Just leave me alone please," she mumbled, putting up her hand. She knew Sandy meant well, but this wasn't the time. *No. Not now.* She heard Genevieve and Benjamin walk past her. Genevieve was afraid to approach her. Josette could feel them staring at her, but she kept her eyes on the slow-moving liquid inside the light blue plastic container. She poured herself another cup of water. She couldn't move. Couldn't blink. Couldn't flinch. If she did, all the tears would come rushing again. She was fragile. She would break into a million tiny pieces if someone so much as touched her. She was the scared little ten-year-old that had been assaulted by an animal. She placed the cup under the spout and lifted the lever again, so she could drink more of the liquid that was stabilizing her emotions. She felt his warm breath on her ear.

"Jo, I need to talk to you. Meet me at the house in an hour… please," Patrick said. It was a quiet command.

Josette didn't move. Didn't respond to Patrick or the words he spoke. *Just let it be over. Please.*

Patrick repeated his request, turning her face towards him. "An hour."

She nodded and all the tears came again. *What does he want with me?*

Josette pulled into the long circular drive of their stately seven bedroom mansion. Patrick's pewter-colored Hummer entered from the opposite direction. He took his time getting out of his truck. His hesitation both irritated and saddened Josette. She put her foot on the brake. She could just leave right now and let it be. But before she had convinced herself to back out of the driveway, Patrick hopped out and walked over to her Range Rover. Josette sat still, refusing the starring role in his melodrama. *Why doesn't he just get it over with? Whatever he has to say he can say right here.*

Patrick opened Josette's door. "Come on."

"Pat, whatever it is that you want to talk about, we can talk about it right here. I need to go home and get some rest. Rough day."

"Jo, come on inside."

"Look, I don't have time for this crap, Pat. Please . . . just say whatever it is you have to say!"

"*Josette,* get out of the car . . . please."

Reluctantly, she turned off the ignition and followed him to the door. She sighed hard to let him know that she didn't want to be a part of whatever was happening right now.

"Come on," Patrick said, allowing Josette into her own home.

The door creaked open and Josette looked at everything as if it were her first time seeing it. She'd forgotten the scent of sandalwood that greeted her in the parlor, and the feel of the cold, black and white marble as she kicked off her boots. A sensuous oil painting of her and Patrick by artist Kevin A. Williams hung opposite the door. Both of them looked heavenly in white, with their lips touching gently. Their images were surrounded by an antique baroque frame. Patrick surprised her with it on their first anniversary. He had been so in love with her then.

Everything in the house seemed new to Josette except for the love she used to share with her husband. It was haunting. The ten-thousand-dollar black glass chandelier that hung in the center of the hall in front of the dual winding staircase captured Josette's attention. It had been imported from Europe. It was the first "millionaire's wife" purchase she made after they'd bought the mansion. She wanted people to be dazzled by something grand when they entered. Patrick hadn't even flinched when she'd told him the price. She'd seen it and she wanted it. That was all that mattered to him. Josette almost smiled at the memory of that day—the day she realized that she and her childhood sweetheart were rich. Patrick looked up at it as if he held the same memory in his mind. Without speaking he motioned her up the stairs.

Josette followed Patrick up the right side of the wide staircase, gliding her hands over the elaborate wrought iron and wood railing. Patrick turned once to see if she was still behind him. She kept following him until he came to their bedroom door. She watched as he opened both sides of the French doors and walked in.

Sometime during the first year of their marriage, they began discussing their "issues" in the bedroom, despite what popular talk-show hosts and television psychologists recommended. Patrick said that it was a good practice that would benefit them when they had children. It was a practice that had worked for them. They hammered out their problems and went to bed without being angry. And it had been convenient. Most of the time, both of them were exhausted at the end of the day, going directly to bed after they'd had their "discussions" seemed sensible.

Now, Josette stood in the hallway. She couldn't go into that room again. The last time she'd been in that room, she and her husband fought like they'd been trapped in some dysfunctional nightmare. Her marriage ended in that room.

Patrick intertwined their fingers, and pulled her in gently. And there were no signs of his rage left. The mirrored wall behind their canopy bed showed no evidence that Patrick had thrown Josette's antique, eighteenth-century, Queen Anne armchair up against it. It wasn't the same mirror that had been shattered. No spider cracks ran across it now. The room was clean, orderly, and peaceful. It resembled the bedroom they used to share except for the walk-in closet that used to house Josette's clothing. It was empty, aside from the wooden hangers and mahogany shelving. No. Josette Kelley didn't live here anymore.

She shut her eyes and tried to pretend that that night had never happened. She prayed that when she reopened them, her life would be normal again. She and Patrick would laugh about some silly movie they'd watched on television, eat a couple of triple-scoop banana splits, and make love afterward. She'd wake up the next morning wrapped around him, and he'd brag about the way he'd put her to sleep the night before. But it was over. Josette stood in the middle of the room, letting go.

Patrick sat on the edge of the bed, staring at the woman who used to own his heart. He'd loved her since he was fourteen. He would have died for her. "Jo, what happened to us, babe? I loved you."

Josette closed her eyes again. Her tears trickled anyway. "I don't know . . . I'm so sorry, Pat."

Patrick's eyes glazed sadly with tears. "How could you do this to me, Jo? Seven years . . . seven years I was in the NFL. And for seven years, it was about *you*. I never strayed on you, Jo—not one single time. From city to city, there were always women. Everywhere I turned there was a woman waiting—trying to give herself to me. But I never got caught up, because the Lord is my judge and you were my wife. When I was tempted, I got down on my knees and prayed, Jo—so I wouldn't sin against my God. So I wouldn't destroy what we'd built."

"I don't know, Pat . . . I just don't know," she repeated. If there were meaningful words she could have said to explain it all, she would have said them. But there were none. She didn't know what had happened or why. All she knew was that she had ruined something beautiful.

"You took something that was so sacred to me and just ripped it apart, babe. You broke our covenant, Jo—our bond. You promised me that this marriage was going to be about *us*. And you never told me about the rape—your mother. I don't even know who you are, babe." His words stung like a whipping.

"Pat, please . . . if it's over . . . let it be over. I just can't take anymore today!" Josette screamed. She turned and ran from the room.

"Jo!" Patrick yelled, running after her. "I'm sorry . . . don't go . . . please," he said, subduing her on the ledge. He pulled her back to him, locking his arms around her, holding her close to his chest. "Please, don't..." he said squeezing her. Josette wailed loudly against him, letting out the pain of regret. Patrick smoothed his hands over her hair and inhaled it. And he held on to the memory of the woman who had been his wife for seven years, kissing her gingerly over her face. He savored the precious moments he'd shared with her over the years, kissing the tears that fell until he could feel the warmth of Josette's lips against his. And he claimed those lips that once belonged only to him.

Slowly and easily Patrick undressed his wife with the gentleness and desire that he'd always loved her with, until every article of Josette's clothing had fallen to a soft pile at her feet. She returned the favor, and a passionate waterfall rushed over them, sweeping them back to a time when love was good. Patrick kissed every part of Josette's bare skin like he'd forgotten the taste of it. He scooped her into his arms, carried her into their room, and laid her on their bed, where words were spoken in graceful movements and short-breath whispers. Josette surrendered sweetly, receiving her husband again, allowing him to love her completely. And together they flew to beautiful places. *Mountaintops. Forests. Canyons. Hills. Creeks. Beaches. Sky. Space. Heaven.* Their tears mingled until they were both spent.

It was after ten p.m. when Josette awakened in Patrick's arms. The darkness was intruded upon by slivers of moonlight that shone through the windows. Realizing that she had not dreamed the last few hours of lovemaking, Josette comforted herself in Patrick's muscular hold, brushing her nose across his solid chest. The smell of his skin was intoxicating. She closed her eyes again, knowing that this stolen, undeserved, and yet prized moment was their good-bye. She wanted to sleep this way for as long as she could and hold on to what used to be. But just two-and-a-half hours later, she awakened again, startled that she could no longer feel Patrick's strong, protective arms around her.

Josette's cheek pressed against the soft white sheet. It was an unsatisfactory substitute for Patrick's chest. She reached out for him, but there was only an empty space beside her. She glided her outstretched hand over the cold area where Patrick's warm body had lain, and lamented. She closed her hand into a fist. She had let their love slip through her fingers. Tears of resignation flowed.

Josette sat up against the headboard, wrapping the sheet around her. Patrick sat across from her in his winged-back reading chair with his Bible on his lap. His eyes were wet with tears. His face glowed from the dancing lights of the fireplace that crackled next to him. The crackling melody had often been a familiar romantic tune; now it sang a song of mourning.

Patrick spoke in a choked up voice. "I've been watching you sleep . . . you're still beautiful."

Josette didn't want to hear him console her with appealing words. "Just say it, Pat."

Patrick's voice was restrained and lowly. "I tried to be the best man I could, Jo. I respected you. I respected this marriage . . . prayed over it. You told me you were *mine*. I can't share my wife."

"I don't expect you to, Pat."

"Jo, I love you . . . but I can't share you. Can't share what's supposed to belong to me and me only. Scripture says that a man can divorce his wife if she commits adultery, Jo."

Josette didn't want to hear anymore. "I know," she said, guiltily. She got out of the bed with the sheet wrapped around her and went into the hallway to retrieve her clothes. She came back and stood before him fully dressed except for her boots that she'd left in the parlor.

"I've been struggling with this thing, Jo. Maybe if you would have told me that you had a problem with me—we could have worked it out, babe. Maybe we should have straightened things out after the incident in New York, in the beginning of our marriage . . . I don't know."

"You knew about that?"

Patrick nodded. "Yeah. *Kenneth Posey.*"

Josette shuddered at the mention of that name. An old ghost.

"He bragged about it to another player he represented and the word sort of traveled until it got back to me. It was an ego thing for him, Jo—just to say that he'd had '*Patrick Kelley's wife.*' I forgave you without even asking you about it. I think a part of me didn't want to believe it. We were twenty-two—just married. I knew you loved me. And I didn't want to believe anything different. I ignored it, Jo. I ignored it so that everything I believed God for didn't come tumbling down. But I can't ignore it this time." Patrick stood up.

"Just say it, Pat."

Patrick's words were final and cutting. "I've filed for a divorce, Jo. I've forgiven you, babe. But I just don't think I could ever love you the same way. It wouldn't be fair to you or to me."

Josette sniffed in deeply. "Okay . . ." *Finally he's said it. It's done.* "Well . . . now at least I know what's going on." She forced a sad smile.

"I love you, Jo. This is not what I wanted for us."

"You don't have to explain anything to me, Pat. I understand," Josette said. "You don't owe me anything. You keep everything. It's yours. You earned it. Let's just get it over with."

Pat enclosed Josette in his arms. He squeezed her to him like he'd never see her again. Josette needed to pull away from him, but she found it hard to leave those arms that made her feel like she was the only woman on the face of the earth. They cried together until Josette couldn't take the stabbing pain anymore.

Josette's plea was a double wound to her own heart. "Let me go, Pat," she said quietly.

Patrick hesitated before releasing her. All his love flowed down his cheeks. "Good-bye, Jo."

Josette refused to say those words. She couldn't make herself say those words. She looked at her husband one last time before leaving her life behind.

Patrick fell to his knees and prayed. "Lord…"

Chapter Twenty

Benjamin had been detached for the past two hours since he and Genevieve returned to their hotel suite from the session. She wanted to ask him how he was feeling, but he'd relegated himself to the desk with his nose stuck in the Bible since they'd walked in the door. Genevieve ordered room service, but Benjamin said that he wasn't hungry. She wondered what he was reading that he hadn't already combed through in the last two hours. She felt like he was avoiding her.

Genevieve sat on the bed and tried to read a magazine she'd picked up in the hotel gift shop. She had to do something to calm her mind. Jody had left a message stating that Sandy had cancelled the family session for tomorrow and wasn't going to reschedule it. She'd said that she was done with therapy and was going to go on with her life. Genevieve had tried to reach her with no success. She knew that the revelation of Josette's rape had pushed her further away from reconciliation with her daughters. The roller coaster ride she'd been on for the last months had halted. And now her husband was emotionally distant at a time when she needed him most.

Genevieve felt insecure—ashamed. She had never felt that way with Benjamin before. But now, he'd heard the worst parts of her past from her daughters. For the first time since she'd known him, she felt dirty and unworthy. What did he think of her now?

"Are you going to read the Bible all night?" Genevieve asked, slipping underneath the covers.

Benjamin turned away from the desk and looked at her. "Did you say something, Sweets?"

"I just wanted to know if you were going to ignore me all night. If something that was said earlier bothers you, we can talk about it, Ben."

"Sorry. I wasn't trying to ignore you. And no, nothing is bothering me, Sweets."

"Well then, tell me why I feel so guilty and ashamed. Are you ashamed of me now, Ben?"

Benjamin looked surprised that Genevieve had asked him such a thing, and immediately rose from the desk and sat next to her on the bed. "Never. You hear me? You are a new creature in Christ, Sweets. I've never thought of you as anything less. *Nothing* will ever change that."

Genevieve wanted to believe him. But she knew it had to hurt. It had to have disgusted him to hear all those sordid details about her former life. "Ben, please . . . if you are feeling something, just tell me what it is. I'd really like to talk about it."

"*Dr. Moss-Carpenter,*" Benjamin smiled, "let's just leave the therapy session back at that lady's office where it belongs. I'm okay. Really."

"Okay," Genevieve said, but she didn't feel settled. She called to check on the twins, who were staying with Benjamin's assistant pastor and his wife. She watched Benjamin take off his clothes, pray, and get into bed. She felt like he was coming to bed just to appease her. But she didn't push. She had enough to think about now. What had it all been for? They'd found her. Now it was back to life without them. Genevieve turned over, closed her eyes, and imagined having lunch with Sandy and Josette; they talked and laughed like normal mothers and daughters. She imagined the three of them shopping afterward to walk off the pounds they'd put on from lunch.

Benjamin had fallen asleep and Genevieve suddenly felt the urgency to bathe. She needed to wash the filth and dirt of her past life off again. She'd repented. Why did she feel so guilty? She was sorrowful about what happened to Josette. A horrible thing happened because she hadn't been a protector. She'd been an addict. She regretted it. But she was still paying for the emotional scars she'd caused her children. And still, she couldn't go back. Couldn't undo any of it.

Genevieve pulled the covers back and got out of bed. She went into the bathroom and looked at herself in the mirror. She searched for that woman, but she couldn't see her reflection anymore. Only the woman God had forgiven. She turned the faucet on high to drown out her frustrated cry.

Benjamin pushed the door open gently. He looked at his wife and said, "Why are you crying, Sweets?"

Genevieve sniffled. "Because this is the first time we've been away from home in a beautiful hotel suite and you haven't touched me, Ben! Why won't you just talk to me?"

"Sweets, I was just trying to give you some space. That's all."

"I don't need space right now. I need my HUSBAND!" Genevieve screamed.

"Sweets, I'm sorry. You've got me...I'm right here," Benjamin said, holding her, reassuring her. He placed his hand on her forehead and prayed fervently for the two of them. And Genevieve took up residence in his arms.

Chapter Twenty-One

Sandy spent the weekend at Lamont's to get away from her life. She'd decided that she was okay without therapy—and Genevieve. She'd written Genevieve a letter telling her that. Jody had recommended that Josette attend group counseling sessions for rape victims. Josette agreed that she would as soon as the John Paul Dozier murder trial was over. Sandy watched the news every day to keep up with the trial updates. But she was happy to be away from home.

Sandy rested in Lamont's main guest room, awakening to the smell of bacon sizzling on the griddle. It was the motivation she needed to get out of bed, grateful that Lamont was an early riser and a man who loved to cook. She showered and came down to a breakfast of bacon, eggs, grits, waffles with strawberry topping and whipped cream, and fresh-squeezed orange juice. Lamont had his back turned to the kitchen entrance. He hadn't heard Sandy. He talked on the phone as he loaded utensils into the dishwasher. Sandy felt like a sneaky eavesdropper, but she remained quiet because his conversation interested her. Mainly because he'd said the word "*baby*" three times so far. It definitely wasn't a business call at seven forty-five a.m. on a Saturday morning.

"Not a good idea," he said blankly. "Because I have compa—ny," he said, noticing Sandy when he turned. "Listen, I've got to go. Talk to you some other time."

Sandy calmed her heart. "Good morning."

Lamont kissed her on the lips. "Good morning, baby."

"*Baby?*"

Lamont pulled out a chair for her. "Yeah. That's what I always call you."

Sandy sat down and scooted close to the table. "Who were you talking to on the phone?"

Lamont was undisturbed by Sandy's questioning. "A friend of mine. Why?"

"I heard you call her *baby*."

Lamont smiled, cutting his waffles in smaller squares. "I didn't mean it like that. It's not a big deal, baby."

Sandy wanted to let it go, but she couldn't. "Who is she?"

"Sandy, it's *not* a big deal, baby, really."

"Okay . . . who is she, then?"

Lamont was uncomfortable. He sighed. "Sandy, baby . . . you are my lady—that's what we said, right? Don't make a big deal out of nothing."

Sandy stood up. "Mont, why can't you just answer my question?"

"Ugggh . . . okay . . . it was Simone. Sit down and eat, baby, please . . ."

Sandy sat. "Simone *who?*"

Lamont scratched his head and grunted. "Simone Montgomery." He took a swig of orange juice.

"Why didn't you just say that in the first place, Mont? What is all the 007 stuff about? Are you seeing her again?"

"What do you mean, *again?* I'm seeing you. I just . . . didn't want you to feel intimidated."

"Huh. I'm not—not by her, anyway."

"Listen, I'm with who I want to be with. You're here. She's there. There's no problem with us, okay?"

An undercurrent pulled at Sandy's ankles, threatening to pull her deeper into a mysterious river of uncertainties. "Lamont, does your talking to her have anything to do with my celibacy?"

Lamont hesitated before responding. "No. She and I are friends. That's it. When your celibacy becomes a *major* problem, or if I don't feel like I can deal with it anymore, I'll let you know. Trust me."

"So it's already a problem, it's just not a major problem?"

"Sandy, I'm not going to lie. We're adults. You are sexy as ever. Beautiful. Desirable. And I love you. And yes, I want to enjoy you. And I want you to enjoy me. It can only strengthen what we already have. And yes, it drives me crazy when I'm with you and I want to express myself physically and I can't. I'm a grown man—I need to be able to do that with my woman."

Sandy was tired of the topic. "If we were married it wouldn't be an issue, Lamont."

"Baby, come on . . . think about it. How can a man really be sure that his woman is *the one*, if he has never even made love to her? I mean, how would I honestly know that you and I are sexually compatible? We're talking about spending the rest of our lives together without knowing first? Honestly, I feel like that could be a disaster."

"And it could be beautiful. I believe that the Lord honors obedience, Lamont. I don't think He's up in Heaven trying to make us miserable down here—living the rest of our lives with a spouse who isn't sexually satisfying. I believe He would bless two people who'd been obedient."

"That may be true, but in the meanwhile . . . just like you need affection and emotional support, I need lovemaking. I mean, I feel like I'm in grade school or something. I'm thirty-eight years old."

"Are you saying that you can't wait for me?"

"I'm telling you that I *don't want to wait*. But that's what I've been doing anyway. I just don't want us to continue this way. I *can't* continue this way."

Sandy heard an unspoken warning. Her anger rose. "Mont, you do what you have to do—if you need it that badly—maybe we need to re-evaluate our relationship!"

Lamont's anger followed Sandy's. "What do you mean if I need it that *badly?* I'm not some sex hound, Sandy! If I want sex, all I have to do is pick up the phone and it's done! It's not about—"

Sandy interrupted him. "Well you do that! Just pick up the phone and make it happen!" She stomped out of the kitchen and up the stairs. She threw her belongings hurriedly into her duffle bag. She was too angry to cry today. Besides, she was tired of being a victim.

Lamont knocked on the door. Sandy didn't answer. She continued gathering her things, laying her jeans and sweatshirt across the bed for the ride back home.

Lamont opened the door and spoke with exaggerated calmness, like she was some bipolar mental patient in a manic state. "Sandy, where are you going?"

Sandy zipped her duffle. "Home."

"Sandy, don't do this. I'm sorry. I don't want to be with another woman. I want to be with *you*. It's that simple. I'm just sexually frustrated . . . I didn't mean to say anything to hurt you . . . I would never hurt you.

Please stay."

"I don't want to keep fighting about this, Lamont."

"We're not going to fight anymore, I promise. Give me some time." Lamont stroked Sandy's hair. "Work with me, baby. This is the first time I've ever felt this way about a woman, and the first time a woman has ever denied me. But I love you," he said, kissing her forehead. "I love you." He caressed her methodically, causing that dizzying sensation that she felt every time he touched her that way. And Sandy succumbed to Lamont's touch more than she wanted to—more than she should have, dangling over the edge of a cliff.

Chapter Twenty-Two

Not Guilty. The jury's verdict caused a roar in the courtroom. "Yes!" Josette said aloud, forgetting herself. That kind of display was not acceptable—especially not in Judge Velasquez's court room. He pounded the gavel. "Order!" he shouted. The court came to a quiet hush. Josette calmed herself and gloated on the inside. Prosecuting attorney Mark Major eyed her reaction from the prosecutor's table. Josette had won the case. She mouthed the words, *"Told you"* to Mark. He read her lips and nodded casually without showing emotion. Josette could get away with anything with Judge Velasquez, Mark couldn't.

The noise level rose again as the courtroom emptied, but J. P. remained doubled over in his chair as if he were in an airplane crash position. It was so noisy that Josette wouldn't have noticed J. P. sobbing like a child if it hadn't been for the fact that his shoulders were hunching up and down. She put her hand on his shoulder and told him again that he was a free man. That it was over. That it was okay now. But perhaps the possibility of facing a life sentence in addition to losing his soul mate plunged J. P. to an emotional release.

Josette spoke in his ear so that her words were heard despite the noise level. "J. P., it's okay. Go home and get some rest."

"Why'd you have to do it, Gina?" he cried to himself.

Josette evaluated his words slowly. "What?" she asked herself, confused.

"Why'd you . . . make me . . . do that? Why . . . couldn't you be faithful t—to me?"

Josette's muscles tightened. She felt like she was having a stroke. Anger shook her like a rag doll. *He did it. He killed her.* The alibis lied. They all lied. The one client she'd believed in had made a fool of her. She clenched her teeth. J. P.'s entourage surrounded him. Josette wanted to beat him over the head with her briefcase. *People are standing around. Stay calm. Back away from the victim. Just back away from the victim.*

"Congratulations," Mark said, sliding his arm under Josette's, leading her out of the courtroom—pulling her away from what could very well have been the next crime scene.

Outside of the court, Mark and Josette were bombarded by a frenzied group of reporters. Court reporter Jason Jefferson was the closest to them. He stuck a microphone in their faces. "The way you two go at it in the courtroom, it's a wonder you guys even talk to one another *outside* the courtroom."

Josette was blinded by the high-beaming camera light. And she was too angry to give an interview. Mark saved her. "It's all in a day's work," he said, smiling professionally.

Josette kept the stupid victory smile on her face. And in a split second, the crowd of reporters rushed in the opposite direction. J. P. had finally pulled himself together enough to exit the courtroom. The reporters deserted Josette and Mark for real sensationalism. Josette felt sick. She ran toward the women's restroom. Mark ran behind her like a bodyguard. And after Josette had vomited the last of her guts out, and brushed her teeth with her mini hygiene kit to get rid of the evidence, Mark was standing on the outside of the restroom waiting for her.

Mark compromised Josette's space so that the words spoken could only be heard by the two of them. "You got burned, Jo," Mark said at a whisper level. "It's your first time, too. It was all on your face."

She stuck her right arm in her coat sleeve. "I don't know what you're talking about, Mark."

Mark assisted her with the other arm as Josette shifted her purse to the other side. "I know that look, baby girl. The one client you believed in the most let you down. I knew it. Tough case to prove, though. Do you see what I mean? Money allows people like him to literally get away with *murder*."

Josette rubbed her hands over her stomach. "I feel like crap," she said, not validating Mark's theory one way or the other.

Mark patted Josette on the back. "Now, this is where you decide what side of the game you're going to play on. That's the bottom line." He hugged her good-bye and headed home.

But Josette had bigger problems than J. P. making a fool out of her. Her real problem was at the early stage. Days went by before she was brave enough to deal with it.

Chapter Twenty-Three

Josette and Sandy sat across from each other at the kitchen island. "I'm pregnant," she said, defeated.

"What?"

"I'm pregnant," she repeated.

It took moments before Sandy could breathe again. Her mouth gaped open. She held her hand over her heart and shot a suspicious look at Josette.

"It's Pat's, so you can take that stupid look off your face. And drop the theatrics, will you?"

Sandy let out her breath. "Whew!" She smiled at Josette slyly, twisting her lips. "And just *how* did *that* happen?"

"Pat asked me to meet him at the house after that session we had, and one thing led to another."

Sandy took two gallons of ice cream out of the freezer. "You didn't tell me that part."

"I didn't think it mattered."

"Sherbet or Cookies and Cream?"

"Sherbet."

Sandy took two crystal bowls out of the cabinet and filled them, then put the ice cream back in the freezer. "So, what is Pat saying about all of this?"

"Nothing—I haven't told him."

Sandy slid Josette a bowl full of Rainbow Sherbet. "What are you waiting for?"

"I don't know."

"How far along are you?"

"Five weeks."

"Well, by the time you miss a period you're usually about four to five weeks. So that sounds about right," Sandy said, sounding like a nurse. "So when are you going to tell Pat?"

"I don't know. I may not tell him at all. I don't think I'm going to keep it."

Sandy scowled. "Are you talking about having an *abortion?*"

"Yes."

"Jo, that is a sin and you know it. No. You cannot do that. Talk to Pat."

"Sandy, Pat has filed for a divorce. There is nothing to talk about. I'm not raising a child by myself."

"Josette Kelley, I don't care if you haven't picked up a Bible or gone to church in ten years; you know full well that what you're talking about doing is not right. Killing a baby is not going to solve all your problems."

"It's my body!"

Sandy's eyes narrowed with aggravation. "Josette Kelley, you need to grow up!"

"You did it; now all of a sudden I'm sinner of the year!"

Sandy paused before she responded. She looked at Josette with disgust. *She didn't have to bring that up.* "That was different and you know it! And it doesn't have anything to do with you!"

"What was different about it? You made a choice that was convenient for you. I'm making one that's convenient for me."

Sandy's eyes filled with tears. If she could take back that sin, that moment, she would. "I regret it too! Every day! Why can't you just listen sometimes? It's always about you, Josette!"

Josette screamed. "Sandy, just LEAVE ME ALONE!"

"You know what? Do what you want. I don't care anymore!" Sandy rose and slammed her bowl hard into the sink. The shattering of the crystal echoed and reflected Josette's life. Josette laid her head on the island and cried. She wondered if her miserable life was amusing to God. She hated the world. Hated Patrick. Hated Sandy. Hated Genevieve. Hated herself. She'd always hated herself. How could she love a baby?

Chapter Twenty-Four

She was meddling. It wasn't her business. But it was. Sandy sat back against the comfortable bronze, gold, and brown paisley print booth cushion, at the lavishly decorated Elephant City restaurant, and tapped her fingers nervously on the brown linen tablecloth. She looked at her image in the mirrored wall across from her. *Traitor.* Josette was going to hate her after this. They hadn't spoken in three weeks, and now they probably never would. What did God want her to do? Wasn't that all that mattered? Sandy ordered a cinnamon spice tea with honey when the handsome, broad-shouldered waiter with the midnight disc jockey voice, approached the table offering her a drink and the Chilean sea bass house special for the day. She told him that she was expecting a guest, and he departed back to the kitchen area after bringing her tea to the table.

Sandy looked nervously at her Movado. Patrick was twenty minutes late already and hadn't called. It was unlike him. She felt guilty about what she was about to do. She'd never betrayed Josette before. It gave her a terrible feeling of angst. She took out her cell phone and dialed Patrick. *Maybe I should just stay out of their business.* She pondered the thought as she listened to Patrick's cell phone ring. She could just tell Patrick to forget about it and make up some excuse as to why she'd asked him to meet her in the first place.

"I'm right here," Patrick said, sliding into the booth. He unzipped his jacket just enough to loosen his cashmere scarf, but not enough to get comfortable. He hadn't planned to stay long. And if what Sandy had to say was about him reconciling with Josette, it would be an even shorter conversation. Sandy had only told him that she needed to discuss something that concerned the three of them. Patrick hoped that Sandy hadn't called him here to try to talk him out of getting a divorce.

Sandy sipped from her tea cup and said, "Look, Jo is pregnant and she's going to have an abortion because of the divorce."

"Pregnant?" Pat smirked indignantly. "By who?"

Sandy didn't have time for the foolishness. "Pat, don't be stupid, okay? You did sleep with her a couple of months ago, right?"

Pat wrestled with the tongue lashing he'd just received. "Sandy, that doesn't change anything. I'm getting a *divorce*. If the baby is mine, I am going to be the man I've always been and take care of my child."

"Did you miss something? I said she's going to get an ABORTION."

Pat rubbed his temples and bit down on his bottom lip. He gulped almost all of the ice water down, and rubbed his temples again. Abortion was against everything he believed in. But if he were able to convince Josette to keep the baby, it wouldn't change the fact that their marriage was over. He would have a broken family. Visitation schedules. Shared holidays. All the things that he vowed would never happen to him when he'd said the words, *"I do."*

"You need to talk to your wife."

"Sandy, this… is really messy."

"You can say that again. Pat, you are a man of God. Do you mean to tell me that there is no way you can work things out with Jo? I mean, after all that came out in that session, can't you see that in spite of what Josette did to screw up your marriage, she has some emotional problems that have never been dealt with—and those may be the reason why she sabotaged the marriage in the first place? She loves you and is sorry for what she's done. She's been to counseling every week and a rape victims' support group trying to get herself together. Doesn't that count for something?"

"Your sister sleeps around with other men. It is my God-given right to divorce Jo. You are not going to make me feel guilty about that."

"I'm not trying to make you feel guilty, Pat. I'm just saying that your wife is just a scared little girl who was raped at ten years old and never learned to love herself. Don't you see? It makes perfect sense now. All the over achieving. The expensive clothes, make-up, and attitude have all been to cover up for the fact that she hates herself for what happened to her. Promiscuity is self-loathing behavior. I've read up on it. A lot of women who have been raped or molested engage in that kind of behavior, Pat—out of self-hatred. And no matter how much love you gave her, it wouldn't have helped her until she admitted that she had a problem with herself. And she's done that now."

"Do you think this is easy for me, Sandy?" Patrick covered his face with his huge hands and rubbed his temples again.

"Pat, do you still love Jo?"

He sighed. "Yes," he said, looking into his glass.

"Are you still in love with her?"

"No," he replied too quickly for it to be the truth.

"Well, why'd you sleep with her?"

Patrick looked at his sister in-law with the eyes of a man whose soul had been uncovered. "It just happened . . . I didn't plan it. I just wanted to say good-bye in person—before she was served with the papers."

"Oh, you said good-bye all right." Sandy looked her brother-in-law over. He was a defeated man. Broken-hearted. "Pat, consider the baby. Don't just allow an innocent child to be killed without pouring yourself out first—without at least trying."

"So Jo is pregnant?" he asked rhetorically, almost smiling.

"Yep." Sandy nodded. "Pat, have you prayed about this thing?"

"Of course I've prayed. I've fasted. This is my life, Sandy. Jo was my life." He looked away.

"Did God tell you to divorce Jo?"

"I have the right to divorce her for—"

"That's not what I asked you. I said, did He tell you to divorce her?"

Patrick didn't answer. He didn't have to. Sandy knew everything he couldn't bring himself to admit. She gathered her purse and coat. "Pat, I know that you're a man of God. I know that you love the Lord. And I know that you're hurting. But the God we serve can fix broken things, broken marriages—broken people—even my little sister. I believe that."

"Sandy, I love Jo. I just don't know if it's enough to make a difference right now."

Sandy thought back to Patrick's overnight guest. "Why? Is there someone else in the picture now?"

"No."

"Pat, what about the girl that was over when I stopped by that day?—between you and me from this day forward."

Patrick shook his head, disappointedly. "That was my cousin Rhonda—one of the anchors on the JCTV Christian Broadcasting Network. You met her a long time ago. She's dating one of my old teammates. I thought it would be better if she spent the night with me, you know—so she wouldn't be tempted to compromise herself," he explained. "I still have not touched another woman. I'm not like Jo."

"Prove it," Sandy said. She walked away from the table.

Chapter Twenty-Five

On a Sunday afternoon, Josette meandered around Saks until she drifted into the children's department. The soft, soothing shopping music nudged Josette deeper into her thoughts as she moved slowly through the racks of miniature designer outfits, contemplating. *What would it be like to be a mother? How could I do it alone?* She wandered around processing those thoughts. Somberly, she curved through the infant section feeling confused. She trailed her French-manicured hands over the soft-to-the-touch cotton blankets and hooded towels. She picked up a receiving blanket and brushed it delicately across her cheek. She tried to imagine holding a baby—her baby—next to her skin, cheek to cheek. She tried to imagine the creation of her and Patrick's genes merged together. She picked up a lavender stuffed elephant and shook it gently, smiling at the rattling noise it made.

Josette touched her lower abdomen, knowing that there was something miraculous growing on the inside of her. She'd thought about it every minute of the day. She was connected to the precious being already. It was a part of her. But she needed to be realistic about her life now. It wasn't the fairy tale that began when she was just fourteen years old.

Her fight with Patrick over the abortion had been worse than the fight that they'd had the night he found out about her affair. He wanted her to keep the baby. "How could you just make a decision to kill my baby, Jo?" he'd said. "What have I ever done to you to make you keep hurting me?" He'd called her selfish and destructive. He'd asked her why she had to destroy every beautiful gift God had given them—first their marriage, now their child. Josette swallowed hard. Patrick's words still tore at her soul. She brushed the back of her hand across her face to wipe away the evidence.

Couldn't Pat understand that it was the fear of being hated, like she hated Genevieve that had kept her from wanting a child? It was the fear of not having the capability to be a good mother. She'd feared that since she could remember. She'd put off having children for that reason. Josette was afraid of who she would become. And yet, she loved the precious individual forming in her womb who caused her to be nauseated every morning, and swayed her emotions like the wind.

She had already made the appointment. It was the third one she'd made. Something inside of her had caused her to cancel the last two. She was scheduled to have the procedure done the coming weekend. It was one frightening ordeal that she would have to do alone. Sandy wasn't going to support her and neither was Faye. It didn't matter about Patrick. Their ties would be severed soon enough.

Josette had scoured the city and surrounding areas searching for a reputable doctor or clinic that would be safe. Sandy and Faye refused to help. They refused to discuss abortion at all—except to remind Josette that it was a sin. They said that they were Christians first and health professionals second. And surely Patrick hated her more now than he had before. He'd wanted to be a father since they married. Maybe he'd have that opportunity with someone else. It wasn't going to happen with her. But the thought of him having a family with another woman—of him making love to another woman, made her sick to her stomach. She could never love another man like she loved Patrick. She felt weak. She held on to a shelf and bent over. She gagged and her eyes misted.

"Miss, are you okay?" a sales attendant asked, rushing toward her.

It took moments for that feeling to subside. Josette straightened herself slowly. "Yes, thank you." *Love sick.* "Just a little bit of nausea," she said.

"Maybe you should sit for a moment," the sales attendant offered.

"No. I'm okay. I just need to get home," Josette said before rushing toward the elevators.

Josette listened to her messages. Patrick's voice clouded her mind. *"Jo, give God a try. Please. Regardless as to what's happening with you and me, don't kill our baby. Please, Jo. Just trust God this one time to work it out . . . please."* Josette wiped tears from her face and dressed in a comfortable jogging suit and a pair of slide-on gym shoes. It was going to be over today. She was going to go through with it this time. Then she was going to start putting her life back together. The first thing she was going to do was find another place to stay. She and Sandy's relationship wasn't going to be the same—ever. They'd barely said three good sentences to each other since she announced her pregnancy.

At a quarter past eight, Josette walked quietly down the stairs. Sandy sat in the kitchen drinking a cup of tea while she read her daily devotional. She glared at Josette. She had a feeling that today was the day Josette was going to kill her little niece or nephew. She'd overheard Josette in her room the day before, confirming her appointment. For the last month, she'd tried to talk to Josette with empathy, humility, and the gentleness of Christ, but none of it had worked. She had to fight to keep her anger from exploding. "Jo, God doesn't want you to do what you're about to do. It's not right," Sandy said, placing her teacup on the saucer. Josette ignored her. She walked past her without looking at her and went out of the door that led to the garage. Tears streamed down Sandy's face. "Lord, Pat and I have both prayed and fasted. We know that this is not Your will. Do something!" Sandy said, exasperated.

The hours ticked away like a time bomb after Josette left. And Sandy's anxiety increased with the movement of the hands over the face of the clock—the gauge for some pre-determined disaster. She hated that she'd made her little sister suffer the isolation and shame of having an abortion without any support. She'd been down that road. She knew how traumatizing it was for a woman to come to that end and live with it afterwards. But she couldn't uphold Josette in something that was against God's will.

Four hours later, Sandy was still planted in that same spot at the kitchen table, fighting with her conscience. She hadn't dressed. She had sat there praying, and meditating on God's Word. Weary, she had rested her head on the table for a moment when she heard the garage door open. She stood up and waited for Josette to walk in, sorrowful that their lives had come to this point.

Josette shuffled in looking haggard, and distraught. Strands of her hair were freed from the neat ponytail she'd tamed it with this morning. She looked as though she'd been in a playground brawl. She trembled as she hung her key on the key hook. Loss was superimposed on her face. Sandy shoved her anger aside and embraced her little sister, and Josette fell limp in her arms.

Josette cried. "My life is such a mess . . . I'm so scared . . . I'm so scared."

"It's okay, Jo. The Lord will forgive you. It's okay," Sandy said, patting Josette. "He is still merciful."

Josette looked up at her sister. "You don't understand . . ."

Sandy pacified her little sister. "But God understands, Jo."

"I'm afraid of being a mother . . . I don't know how to be a mother," Josette sobbed. "I don't know what to do. I don't know how to do this without Pat. I don't know what to do with this baby."

Sandy's heart jumped joyously. "You didn't do it?"

"No . . . I couldn't," Josette cried.

"Oh, Lord God . . . thank You, Lord God," Sandy said, wiping the waterfall from her eyes. "I'm gonna be an auntie?"

Josette nodded. "Yes . . . you're going to be an auntie."

Sandy shouted. "Oh, praise God! Thank You! Thank You!"

Chapter Twenty-Six

Genevieve sat at her desk immersed in her task. Her brows furrowed as she flipped through the papers scattered across her desk. Her office phone beeped. She took her black designer reading glasses off and placed them on top of the grant proposals she'd been dissecting. It was almost eight p.m. She smiled. "Yes, honey."

Benjamin laughed. "When are you coming home?"

"Soon. I was just going over some grant proposals. Why? Do you miss me?"

"Yes. And Faith and Joshua just left to go roller skating with the Johnson family. The Johnsons said not to expect them back until eleven. They have a bunch of kids to drop off at home afterward."

"Mm-hmm. And you were thinking what?" Genevieve smiled.

"I was thinking that I could have you to myself for a couple of hours."

"My, aren't we greedy?"

"Guilty as charged."

Genevieve was back on an emotional down slope, but she was going to work through it this time. She didn't want her and Benjamin's relationship to suffer like it had in the past. "I see . . . give me twenty minutes to finish up, and I'll be right home. I just need to straighten up a little and lock up."

"You promise?"

"Promise." Genevieve stood up and stretched.

"Hey you," an upbeat voice said from the doorway.

"Well, hello. How are you doing?" Genevieve said after her heart slowed. She'd been startled momentarily.

"I'm good. You still haven't learned to go home at a reasonable time on a Friday night?" Dr. Banks asked, walking over and sliding her rear on the corner of Genevieve's desk.

"Well, Ben just called, so I'm on my way home now. What brings you by?"

Dr. Banks shifted. "I came to see how things were going with you."

Genevieve raised her brow. She knew that something was up. "You could have called."

"Yes. But I thought it would be better if I stopped by in person this time."

"Oh?"

"I *heard* that you haven't been yourself around here lately," Dr. Banks said gently. "Your staff is a bit worried about you."

Genevieve grew concerned. "Well, what did they say?"

Dr. Banks was serious. "Listen, Vee, they weren't telling on you. They just said that you'd been a little short-tempered at times. And that doesn't sound at all like you. They're really worried."

Genevieve sat down at her desk, disappointed that her mentor and friend had to have this conversation with her. She felt guilty that she'd offended someone. It wasn't her nature to be mean-spirited. She let out a sigh. "Okay, my personal life has been in *shambles*. Ben and I *just* started being intimate again—which has been a major strain on our marriage. Trying to work it out is twice as difficult, because now I feel like I have to work extra hard to show him that I am committed to us as a couple—which has put a lot of pressure on me. Second of all, my daughters found me some months ago, and I thought I was going to have the chance to start over with them. But instead, it's been one disappointment after another. And I don't know what I've done wrong for the Lord to deal with me this way. It's affected everything—my relationship with Ben, and now my work here. I love my staff. I hate to think that anyone has been walking on eggshells because of me—that's not me. I would have talked to you about it earlier, but I just wanted to have something positive to say."

Dr. Banks nodded. "Vee, we are all human. Christians or not. We have bad days just like the rest of the world. We just know who to go to in order to straighten everything out."

"I just wanted things to be different between my daughters and me. I had so much hope when Sandy called me. I thought it was a second chance for me to start over fresh, you know? I didn't want us to have the same raggedy, painful relationship that I had with my mother, Grace. And now we do."

"You've never talked that much about your mother, Vee."

"She died while I was in my habit. But I had tried to make amends with her after the girls' father put me out. She was just so cold," Genevieve said softly, shaking her head. "She just couldn't love me. It's like there's a generational curse on my family. I understood her and I forgave her. But she never loved me."

Dr. Banks nodded. "I understand. Why do you think that was—that she never loved you, Vee?"

"Well, when Lou put me out with the girls, I was penniless. I could only think of one person to call for help—that was Ms. Lucille, Grace's next door neighbor. Ms. Lucille allowed me and the girls to spend the night with her that night. But she wanted so badly for Grace and me to have a relationship. Ms. Lucille had never been able to have children, so I guess it was important to her. So anyway, she arranged a meeting between me, Grace, and the pastor of their church." Genevieve paused in thought for a moment. "I think his name was Pastor McKinney . . . yes. That was it. I didn't want to go through with the meeting at all. I was just hoping the man could find me an apartment or something. But he met with me first, then Grace. And when he talked to Grace, I stayed on the outside of the door, listening. I needed to know why she hated me so much."

"Did you find out the answer to that question?"

"Oh, yes. But it was still painful. Grace's biological father died of a heart attack when she was thirteen. My grandmother remarried a Baptist preacher of a dirt road church in Mobile, Alabama, when Grace was sixteen. I heard Grace say that she loved him—loved him as if he were her own father. But he betrayed that trust," Genevieve said, looking toward the window. She unscrewed the top of her bottled water and refreshed herself. "I heard Grace tell Pastor McKinney that her stepfather forced himself on her one evening—at the church of all places." Genevieve rolled her eyes and twisted in her chair. "She became pregnant with me. She was too ashamed to tell anyone what had happened. The people in the community respected him. She felt that no one would have believed her. And he warned her that if she ever told a soul, he would say that she seduced him."

Dr. Banks looked sympathetically at her protégé. "My goodness. That must have been awful for an innocent young girl to deal with."

"I'm sure. Somehow Grace thought that if she ignored it, the pregnancy would go away, but her belly kept growing. When Grace told him that she thought that she was pregnant, he suggested to her mother that they send her up north to live with a relative. Allowing her to stay would have raised too many questions, I guess. And I'm sure he was afraid that the truth may have come out eventually."

Dr. Banks shook her head in disgust. "What a shame to put that burden on her, when she was taken advantaged of—raped. That's horrible, Vee."

Genevieve's eyes watered. "I know. That's why I had so much empathy for her." She plucked a tissue from the floral designed box on the corner of her desk. "Grace couldn't bear to hurt her mother with the truth, so she allowed her to believe that she had sinfully given her virginity to one of the boys in town. I understood why she hated me. Why she'd locked me in closets and beat me all those years—I was a reminder of that betrayal she experienced at sixteen."

"Yes, you were." Dr. Banks nodded in agreement with Genevieve's assessment.

"And I started another ugly life with my children. It's like a cycle—a curse."

"You listen to me," Dr. Banks said, with her hands gently lifting Genevieve's chin, "God is a cycle and curse-breaker. Give it to Him."

Genevieve cried openly. "I feel . . . like I'm falling apart. I am falling apart."

Dr. Banks patted Genevieve's hand. "No, you're not. You're just being human."

"I have so much love to give those girls, Denice. If they would allow me the opportunity to show them that I am different—and that I'm sorry for whatever hurt I've caused them."

"Vee, I wish I knew the right words to tell you. Not one degree qualifies me to solve this one. Your mother had every right to feel the pain she did—not to hurt you—but she had the right to hurt for what had been done to her. And you, there was virtually no way you could have made it through that kind of abuse unscathed. Self-hatred was embedded in you from the beginning. And now we have two beautiful young women who were just as emotionally scarred as you and your mother were. And that brings me to one conclusion; this is a God problem, Vee. This is not a Dr. Banks or a Dr. Moss-Carpenter problem," she smiled. "But now, until God works this thing out for you, take all that love that you want to give to those women, and channel it to the man who loves you. He's a man of God—but he's a man. And he still needs to know that no matter what, you are his. Intimacy with you validates that."

"Spoken better than Dr. Phil." Genevieve smiled.

"He better ask somebody," Dr. Banks joked. "Now get on out of here and go home and have fun."

"Okay. What about you? What are you doing out this way?"

"Honey, Charles and I are just taking a romantic drive—who knows where we will end up tonight. He's downstairs looking around. I told him to stop here for a moment."

"Well then, *you* better get out of here."

"You're right."

Chapter Twenty-Seven

Sandy stood over the stove sautéing mushrooms, with the phone cradled between her neck and shoulder. "Yes, girl. Can you believe it? Josette has me in here cooking for her. I told her she better call and see if her and Patrick's chef, Franklin, can work over here a couple of days a week—'cause shoot, I am no cook—especially not a gourmet cook," she said jokingly to Samantha Cross, her co-worker and close friend. She beamed with pride. "If the media stays out of their business, maybe she and Pat can work things out. Jo's pregnancy has created more speculation about the reason for their divorce," Sandy said, lifting the pan off the flame.

News of Josette and Patrick's divorce had played out in the media weeks ago, but her pregnancy had tossed more logs in the fire. And how the news leaked out was still a mystery. Everyone was wondering what was going on with their former star football player and his wife. That was the one thing Sandy didn't envy about her sister's life—the fact that because of who her husband was, people felt it was their right to delve into their personal business. The truth of the matter was that they were just like everyone else. They just happened to be famous.

Sandy sat down at the island. "Well, Jo says the news reports are not bothering her, and that they'll find something else to report on in a couple of weeks. And I hope so, because it does bother me. No matter how badly she gets on my nerves, she's my little sister and I love her. She's got enough on her plate right now—dealing with a divorce and becoming a single mother," Sandy said, noticing that it was time to check the steaks she'd put on the grill. "Well, girl, let me get off this phone, I have steaks on the grill outside—yes, in this cold weather. Shoot girl, this is Michigan. Spring don't mean nothin'. But Jo wanted a charcoal flavor. She said she was craving it. So talk to you later. Bye now." Sandy placed the phone on the base and slid her patio door open. She lifted the long barbeque fork from the side rack and opened the grill top. Turning the porterhouse steaks over, a thought popped in her mind that she suppressed. She had to concentrate on other things—things that didn't make her cry—like becoming an auntie.

She replaced the worrisome thought with the memory of her and Josette at the meat market yesterday. She smiled, and chuckled about the way Josette had vomited all over Angelo's floor. She'd begged for fresh catfish, so the two of them had gone to Angelo's Meat Market to pick out some large filets for Sandy to fry. Both of them were convinced that Angelo had the freshest meat of all the markets in the city. But as soon as Josette walked in Angelo's door and got a whiff of all that raw meat, she puked all over his floor. She'd tried to make it outside, but hadn't run quickly enough.

Sandy told Angelo that Josette was pregnant because Angelo didn't watch television. She figured that he hadn't been privy to all the media coverage. Angelo had put his hands over his own expectant-looking belly and laughed heartily as his youngest son mopped up the mess. His round face was jovial. "Jo's having a boy, I tell ya. They start giving their mothers grief before they even get here," he'd said happily.

Josette couldn't even eat the fish after Sandy had fried it. She'd said her stomach was too upset. Sandy had fussed playfully about stinking up her whole condo for nothing. She had to spray Lysol and open most of the windows to release that fishy smell. Josette was lucky she was pregnant. That was the one thought Sandy could hold onto to keep her sane.

Sandy wanted Josette to stay with her until the baby was old enough for her to handle alone—maybe when he or she was five or so—maybe when he or she went off to college. She was excited about the company of a new baby. She'd wanted that for herself for so long. But she would share in the joy of experiencing motherhood through her little sister until the Lord blessed her personally—if that was His will. She still hoped it was.

She and Josette were in the process of turning Sandy's den into a nursery. She'd moved the convertible sofa to the sitting room in the master bedroom. She had sold the rest of the furnishings to one of the young nurses at the hospital who was just striking out on her own. Sandy and Josette had been to every high-end furniture and wallpaper store looking for decorations for the nursery. Josette finally hired Beverly Mason, the interior decorator who was responsible for decorating some of the most posh homes and businesses in the city—including the mayor's mansion and the models for several multimillion-dollar apartment complexes and subdivisions that were attracting people back to downtown Detroit. Beverly's assistant, Jeffery, had already been out to "assess" Sandy's "dwelling place."

Sandy didn't want to know what the bill was going to be for all that bourgeois service, and didn't care, since Patrick was picking up the tab. She didn't think it at all necessary to hire an interior decorator for such a small task—rather excessive, even. But that was Josette. If it had been left up to Sandy, the little rascal—he or she—would be "dwelling" in a room courtesy of Target or JCPenney.

Josette had already begun purchasing baby clothes and accessories from stores that most grown people couldn't afford to shop in. And sooner or later, Josette had to realize that with her and Patrick divorcing, and her refusing any type of settlement, her lavish lifestyle was going to have to change. She earned a low six-figure salary as an attorney, but it could in no way compete with Patrick's millions and the lifestyle that his kind of money afforded her. Their home in Michigan alone was worth $15.5 million. The two villas and beach front land they owned in Turks and Caicos was worth a cool $7 million. And Patrick still had lucrative endorsements even though he was retired. He had properly invested his earnings over the years, and his portfolio was solid. And he was a man of his word. The baby would surely be well taken care of, but Josette—she was going to have to stay out of Saks and Neiman's—forget about Gucci, Versace, and Manolo. They couldn't continue to be her friends. High consumption without the cash to match equaled debt. Sandy had tried to mention it to her little sister in a casual kind of way without adding any additional stress on her. She knew it was going to take awhile for Josette to "unlearn" the lifestyle she'd had for the last seven years.

The sound of rain pouring down authoritatively made Sandy think of Lamont. But instead of stirring thoughts of kisses, touches, and smiles, she was disheartened. She'd been suppressing the thought of him for the last eight days in order to rejoice over Josette's gift from God—in order to keep from falling apart like she'd seen her little sister do when the reality of her marriage had shifted from rose-colored to gray.

She hadn't heard from Lamont in eight days. She'd left messages and e-mails. Her stomach had been tied securely in love knots—the kind that made her want to stop breathing. There'd been no rest for her tonight either, despite the lovely meal and conversation she'd enjoyed with her sister, talking about the baby's future. She was a restless bag of nerves. The pain in her stomach kept her from sleeping. If this continued, a panic attack would sneak up and catch her. She'd given up the Zoloft for good, and was hoping she'd never have to take it again—ever.

She went downstairs to the kitchen, took a bottle of Maalox out of the refrigerator, and drank some down like it was a cool, refreshing drink. Then she climbed back in bed and tried to beat the Insomnia Monster at his own game. An hour into their duel, Sandy was thrown out of the rink by the terrible sound of banging and ringing. Her heart sprinted. She checked her pulse with the normalcy of a nurse and looked at the clock, realizing that she was dreaming. It was exactly 3:15 a.m.—the time all the murders occurred in her old childhood scare, Amityville Horror. She chided herself. "Dream something else," she whispered, dazed. But when she covered her head with a pillow, the ringing and banging persisted.

Sandy sat straight up in the darkness, assessing her surroundings again. *Home. Not dreaming.* Zombie-like, she threw her comforter back and swung both of her legs over the side of the bed in unison. She willed herself to her bedroom door, snatched her housecoat off the hook, and put it on clumsily, squeezing the belt tightly around her waist. Sleepiness gave in to sheer fear. *Fire. War. Escaped mental patient.* She poked her head in the guest room where Josette was sleeping peacefully. She called out to her, just so she'd be alert in case it actually was some psycho at the door with an ax. At least Josette could call the police. She'd be dead. But

Josette was a hard sleeper. She mumbled something and turned over on her side. Maybe sleeping for two was a lot more taxing than sleeping for one.

Sandy trotted down the stairs so quickly that she lost her balance. She steadied herself with the handrail. She jumped the last two steps and ran into the kitchen to answer the phone, because it too was participating in the noise drama. "Hello!" Sandy barked. The caller was frantic.

"Cassandra, there is a *black* man banging on your door!" Sandy's next door neighbor, Zelma, informed her, forgetting perhaps that Sandy was black too. Zelma was a retired widow who stayed up all times of the night, but she was protective and sweet. Sandy wondered why Zelma wasn't sleeping on a cold and rainy night like tonight. Maybe whoever was at her door had awakened Zelma too. "He's been out there a few minutes," Zelma warned.

"Thanks Zelma," Sandy said, pushing the disconnect button. She clutched the phone in her hand and raced to the door. Her heart hoped it was Lamont. Yes. Certainly it was him coming to explain what terrible incident had kept him away for eight whole days with no communication. Sandy looked out of the peephole and sighed. *Relief. Anger.* She snatched the door open. "Are you crazy! It is three o'clock in the morning. What is your problem?"

"I'm sorry," Patrick said. "I left my cell phone at home. I need to talk to Jo—it's important."

Sandy opened her eyes wide and scratched the top of her head with the short, stubby antenna of the cordless phone to stimulate her brain. She wanted to tell Patrick that this could have waited. But the serious look on his face conveyed that it couldn't have. His jeans were soggy at the bottom from the rain. And the hooded raincoat he'd paid a couple thousand dollars for was just as soggy.

"Pat, Jo is asleep. That's what we usually do around here this time in the morning," Sandy said, locking the door behind him.

"No, I'm not," Josette said, standing at the bottom step looking sleepy and disoriented. "What do you want, Pat?" she asked flatly.

Patrick pulled the hood of his jacket away from his face and spoke in a low, urgent voice. "I need to talk to you, Jo."

Josette stood with her fists balled on her hips. "About what?" she snapped. But she looked a lot less intimidating with the short, lavender Victoria's Secret baby doll on.

Patrick glanced at Sandy like she was interrupting. But she didn't leave because it was her house and her little sister. And whatever Patrick had to say so badly that he had awakened her out of her sleep this early in the morning, she was going to hear—or at least part of it, anyway.

Patrick sucked in air, let it out, and spoke cautiously. "Jo, I . . . want you . . . to come home . . . I'm sorry. I'm sorry about everything," he said. He bowed his head as the tears flowed. He sniffed in and looked up at Josette again. "I want to work it out. I want us to be . . . a family."

A lone tear crept down Josette's face, but she remained silent. Still. So still that Sandy couldn't tell if she was breathing. And she did not look at all impressed with Patrick's a.m. drama.

Patrick took humble *"Mother, May I?"* steps past Sandy and up to Josette and said, "Jo, I love you. I am *still in love* with you. I don't want a divorce, babe. I want you to come home." All the man in him was locked in every tear that slid down his cheeks. "I've been stupid and prideful, I know. But this thing—me and you not being together—has been killing me. I know we can make it better. Let's make it better, babe."

The knots in Sandy's stomach tightened. She sensed that Josette was going to turn around and go back up the stairs, tell Patrick to get out, and then go back to being without him, like she'd been for almost a year. The three of them were suspended in the moment, waiting to see where the next second was going to take them. It was so quiet in the room that Sandy could hear every one of the billions of drops of rain beating against the doors and windows.

Unpremeditatedly, Josette flung her arms around Patrick's neck—soaking wet and all. Patrick squeezed her to his body, lifting her off of her feet. They cried on each other. And Sandy, the voyeur, shed her tears as well—for the sake of good, committed love. Then and only then did she walk away and let them have their moment. She was halfway up the stairs when the doorbell rang again. She rushed to the door again, because Patrick and Josette were in their own world, kissing, squeezing, and talk-crying. Sandy looked out of the peephole again. This time it was the police—two white policemen. One looked to be in his late forties, and the other about twenty-seven. As soon as Sandy pulled the door open, the older one asked if she was the owner of the residence.

"Yes, I am," Sandy said politely, looking at their badges and nameplates.

They introduced themselves as Officer Bryant and Officer Stokes.

"And what is your name, ma'am?" Officer Bryant asked.

"Cassandra Moss."

"Ms. Moss, we got a report that a suspicious looking . . . man was hanging around outside your home—banging on the door and disturbing the peace," Officer Bryant explained.

Sandy covered her mouth to keep from laughing. If she were back in the 'hood, the operator would have told Zelma to tell her to let her cousin in. But out in the 'burbs, a black man banging on a door at three a.m. was cause for the police to come right away.

"It was just my brother-in-law coming to pick up my sister," Sandy explained.

"Is he still here?" Officer Stokes asked.

"Yep. Sure is," Sandy said stepping back, allowing them in. *Nope. There is no domestic violence going on here.* Patrick and Josette separated.

"Sir, we just want to—" Officer Stokes stopped mid-sentence when he recognized Patrick. His youthfulness and fanaticism for sports elevated his voice. "Hey . . . *Patrick Kelley* . . . how are you?" he asked. Both he and Officer Bryant shook hands with Patrick. Officer Bryant continued the questioning because Officer Stokes was star struck.

"Mr. Kelley, sir, is everything okay?" Officer Bryant asked.

"Yeah—everything is fine . . . fine," Patrick said, looking back at Josette. "I just came by to pick up my wife."

"Are you okay, Mrs. Kelley?" Officer Bryant continued.

"Yes, sir," Josette blushed.

"Get dressed, babe," Patrick said quietly to Josette, because Officer Stokes could not keep his eyes from wandering over Josette's Victoria's Secret special. Obeying, Josette sprinted up the steps with newfound energy. "Jo, slow down!" Patrick said, worried about the baby. She slowed and walked up the next few steps.

"Well, it seems like everything is okay here," Officer Bryant and Officer Stokes said at the same time.

"Yeah, my wife and I had some problems, and she's been staying here with my sister-in-law for awhile. But we decided that we're going to work things out—we're expecting a baby!" Patrick volunteered proudly. There was no doubt that Officer Bryant and Officer Stokes had heard about it in the news, but Patrick seemed content to give it to them firsthand.

"The Lord has been my strength through our separation, you know. And He has been speaking to me about me. Showing me myself. He put a question on my heart that caused me to realize that my marriage was worth giving another try." Officer Bryant and Officer Stokes listened intently. Patrick couldn't pass up an opportunity to witness. "The question was simply, *'Is anything too hard for God?'*" Patrick said.

"Wow. Well, we know the answer to that, don't we?" Officer Bryant said. "And congratulations, Mr. Kelley. I'm not supposed to talk about this when we're on duty, but I'm a saved man myself. And I know firsthand what the Lord is capable of doing. My wife and I have been married for twenty-eight years."

The three of them stood there shooting the breeze about Patrick's retirement, his new restaurant, and his plans for his and Josette's future. Patrick signed autographs for both of them, and Officer Bryant's son before they left. Then he took his wife home where she belonged.

Alone finally, Sandy sat on her bed and cried. Her tears were a symptom of something she didn't want to face. The logical part of her heart was stirring a truth that could not be disregarded. She needed to know what was going on with the man she loved. They'd talked every day several times a day since they'd met last September. Now he'd vanished, filling every sweet word he'd ever spoken to her with bile. By four a.m., she'd decided that she was going to face him, even if he didn't want to face her.

Sandy arrived on the doorstep of Lamont's greystone at exactly 8:37 a.m. She pressed the doorbell without letting up. The fact that she had driven over two hundred miles had simmered over the past four hours and was now boiling. She knew he was home and she knew he was awake. Lamont was not at all happy to see the woman he'd asked to be "his lady." If he could have disappeared, he would have. But Sandy was not an apparition he could blink away. She was right there, staring at him with those eyes he'd said were the most beautiful he'd ever seen. He didn't invite her in.

"Am I supposed to talk to you out here?" Sandy asked in smoke ringlets from the cool morning air.

Lamont questioned her like she was a stalker. "Why are you here, Sandy?"

"No, the question is, why have you been avoiding me? If there is something that needs to be said, then say it. You don't have to run, Lamont."

Lamont was unfeeling. "I haven't been running. I've been busy. I run a company," he said.

"Too busy to return *one* phone call?"

Sandy's breath was snatched away in an instant. The *reason* walked up behind Lamont wearing a long, see-through mesh gown, with her breasts spilling over the edge of the push-up front. Sandy blinked twice. Collected her thoughts. Was this woman the reason she hadn't heard from Lamont in eight days? The reason that he had reduced her to standing outside in the cold like a nuisance?

"Mont, what's going on?" Simone Montgomery asked, tossing her hair like she was in a Pantene commercial.

Sandy couldn't hold her tears. She looked between the two of them, unbelieving. "Yeah, *Lamont*, what is going on?"

Lamont attempted to make the situation casual by allowing Sandy in. "Baby, this is my friend Sandy," he said to Simone.

"What!" Sandy said incredulously. "No, I am NOT your friend! You said we were *together*."

"Are you with her?" Simone snapped, forcing Lamont to declare his alliance with one country or another.

"No. I'm with you," Lamont said to Simone, without a hint of remorse for the fact that he'd just butchered Sandy.

"So then you need to leave," Simone said dryly.

Sandy wanted to fight. She wanted to hit him. She wanted to hit Simone. But neither one of them was worth humiliating herself or polluting her testimony. She looked at Lamont long and hard, with his exposed bare chest and white Ralph Lauren pajama bottoms. She glowered at him, waiting for him to say something. But he didn't. His silence was condemning. "Thank you," Sandy said to both of them before Lamont shut the door. She walked back to her car and got in. She started the ignition and put it in gear robotically.

Why hadn't he just told her that he couldn't deal with her celibacy anymore—like he'd said? He was with *her?* Was that all she deserved? Sandy pulled over down the road because she felt her chest caving in. She cried hard on the steering wheel, beaten by God's cruelty. She loved him. What had she received in return? He was with *her.* A panic attack seized her without warning.

Chapter Twenty-Eight

Home. It was good to be home. The first order of business was to meet with Reverend Kelley for counseling. Having a session with him was going to be awkward for Josette, but Patrick was adamant about not seeing another minister. He trusted his father's objective judgment and his relationship with Christ. Besides, Patrick couldn't bring himself to discuss the intimate details of his and Josette's marriage with anyone else but his father. They'd shared that kind of relationship all of Patrick's life. Reverend Kelley had provided their premarital counseling, and Patrick saw no reason for things to change. Josette didn't have any valid objections to having counseling sessions with Reverend Kelley, except for the fact that she was immeasurably embarrassed by what she'd done.

She and Patrick entered through Reverend Kelley's private office entrance in the back of the church, holding hands. Pat tapped a musical tune on the door.

Reverend Kelley answered it on cue. "Welcome. It's nice to see that some people would rather be at church on a Friday evening than at the movies or something," he joked.

Josette smiled nervously. "Hey, Dad," she said, kissing him on the cheek.

"Hey, precious," he returned, embracing Josette.

Reverend Kelley was handsome, with the same honey brown complexion as his son. His face held the same masculine softness. And though his salt and pepper fade distinguished the two, there was no mistaking that he was Patrick's father. Josette looked at her father-in-law and saw her husband years from now. He and Patrick shook hands before they hugged each other lovingly.

"You lookin' pretty good, old man," Pat joked, noticing that his dad was wearing a pair of beige linen slacks, matching shirt, and sandals. "You smell good too. You been by Keturah's place lately?"

"Shoot, naw. She is too expensive for my blood! What you smell is the same bottle you and Josette gave me a couple Christmases ago. I only wear it on special occasions."

"Oh, yeah?" Patrick said curiously, looking his dad over again. He smiled. "It might be a story behind all this."

"None you gonna hear tonight, son," Reverend Kelley smiled. "Let's get started. We've got an hour. And I want to be orderly," he said, winking at Josette.

Josette knew that wink meant that Reverend Kelley had something else important to do as well—like maybe a date afterward. She winked back knowingly. Reverend Kelley led the three of them in prayer. When they finished praying, they took their seats at Reverend Kelley's small round table.

"Before we get started, I have to get something off my chest," Reverend Kelley said. He looked at Josette. She cringed, not knowing what to expect. After all, he was Patrick's father. "Jo, I was angry and disappointed—not by what happened between you two, but because you didn't return any of my calls during the time you and Pat were separated. No matter what happens, nothing should keep family from communicating, understand?"

"Yes," Josette answered. Patrick squeezed her hand and kissed it softly.

"In the sight of God, both of you are my children. I'm in no position to condemn anyone, Jo. As closely as I have walked with the Lord, I have sinned just as greatly over my lifetime—just like the next man, but I keep my eyes fixed on Him," he said, opening the Bible. "Now that that's over, how do you feel, Jo—about what is happening with you and Pat now?"

Josette searched Patrick's eyes tenderly. "I feel like I've been given a chance to start over with Pat."

"Have you started over with God, Jo?"

Josette wiggled in her seat. "I don't know. I have confessed to Him that I am so sorry for what I did to my husband—to our marriage. I've asked for God's forgiveness and Patrick's forgiveness. But I cannot say for sure that I've started over with God. I don't know where I am in terms of my true feelings about religion," Josette admitted. "To be honest, I don't know where I was in the first place."

"Jo, you need to know that your marriage can't grow properly without God," Reverend Kelley said. "He's the one that designed it. It's like taking your Range Rover to a Chevy dealer for service. They wouldn't have the expertise to do what needs to be done. You may have mouthed the words when you were a girl, telling the Lord that you confessed your sins and that you accepted Him—but if you did it for Linda and Roger, or even for Pat, you haven't done anything. If you didn't believe, you still don't have His salvation. Salvation is granted on the faith of your heart. That is the only way. You've got to understand that, daughter. Now, I'm going to give you some verses to study, and I want you to be able to tell me how they relate to you, Jo."

Reverend Kelley went through his Bible pointing out key passages for both Josette and Patrick to study separately and together. He discussed the challenges they were having and their plans for fortifying their marriage. After an hour, he was satisfied that they'd gotten off to a good start. He ended their session and scheduled them for four more, letting them know that it would be a long and sometimes painful journey to get back to where they'd been before the affair.

Spring had given way to the beginnings of summer. Josette washed the last of the Sunday breakfast dishes by hand. She and Patrick had left church right after eight o'clock service and had eaten breakfast together. Patrick had gone out to run a few errands and visit Keith. Josette looked out at Long Lake from the kitchen window as she slid it open. Life felt fresh and new. She imagined her, Patrick, and the baby having a picnic out by the lake. The whole terrible situation with her marriage had caused her to reevaluate what she truly wanted out of life—what she wanted to look back and see when it was all over.

Josette decided that she wanted her family. She wanted to look back and have all the memories of her baby's childhood, every detail—the first word, the first step—all of it. She didn't want to miss anything. She wanted to have the family she should have had growing up, without all the scars. She'd been home for a little over two months now. She was five months pregnant, barely showing, but still, she had made a lot of life-changing decisions in that short period of time. She and Patrick would explore some of those things tonight over dinner. Josette had allowed their Panamanian housekeeper, Cuca, and their chef, Franklin, to go home early. She wanted her and Patrick to have complete privacy for the conversation that needed to take place.

Josette was still considering everything she'd been learning about herself in rape counseling and in sessions with Reverend Kelley. She was making progress. She and Patrick were talking openly about their relationship, and the pain that came along with it when the subject came up. It was crucial to Patrick that Josette developed a real relationship with God. He didn't want to push her into it, but it was the foundation of almost every discussion they had about their future. Josette wanted desperately to please him this time, but now she understood that he couldn't be her motivation for building a relationship with God. She didn't want to lie and say something she wasn't feeling. And she wasn't quite feeling "it" yet—whatever it was that drew people to God. And that was just one hurdle.

It was clear that she and Patrick had a long way to go. Scars had to heal and trust had to be reestablished. It was an uphill battle. Since she'd been back at home, Patrick had been sneaking up on her whenever she was on the phone. When she wasn't home, he called her excessively. Josette felt like she was being hunted at times—spied on. In addition, their lovemaking had suffered too.

The last time they'd been intimate, Patrick had stopped abruptly in the middle of their lovemaking, leaving Josette wondering if she had said or done something wrong. She'd learned the next day, by Patrick's own admission, that her zealous passion for him the night before had made him suspicious. He'd wondered if she'd been that *free* with her lover. He said he couldn't get those images out of his head. And how was she supposed to combat her husband's imagination? Even her desire to please him physically was backfiring on her. She hadn't brought this concern up for discussion yet, because she didn't want to make waves. They were in such a delicate state now. She didn't want to do anything to impart the idea that she was revolting against him in any way. She'd made a mess, and now she had to clean it up by slowly earning her husband's trust back.

Josette took a short nap, and then began preparing Sunday dinner. She cooked shrimp pasta, grilled salmon, and peach cobbler. She silently thanked Linda for insisting that she learned how to cook. Even Franklin's best gourmet dishes weren't as delicious as some of Linda's recipes.

The dining room table was set for royalty with decorative silk and linen placemats, solid gold napkin holders, and gold-plated silverware. Josette took the crystal stemware, a clear glass plate, and a vase from one of the china cabinets which contained only Lalique pieces. She put fresh orchids in the vase and placed it on the table in between four dinner candles. She nodded with accomplishment. She took off her apron and went upstairs to shower while her cobbler cooled. She came back down a half hour later and sat in the kitchen watching cable, waiting for Patrick. He'd promised to be home by six o'clock. He'd said that he had to stop by the restaurant to retrieve some documents. Their Grand Opening was just two weeks away.

When the phone rang, Josette hoped it wasn't Patrick telling her that he was going to be late. She heard the door to the garage creak open. She recognized the caller's voice before he identified himself. It was Jeffery, Beverly Mason's assistant from the design studio. In his over-exaggerated feminine drawl, he told Josette that the wallpaper for the nursery had arrived the day before, and the drapes were ready as well. He said that he would have the installation team over tomorrow by noon. He wanted to make sure someone would be home.

"Okay, no problem. Thank you for the rush delivery. I'm getting excited."

"Josette, you are one of our best customers, honey. Anything for you. I'll be by tomorrow with some more pictures of furniture samples, or if you want, we can have something made. Just give me an idea of what you want," Jeffery said.

"Sounds good, hon. See you tomorrow," she said, rushing Jeffery off the phone. He had a tendency to be hyper-verbal. And besides, Josette wanted to see the look on Patrick's face when he stepped into *Dinner at Jo's place*. She hung up the cordless and set it on the counter. "Surprise!" she said excitedly. She waited for Patrick's response, but he was distant. No expression surfaced on his face. He walked right past her. There was no smile of appreciation for all her domestic labor. "Baby, what's the matter?"

Patrick huffed and bit down on his lip. He counter-questioned his wife. "Who were you talking to, Jo?"

"Huh? It was just Jeffery from the design studio, letting me know that the baby's wallpaper is in."

"Why'd you hang up so fast? You hung up that phone as soon as you heard me come in this house, Jo."

"Pat, no. I was just trying to keep Jeffery from rambling—that's all."

"Don't lie to me, Jo!" Pat was in her face—invading her parameter like she was some child forced to come clean with a confession.

"Pat, baby, I swear . . . It was Jeffery."

Pat sighed. He looked around the kitchen. Refused to look at his wife. He smirked, unbelieving. "Well then, get him on the phone, Jo," he said, taking the cordless off the counter and handing it to her.

Josette refused to take it. Not because she didn't want to prove to her husband that she was sincere about doing right by him this time, but because she knew that if she allowed him to do this to her every single time, it would tear at her and eventually destroy what she was trying to rebuild. "Pat . . . you've got to trust me, baby . . . please."

"Call him," he ordered for the second time.

Josette shook her head slowly. "No," she said just above a whisper. She was not going to let him do this to her. For a moment, she wished that they had that stupid Caller ID service that Patrick, himself, felt was insulting. Then they could just settle this without any accusatory exchanges and eat the dinner she'd prepared.

"That's what I thought," he said, dropping the phone on the floor.

The sound of it clashing against the imported Spanish tile sent a message to Josette that maybe their marriage *couldn't* work. Maybe it was too damaged to work. It was never going to be the way it was when they were young. And if that was the case, Josette would rather be alone. She couldn't do this every day for the rest of her life with him. Without saying anything, without pleading, without proving her innocence with a simple phone call, she took her keys out of the drawer near the refrigerator and left.

Right back on top of the *Table of Pain* in the picnic area of Belle Isle is where Josette took her refuge from Patrick. She wondered if the tear stains from last year were still here. She lay atop of it without the worry of snagging her already worn Levis, and watched the sky change from blue, to orange-ruby, to gray, to black, wrapped inside the checkered picnic blanket that she kept inside the trunk. She examined the stars that weren't visible earlier, and laughed a deranged laugh as she thought about the possibility of really having a conversation with God. The probability of God's voice booming out of the night sky was zero. "Yeah, what do you have to say about tonight, huh? Was I wrong? No. Your homeboy Pat was wrong—that's who was wrong! Am I supposed to just let him bully me into proving my worthiness at his every whim, huh? Answer me! ANSWER ME!" Josette yelled into the sky before she broke down crying.

It was an irony of sorts that she was back in this space again. She didn't know what was worse, not having Patrick, or having him with all of his overbearing suspicions. What did restoration mean? Was it just a restoration of words? It seemed that way in their case. Josette had wanted to do exactly what they said they were going to do—start over. But reality had proven stronger than the heart. So she just cried, ignoring the danger of a woman being in a park alone this time of night. She would have gone home, but she didn't know where home was. Concern for her safety was pushed into oblivion by thoughts of her self-imposed exile and her subsequent plans. She drifted slowly to a place where life was perfect—where she and her husband still made love in the morning before breakfast and cuddled at night, sharing stories of their adventures and stresses. Someplace where they still made each other laugh, and didn't rip each other's souls apart.

Patrick's hands shook Josette gently at first, then more fervently. Drowsily, she opened her eyes, trying to connect time and place. That is when she realized that the hands shaking her were not those of her husband, but a stranger. She screamed loudly as she attempted to unravel herself from the blanket. In her hysteria, she tumbled off the Table of Pain onto the ground, bumping her head. The stranger continued to approach her deliberately, speaking words Josette could not hear over her own screams. She screamed more loudly and kicked with such force that the blanket loosened its grip on her, and her house shoes flew off of her feet. The man threw his hands up in front of him, backing away from her slowly, yelling over her screams.

"Young lady, I'm not gonna hurt you! I wasn't tryin' to hurt you. This park ain't safe for no woman this time of night. I's just trying to tell you that—that's all. I'm not gonna hurt you. Just calm down!" He repeated himself until Josette was able to decode the movement of his lips. "My name is Willie. I was out here fishin'. Seen you layin' on this picnic table. Didn't know if you was okay or not. When I realized you were sleepin' I tried to wake you up. Didn't want to leave no woman out here sleep like that. Terrible thangs could happen," he said.

Josette had quieted, but her heart was still trying to force its way out of her chest.

He bent over and picked up Josette's house shoes. "I'm sorry if I scared you. Boy, you sho'nuff a fighter," he chuckled. "You okay now?"

"Yes, sir. Thank you." Josette rubbed the side of her temple where a nice knot was forming. Quite embarrassed, she picked up her blanket and wrapped it around her to defend herself from the unfriendly chill.

Mr. Willie, a man about seventy years old, with a head full of white hair, was fixated on Josette's wedding ring as she pulled the blanket closed.

"Your husband shouldn't have let you run off like that. I don't know what to say for these young fellas today," he said, looking up at the glow of God's creation in the sky.

"How do you know I *ran off?*" Josette said, sitting back on top of the Table of Pain.

"Well, you ain't got no jacket or purse with you. And you still got your house slippers on. You dressed like somebody that done run off," he smiled, taking a seat next to Josette.

"We had a disagreement."

"Well, disagreements are meant to be resolved. You can't run from trouble. You gotta deal with it. How long you been married, young lady?"

Josette couldn't explain herself, but she divulged all of her personal business to Mr. Willie. She told him the whole horrible story about her affair and Patrick's three a.m. Harlequin Romance rescue. Even the reason she'd ended up out here tonight. He was a total stranger—someone she'd probably never see again. So it didn't matter what he knew about her. His ears were as good as any right now. And maybe in his aged wisdom, he could give her some advice that could help her decide what to do next. He couldn't be anything but objective because he was a stranger.

"That don't seem unfixable to me at all," he said. "Time and trust go hand in hand. What you gotta do is go on back home and tell him you gonna stick it out with him. Tell him that you love him, and you wanna work it out and stick it out. Don't matter who was right or wrong. Don't matter at all. Just gotta stick it out. You gotta go on back to your husband, Josette."

Josette's heart quickened again. He'd called her by her name. But in all the chaos, she hadn't told him her name. She scooted away slowly.

He looked curious. "What's the matter?"

"You called me *Josette*. I haven't told you my name," Josette said, standing.

Mr. Willie looked puzzled. "Hmph. Did I say that?"

"Yes, you did," Josette said uncomfortably.

"Well, it musta just slipped out. I knew a young woman back in my day named Josette. She was feisty like you. I guess she crossed my mind," he nodded to himself.

"My name is Josette," she said, tracing the wrinkles of Mr. Willie's face with her eyes.

"You must be kiddin' me."

"No. Really."

"Ain't that somethin'? The Lord sho' is powerful, ain't He?"

Josette gazed in awe at those shining diamonds that dotted the sky. "I guess."

"Well, Ms. Josette, it's almost midnight," Mr. Willie said, looking at his Timex. "You best be gettin' on home. Your husband is probably worried about you."

"I don't know about that."

"I do," Mr. Willlie said, walking towards the road. He watched Josette get into her truck.

Josette strapped on her seat belt and adjusted her rearview mirror to watch Mr. Willie, but he was gone.

Patrick was sitting at the dining room table alone, praying. Billie Holiday's "Come Rain or Come Shine" played softly in the background. The dinner candles had burned halfway down. The flickering of the firelight cast Patrick's shadow against the wall. He rose from the table with his head hung low. He waited for her to speak first—for her to argue with him and tell him how stupid he'd been earlier—how she wasn't going to put up with all the distrust and the spying—that she was sick of the crap. But Josette didn't open her mouth to speak one word of condemnation. Instead, she walked over to him, reached her hand out, and stroked his face.

"Pat, I love you," she said softly. "I'm gonna stick this out. I'm gonna make this work."

"Jo, babe . . . I'm sorry. I feel like I'm going crazy sometimes . . . thinking about you lovin' someone else . . . forgive me . . . please."

Josette hushed his lips with her fingertips. "Just tell me you love me."

Patrick held her. "I love you . . . I love you . . . I love you . . ."

"Jo, get up, babe. You're gonna be late for work. Jo . . . wake up. It's eight o'clock," Patrick said while nudging her, half asleep himself.

"No work today, baby," Josette mumbled into her goose-feathered pillow.

"Jo, you're dreaming. Get up babe. You gotta get to work."

Josette twisted beneath the covers. "No work," she mumbled again, still exhausted from the previous evening.

"Yes, work," Patrick said, turning Josette toward him.

"No more work," she said, sitting up on her elbow and facing him.

"What did you do, take a vacation this week?" Patrick said, sitting up.

"Yep. Permanently." Josette scratched her head and yawned with her mouth covered. "We talked about this last night, baby . . ."

"Jo, babe, we didn't get much talking done last night. Whole lotta lovin'—no talking," Patrick said as he kissed her forehead.

"Really? Well today, Mr. Kelley, I am officially a housewife—I quit the firm."

"Are you serious? You didn't have to do that for me—I told you we could work something out if you want to continue practicing law."

"Well, I've decided that I don't want to work. I want to be a mommy.

I don't want to miss anything. I turned in my resignation a couple of weeks ago. I wanted to surprise you."

Patrick's smile glowed. "So, no work today, huh?" he confirmed.

"Nope."

"Well, what you waitin' on, woman? Get me my breakfast!"

Josette hit him with a pillow.

"Gimme kisses," Patrick said, puckering with fish lips.

Josette cooked her first housewife breakfast, and afterward, she and Patrick hit the malls for baby clothes. They had lunch at Elephant City when Josette was done attacking the sales racks and no-sales racks.

"Now I remember why I don't shop with you that often," Pat said, looking up from the menu. "My feet are more tired than they used to be from football practice. I ain't kiddin'. I should call coach up and tell him that the team needs a shopping drill."

"Hush."

"Well, hello, *Mr. and Mrs.* Kelley, how is everything going?" Paco asked, giving them a personal greeting. "I see that life is back to normal. Congratulations."

Patrick stood up and gave him the Brotha Greeting with the four-part handshake and hug. "Fine, thank you. And I owe you an apology."

"Everything's fine. No apology necessary. Lunch is on the house today," Paco said. He walked over to the next table to greet more of his customers.

Patrick went to the restroom and Josette ordered him his favorite meal, grilled chicken fettuccine. That's when she saw him. She stood up from the booth to get a better look. She couldn't believe her eyes. It was him.

He walked alongside a group of businessmen. There were so few people in the restaurant, the two of them couldn't help but notice each other. He was staring at her just as hard as she was staring at him. He rushed over to the table.

"Heey, girl!" he said, hugging Josette. "I thought that was you."

Josette eyed his expensive business suit, well-groomed hair and mustache. "Look at you! All grown and stuff. Looking handsome."

"Thanks," he smiled.

"What are you doing here?"

"I'm here on business. I'm thinking about relocating here and franchising my shop. I tried to look you guys up, but it's like you two work for the CIA or something. I couldn't get any information."

Josette smiled. "We're a bit private, yes. But here I am, in person."

"You look good."

"So do you."

"How's Sandy doing?" he asked, looking back over his shoulder at the group of men who were waiting for him.

"She's doing fine. Just fine."

"I wish I could talk more. I need to make a good impression. Those are my potential investors. Here's my card. Give me a call and we can catch up."

"That sounds wonderful."

He kissed her cheek and hurried back to the group of businessmen.

Josette was so excited that she started planning something special in her head. She was starting to believe that God *was* good.

Chapter Twenty-Nine

Genevieve left the radio interview for HOT Detroit where she'd been promoting a mental health conference for black women. She was scheduled to speak at Cobo Hall in the morning. She scooted into the back of the chauffeured Yukon Denali and laid her head back. She tried to ignore what had been on her heart for the last hour or so. She had the feeling that the Lord was leading her to call Sandy. She hadn't spoken to her in months because Sandy had asked her to respect the fact that she didn't want her to be a part of her life anymore. She'd made that clear in a six-page, detailed letter written on white linen stationery. Benjamin warned her more than once to leave it alone—not to make things worse. He said that she needed to respect the girls' wishes. The revelation of Josette's rape was the last straw. Sandy blamed herself for what happened to Josette. But she blamed Genevieve more.

In a matter of minutes, Genevieve was back in her hotel room, trying to get comfortable. But its mundane décor and familial emptiness made her realize that she'd rather be home. She had to be up early in the morning to prepare for the conference, so she lay in the bed trying to relax her mind and forget about the nagging uneasiness in her spirit. Her stomach churned. She had an awful feeling that something was wrong with Sandy or Josette. It pressed heavily upon her, becoming clearer. She couldn't keep ignoring it. Why was God doing this to her? She didn't want to call Sandy. Of all people, she understood what it meant to back off when someone had had enough. But her obedience to Him made her dial Sandy's number anyway.

The phone just rang. For that, Genevieve was grateful. She toyed with the curly cord of the phone nervously. She couldn't stand to hear Sandy say again, that she didn't want to have anything else to do with her. Sandy's answering machine picked up. Genevieve wanted to hang up, but that little voice inside of her prompted her to leave a message. She started talking to the contraption with reservation. "Sandy, I really want to respect your wishes . . . I do. But I feel that the Lord is leading me to call you this evening. You may not believe that or understand that, but it is the truth. I love you . . . and . . . um . . ." Genevieve stuttered. "I really don't know what else to say. I'm just trying to obey what I feel on the inside. And I want to make sure that everything is okay with you and your sister. If you don't want to talk to me, maybe you could just leave a message at the desk of the hotel. I'm at the Atheneum. Please just do this one thing for me, and I will stay out of your life for good, if that is what you want . . . please Sandy."

Sandy picked up in a weary voice. "Hello." The words dragged out like it pained her to speak them.

"Hi . . . I'm sorry. I've been having this terrible feeling. Are you okay?"

"No . . . nothing is okay," Sandy said, muffled. "My heart is so . . . broken."

Genevieve listened to Sandy's sobs, cringing. She knew what the tears were for. "Baby, what's wrong? What happened?" she asked anyway.

"I . . . am so tired . . . of being used . . . and . . . mistreated . . ." Sandy cried. "I'm just tired!"

"I can come over, honey. You shouldn't be alone right now."

"No, I need to get out of here. I can't take it any more."

Genevieve gave Sandy her room number and waited for her to arrive. She prayed and asked God to give her the right words to say to her daughter. She felt overwhelmingly guilty because she'd known Sandy and Lamont's relationship would end this way. The Lord had spoken to her the day the two of them had eaten breakfast at the Flap Jack Shack. Genevieve knew then that Lamont was not the one for Sandy. She knew that despite the excitement Sandy had for him, their relationship would end in disappointment for her. The trips and expensive gifts were just traps used by Satan to draw Sandy into something that God didn't want for her. Genevieve took her study Bible out of her suitcase and read a few of the Psalms. She prayed them fervently, giving God's Word back to Him. She was fully fortified in spirit when Sandy arrived.

Genevieve opened the door and was dismayed by what she saw. There was no glow on Sandy's skin. Her eyes were empty—hollow. No care had been taken by her to tame her frizzy mane. She was dressed in an ill-fitting grey jogging suit, which did nothing to liven up her tattered look. She was a woman scorned. She looked tired—exhausted from all of life's cruelties. Genevieve could see that by looking into her face. She swallowed hard and wrapped her arms around Sandy.

"Oh . . . Lamont hurt me . . . so bad . . ." Sandy cried loudly. "I don't know what happened. He won't even talk to me anymore...and he's with someone else. I thought he loved me. He said he loved me," Sandy sniffed.

Genevieve rubbed Sandy's back. A part of her was furious. Another part of her shared her daughter's hurt. She remembered how Sandy had giggled with schoolgirl excitement. She remembered the confidence Sandy seemed to have because of him. Now, Sandy was filled with defeating thoughts of unworthiness. Genevieve could feel all of them as she touched her. "It's okay, baby," she comforted. "You'll be fine. Just trust God. Trust the process." How many times had she reminded herself of that same thing? Genevieve pulled apart from Sandy and looked at her again. Her eyes were full of a mother's pain. "Baby, you didn't compromise yourself did you?" She asked.

"There were times I just wanted to make him happy—to please him, but I didn't," Sandy said. She had come close to compromising once, but at the last minute, God had pulled her from the edge of that cliff. Now, she was glad that she'd chosen to please God instead—but the pain was still there.

They sat next to each other on the edge of the bed. Praise for God circulated through Genevieve. She stroked Sandy's face. "Then you haven't lost anything, sweetheart. God protects us because He loves us."

"Every person I've ever loved or trusted on this planet has hurt me. Every single one."

Genevieve took Sandy's hands gently in hers. Those words stung. That *"everyone"* included her. Hearing Sandy say that took Genevieve back to the day she'd overheard Grace confessing the betrayal against her. Grace had brought so much pain on Genevieve because of it. And Genevieve had brought the same pain on Sandy and Josette because of her misery. Betrayal, rape, and self-hatred had all been strongholds in the lives of the women of their family. It had to stop. Secrets. Lies. Infidelities. The aftermath was still destroying them spiritually. Holding Sandy, Genevieve said, "Sandy, I promise you, it's going to be all right."

Sandy lay across Genevieve's lap and cried harder. "I love him so much, Mama. How do you just stop loving somebody?"

Mama. She'd called her *Mama*. Genevieve hadn't heard Sandy say that word to her since she was twelve. Her heart leaped. She stroked Sandy's face with the same softness she'd stroked it with the day she was born. For all the years Genevieve had wasted, unable to be the mother she should have been; for every storm Sandy had weathered without her support, Genevieve poured out her love. And she promised Sandy that even in this weak, broken moment, when she was feeling that she'd never have the capacity to love another man—or be loved by another man—the Lord would break the chains of bondage. He would make provisions. "The Lord always has a ram in the bush, sweetheart. He knows your innermost thoughts. He will restore," Genevieve said, lifting Sandy's face. "God is still God," she smiled.

The months without Lamont seemed more like a punishment than God's protection. Sandy felt isolated. Loving the Lord with all her heart and knowing that He loved her, did not immediately dissolve the torment of losing the man she loved. There were days when she second-guessed herself and regretted that she hadn't given Lamont what he'd wanted. She'd been on both sides of the "celibacy" fence since she'd been saved, and it seemed that the pain of obedience equaled that of disobedience. When was God going to restore? Genevieve had told her that God would reward her for her faithfulness to Him. And somewhere underneath a mess of tattered nerves, Sandy knew that He would. But she felt the loss of her relationship with Lamont just as strongly as if it had been consummated.

Everything reminded her of Lamont Drake. And when there was nothing to remind her, she created something. She had lain in the dark many Saturday nights, torturing herself by listening to some CD that she and Lamont had listened to during some sweet interlude. She'd get up, go to church, and praise the Lord with her whole being the next morning; and then after service, she'd get in the car and lose herself at a red light because the DJ had played one of those stupid love songs that Lamont used to sing to her.

It was a sick joke, all the time she'd spent with him. He walked out of her life like she had never existed. Sandy rewound conversations in her mind, trying to make sense of the way he so easily slithered out of her life without any explanation. Why had he chosen her to be a victim in his twisted little soap opera?

She wrote to him because her tears and calls were never acknowledged. She poured herself out on paper. Told him that she was still in love with him—that she needed him. That he had a right to be with any woman he chose, but she just needed to know *"why?"* She needed to know why her future disappeared when he closed the door on her that day in Chicago. How had she ended up back in the same punishment circle she had escaped after her ex-husband, Terell? She felt rejected all over again.

After all their talks about her past, Sandy believed that Lamont would show a little sympathy for her—at least enough not to abuse her love. But that's what he'd done—abused her love. Those Blockbuster evenings, laughs, and cuddles on the chaise lounge meant nothing in the end. She wondered who that man was whose own mother told her that she was *the one* for him. She wondered who that man was who used to call her first thing in the morning just to tell her that she was beautiful and that he was thinking about her. The same one who called her every night before he went to sleep, claiming that he couldn't sleep without hearing her voice first. The one who took her on trips and spoiled her with flowers and cards. Had she dreamed the whole thing? Had she just been a stand in for the times when the woman he truly loved wasn't available? Had his love been inflated full of surface feelings—empty lies to entice her to sleep with him? There was no healing and no answers.

Chapter Thirty

Josette and Patrick renewed their vows in a quaint ceremony at Morning Star Baptist Church. Reverend Kelley presided over the nuptials. Patrick insisted that Josette keep the guest list down to a maximum of twenty-five close friends and family. He didn't want another one of Josette's major, Hollywood productions to overshadow their testimony. The only exception had been allowing an entertainment network to film their nuptials. Patrick promised the producers an exclusive interview after he and Josette had returned from their honeymoon.

An eight-course dinner reception was held at Pat's Place. Patrick and Josette honeymooned in a cabin in Escanaba, Michigan, owned by one of Patrick's former teammates. The cabin was modest and secluded, containing none of the luxury amenities that Josette had been spoiled by at five-star hotels and resorts. There were no cell phones or televisions to distract her and Patrick from one another. Their mornings began with spontaneous strolls on obscure trails and walks along the riverbank, taking in nature's beautifully painted canvas. Their nighttime entertainment was long conversations and chess games in front of the fireplace. This quiet time together was the beginning of a new relationship engineered by God.

Patrick and Josette sat lovingly close on their cream-colored suede sectional in the living room of their fifteen-million-dollar mansion, with their hands clasped together. The camera lights shone brightly on them as they prepared for their exclusive interview with Taylor Rankin, host of The Know Network, an entertainment affiliate of NBC News. Make-up artist Monica James-Alexander dusted Josette's face with loose powder again, before placing the large brush into one of many pockets on her smock. Josette adjusted herself against one of the crimson throw pillows and rubbed her sweaty palm over her bulging belly.

Patrick looked concerned. "Everything okay, babe?" he whispered.

"He's kicking up a storm. I think I'm making him nervous," she said, continuing to rub her hand over her stomach.

Patrick covered Josette's hand with his, following her circular rubbing motion. "Hey, man, mommy's okay. Calm down," Patrick said lovingly to Josette's belly. He looked around for their housekeeper, who had instinctively gone into the kitchen to retrieve purified water for him and Josette. She pushed her short, round body through the crowd of strangers.

"Here you are, Mr. Kelley," Cuca said handing Patrick two glasses.

"Thank you, Cuca," Patrick said, handing one of the glasses to Josette.

Josette sipped from the glass and placed it on the table behind the sofa. Cuca disappeared back into the kitchen where Franklin was finishing a post-interview meal of roasted lamb chops stuffed with black olives and goat cheese, with grilled asparagus and overstuffed baked potatoes, for Taylor Rankin, the camera crew, and the production assistants.

Minutes later, Patrick and Josette were live on national television, divulging the intimate details of their private life before millions of viewers. America's former number-one running back and his wife bared all. There were uncomfortable moments. Josette discussed how being raped as a child subsequently caused her to sabotage her marriage. Patrick spoke candidly about dealing with Josette's infidelity on an emotional level and how he felt about the news of their divorce being sensationalized by the media. Taylor Rankin's eyes watered on more than one occasion as Patrick and Josette talked about their challenges as individuals and as a couple. She fought hard to maintain her professionalism.

Mid-interview, Taylor Rankin leaned in and asked the question that she had been waiting for the opportune moment to ask. "Pat, I've got to put this one question out here, because my viewers want to know—especially my female viewers. Why would a wealthy, attractive man like you put up with infidelity? I mean, there are thousands—millions of women out there who would be willing to take Josette's place in a heartbeat," Taylor said, snapping her fingers for emphasis. "Just last year, Popular Magazine voted you the Sexiest Man Alive. Help me out."

Pat considered the question carefully, kissing Josette's hand. He'd known that the probability of Taylor trying to steer the interview away from God in lieu of gossip and media hype would be high. He took his time steering it back. "The union I have with my wife, and what we are able to accomplish because of my relationship with Christ, is a testimony to any couple out there who is facing what we faced—whether it be infidelity, divorce, or anything else that threatens to destroy what God created for us to enjoy. The fact that we were able to get through it with Christ in the middle, lets other people know that they can get through it too." Patrick gazed at Josette, and looked back at Taylor. "I know this woman loves me with all her heart. She's not perfect—and neither am I. But what I do know is that every day that I wake up to my wife, I am more of the man God has called me to be than I was the day before. And more fully do I understand His purpose for me—that being to glorify Him," Pat said, pointing upward. "To proclaim Jesus and His salvation—and demonstrate what His power can do—that is what I'm here for. This marriage is solid proof of what God can do. I love my wife. And there is no other woman on this planet that I would rather spend the rest of my life with. What I need is what God has already allowed me to have—sitting right here next to me," Pat said, controlling the interview.

A different Josette listened with admiration. She was softer, more reserved. Humbly, she held her husband's hand. Her warm, resplendent glow came across as strength in the face of adversity, but she allowed Patrick to guide the interview in order to get his message across—God's message. She was proud of her husband and appreciative of the honor of being his wife. It was made clear on Primetime that God—and only God—received the glory for the trials and tribulations of the Kelley family.

Finally, after an hour of one of the toughest things Josette had ever done, she ended the interview with a final comment. "I am very blessed to have this man. I know this," she said, dispelling doubts. "The problems we've had have strengthened us in ways I never imagined they would. I believe that we are better than we were before. And now that God has blessed us with a son that's due any day now, we have a greater commitment to see this union through. I'm going to be here up until they bury one of us—or both of us. I'm not going anywhere," Josette said.

During the interview, Sandy had received several calls from women who were genuinely interested in knowing what could have caused her little sister to slide out on a man like Patrick Kelley. They wondered if he was some psycho masquerading as Mr. Perfect.

"I'm telling you like I told everybody else—Patrick is the real McCoy," Sandy said to her co-worker, Samantha.

"Girl, they need to duplicate him, package him up, and sell him. I'd be the first one in line buying him," Samantha joked.

Caleb David Kelley pushed his way into the world on a Friday morning at 7:22 a.m. weighing seven pounds, at twenty-two inches long, just two weeks after his mommy and daddy's interview on national television. Sandy witnessed one of God's finest productions firsthand. She was officially "Auntie Sandy" now. And Caleb was the most precious thing she'd ever seen or held. He was a cocoa brown bundle of pure joy. Each time Sandy cradled Caleb in her arms, she felt an inexplicable sense of newness. And she also expected a miracle from the Lord, because although she loved her role as auntie, she wanted to bring forth fruit from her own womb. She reminded the Lord of that from time to time, even though she knew He didn't need reminding. In fact, she was reminding Him at the moment as she stood next to Josette during Caleb's christening. Linda and Roger stood proudly next to Patrick as Reverend Kelley christened his grandson. The family formed a small, united circle around Caleb. The two-thousand-seat sanctuary was full. Reverend Kelley's face beamed with pride as he held Caleb up in the air for the congregation to see. Caleb's face appeared on the two large monitor screens on either side of the sanctuary. The congregation roared with applause and hallelujahs.

After Caleb's christening, the family took their places in the second row of the center pews to hear Reverend Kelley's sermon for the morning. Patrick held Caleb in his arms, periodically sharing him with Linda and Sandy, who were whisper-arguing over whose turn it was to hold him next. Josette's attention was not on Caleb. It hadn't been since she'd handed him over to his daddy. She sat serenely, entranced by the message.

"I can't take credit for this sermon," Reverend Kelley said, smiling at his congregation. "Nope. This is God's sermon. He gave me this Word to give to you. God wants to ask each and every one of us here today one simple question," Reverend Kelley said, looking out at the congregation. "And the question is: 'Is anything too hard for God?' Turn your Bibles to Genesis 18:14."

Josette was engrossed in the message. She opened her Bible and read the scripture. She felt something different today—a high. Was it Caleb's christening? Or was it something more profound? She stole a glance at her husband. She loved him so much. But not even he was responsible for what she was feeling right now. It elated her and frightened her. She sat back against the pew, reeling, allowing the Word of God to penetrate her soul. She sat through the entire sermon being drawn. When the choir began singing the Hymn of Invitation, "I Love the Lord," the melody resonated. Josette felt it in the pit of her belly and throughout her limbs. Sister Cora Carter belted it out with angelic soul. Josette shook involuntarily as the layers were stripped away.

"God is still waiting on you," Reverend Kelley said with his hand extended. "You read it. Now receive it, because it's true. Ain't nothin' too hard for Him! Give Him a try, won't you?" He searched the congregation for any drawn soul.

It seemed that the choir became increasingly loud because Josette couldn't hear her own thoughts anymore. She couldn't hear the words to the song. Only the scripture saturated her mind. She wrestled in her seat, wiggling nervously, before finally standing to her feet. She climbed past her husband and walked slowly up to the front of the congregation, with tears streaming. She let them flow as she continued her journey. With blurred vision, she kept her eyes on the bronze cross hanging behind the altar. She believed.

"Hallelujah! Yes, Lord!" Reverend Kelley shouted, squeezing Josette when she stood before him. The congregation praised the Lord with reverent hand clapping and shouts of thanks. The praise of the congregation rose gloriously higher as Patrick stretched himself before the altar of the Lord with a man's praise. He had trusted the Lord to answer his prayers and they'd been answered.

Chapter Thirty-One

Sandy sat propped up against her headboard, reading a novel. She laid her book on her lap for a brief moment, picked up the oversized coffee mug on her nightstand, and held it with careful hands. She drank the remainder of her hot apple cider and placed the mug back on the night stand. She gazed out of the window, where she spied a deer ducking bashfully behind a tree in the backyard. His freshly made tracks looked picturesque in the virgin snow.

It was hard to believe that more than a year had gone by. Sandy had found her mother, been in love and out of love, and been made an auntie. Just months ago, she'd felt completely destroyed. But God had healed her. She felt complete in Him. She'd surrendered to His will, turning her desires over to Him—even that of wanting a family. When she found herself doubting, she reminded herself that God loved her and wanted the best for her. She'd made peace with her singleness.

The doorbell interrupted a hilarious scene in her book. She was still laughing as she walked down the stairs to find out what villain had stopped by unannounced. From time to time, she fantasized about Lamont showing up on her doorstep to reclaim their love. But every time that thought came, she let it pass, knowing that it wasn't God's will. She twisted her lips when she looked through the peephole at Josette and Patrick, both grinning ear to ear.

"What are y'all doing poppin' up on people, and where is my baby?" she asked, opening the door.

"We came by to bring you a surprise!" Josette said excitedly. "And Caleb is with Linda and Roger this weekend because I'm going on a weekend getaway with my man."

Patrick took a paisley print cotton scarf out of his jacket pocket and covered Sandy's eyes with it. "But first, we need you to put this on."

Sandy smacked her lips. "Y'all better be giving me the keys to a new Lexus for all this drama."

"This is better than a Lexus," Josette giggled.

Patrick and Josette were silly teenagers, spinning Sandy around several times, insisting that she had to endure this in order to receive her surprise. Sandy gave in to her inner child and allowed them to treat her like a contestant on a game show. Their silliness rubbed off on her, and she laughed just as much as they did because she imagined how ridiculous she looked. She heard her door open again and felt the cold air. "I hope y'all have not brought me a pet, because I already got rid of Josette."

Josette stomped her feet. "Now, that is cold!"

"You'll see in just one second," Pat said, stepping behind Sandy to remove her makeshift blindfold.

"Surprise," an all-too-familiar baritone voice said coolly.

"Oh, my goodness! This is unbelievable. Oh, my goodness!" Sandy said, touching his face to assure herself that he was real. Without words, they hugged and squeezed tenderly like characters in a Sunday afternoon movie.

Josette stood to their left with a video camera she'd taken from behind her back. "Aw, that is so beautiful," she said, taking one hand off of the camera and wiping her eyes.

"Hey, cut it out. I'm a man. I can't be up in here cryin'!" Patrick said.

Sandy hoped she wasn't dreaming. If she was, she refused to wake up. She had received a personally delivered present from God. Gently, she released B. J. just to say, "Wow, this is great!"

The four of them brought each other up to date over a Papa Ramano's Garbage Can Pizza. When Patrick and B. J. started debating about which team was going to the Super Bowl, Josette and Sandy crept upstairs to talk alone.

Looking at her sister, Sandy could see the softness that carrying a baby and becoming a mother had created. She could see the gentleness and maturity of a woman who had put her life and her family in the hands of God. "Thank you, Jo. I needed this."

"I know. You're a strong woman, but you've been through a lot—we've been through a lot. And I feel like life is going so well for me now. I'm really happy. I mean, I have joy. And I want you to experience happiness and joy on the same level." Their roles had switched over the last year, with Josette becoming the comforter and supporter instead of the receiver.

Sandy bumped her forehead gently against her sister's. "I love you, Jo. I've got the best little sister in the whole world."

Sandy and B. J. sat on the floor trying to fit all the details of the last several years of their lives into their conversation. She avoided the painful parts on purpose so that she didn't kill the mood. Seeing B. J. again, after all those years, was yet another sign that God was still in the blessing business. They'd changed externally, but on the inside, they were still the same goofy little kids who'd started kindergarten together.

"So, how did it happen for you—being saved—starting your own business?" Sandy asked, held captive by B. J.'s grey-green eyes. His potent handsomeness was difficult to ignore. He was a mature version of the good-looking twenty-year-old she remembered.

B. J. smiled an easy smile. "I guess Big Mama's prayers paid off. It was about seven years ago—right after I had left some wild party. I was too drunk to drive, so a friend of mine had to drive me home. On the way, something came over me and I started to cry, you know? My buddy thought it was because I was drunk, so he started laughing. But I realized right then that my life was going nowhere. And I was like, 'God, what do you want me to do? Because I don't want to keep living like this.' When I got home, I just got on my knees and prayed. I asked for forgiveness for all the things I had done—the way I had been living. The next morning I got up, went to church, and turned myself in. I started going to community college that next semester, then transferred to a university later on. I kept my job at the auto repair shop to help pay for my classes, and when I was done, I took what little I had left of Mama's life insurance money, along with some money Big Mama had saved, and opened B. J.'s Auto Repair and Restoration. And the rest, they say, is history," he said, taking another slice of pizza out the cardboard box.

"I am so proud of you. I used to think about you a lot—wonder what you were doing."

B. J. thought back over the years. "I used to wonder about you too. Of course I knew you'd gotten married, but I didn't know you'd gotten a divorce. I would have called." His eyes were sincere.

"It's okay. Can't change the past," Sandy said. She'd learned that. Accepted that. Because of it, she had a beautiful relationship with her mother now.

"You're right."

"So, how does it feel to be your own man?"

"Great. I never thought I'd be making so much money doing something that I love to do. It's crazy."

For a millisecond, Sandy had a flashback of Lamont speaking those same words. Then she let the memory out of the window of her mind. "That's awesome."

"That's why I was hesitant about leaving Florida," B. J. said. "I had a good client base there, but it never felt like home. Then I restored a classic for this guy who turned out to be a businessman and investor. He talked to me about franchising my business like McDonald's. He told me he had some friends in Detroit who could help me out," B. J. said, trying not to stare at Sandy, who was taking in every word with her beautiful self. "I felt like God was speaking to me because I had been thinking about moving back here for the last two years," he continued. He held her in his eyes and looked away, denying his weakness for her.

"Well, I'm praying that my purpose is revealed to me—because right now, it's kind of fuzzy." Sandy squeezed a toss pillow to her chest. She looked innocent doing that.

"Well, what do you like to do?"

Sandy drifted back to the time they'd spent together after Sarah's funeral. The question he'd just asked had slipped from her mind.

"What do you like to do?" he repeated.

Sandy chuckled. What she was thinking about was so silly.

"Come on, what is it?"

"To be honest, I like going to the spa—and that is about it for hobbies," Sandy admitted. She smiled uncomfortably. "I know it's silly. You can't make a living out of going to the spa."

He didn't laugh at her answer. "Actually, you could make a career out of going to the spa. Have you ever thought about *owning* a spa?" He sounded like a patient career coach.

"Not seriously. I don't like managing other people."

"Okay, so maybe owning a business is not what you should do. But there's got to be something you really want out of life—whatever that is, you've got to concentrate on it."

Sandy brought her knees to her chest and shut her eyes. *My little sister has the life I want.* She didn't want a new career. Forget about a stupid job. She wanted to be a mommy. She wanted to be a wife. "I want a husband. I want babies. I want a family," Sandy said, exasperated. "Those are the things that I am trusting God for. I don't want anything else."

The tone in the room had changed. B. J. sat with his legs stretched out in front of him; his feet were crossed at the ankles. He studied her, giving careful thought to what she'd said. He stood up. "I'll be right back. I've got to get something out of my truck," he said. He returned with a large study Bible with his whole name engraved on the front. Standing, he read Psalm 37: 4-6. *"Delight thyself also in the Lord, and He shall give thee the desires of thine heart. Commit thy way unto the Lord, trust also in Him, and He shall bring it to pass. And He shall bring forth thy righteousness as the light, and thy judgment as the noonday."*

"You know, I've been trying really hard to do that. But my wants get in the way sometimes."

B. J. sat down next to Sandy and said, "Trust God, Sandy. I've been through many things, and I can sum up my whole life in two words—

trust God. Big Mama taught me that when I was a young man. I live by it. I'm not disregarding anything you've just shared with me. But when you can't see the light at the end of the tunnel, you have to just trust God." He took Sandy's hand in his and prayed. It was after midnight when they said good-bye. Sandy stood in the doorway watching him walk across the street to his blue Dodge Ram 1500.

"Hey, I'll call you tomorrow. I'd like to take you out to lunch or dinner one day this week," he said sliding inside.

Sandy shouted over the loud roaring of B. J.'s engine. "Sounds good. Good night!" She shut the door and leaned against it. She crossed her arms over her chest, and thought about holding her own baby.

Josette held Caleb in one arm and unpacked her overnight bag with her free hand. "So how old is his kid now?" she asked.

"The baby wasn't his," Sandy said, adjusting the phone. "No kids. Never been married. Not involved in a serious relationship. Will you stop trying to marry me off to the first man you see?"

Josette talked loudly into the phone over Caleb's cries. "He is a good catch. And he never looked *that* good when we were growing up. Maybe something could happen. You never know."

"What are you over there doing to my baby?" Sandy asked, maneuvering Josette away from the conversation she didn't want to have.

"Nothing. He's hungry."

"Well, feed him."

"I will as soon as I get this shirt unbuttoned." Caleb quieted, satisfied. "*We* need to get some more info on B. J." Josette said, returning to her conversation.

"No *we* don't. Things are different. We're adults—life has changed."

"Did you guys see each other again?"

"No. We made plans to, but something came up."

Josette contemplated. "Hmm…"

"We have a friendship, Jo—that's it. And that is all it's going to be. Apparently, that is all that God wants me to have at this point in my life."

"Hmm . . ."

"Jo, don't worry about me. I'm fine. I just have to trust God. When it's time, it'll be time."

"I guess you're right," Josette said reluctantly.

Sandy didn't want to keep talking about her life. "Hey, I'll see you at Bible study."

"Okay, save me a seat."

Chapter Thirty-Two

Josette slipped into bed after a long bubble bath, having enjoyed the temporary freedom from motherhood. Finally, Caleb was resting peacefully, and so was his daddy. Carefully, she pulled the covers back on her side of the bed so as not to awaken Patrick. She scooted in with her back to him. But as soon as she found a snug spot, Patrick reached over and pulled her close so that her back rested against him. He lifted her hair and kissed the nape of her neck. Josette smiled. He definitely was not asleep. He was a wild animal stalking his prey.

"What can I do for you, Mr. Kelley?" Josette whispered, fitting the curves of her body into his.

Patrick kissed Josette's ear. "I want to talk to you about something," he said.

Josette giggled. "About what? Some anatomy?"

"Not quite. But that would be nice afterward, if you're not angry," he said resolutely.

"Pat, what's the matter?" Josette asked, turning toward him. "Why would I be angry?"

Patrick caressed Josette's shoulders and allowed his nose to brush gently across her collarbone. He kissed her forehead. Josette sensed that he was stalling. She flipped through her mental note pad, trying to recall if she had said or done something wrong today that would warrant him discussing a problem in bed.

"Pat..."

"Babe, you're a good mother," Patrick said, stroking Josette's face lightly with his thumbs. "You've been doing a heck of a job with Caleb. I want to let you know that first and foremost. But Jo, he deserves to have the best. I just want him to have the best, Jo."

"Pat, what are you talking about? I have been giving him my best. I've been giving you my best," Josette testified, feeling like she was being accused of some unknown offense.

"Babe, you're not giving him all that he deserves. Roger and Linda are beautiful—they are," he said. "They're excellent grandparents. And my dad too. They all do a great job with him. But Caleb deserves to know his other grandparents too, babe. It's only right. You are keeping him from a part of who he is."

"Are you talking about Genevieve and her family?"

"That is exactly what I'm talking about, Jo."

Josette sat up in bed and lightly touched the mood lamp. Instantly, it shone light on her face. She didn't know what to make of what she'd just heard her husband say. And an argument three hours before Caleb awakened for his next feeding, would ensure that she didn't get any sleep tonight. She calmed herself before she spoke—thought about how she was going to respond. She tossed the words around carefully in her head to see how they sounded. She didn't want to be disrespectful to her husband. "Pat, not knowing Genevieve is not hurting Caleb in anyway. It is my decision—and my decision only—to decide if I want to have anything to do with a mother who abandoned me and is the sole cause of me being raped. Now, I'm sorry if you don't understand that!"

"Jo, when you cheated on me . . . you hurt me very deeply. Worse than I've been hurt in all my life."

"Pat, why would you even bring that up? Why would you even say that? I know that. That doesn't have anything to do with what we just talked about. So why are you bringing that up?"

"Jo, it has everything to do with what we just talked about, because I forgave you, babe, so none of it matters. When we come together, babe, it's about you and me, Jo. There is nothing else on my mind. I wouldn't let anything hold us back from where God wants to take us. That is forgiveness."

Josette threw the covers back to get out of bed. The climate had to be better in Caleb's nursery. "If your intent was to make me feel like crap, give yourself a hand."

"Jo, where are you going?"

"I'm going to go sleep in the nursery," she said, standing.

"No you're not."

"Excuse me?"

"You heard what I said, Jo. You are going to stay right here and talk."

Josette walked toward the door anyway. She didn't want to go there with him tonight.

"Josette Kelley, DO NOT leave this room. I mean it!"

Josette snapped her body around. "I'm not your child, Pat. Yes, you are the head of this house. I respect that. But I'm not a child!"

"Well, you need to stop acting like one. You can't run away when it's time to solve a problem."

Josette could have screamed and shaken all the expensive oil paintings off of their bedroom walls. Pat had taken his spiritual authority beyond boundaries. She ran her fingers through her hair. Counted to ten silently. She didn't like to be ordered around like some puppy. She ran her fingers through her hair again and counted over again. "You want Caleb to know Genevieve and her family? Fine. You work it out. I'm not going to be involved." She plopped down on the bed. "Good night." She lay as close to the edge as possible and buried her head in her pillow.

"Tell me something, Jo. How is it that you can accept my forgiveness of you—after all we went through—but you can't extend it to your mother? According to the God you gave your life to, you are being a hypocrite," Pat said. Josette tried to quiet her frustration by crying into her pillow.

"Come here babe . . . don't cry," Pat said, cuddling Josette. "I'm sorry if I hurt you. But it is my responsibility as the head of this family to tell you the truth."

"You don't understand about her . . . you don't understand how I feel."

"Jo, I felt everything you're feeling. Believe that. But babe, you have to do what is right. Let's not sleep on anger. I love you," Patrick said, pulling Josette atop his chest.

Despite their lovemaking, morning renewed the frustration between Josette and her husband over what she had deemed a non-negotiable subject. Patrick held Josette in his arms, stroking her tenderly. "I want you to give some serious thought to what we talked about last night, babe," he said, reopening the can of worms Josette thought she'd put a lid on. She was relieved that Caleb awoke an unhappy camper. His cry grew more boisterous. "I'll get him," Patrick offered before Josette could move.

Josette pulled her silk housecoat from the chaise lounge and put it on to shield her body from the morning cold. It hung loosely on her body as she sat on the edge of the bed. Caleb's cries increased. Josette could faintly hear Patrick speaking hush-hush words that didn't quiet Caleb's ire. She headed into the bathroom to brush her teeth before Patrick brought him in for his feeding. Earlier in the morning, Patrick had fed him the last bottle of pumped milk. Caleb's cries elevated to aggravated screeches. Patrick hurried into their bedroom with Caleb over his shoulder, bouncing him gently.

"He's hungry," Patrick said into the master bathroom.

"I hear. Can't you wait for mommy to brush her teeth?" Josette asked, washing her face with a disposable cleansing cloth. Caleb continued his display of dissatisfaction. "Okay, I guess not," she said, taking him from Patrick and holding him to her breast. She sat down on the bed. Caleb latched on instantly and his cries quieted to a soft cooing sound.

Patrick stood over them, watching them bond. "That is so awesome, babe. God is so awesome."

"Yes, He is."

Patrick showered and dressed before Caleb was done with his breakfast. He took Caleb downstairs with him while Josette showered. Josette sat at her antique vanity table combing her hair, trying not to think about what her husband wanted her to think about. Downstairs, she was surprised to see B. J. sitting at the breakfast nook with Patrick, while Caleb swung gleefully in a motorized doo-dad Sandy had bought.

B. J. stood up. "Good morning," he said, hugging Josette.

"Morning. I didn't know we were having company." Josette kissed B. J. on the cheek. She scrutinized him delightfully. He and Sandy would be a good match. B. J. was casually dressed in a pair of khakis and a baby-blue button-up shirt. He had a fresh, unassuming look about him. Just what Sandy liked. Josette had plans for the two of them whether they were aware or not.

"Oh, babe, we have the Brother-to-Brother meeting here in an hour. I asked B. J. to come by early so that we could have a chance to talk before the rest of the crew gets here," Patrick said before kissing her.

"So I guess I need to get lost, huh?"

"No. But I thought you could use some time alone. I was planning to keep Caleb here with me."

"While you're having your meeting?"

"Yeah. You did it with your sorority sisters. I figured I could handle him too."

"Well, go ahead, black man. I'll pump some milk for you."

Caleb had grown tired of swinging and started a whiny cry to let his mommy and daddy know that. Patrick lifted him out of the swing and cradled him in his arms. "Hey, man, you ready to hang out with the fellas today?"

Caleb looked as if he were smiling at his daddy. Patrick was full of pride, looking at him wide-eyed. Caleb's tiny hand held a tight grip on Patrick's thumb. B. J. watched the two of them, slightly envious. Josette sat down at the table where Patrick had prepared a breakfast of Belgian waffles and sausage links. She spread the rose-colored linen napkin across her lap, winking at B. J.

"Man, this is beautiful—your home, your family. You two really seem to have a good relationship. I can't wait to have a son one day," B. J. said, admiring his surroundings. Their mansion was one of the most beautiful homes he had seen—down to the intricate details of their kitchen cabinetry and stone hearth. It represented a time period when fine workmanship was prized. B. J. took the same type of care when he restored classic vehicles. Patrick had promised him a tour of the entire house once Josette was dressed. But what he'd seen so far was impressive.

"You want to be a daddy, B. J.?" Josette asked. Patrick gave her the *look*. She read his mind, saying, *"Mind your business."* But she ignored the warning.

"Definitely. Just waiting for the right woman to come along," B. J. answered.

"Is that right?"

Patrick threw Josette another cautious look, knowing full well that the little wheels in her head were turning at full speed.

"Yeah. I'm not getting any younger. I'm looking forward to it."

"You mean to tell me out of all these beautiful women in this city, you haven't found *anyone* compatible?" She sipped her cappuccino and waited for him to satisfy her curiosity.

B. J. picked up on Josette's steer of the conversation. "Well, timing always plays a big part in a relationship," he said.

"Mm-hmm…"

"Jo, I'm 'bout to put you outta here," Patrick teased, shaking a sausage link at her.

B. J. laughed. "It's okay, Pat. She hasn't changed a bit."

"Okay, so now that we have that established, what is going on with you and Sandy? Because from my personal experience, I can tell you that best friends make the best lovers," Josette said.

"Jo . . ." Patrick warned again.

"That's a fair question, Pat. Sandy is her sister."

Josette tilted her head.

"To be honest, Jo, I care for Sandy a great deal. I love her. Always have," he said smiling. "I'm talkin' since kindergarten. She's beautiful. And she's a good woman. I know she'd make any brother a good wife. No doubt. But she still needs more time to heal. I sense some residue from her previous relationship. I've been there before with someone I cared about and it just busted our relationship up. And I don't want to get involved with anyone if it can't lead to the kind of relationship and family that God has planned for me to have. I've learned the hard way that when a woman has residue, it's best to let her work through it without complications. Starting a new relationship is complicated—saved or not. That's all."

Josette couldn't argue with anything B. J. had just shared. She and Patrick had this same conversation about Sandy when they'd entertained the idea of introducing her to someone they knew. "Well, she thinks that you are a really special brother, B. J. And that is saying a lot coming from Sandy," Josette said, placing her dishes in the dishwasher. Patrick held Caleb in one arm and helped to clear the table with the other.

"I'm honored. I think she's special too—trust me. And *f-i-n-e*—whew!" B. J. chuckled.

Pat laughed. "I think that runs in the genes, man," he said, pinching Josette's behind as she passed him.

Josette turned around slowly. "Don't get into trouble. You know you've got company coming," she teased.

Patrick pulled Josette closer to him and kissed her softly. Caleb was planted securely between them. "What are you doing tonight?" He sounded like he was asking a stranger on a date.

"Whatever you're doing," Josette said, kissing him again.

"Good. I'll see you home around six."

"That gives Sandy and me plenty of time to do some serious shopping."

"I bet."

"Love you."

"Love you," Patrick said. He watched pleasingly as his wife sauntered out of the kitchen. His eyes were locked on her.

Josette turned back around because she could feel him staring. She blew him a kiss. "See ya later B. J. I'll tell Sandy you're thinking about her, and that she's *f-i-n-e*," Josette teased.

Chapter Thirty-Three

Genevieve sat at the nook looking at pictures of Caleb that Sandy had secretly sent. She was teary-eyed. She didn't know how she felt about being a grandmother. She would probably never see her only grandchild. Normally, bragging rights and extensive photo albums came along with the title. She had neither. Josette had locked her out of her and Caleb's life. There'd been no miracles and no breakthroughs.

Benjamin looked on empathetically as Genevieve wiped her tears with the sleeve of her pink velour robe. She slid the pictures across the glass-top table. Benjamin picked them up, careful not to smudge the photos with his fingerprints. He smiled. "He's a handsome little fella. Sort of reminds me of Joshua," he said, looking through various pictures that Sandy had taken.

"I feel so left out, Ben. God is a God of restoration. Where is mine? I feel like I've paid a hundredfold for my sins already."

"Sweets, don't get discouraged. Try to focus on what the Lord is telling you through this trial."

Genevieve was irritated. She wanted a quick-fix answer. Something tangible. "I don't know what He's telling me. If I knew, I would do it—

whatever it is, because this is so disheartening."

Benjamin reached across the table and held Genevieve's hand, bringing it to his lips. "I know," he said, kissing her hand. "Did the Lord reveal anything to you during your fast, Sweets?"

"No—I don't know. Maybe I haven't been listening because of all the nightmares."

"Nightmares about what, Sweets?"

"Mother. Three nights in a row I dreamed that I was a little girl again and was back at home with her. It was horrible. But Ben, that's not a revelation, that's just the way it was."

"Well now, hold on, Sweets. Don't just overlook it. Maybe this is something we need to pray about. Why do you suppose you've been dreaming about her all of a sudden?"

"I don't know honey . . . the excitement of being a grandmother—or the pain of not being a grandmother. I have no idea."

Ben held Genevieve's stare. "Sweets, how do you feel about your mother now that you've had a chance to reconcile with Sandy?"

"I don't feel any differently than I did before, honey. I forgave her a long time ago. It's not something I think about day to day. It's just a part of my past—that's all. To be honest, I try not to think about Mother much."

"Have you forgiven her?"

Genevieve nodded, "Yes, I have."

"Sweets, have you truly forgiven your mother, or have you just convinced yourself that you have? That could be holding you back. True forgiveness doesn't leave scars."

Genevieve looked away. She needed to let that thought marinate. Benjamin rolled up his newspaper and left her alone with God. Truth was a delicate thing; it was just as chastening as it was cleansing. Genevieve covered her face and wept. She wept for the abused little girl who became an addict. She pictured complete healing—a family that included all of her children. Softly, what needed to be done was laid on her heart. She had to make the necessary arrangements while she still had the courage.

Genevieve and Sandy trekked through the soft snow at Eastbrook Cemetery. The tree branches looked as though they were decorated with cotton. It was a serene image of death. Sandy held Genevieve's hand, buffering her. She squeezed her mother's hand as Genevieve counted the trees past the hill. Her tears fell before she could count the tenth one. That is where her mother's grave was. The headstones looked identical as Genevieve passed each one, searching for Grace's. When she came across it, she clinched the roses she'd brought with her. She let go of Sandy's hand to wipe her eyes, then gripped it again. Genevieve kneeled down in the snow and touched Grace's headstone. She rested her head against it as if it were mother's bosom and grieved until Sandy pulled her from the cold concrete.

Genevieve stood up tall in front of Grace. "Mother . . . I came to tell you that I'm okay . . . I'm okay. I'm not evil. I'm compassionate and loving. I have always been a loving person. I was just a child . . ." Genevieve swallowed. She looked at Sandy, who encouraged her with loving eyes to finish what they'd come for. "You hurt me, Mother. I hurt my children . . . I wasn't a good mother. I didn't know how to be a good mother. I wish you had taught me to love myself. I wish you hadn't hated yourself so much. I'm sorry for what happened to you, Mother. I brought my daughters—my daughter, Sandy, with me today. We came because we want to let go of the generational pain. We don't want to live in the past anymore. We came for closure." Sandy rubbed her hands over her mother's shoulders. Genevieve looked up at the winter white sky through stinging tears. She looked back to Grace's headstone. "Mother, I forgive you. I forgive you for every beating . . . every harsh word. I forgive you for not loving me. I understand that you just…didn't know how to love me. But today, I forgive you. And I love you . . . I still love you. I came by to tell you that," Genevieve said, laying the roses on the ground in front of the headstone. Sandy hugged her mother and Genevieve buried her face in Sandy's wool coat. The feeling of another presence caused them to separate. Tears blurred their vision, but it wasn't difficult to make out the image that was moving toward them. Genevieve and Sandy waited breathlessly, holding hands.

Josette stopped before them. "Did I miss something?"

"No. We were just about to pray," Genevieve said joyously.

Josette hugged her mother and sister, and the three of them huddled together in prayer, giving thanks to God for family, forgiveness, and love. Especially love.

Chapter Thirty-Four
Genevieve's Journal

Dear Lord,

Years zoomed by like the change of seasons. Tonight was prom night for Faith and Joshua. Someone would have thought it was a family reunion because everyone was here. Faith's date was Cameron Giles—Deacon Giles's grandson. He looked so handsome in his tuxedo. He nervously pinned Faith's corsage on her, while Ben and Deacon Giles looked on, teasing. Two weeks ago, Faith informed me that they are officially a couple and will both be attending Howard in the fall—both studying pre-med.

Joshua escorted Patricia Doty, his high school sweetheart of the last four years. They are planning to attend Howard in the fall too. Joshua wants to study religion—says he is going to go to Seminary after college. Patricia wants to be a teacher. Joshua is talking about getting married already. I pray that the two of them can keep their hormones under control. If not, wedding bells will be ringing, because Patricia is just as adamant about remaining chaste as Joshua is.

The twins left here in a super-stretch limo that was fit for the Grammy's or the Academy Awards. And their big sisters, along with their husbands and children, were here to see them off. Josette, Pat, Caleb, and baby Cassandra are camping out in Joshua's room. Sandy, B. J., Brian Jr., and Celeste have the guest room. B. J. convinced me to let them have it because it has a king size bed—more accommodating for Sandy's belly, which seems to be growing by the day. Her doctor says that she is expecting twins. She says this is it. But that's what she said the last time she came out of the delivery room. And she and B. J. have the nerve to be frisky with one another. I told them to cut that stuff out before they mess around and have quintuplets.

Josette says that she and Pat are definitely through in the baby department. She says a boy and a girl are good enough for them. So Ben and I are grandparents four times over, with two on the way. And we are getting younger every day. Yes, the fire is still burning. And God, You are still God. Thank You for these gifts.

In Jesus' Name,
Amen.

Reading Group Guide

1. While in recovery, Genevieve made the decision not to contact Sandy and Josette, but instead allow everyone to "start over." Do you think that it was a poor choice on her part? Would her relationship with Sandy and Josette have been different if she had contacted them as opposed to waiting until they found her?

2. Sandy criticized Josette for being self-centered, yet she envied her lifestyle and her ability to attract men who truly loved her. Do you think this is contradictory? Explain.

3. Josette's husband, Patrick, demonstrated on a number of occasions that he had a bad temper, yet he was considered to be a man of God. Was his anger justifiable? Do you feel that his actions were representative of a Christian man? Explain.

4. At the beginning of the novel, Genevieve, Sandy, and Josette are at different stages of their lives. Genevieve is experiencing overwhelming success, Sandy is dealing with disillusionment, and Josette is suffering from the consequences of her actions. How did finding Genevieve affect or change all three of their lives?

5. How did Genevieve, Sandy, and Josette's relationship or lack of a relationship with God affect their actions throughout the novel?

6. Was Sandy and Josette's hatred toward Genevieve justifiable? Why or why not?

7. Do you feel that Patrick took advantage of Josette's vulnerability

after the family session? Explain.

8. Josette's pregnancy brought up questions of morality and spiritual values, subsequently causing her to examine right and wrong from God's perspective. Have you ever had to forego your own ideals of morality to accept God's will?

9. Do you think that Patrick would have divorced Josette if she hadn't become pregnant with his child?

10. Sandy spent the night at Lamont's house on several occasions due to them having a long distance relationship. Although she slept in a separate room, do you think that this is advisable for a Christian woman? Why or why not? List any scriptures that you feel support your answer.

11. It appears that Sandy's decision to obey God and remain celibate until marriage causes Lamont to become involved with Simone Montgomery. Do you believe that Lamont would have married Sandy if she had compromised and had sex with him? Did he truly love her? Was his turning to Simone based on sex alone? What are your personal feelings regarding celibacy as it relates to God's Word? *See 1 Corinthians 6:18*

12. Betrayal, rape, and self-hatred were strongholds in the lives of the women of Genevieve's family. Do you feel that strongholds are common in most families today? How can they be dealt with biblically?

13. The themes of betrayal and forgiveness are prevalent throughout

the novel. Discuss and compare biblical accounts where betrayal and forgiveness are present. How are these incidents applicable to experiences you have had?

Printed in the United States
118087LV00003B/44/A